LOVE IS ALL YOU NEED

Also by Deb Caletti

The Queen of Everything

Honey, Baby, Sweetheart

The Fortunes of Indigo Skye

The Secret Life of Prince Charming

The Six Rules of Maybe

Stay

The Story of Us

LOVE
IS ALL YOU NEED

Wild Roses · The Nature of Jade

DEB CALETTI

Simon Pulse
NEW YORK   LONDON   TORONTO   SYDNEY   NEW DELHI

SIMON PULSE

An imprint of Simon & Schuster Children's Publishing Division

1230 Avenue of the Americas, New York, NY 10020

This Simon Pulse paperback edition January 2013

Wild Roses copyright © 2005 by Deb Caletti

The Nature of Jade copyright © 2007 by Deb Caletti

SIMON PULSE and colophon are registered trademarks of Simon & Schuster, Inc.

For information about special discounts for bulk purchases, please contact Simon & Schuster Special Sales at 1-866-506-1949 or business@simonandschuster.com.

The Simon & Schuster Speakers Bureau can bring authors to your live event. For more information or to book an event contact the Simon & Schuster Speakers Bureau at 1-866-248-3049 or visit our website at www.simonspeakers.com.

Designed by Mike Rosamilia

The text of this book was set in Scala.

Manufactured in the United States of America

2 4 6 8 10 9 7 5 3

Library of Congress Control Number 2012938631

ISBN 978-1-4424-6636-4

ISBN 978-1-4424-6637-1 (eBook)

These titles were previously published individually by Simon Pulse.

Wild Roses

To my family, with love and gratitude.

ACKNOWLEDGMENTS

Thank you to my dear friends and partners—Ben Camardi and Jen Klonsky. It's a privilege to be part of your intelligence, humor, and insight. Thanks as well, to Jenn Zatorski, Leah Hays, Sam Schutz, and all the fine folks at Simon & Schuster—you guys are the best. Gratitude also to Kirsty Skidmore and Amanda Punter and U.K. Scholastic.

Doug Longman, music teacher extraordinaire—thanks for essential information, and for your dedication to teaching. And to all those organizations that assist writers and, more importantly, get the word out about books, my appreciation and admiration. Thank you Artist Trust; National Book Foundation; PNBA, with special thanks to Rene Kirkpatrick; California Young Reader Medal Program; PSLA; International Reading Association; YALSA, and to libraries everywhere, particularly King County Library System. Librarians are awesome, and KCLS is home to my favorites.

Anne Greenberg; the beautiful and singular Muriel Diamond; "Magic" friends; Rick Young; and the Flo Villa houseboat gang—life is happier with you in it. Love and endless thanks to my clan in Virginia, California, Chicago. And to my new family in Denver, Seattle, Phoenix, L.A., and Mineral Point—oh, lucky girl am I.

Finally, deep and forever love and gratitude to Evie Caletti, Paul and Jan Caletti, Sue Rath and family. And to my Sam and Nick, who make every day a present.

Chapter One

To say my life changed when my mother married Dino Cavalli (yes, *the* Dino Cavalli) would be like saying that the tornado changed things for Dorothy. There was only one other thing that would impact my life so much, and that was when Ian Waters drove up our road on his bicycle, his violin case sticking out from a compartment on the side, and his long black coat flying out behind him.

My stepfather was both crazy and a genius, and I guess that's where I should start. If you've read about him recently, you already know this. He was a human meteor. Supposedly there's an actual, researched link between extreme creativity and mental illness, and I believe it because I've seen it with my own eyes. Sure, you have the artists and writers and musicians like my mom, say, who are talented and calm and get things done without much fuss. The closest she gets to madness is when she gets flustered and calls me William, which is our dog's name. But then there are the van Goghs and Hemingways and Mozarts, those who feel a hunger so deep, so far down, that greatness lies there too, nestled somewhere within it. Those who get their inner voice and direction from the cool, mysterious insides of the moon, and not from the earth like the rest of us. In other words, brilliant nuts.

I guess we should also begin with an understanding, and that is, if you are one of those easily offended people who insist that every human breath be politically correct, it's probably best we just part company now. I'll loan you my copy of *Little House in the Big Woods* (I actually loved it when I was eight) and you can disappear into prairie perfection, because I will not dance around this topic claiming that Dino Cavalli was joy-impaired (hugely depressed), excessively imaginative (delusional), abundantly security conscious (paranoid as hell), or emotionally challenged (wacko). I'm not talking about your mentally ill favorite granny or sick best uncle—I'm not judging anyone else who's ill. This is my singular experience. I've lived it; I've earned the right to describe how it felt from inside my own skin. So if your life truths have to be protected the same way some people keep their couches in plastic, then ciao. Have a nice life. If we bump into each other at Target, I'm the one buying the sour gummy worms, and that's all you need to know about me.

Anyway, madness and genius. They're the disturbed pals of the human condition. The Bonnie and Clyde, the Thelma and Louise, the baking soda and vinegar. Insanity just walks alongside the brilliant like some creepy, insistent shadow. Edgar

Allan Poe, Virginia Woolf, Charles Dickens. William Faulkner, Dostoevsky, Cézanne, Gauguin. Tolstoy, Sylvia Plath, Keats, and Shelley. Walt Whitman and F. Scott Fitzgerald and Michelangelo. All wacko. And we can't forget the musicians, because this story is about them, especially. Schumann and Beethoven, Chopin and Handel, and Rachmaninov and Liszt. Tchaikovsky and Wagner.

And, of course, Dino Cavalli.

In that group you've got every variety of creation: the ceiling of the Sistine Chapel and *Farewell to Arms* and the epic poem, "Ode on a Grecian Urn," which, if you ask me, finds its true greatness as a cure for insomnia. You've also got every variety of crazy act. You've got the gross—van Gogh slicing off his earlobe and giving it to a woman (you can just hear her—*Damn, I was hoping for chocolates*), and the unimaginable—Virginia Woolf filling her pockets with stones to hold her down in the river so that she could do an effective job of drowning. And even the funny—the reason our dog is named William, for example, is because Dino Cavalli bought him during a particularly bad bout of paranoia and named him for his enemy and former manager and agent, William Tiero. He liked the idea of this poor, ugly dog named William that would eat used Kleenex if he had the chance. He liked yelling at William for getting too personal with guests. I can hear his voice even now, in his Italian accent. *Get your nose out of Mrs. Kadinsky's crotch, William,* he'd say with mock seriousness, and everyone would picture William Tiero with his bald head and beetle eyes, and they would laugh. Man, oh, man. You didn't want to get on Dino Cavalli's bad side.

Some people think the brilliant have been touched by God,

and if this is true then Dino Cavalli got God on the day he was wearing black leather and listening to his metal CDs, feeling a bit twisted and in the kind of mood where you laugh at people when they fall down. God wearing a studded collar. Because, sure, Dino Cavalli was a world-renowned composer and violinist, a combination of talent virtually unheard of, but there were days he didn't get out of bed, even to shower. And, sure, he wrote and performed *Amore Innamorato,* said to, "have moments of such brutal tenderness and soulful passion that it will live forever in both the hearts of audience members and the annals of modern composing,"[1] as well as the unforgettable *Artemisia* ("breathtaking and heartstopping work with the brilliance of the seventeenth-century masters."[2]), but he also had the ability to make you feel small to the point of disappearance. His perfectionism could shatter your joy like a bullet through a stained glass window.

What I'm saying is, he possessed magnificent and destructive layers. Either that or he was just plain possessed. I mean, it all got toned down in the papers, but we all know what could have happened to William Tiero that day. We all now know what happens when you self-destruct. Yet I've got to say, listening to his music can make you cry. Goose bumps actually rise up along your arms.

Everyone wants to get close to genius and fame, claim pieces of it, mostly because it's the closest they'll ever get to fame themselves. You learn this when you live with someone renowned. Those who know that Dino Cavalli was my stepfather think

---

1. Dawson Cook, "Cavalli Strikes a Perfect Note" *Strad Magazine* (April 1996): 12–15.

2. Alice Lambert, "The Season's Best" *Strad Magazine* (May 1989): 20–22.

I'm near enough to fame to call it good. Fame, the nearness of it, the possibility of it rubbing off, seems to turn people into obsessed Tolkien characters, hypnotized not by a ring but by the thought of getting on TV. Luckily at my school, most of the kids who hear the name Dino Cavalli will think it's some brand of designer shoes. To the majority I am just Cassie Morgan, regular seventeen-year-old trying to figure out what to do with my life and hoping my jeans are clean and swearing at myself for cutting my own bangs again. Few know my stepfather was once on the cover of *Time* magazine, or was also well known for the journals in which he wrote of his sexual adventures as a young composer in Paris. Everyone is too involved in the school game of How Orange Is Tiffany Morris's Makeup Today to care, even if they did. But the teachers and orchestra students, they know who I am, and I see what it means to them. Once during a school concert this kid was staring so hard at me that he accidentally stepped into an open viola case and wore it like an overgrown shoe for a few seconds on the gym floor.

And then there's Siang Chibo, who used to follow me home every day. She would walk far behind me and duck behind trees when I turned around, like some cartoon spy. She once tripped over a tree root in the process and spewed the contents of her backpack all over the place. You couldn't find a more incompetent stalker. I went over to her after she fell, and her palms even had those little pockmarks on them from landing on gravel. Now we have a Scrooge–Tiny Tim partnership of reluctant giving and nauseating gratitude. To Siang, I'm second in line in the worship chain of command, right after Dino. If people look at the famous as if they've been touched by God, then they look at those close to the famous as the ones who have seen Jesus' face in the eggplant.

You would have never recognized the Dino I lived with in the books that had been written about him before the "incident." No one had a clue. No one seemed to see what was coming. His demons were the real truth, but those who clutched at his fame made him into someone else. Just listen to Irma Lattori, a villager from Sabbotino Grappa, interviewed in Edward Reynolds's *Dino Cavalli—The Early Years: An Oral History*, the much-quoted source of Dino's childhood. It's his only authorized biography, in which the people who knew him then tell the events of his life.

Everyone in Sabbotino Grappa knew Dino Cavalli had that special light, Irma says in the book. *From the time he was an infant. I would see his mother, Maria, walk him around in his carriage. She was a beautiful woman with round, warm eyes. She always dressed elegantly, oh, so rich. She had tucked a peacock feather in the back of his carriage. It rose up, like a grand flag. You want to know where he got Un Cielo Delle Piume Del Peacock? That was his inspiration. Maria always appreciated the unusual. She wore hats, even when no one wore hats. Stunning. No wonder he became a ladies' man. He was born, you see, taking in the world and using it in his work. Born to beauty and greatness. He couldn't have been more than six months old, this time I am remembering. He reached his hands up to me when I bent to look at him. He wanted me to hold him. He wouldn't let my sister Camille go near him.*[3]

---

3. *Dino Cavalli—The Early Years: An Oral History.* From Edward Reynolds, New York, N.Y. Aldine Press, 1999.

And Frank Mancini, gardener, another one of the villagers from tiny Sabbotino Grappa: *A beautiful garden, beautiful. Four hundred years old. Magnolias in the spring. Plumbagos, hibiscus in the summer. Lemon trees and figs. An olive garden. I worked my fingers to the bone. Now I cannot tie my own shoe, my fingers are so crippled. But it was a beautiful garden, and you could hear the child playing the violin through the open window. Small boy, not more than four years old, and he played the violin! A divine gift. His mother played the piano. Music was in his veins. And the smell of lemon trees. I didn't mind that the father was cheap and barely paid me enough to buy food.*[4]

All in all, as gagging as a dental X-ray.

"No one ever mentions that he is a wife-stealing psycho," my father said once after Dino was featured in the entertainment section of the newspaper—FAMED MUSICIAN SEEKS LOCAL INSPIRATION. He tossed the paper down on his kitchen table. "With bad breath."

"You haven't even been close enough to him to smell his breath," I said.

"Who says you have to be close," my father said. Let's just say my father didn't read the divorce books that say you are not supposed to talk badly about the other parent and the other parent's partner. Actually, I think he probably did read them, but has somehow convinced himself that only my mother is required to follow these rules. He ignores the other Divorced Parenting Don'ts too, the ones where you aren't supposed to grill your kid

---

4. *Dino Cavalli—The Early Years: An Oral History.* From Edward Reynolds, New York, N.Y. Aldine Press, 1999.

about what happens in the other home. Sometimes he tries to be casual about his fishing around, and other times it's like I'm in one of those movies where the criminal sits under the bare lightbulb in a room and after twelve hours confesses to a crime he didn't commit.

My parents were divorced three years ago, and my mother married Dino five days after the divorce was final. Do the math and figure out what happened. If you've been through this, you know the vocabulary. Parenting plan, custody evaluation, visitation, court orders, mediation, transfer time. And can anyone say *restraining order*? I can talk with my friend Zebe about these things. Ever since I met her in Beginning Spanish we've spoken the same language, in more ways than one. Her new stepfather may not be famous, but we understand the most important things about each other. She knows that you really don't give a crap about who gets you on Labor Day, that *no-fault divorce* are the three stupidest words ever spoken, and that you are not split as easily as your parents' old Commodores albums, and there was even a war over those.

"Barry Manilow, in my house. Not Commodores," Zebe told me once. "Which they both hated, by the way. For a week they were flying e-mails at each other over the goddamn F-ing *Copacabana* LP. They each accused the other of taking it. 'Did your mother find my "missing" album yet?' 'Next time you go to your father's, look for my stolen record.' God."

"Was anyone hurt?" I asked.

"Aside from the e-mail bloodbath, the only thing that was hurt was both of their egos when one of them finally remembered that they brought the album to some party back in the seventies and left it there on purpose."

"You wonder why they ever got married."

"Mi mono toca la guitarra," she said. *My monkey plays the guitar.* It's what she wrote on every Spanish test question she didn't know the answer to. I cracked up. Zebe's the greatest.

If my father treated my time at my mother's house as if he were the gold miner panning for The Dirt of Wrongdoing, my mother, on the other hand, would listen to any news of my father the same way someone who had plans to stay inside listens to a weather forecast. Hearing just enough to make sure there was no tornado coming. This is one difference between the leaver and the left, the dumper and the dumpee. The dumpee has the moral righteousness, and the desire to hear every dirty fact that will prove that *You get what you deserve in the end.* The dumper has the guilt, and wants to know as little about the other party as possible, in case they hear something that will make them feel even more guilty.

"Dad's got a new client. Some big Microsoft person," I told Mom once. It was after she and Dino had first gotten married, and I was starting to get a real clear picture of what she'd gotten us into. I guess I was hoping she was seeing, too, and that a little nudge in Dad's direction might help along the underdog. I hadn't learned yet that in terms of divorce, your only real hope is not to play team sports.

"Oh, really. Good for him," she said. She was braiding her long hair. She had a rubber band in her teeth. *Oh, weewy. Ood for him.* She finished the braid, put her arms down. "I need to find my overalls. I'm planting tulip bulbs today. Planting just calls for overalls." She went to her closet, flung open the doors.

"It'll bring him a lot of money," I said. My father was an accountant. He was a white undershirt in a world of silk ties and berets and pashmina. He was a potato amongst pad Thai and curry and veal scallopini. He was still madly in love with my mother. He didn't have a chance.

"Great," she said. "My God, look at this mess. The man is incapable of hanging anything up." She said this with a great deal of affection, poked a toe at a pile of Dino's shirts. "Overalls, over-alls. Bingo." She held them up.

"You're not even listening."

"I'm listening, I'm listening. You're just making me feel like I'm in some *Parent Trap* movie. You're not going to put frogs in Dino's shoes or something, are you?"

Mom's unwillingness to get involved may have also had to do with her own experience of her parent's divorce. Thirty-two years after the end of their marriage, she still can't tell one of her parents that she's visiting the other, or she'll be punished with coldness, hurt, and upset. Thirty-two years later, and her mother still refers to her father's wife as That Tramp.

"I thought you'd like to know. Jesus, Mom."

"Good. Thanks for telling me. You're not the *Parent Trap* type anyway. What was the name of that actress? Started with an H. Heather. Hayley! Mills. God, how'd I remember that? You, girl, are not Hayley Mills. I'd like to see them put you in a remake. Disney'd ditch the hemp bracelet. Don't you think? Too edgy."

"I hope squirrels dig up your tulip bulbs," I said.

She socked my arm. "You know how much I respect you. I *like* your hemp bracelet."

Respect—that was what was lacking in the other member of our household. Dino didn't respect me, or my mother, either, for that matter. Or anyone who wasn't his own perfect self. See, Dino hadn't always acted crazy. For a while, he was just plain arrogant. Dino was fluent in criticism, as generous in spirit as those people who keep their porch lights off all Halloween. If my mom was dressed up to go out and looking beautiful, he'd point out her pimple. If you opened the wrong end of the milk carton, he'd make you feel you were incapable to the point of needing to be institutionalized. After I'd bought this jacket with fur around the collar and cuffs at Old Stuff, Dino had pointedly told me that people who tried to make some statement of individuality were still only conventional among those of their group.

"I'm not trying to make a statement," I said. I was trying to keep the sharpness out of my voice, but it was like trying to hold water in your hands—my tone was seeping through every crack and opening possible.

"I didn't say you were. Did I say you were? It was a commentary on dress and group behavior," he said in his Italian accent. He chewed a bite of chicken. He was a loud, messy eater. You could hear the chicken in there smacking around against his tongue. His words were offhand, casually bragging that they meant more to me than they did to him. "By avoiding conventions, one falls into other conventions." He plucked a bit of his shirt to indicate someone's clothing choice. I felt the ugly curl of anger starting in my stomach.

"I'm sorry, I just don't want to be one of those See My Thong girls who bat their eyelashes at boys, rah rah rah, wearing a demoralizing short skirt and bending over so a crowd sees their butt," I said. "That's convention." Anger made my face get hot.

"Be who you like. I was simply making an observation. You don't need to bite me with your feminist teeth."

Honestly, I don't know how my mother didn't poison his coffee. Certainly I wondered what the hell she was thinking by loving him. If this is what could happen to a supposedly charming, romantic guy, then no, thank you. And this was before everything happened, even. Before Dino's craziness became like a roller coaster car, rising to unbelievable heights, careening down with frightening speed; before he started teaching Ian Waters; before he began composing again and preparing for his comeback after a three-year dry spell. But in spite of what must have been perfect attendance in asshole classes, Dino was one of those people who got under your skin because you cared what they thought when you wished you didn't. So after that conversation I did the only thing I could. I wore the coat the next day, too. The truth was, I wasn't sure I liked it either. It was vaguely Wilma Flintstone and Saber Tooth Tiger. Little hairs fell into my Lucky Charms.

Because I wanted his approval and hated that fact, I did what I could to make sure I didn't get it at all. One of those things you should be in therapy for. Before I met Ian Waters, for example, I had no interest in music, which was an act of will living in a house where my mother was a cellist and my stepfather a prominent violinist and composer. But Ian Waters changed that about me, and everything else, too. Before I met Ian the music I liked best was something that sounded, if Dino was right, *like your mother hunting for the meat thermometer in the drawer of kitchen utensils.* My interest was in astronomy—science, something that was mine and that was definite and exact. I felt that the science of astronomy existed within certain boundaries that were firm and logical. If you think about how vast the universe is, this gives you some idea of how huge and wild I thought the arts were.

After three years of living with Dino Cavalli, I had had enough of people of passion. Passion seemed dangerous. I'd seen the tapes of his performances, the way he had his chin to his violin as if he were about to consume it, the way his black hair would fly out as he played, reaching crescendo, eyes closed. It made you feel like you needed to hold on to something. I'd never felt that kind of letting go before. It all seemed one step away from some ancient tribal possession. And that crescent scar on his neck. That brown gash that had burned into him from hours and hours and hours of the violin held against his skin. He had played until the instrument had made a permanent mark, had become part of his own body. If Chuck and Bunny are right, and everyone should *hunger for life and its banquet,* I would rather have the appetite of my neighbor Courtney and her two brothers, over Dino's. All Courtney and her brothers hungered for in life was a box of Junior Mints and MTV, fed straight through the veins. Dino, he could inhale an emotional supermarket and still be ravenous.

Right then, the only thing I was hungry for was to have Dino Cavalli, this flaming, dying star, out of my universe. It was the only thing I would dare be passionate about. That is, until Ian Waters veered into our driveway on his bike, his tires scrunching in the gravel, scaring Otis, the neighbors' cat, who ran across the grass like his tail was on fire. Otis was running for his life. In a way, that was when I began finally running to mine.

Chapter Two

Edgar Allan Poe watched his mother bleed from the mouth as she died from consumption, as he and his two siblings lay in bed beside her. Hemingway committed suicide with the same gun his father had used to kill himself. Lord Byron's father had an incestuous relationship with his own sister, and his mother's relatives were a toxic mix of the depressed and suicidal. When you look at the families of crazy geniuses, you start to understand where their pain comes from. You start to get their need to paint it away, write it away, compose it away.

But Dino Cavalli's childhood in Sabbotino Grappa (population 53) sounded like one of those lush movies filmed in hazy golden-yellows with a sappy soundtrack that makes you cry even though you know it's just music manipulation. It sounded close to perfect. Reading *The Early Years* snapped me right up from Seabeck, the island where we live, just a ferryboat ride from Seattle. It lifted me from the salty, wet air and the ever-greens and the cold waters of the Puget Sound, and landed me in the warm orange tones of a Tuscan hill town. *I would open the shutters in the morning,* said Antonia Gillette, wife of town baker Peter Gillette. *And I would see little Dino walking to school in his white shirt, holding his mother's hand. I remember the smell of the lemon trees, and the smell of the baking just done, coming up warm through the floorboards. Peter would hurry out to give a frit-telle to Dino, and one to his mother, no charge. Always no charge. He should have charged the mother, but she was too pretty. And the father—ah. Handsome, like from a magazine. And a beautiful voice. Dino, we all knew he was special. His hair shined; his fingers were magic on his little violin. We knew he would bring us fame. I heard him from the open window, Grazie, Zio. That's what he called Peter. Uncle.*[5]

"It's too good to be true," my father said once. "You mark my words. If it sounds like a duck and looks like a duck and smells like a duck, it *is* a duck."

"Quack," I said.

The stories of Dino's childhood glowed like firelight or radiation, one or the other. You could see those townspeople sitting at their kitchen tables, remembering a time past, smell-ing of wine and salami, a thick, wrinkled hand grabbing the air to emphasize a point. You grew to love those old Italians, and that ragged town with its winding streets and good intentions, more than you liked Dino himself. I did anyway. The only real

---

5. *Dino Cavalli—The Early Years: An Oral History.* From Edward Reynolds, New York, N.Y. Aldine Press, 1999.

nasty thing that was said came from Karl Lager, Sabbotino Grappa grocer. *The child was a monster. Spoiled and sneaky. He stole candy from me. Later, cigarettes. Slipped them up the sleeve of his jacket as he looked at me and smiled. I tried to grab him, took off that jacket, but nothing was there. Born of the devil, and any idiot could see it.*

Karl Lager is a drunk and a bastard, Antonia Gillete said. *He'd accuse the pope of stealing.*

Karl Lager had no business in Sabbotino Grappa, Peter Gillette agreed. *He is a German, after all.*[6]

You imagined a childhood like that creating a genius. You did not imagine those two beautiful and perfect parents and the adoration of a village creating a Prozac-ed pit bull.

"Is Mr. Cavalli home?" Siang Chibo said the day that I first saw Ian Waters. She was whispering, following me around the house as I dropped my backpack on a kitchen chair and looked around in the fridge for something that might change my life. If you want a good picture of Siang Chibo, imagine that little boy in *Indiana Jones and the Temple of Doom,* that kid that rides around with him in the runaway mine car. She's not much taller, and has that same squeaky voice—*"Indy, Indy!"* But Siang's surprised me a few times. For example, she and her father love to watch monster trucks on the weekends. For another example, she's a fierce flag football player. I once saw her nearly knock out Zane Thompson's perfect teeth as she reached up to catch a pass in tenth-grade PE. Zane had to rush to a mirror to see if he was still beautiful. Go Siang.

---

6. *Dino Cavalli—The Early Years: An Oral History.* From Edward Reynolds, New York, N.Y. Aldine Press, 1999.

"Dino's at the symphony offices," I said. I didn't want to let Siang down, but the truth was, I had no idea where Dino could be. He might have been at Safeway, for all I knew. Being a violinist was not a regular nine-to-five job, I guess—in fact, lately he didn't seem to have any job at all except for being famous and giving interviews about his past glory days. He gave one concert that I knew of, traveled to Chicago for it with Mom. I stayed with Dad a few extra days, days that were mostly spent trying to talk him out of searching the Web for every nasty comment or review about the event. He even printed out one *Chicago Tribune* article and posted it to the fridge with this glittery macaroni magnet I made in preschool. RERUN PERFORMANCE BY MASTER DISAPPOINTS.

What Dino spent most of his time doing was hiring and firing new managers. Since he ditched William Tiero three-plus years ago, he just went through these poor guys like you go through a bag of M&M's when you've got your period. Consume, and on to the next. One of the first exposures I had to Dino's temper was when we had all just moved in together and this manager got booted. I heard only a part of the enraged conversation before I left and walked down toward the water, went far enough so that the cries of the seagulls and gentle voices on the beach—*Olivia! Roll up your pants so they don't get wet*— replaced Dino's shouts. The few pathetic imaginings I was trying to hold on to about a stepfather—new beginnings, new adventures, new life—were instantly shot to shit and replaced with a deep distrust of the word *new*. It is bad enough to be suddenly (even if it is not so sudden, it feels sudden) living with a male stranger who sleeps in bed with your mother and eats off of your forks and who farts with an unearned degree of familiarity. But when the male stranger *yells* loud enough to shake your baby pictures in their frames too, then, God, where have all the boarding schools gone?

Anyway, almost six months before Ian Waters first came, Dino got this new manager, Andrew Wilkowski, this skinny guy with music notes on his tie. It was practically a long-term relationship. Andrew Wilkowski flattered Dino's ego, talked to him about writing again. I heard them when Andrew came over for dinner. They could take it slowly, he told Dino. But the world was ready. Dino was ready. I'm sure Andrew Wilkowski only had staying power because his ass-kissing skills were so perfected, his lips were chapped.

If I had to create a job description based on Dino's behavior before he really went nuts, I'd say being a violinist and a composer meant spending some days in bed, some holed up in your office, occasionally playing music and stopping over and over again, and storming around the house as your wife walked on eggshells. Oh, and seeing your psychiatrist. Mom said this was necessary for Dino to deal with the stresses of his work, but to keep that information private for the sake of Dino's reputation. It was okay to look like a tyrant, I guess, but not to talk with Freud about what your id did. Basically, a genius composer/violinist meant being a tantrum-throwing toddler with an expensive musical instrument. My mother should have given him the spaghetti pot to pound on with a wooden spoon instead.

I wouldn't tell Siang any of those things, though. I could have destroyed him in an instant for her, but it seemed too cruel. To her, not to him. "Apple?" I offered. Mom was on a diet kick. I hated when the adults in my life went on a diet kick. There was never anything good to eat in the house. I hoped Dino *was* at Safeway.

"Okay," Siang said. She took the apple, but didn't eat it. She put it in her sweatshirt pocket. I imagined a Cavalli Collection— empty TP rolls from our bathroom, pebbles from the insides of Dino's shoes left by the front door, William's squeaky rubber hamburger dog toy that had vanished without a trace. "Can we go in his office?"

"I worry about you, Siang, I really do."

I took the key to Dino's office out of the sugar canister that was empty of sugar. Mom put it there because she was sure that Dino, in a distracted state, was going to one day lock himself out. That there was a key at all should tell you that Dino would have gotten furious had he known we were in his study, but I couldn't let Siang down. I had a little problem saying no to people with eyes as pleading as in those ads FEED A STARVING CHILD FOR AS LITTLE AS ONE DOLLAR A DAY. She practically left offerings on his desk blotter.

The room always felt cool when you first opened the door, cool and musty. There was a fireplace in that room, though it was never lit except when guests came over. The fire showed off the room for what it was—one of the best in the house, with big windows that had a peek of the waters of the sound, if you stood on your toes and looked high over the neighbor's hydrangea bush. His desk was dark walnut, and a mess—papers and books, mail and clippings, piles of sheet music. There were three clocks on it, only one which you could hear ticking, sounding like a metronome, and an old coffee mug with a ring of dried brown on the bottom. Assorted objects lay among the clutter—a robin's egg, a golf tee (Dino was not a sportsman), a cigar box (Dino did not smoke cigars). There was a paperweight with a white dandelion puff saved perfectly in glass, and a spare pair of Dino's glasses worn sometime in the seventies, if you judged by their size and thick black frames. Above the desk was a painting of white flowers against a dreary green background, and in the corner of the room sat a globe that always settled toward the side revealing the African continent. An antique music stand, ornate silver, delicately curved, stood in another corner, and there was a bookcase, too, filled with Cavalli biographies, volumes of music theory, history, and art, and one of those enormous dictionaries.

Siang strolled by the desk, her fingertips lightly touching the edge. She looked up at the painting, tilted her head to the side and examined it for a moment. Her eyes moved away to a frame facedown on the desk. She took hold of the velvety frame leg, rubbed her thumb along it. "What's this?"

"How am I supposed to know?"

Siang raised the picture carefully, the way you lift a rock when you're not sure what's underneath. It was an old black-and-white photo of a young man. He was standing in front of a building, a theater, maybe, as you could see a portion of a poster in glass behind him. He was beaming, hands in his pockets.

"That's William Tiero," I said. "At least I think it is." I squinched my eyes, looked closer. "Same beaky nose. A much younger William Tiero. He still had hair. I never knew the guy ever had hair." I chuckled.

"William Tiero became Dino Cavalli's agent shortly after Cavalli won the Tchaikovsky competition in Russia when he was nineteen," Siang said.

"Jesus, you give me the creeps sometimes," I said. "Put that back down."

"They say it was a partnership made in heaven." Siang set the photo on the desk the way it was.

According to Mom, William Tiero had been dismissed no fewer than five times before the final break a little more than three years ago. I could only imagine what that firing must have been like. Before Andrew W. came on the scene, the last poor manager that was booted got a wineglass thrown in the direction of his head. I saw the delicate pieces of it, sitting on top of the garbage can, and felt the silence that lay heavy as a warning in the house. I remember the drops of red wine on the wall, looking as if a crime had been committed there. If being fired five times by Dino was a partnership made in heaven, I wondered what a bumpy working relationship would look like.

"Siang, really. You need a hobby or something. Crochet a beer-can hat. Learn fly-fishing. Whatever."

"The pursuit of understanding genius is always a worthwhile endeavor," Siang squeaked in her *Temple of Doom* voice.

"Did some famous person say that?"

"No. I just did."

"Shit, deprogramming necessary. We are going to walk down to 7-Eleven. We are going to have a Slurpee. Corn Nuts. Or one of those scary revolving hot dogs. We are going to take an *Auto Trader* magazine, just because they're free."

"I hear the door," Siang said.

I froze. Listened. "You're right. Damn it, get out of here."

We hurried out. My heart was pounding like crazy, and my hand was shaky on the key as I locked the door again.

"Cassie!"

"It's just Mom," I said.

My chest actually hurt from the relief. We walked casually into the kitchen. At least I did. God knows what Siang was doing behind me—probably putting her hands up in the air like a captured criminal in a cop show. Mom was filling a glass of water. Wisps of her hair were coming loose from her braid. "What are you doing here?" I asked. Mom was in a rehearsal period with the theater company of her current job. By the time she took the ferry home from Seattle afterward, she didn't usually arrive until dinnertime.

"Hello, my wonderful mother. How was your day?" she said.

"That too," I said.

"I got off early," she said. It seemed like a lie, but I let it pass. "What are you two up to?"

"I was just heading home," Siang said. "Chemistry test to study for."

Mom shuddered. "God, I'm glad I'm done with school."

"Then she's starting a new hobby," I said.

"Crafts," Siang said. I smiled. It was pretty close to a joke.

"Puff paint. Shrinky Dinks," I said.

"Cool," Mom said. She took a long drink of water. You could usually count on her to make her best effort to one-up your jokes. Obviously she was distracted.

Siang left, and I went up to my room, turned on a few of my lamps. My head was achy and tired—I'd slept like shit for the past few nights. Dino kept turning down the heat below zero to save money, and in a few days my nose and toes were going to turn black and fall off from frostbite. Far as I knew, Dino had a lot of money, but he was really attached to it. Any time he had to spend any, he acted like he was parting with his cardiovascular system.

I looked at my homework and it looked back at me, flat and uninspiring, growing to impossible proportions right in front of my eyes. Sometimes a little math and science is as easy as tying your shoes, and other times, it feels like an Everest expedition, requiring hired Sherpas and ropes, oxygen bottles, and crampons, which always seemed like an especially unfortunately named word—a mix between cramps and tampons. I picked up a book of poetry beside my bed instead, thumbed through e.e. cummings, my favorite poet for probably the same reason he was other people's favorite poet—he chucked grammar and got away with it. It was like thumbing your nose at every one of those tests where you had to underline once the main clause, and underline twice the prepositional phrase. I stank at those. Grammar words were so unlikable—*conjunctive*, some eye disease you need goopy medicine for; *gerund*, an uptight British guy. *Gerund would like his tea now!*

I amused myself with these inane thoughts until I heard Dino's car pull up. He had a Renault, and it made a particular *clacka-clacka-clacka* sound so that you always knew it was him (okay, *he*, for the above-mentioned grammar neurotics, although no one really talks like that). The engine was still on when he came through the front door. Then he went back out again and shut it off. It was entirely possible that he forgot that he'd left the engine running, as this was pure Dino, distracted to the point of barely functioning in the real world. Mom sent him to the store once for dinner rolls for a small party they were giving, and he came back two hours later with a glazed expression and a pack of hot dog buns. Another time, he tried to catch a bus from one part of Seattle to another, and ended up across the lake, calling my mother for rescue from a phone booth. He can play the first page of any major concerto off the top of his head, but doesn't understand that it's time to cross the street when you see the sign change to the little walking guy.

I heard my mother and Dino talking downstairs, which for some reason actually spurred my sudden desire to do my homework after all. We were maybe a month into the school year, and every teacher was beginning to pile homework on as if they had sole responsibility for keeping you busy after school and therefore out of jail and drug-free. My head was really hurting now. I worked for a while, then I heard the crunch of bike wheels down our road. This was not an uncommon sound, as Dino also often rode his bike; we Americans drove our cars too much, he said. Growing up in Italy, it was the only way people got around, he said. It was no wonder Americans had such fat asses, he said. You could often see him pedaling to town and back with a few grocery items in his basket. Yes, he had a basket on his bike. It wasn't a tacky one with plastic flowers or anything (thank God), but a real metal basket. The whole bike itself, old and quaint and squeaky, looked snitched from some clichéd French postcard, or stolen from some History of Bikes museum.

The sound of bike wheels on gravel might not have been out of the ordinary, but Dog William (versus Human William) barking crazily at the sound *was* unusual. I pulled up my blinds and here is what I saw: the curve of our gravel road, and the line of maple trees on each side framing the figure in the center. I saw a boy about my age, in a long black coat, the tails flapping out behind him, with a violin in a black case in a side compartment. I saw a yellow dog running alongside him grinning, his tongue hanging out in a display of dog joy.

I cannot tell you what that moment did to me. That boy's face—it just looked so *open*. It was as if I recognized it, that sense he had—expectation and vulnerability. He looked so hopeful, so full of all of the possibilities of a perfect day where a yellow dog runs beside you. The boy's black hair was shining in the sun and his hands gripped the handlebars against the unsteadiness of the bike on the dirt road. Are there ever adequate words for this experience? When you are suddenly overwhelmed by a wave of feeling, a knowing, when you are drawn to someone in this way? With the strength of the unavoidable? I don't know what it was about him and not someone else. I really don't know, because I'm sure a thousand people could have ridden up that road and I would not be abruptly consumed with a longing that felt less like seeing someone for the first time than it did meeting once more after a long time apart.

I watched him as he veered into our driveway, causing a snoozing Otis to bolt awake and flee maniacally across the lawn.

What was he doing here? He was about my age, but I'd never seen him before. Was this a Dino pilgrimage? A fan wanting his violin signed? He parked his bike, set it on its side on the ground. He said something to his dog, who looked up at him as if they'd just agreed about something. The boy lifted his violin case. He ran his fingertips along it, as if making sure it was okay—a gentle touch, a caring that made me rattle the blind back down and sit on the floor suddenly like the wind had been knocked out of me.

Here is something you need to know about me. I am not a Hallmark card, ooh-ah romance, Valentine-y love kind of person. My parents' divorce and my one other experience of love (Adam Peterson, who I really cared about. Okay, I told him I loved him. We hugged, held hands. He told me I was beautiful. He told half the school we had sex.) has knocked the white-lace-veil vision right out of me. Love seems to be something to approach with caution, as if you'd come across a wrapped box in the middle of the street and have no idea what it contains. A bomb, maybe. Or a million dollars. I wasn't even sure what the meaning of the word was. Love? I loved my telescope. I loved looking out at the depth of the universe and contemplating its whys. But love with someone else, an actual *person*, was another matter. People got hurt doing that. People cried and wrapped their arms around themselves and rocked with loss. Loving words got turned to fierce, sharp, whipcracks of anger that left permanent marks. At the least, it disappointed you. At most, it damaged you. No, thank you.

So I sat down on that floor and grabbed my snow globe, the one that had a bear inside. I have no idea where I got it; it's just something I've always liked and have had forever. Just a single bear in the snow. He used to be anchored to the bottom, but now he just floated aimlessly around, and maybe that's why I liked him so much. I related. I turned it upside down, let him float and drift as the snow came down, down. *Oh shit*, I thought. *Holy shit*. My heart was actually thumping around in some kind of heaving-bosom movie-version of love. I could actually hear it. God, I never even came close to experiencing anything like this for Adam Peterson, and look where that got me. I breathed deeply, but it was like a magnet had been instantly surgically implanted in my body, drawing everything inside of me toward that person out there.

My headache had hit the road, replaced with some super energy surge. I told myself I was insane and an idiot and a complete embarrassment to my own self. The snow settled down around the bottom of the globe as the poor bear just floated, his head hitting the top of the glass as if in heartfelt but hopeless desire to rise above his limited world. I got back up and peeked out the blinds. The yellow dog sat on the sidewalk with the most patient expression I'd ever seen on animal or human—just peace and acceptance with his waiting, appreciating the chance to enjoy what might pass his way. The boy had come inside, I guess. And then it finally occurred to me—he'd come inside. True enough, there were voices downstairs. I opened my door a crack, heard Dog William being forcibly removed from the house, his toenails sliding against the wood floor.

"We'll work in my study." Dino.

"Can I get you or your dog something to drink?" Mom asked.

"That'd be great—my dog would love some water," the boy said.

"What's his name?" Mom again.

"He's a she. Rocket."

"Shall we not waste valuable time?" Dino said. You should have heard his tone of voice. That's what could really piss you off. I sent a silent curse his way, that his tongue would turn black and fall out. I heard my mother fish around in the cupboard, probably for a bowl for the water. My heart was doing a happy leap, prancing around in a meadow of flowers, tra la la, without my permission. His dog's name was Rocket. I liked astronomy. It was that thing you do when you first fall in love. Where you think you must be soul mates because you each get hungry at lunchtime and both blink when a large object is thrown your way.

I started to put the pieces together. Boy with violin, Dino and his study. Maybe Dino was giving him some kind of lesson. But Dino wasn't a teacher. First, the best music teachers weren't necessarily virtuoso players. I knew that. Teachers are usually teachers and players are players. As far as I knew, Dino had never taken a student before. But more importantly, Dino didn't have the patience instructing would require. He would get irritated when he couldn't figure out how to turn on the television, for God's sake. You'd think he of all people could locate a power button.

I got a little worried for that boy now, alone with Dino in his office. I went downstairs, caught Mom coming back inside from giving Rocket her water. She had little gold dog hairs on her black skirt.

"What's going on?"

"Dino's taking a student," she said to me.

A student. He was going to be Dino's student. I thought

about what this would mean. He'd be coming back. And back again. I swallowed. Wished my jeans were a size smaller. Wished my hair was something other than brown, that I had a better haircut. Shorter, longer. Anything other than medium length. I forced the casual back into my voice. "Why's he taking a student? He's not a teacher."

"Well, one, because the opportunity came up, and two, the boy needed someone."

"Dino's not exactly patient," I said.

"He's a master. The boy's lucky to have him. And Dino's not charging a cent. A friend of Dr. Milton's set him up." Dr. Milton was Dino's psychiatrist. "God, I'm starving. It's a good thing I'm not home during the day. I'd weigh three hundred pounds." Mom rooted around in the cupboards.

Dino teaching for free surprised me. I knew how he glared when I threw away a bread crust. "That's generous of Dino," I said.

"Well, they both get something out of it. Andrew Wilkowski's got this deal in the works with Dino's old record company and the Seattle Symphony. He's got to have three pieces ready to perform for a taped concert to be held in March. He's got two that he started a long while back, but they need more work. I guess the composing has been torture in the past and he's only got six months."

"So, what, the student helps him?"

"Aha!" she said, and held up the last Pop-Tart she found. She removed it from the foil, threw away the empty box, and took a bite without bothering to warm it up. "No, the student doesn't help *literally*. The lessons just provide a structured environment—another focus, a place he's got to be. They're trying to avoid all of this open time spent obsessing about creating and not creating."

"Maybe he should pay the student, then."

Mom devoured the Pop-Tart like Dog William devours a . . . well, anything. "Ian needs Dino. That's his name. Ian Waters. He's preparing for an audition that's coming a couple of weeks before Dino's concert. Sometime in March too, I think. You know who he really should have? Someone like Ginny Briggs. He's that good, from what I hear. But you've got to mortgage your house to get her."

"What's he auditioning for? The youth symphony?" I asked. It was a hopeful question. If he was that good the answer could be Julliard, which meant he was heading to New York.

"No. Curtis."

"Wow," I said. My heart sank. It more than sank; it seemed to clutch up and evaporate. The Curtis Institute of Music. Only the best of the best went there. Better than Julliard, lots of people thought. Every student was on full scholarship. He was heading to Philadelphia.

"Yeah. Ian was asked to perform at the Spoleto Festival in Italy last year. He was only sixteen. You know who else performed there at that age."

"Clifford, the Big Red Dog?" I guessed. "No, wait. Donny Osmond."

"Very funny," Mom said.

"Is it George Jetson?" I'm sorry, but it just always bugged me how everyone was supposed to know Dino's entire history. Dino composed his first piece of music at twelve. Dino made his first armpit fart on June 12, 1958.

"Okay. Never mind," Mom said. "You asked."

"No, I'm sorry. Okay? I'm sorry."

"Anyway," Mom said. She paused for a moment, deciding whether to forgive my brattiness. "That's why he's taking Ian on. He and his mother moved here when she lost her job. From California. You know that little house by the ferry terminal? Shingles? The one that used to put the sleigh in the yard at Christmas?"

"And keep it there until spring? Yeah."

"They moved in there. Whitney Bell taught him in California. For little or nothing."

"He'll be going to my school."

"Kids like that don't go to school. They have tutors. They learn at home. He's probably working on his GED now. They get into college early. More time for the music. I think the plan is, he applies in March and if all goes well, he moves to Philadelphia in June."

"Lucky," I said. Nine months. That's as long as he was going to be here.

"I don't know. This prodigy business . . . look at Dino. The ultimate love-hate relationship with that violin. I hope this teaching really does help. He'll have to start writing, and he hasn't picked up his instrument in weeks."

"Or his socks," I said. Lately, whenever Dino arrived in the front door, his shoes and socks would come off immediately.

They lay in the entryway like they'd just had a thoroughly exhausting experience.

"He always went barefoot growing up. It's hot in Italy."

Italy, Italy. That was another thing you got sick of hearing about in our house. How much better it was than evil and endlessly annoying America. How Italy had per capita more beautiful and intelligent people than here, how they invented the human brain, how they could take over the world using fettuccine noodles as weapons if they wanted to.

"Well, I hope Dino's nice to him," I said.

"I know."

"So *that's* why you're home early."

"Just keeping an eye on things."

It was my personal opinion that my mother didn't have a relationship as much as she had a babysitting job.

Mom went upstairs, probably reading my mind and trying to prove me wrong. From the kitchen I couldn't hear anything coming from Dino's office. I lingered outside the door for a while, listening to the rumbles of conversation without the definition of actual words, and then I heard the tuning of a violin. I did something I shouldn't have. I sat down right there with my back against the door so that I could hear better. They discussed music, what piece the boy should begin with, and then he began to play.

I can tell you that I have heard Dino play many times, and have heard the best of his performances on his recordings. As I've said, they send chills down your spine, even for someone like me who still chuckles when some musician mentions the

G string or the A hole. Dino's playing was a storm thrashing waves against rocks; all of the earth's emotion jammed into a cloth bag, then suddenly released.

But Ian Waters's playing was different. It was tender as that hand brushing the violin case, as open as his face as he rode down that road with the maple trees on either side. There was a clarity, a newness. A hopefulness that made your throat get tight with what could be tears.

From what I have learned from my mother all of these years, no one pretends to understand musicality, that certain something that a human being brings to the playing of his instrument. A machine can play an instrument, but it is that something of yourself that you bring to it that makes a player really good. That piece of your soul that you reveal as the music comes through you. I know nothing of this personally—I played the tissue paper comb in the kindergarten band—but you can hear it. You may not have words for it, but you can hear it. Maybe *feel* it is more accurate. There is a communication going on at some ancient and primitive level when music is played from somewhere else other than simply the fingers. This playing—it was his energy and heart rising from the notes. His dreams lifted from the instrument and carried out to where I heard them.

I don't even know what he was playing, and that's not even the important thing to this story anyway. I shut my eyes; it was as if he was painting with sound. I saw tender, vulnerable pictures. I was a child in a village, a child who'd just plucked a tangerine from a tree. Around me were the sounds of a town, Sabbotino Grappa maybe, voices speaking in Italian. I watched other children playing under a fig tree, and because it was so orange and shiny, put my teeth into the tangerine peel before remembering that this is not a good thing to do; it tasted terrible.

"Stop, stop, stop." This I heard loud and clear. Dino's authoritative voice could be heard two states away.

"Technically nearly perfect. But *purpose*. There is feeling, yes. But no purpose. You must have it. Without direction, you will drown. You may be young, but you don't need to hesitate. If you don't give everything to your playing, Ian, you will go hungry."

"I know."

"Hungry."

"All right."

"You know what I am talking about."

"Yes, I do."

Ian started to play again. The paintbrush stroked the canvas. I peeled that tangerine, broke off a sticky segment and popped it into my mouth. It was juicy and warm. The juice trickled into the tiny hammock between my fingers. I watched two old Italian women cross the street while arguing. One wore kneesocks that had given up on the job and gathered in clumps at her ankles. The other had a bad dye job—her hair was blacker than a briquette while her face was older than time. Everyone knew her hair hadn't seen that color since dinosaurs roamed the earth.

The music filled me with vivid-dream drowsiness. I watched two teenagers snitch a bicycle from the street, running like anything to the canal where they would toss it. Just like Dino's stories. When it was summer and the boys had too much time on their hands, the canal was filled with bicycles. A grandfather leaned down to speak to me. His breath smelled of a wine-soaked cork, his chin had a dent in it that split it right in half. . . .

I fell backward suddenly, jolting before my head hit the ground. Shit, I had fallen asleep, right there against the door, and Dino and Ian came out of the office and nearly stepped over my tumbling body. Oh, God, I could be such an idiot. I had fallen asleep, *right there*, and the first impression I left with Ian Waters was my body rolling into the room like the corpse in some Agatha Christie novel.

"What have we here?" Dino said. "Either a very bad Romanian gymnast or a spy."

Oh, the humiliation. I gave him the black-tongue curse again, added an essential part of the male anatomy.

"Guilty on the spy thing," I said. I hoped to sound casual, which is tough to do when you are reclining on one elbow and your face is hot enough to ignite a Bunsen burner. I struggled to stand. "Actually I was listening. I'm sorry. It was really beautiful. I must have fallen asleep."

"Rule one. Keep your audience awake," Dino said.

Ian grinned. I wondered if I should hate him for colluding with Dino. Then he said, "Classical music can do that. Someone ought to put lyrics to it." He smiled.

"Ah!" Dino said in mock horror, and pretended to strangle Ian. "This is Cassie Morgan, astronomer. Ian Waters, talented, struggling musician. And heretic." All right. Since Dino attempted to restore some of my dignity, he could have his penis back.

"Astronomer," Ian said. "Wow." His eyes were a very gentle brown; his black hair threatened to swing over them. An angular face, long legs. He was tall and thin. In spite of performing before what must have been hundreds of people, he seemed shy, poetic.

"Still learning," I said.

"Tuesday, then?" Dino said.

"Tuesday," Ian said. "Thanks for listening," he said to me.

"Next time I'll stay awake," I said.

"No problem."

God, I was still kicking myself. That feeling of something being done wrongly, left unfinished, needing to be recaptured and played again, started churning inside as they headed out. Jesus, I should be put on some island for the terminally socially inept. Fuck-Up Island. It could be another perverse reality TV show. Mom came down the stairs, called a good-bye, and checked them both surreptitiously for blood and scratches.

Dino clapped Ian on the shoulder three times at the door before Ian left. Dino shut the door behind him, looked up at my mother, and smiled. "His mother is Italian." Dino beamed.

I went out to let Dog William back in. He was peering through the slats in the fence, no doubt watching as the figure of Rocket got smaller and smaller in the distance. I took a spot next to him, and through the narrow slat watched the black speck of Ian until he was gone. Dog William sighed through his nose as if saying farewell to the most interesting day of his life. I patted the top of his ugly head.

"I know it," I said to Dog William.

Chapter Three

My father's house is also on Seabeck Island, and both of my parents live here to Minimize the Impact of Divorce. We all used to live together on a street not far from here, but Mom sold the place after she got together with Dino. Dad now lives in the house he grew up in, right on Outlook, one of the nicest streets in town, where a row of Victorians sit overlooking the waters of the Puget Sound. From his porch you can see the ferries gliding to and from Seattle, and he has a front-row seat every March, when some thirty-two thousand gray whales migrate down the coast and a gazillion tourists come to town to watch. Dad bought the house from Nannie, his mother, who now lives at Providence Point Community for Seniors. But Nannie comes over a lot and rearranges things back the way they were when she lived there. She's been forbidden to empty the dishwasher after she reorganized every kitchen cupboard when Dad was out mowing the lawn. He couldn't find the cheese grater for two weeks. Once we caught Nannie in the living room, trying to shove the couch back against the window where she'd had it for forty years. She did pretty well too, for someone who must weigh about eighty pounds—she had it about halfway across the floor.

Mom and Dino bought the house we live in now on Mermaid Avenue (yes, it's really called that) shortly before they married. It's bigger than our old house, which was materialistic consolation for about a week or so, until real life set in. The divorce, the wedding, it all happened quickly. So quickly that you sometimes got the feeling that Dino was looking around with no small amount of resentment, wondering how he got from there to here. There being New York City, where he lived with his third wife, to here, a small island in Washington State, tucked far away from the center of the music world, married to a good but not great cellist, with a daughter who didn't appreciate what an astounding human being he was (i.e., hated his guts). How they got here was a tempestuous affair from what I have heard, although you don't want to think of your mother that way. It's okay to think of mothers in the same sentence as *lunch box* and *garden gloves*, but not in the same sentence as *passionate* and *tempestuous*. I will spare you the gory details of that time, the craziest, messiest kind of hell and chaos you never imagine for your life. Okay, one gory detail—my father, who takes insects outside when he finds them in the house, who rides them out on an envelope or some other handy airborne insect express material and gently lowers them to the ground, actually smashed his fist through his car window at the height of his anger and loss. Glass shards poked from the skin, sent blood down his Dockers.

Not that I blame my mother, not really. First, she's my mother and I love her and she's mostly a terrific person. But aside from that, it sounds like Dino chased after her with the determination of those dogs that travel thousands of miles to find their way back home after they tumble out of the back of a pickup. My mother, Daniella Morgan Cavalli, is, after all, a rather beautiful woman. Not in the sexy Barbie way, but like a medieval princess. Long, dark, curly hair. Dark eyes, a serenity that seems mysterious. People look at her, I know that. I have her eyes, I am told, but my hair is brown like my dad's, and is straight but not long enough to quite hit my shoulders. We both tend toward being full and curved and have to watch what we eat, but I distinctly lack that serenity people seem to find so alluring. She and Dino met when she was substituting for a cellist on maternity leave with the Seattle Symphony, and he appeared as a guest for three nights, performing *Amore Trovato* (Love Found), written for his third wife. In spite of this, my mother fell for him as if she had been kidnapped and brainwashed, and my father was sure this is what had actually happened. Dino's charm must have been intense, as prior to then my mother was a practical person who barely sniffed at a sad movie. My mother's charm mustn't have been too bad either—Dino stayed for three weeks, went back to New York only long enough to pack up his things. Lesson learned—charm is a one-way ticket to hell. Better to fall in love with a man who is dull as a pancake than one with *charm*.

Still, if I'm honest, I can't exactly blame Dino entirely either. Blame is so satisfying that you can forget it's actually useless. The truth is, there are a thousand reasons my parents aren't together anymore, and nine hundred ninety-nine of them I don't even know about or fully understand. I do know, though, that there are essential differences between them that I've noticed over the years: my father reads a map, while my mother doesn't mind getting lost; my father is consistently a believer, while my mother uses religion like some people use vitamins—when they feel an illness coming on. Before he paints a room my father tapes the edges and covers everything as thoroughly as an Egyptian mortician, while my mother's only preparation for the same job is to put on old jeans and take off her socks so she can tell if she's stepped in a paint drip. He cuts a peach; she bites it whole. The practicality I thought Mom had was maybe more an adaptive response to living with Dad, rather than her original, true self. Something like those fish that go blind after living in a dark cave.

Whatever the reasons for their split, I now go back and forth between locations, same as a letter with a bad address. I refuse, though, to be a messed up Product of Divorce, which some people think should be stamped on the side of you MADE IN MALAYSIA–style before they stick you in a crate and pack you off to the Land of the Damaged. Broken home, remember? The message being that because a marriage is broken, everything in the home is broken too, including you.

But there is one thing that I would say about the going back and forth, and that is, you wonder if the adults would ever get divorced if they had to be the ones to change homes every week. This is all supposed to be all right, and we are required to be okay about it, but it's not okay. Not really. We can handle it, don't get me wrong. But the truth is, it's *not okay*. The truth is, you just start to get comfy, when suddenly you've got to pack up and remember to bring your book and your favorite earrings and your notes for your paper for humanities. You've got to readjust to your surroundings—the parent, the pet, the stepsiblings or lack of them, who has bagels, who runs out of milk, which drawer to reach for when you want a spoon. The truth is that you have a day on either side where it feels as if you've just come home from vacation. You've got to remember where things left off. Oh yeah, that's right—my room's a mess. Oh yeah, that's right—my CD player's batteries are dead and I haven't read my new magazine yet and I'd gotten in a fight with Mom before I left. And the truth is, as soon as you arrive "home" you are too often pulled into the perverse divorce game, Who Do You Love More. It begins with what looks like an innocent question: "How did it go at Mom's/Dad's?" It ends with this reverse *Sophie's Choice*, where instead of a mother choosing between children, you are asked to choose between parents. If anything, all this divorce stuff made you feel that if you were anywhere near love you ought to don one of those suits those people wear from the Centers for Disease Control.

That's why I was trying to get thoughts of Ian Waters out of my mind that day I went to my dad's for the weekend. Real simply, I didn't want to get hurt by the power of my own emotions. I wasn't doing a very good job of erasing him from my head. I'd stooped to the lowest depths of thoughts, pictured him kissing me deeply before leaving on a plane for Curtis, me sobbing miserably in an airport chair as his plane pulled away from the doorway. I mean, I knew how this story would have to end, if there was even to be a story at all. It was not an end I wanted to willingly walk toward.

Dad wasn't home when I got there, so I went out to the porch and sat in the swing and looked out toward the sound. At that time of year you had your occasional humpback, otters, and sea lions, and I watched for the odd shape in the waves, a break in the pattern that meant some creature was there. It was colder than hell outside, and everything was painted in the Northwest's favorite color, gray. The water was steely, and the sky a soft fuzz, but it was still beautiful out there. A kayaker with a death wish was bobbing around on the water, his boat a vivid red spot in a silver sea. For the millionth, compelling time, I saw those fingers stroke that violin case.

"Look who's here!" my father called out.

I went inside. My father had one arm around Nannie and the other around a fat bag of groceries.

"He thinks he's made of money," Nannie said.

"I bought her a *People* magazine," Dad said.

"That's hard-earned dollars you spent on that trash," Nannie said. I kissed her cheek, helped her off with her coat, which wasn't too necessary. She was flinging it off like an alligator wrestler in her eagerness to get to the bag Dad had set on the counter. She fished around inside with one thin arm, plucked out the magazine, squashing a loaf of bread with her elbow in the process.

"I don't even know who these trollops are," she said as she eased into a corner of the couch and stuck her nose in the pages.

"Hey, Cass. How about sweet-and-sour chicken?"

"Yum."

Cooking was one of Dad's post-divorce hobbies. Before that, his specialty was cornflakes with bananas on them. Now he was really into it. He cooked better than Mom ever had, which was probably the point. He has all of these fancy knives and pots, and various, curious utensils good for only one weird purpose— skinning a grape, say. I could have written a confessional *My Father Had a Spring-form Pan*. He built a shelf in the kitchen for all of his cookbooks, and Nannie kept bumping her head on it. *Who put this thing here?* she'd grouse, knowing full well who did it.

We had dinner and watched a movie, some PG thing about misfit boys who go to camp, which ended with the two parents who'd both lost their spouses deciding to marry. Of course there were two white kids (one good, one evil), a black kid, an Asian kid, one fat kid, and one girl with glasses. It was worse than those movies where a dog wins a sports championship.

"Sex, sex, sex," Nannie said when the happy couple kissed at the end. "That's all you see in movies anymore." I guess that's why we weren't watching *The Rocky Horror Picture Show*. "I'm going to bed."

"Dishes await," Dad said after Nannie's flowered housecoat disappeared slowly up the stairs. "Would you go and check on her? I'm worried that by the time you get there Grandpa's photo will be up on my nightstand and her Poligrip will be in my medicine cabinet."

"No problem," I said.

I trotted upstairs, checked the guest room, but didn't find Nannie. I went to Dad's room to see if he was right. I was expecting to catch her red-handed, an unrepentant criminal of living in the past.

That's when I saw it—part of the cover of Dino's biography sticking out from under Dad's bed. It was splayed open to keep his place. I was sure he'd read it before, when all of the awful stuff was happening, but why was he reading it now, three years later? I walked over to his bed, looked underneath. There was a nest of papers, notes in Dad's handwriting, other books. *Composers Speak—Part 2 in the Young Musicians Series*, with that famous picture of Dino on the cover, looking sultry and young, during his days in Paris. And there was *Culinary History—Authentic Tuscan Recipes*. What was he doing, writing the Dino Cookbook? I wrestled with my conscience about sitting down right then and reading those notes. Guilt convinced me that Nannie would fall and break a hip or something if I did, so I left to find her. I saw the light on under the bathroom door.

"Are you okay in there?" I called through the door.

"Yes, thank you," Nannie said primly.

I waited until she came out and got settled into the guest room bed. She was propped on the pillows as if waiting for visitors when I kissed her cheek and turned off her light.

"What a day," she said.

"Good night, Nannie," I said.

"Good night, my special dear," she said. She was always a little sweeter at night. Maybe it was the nightgown with the bow.

I wanted to go right downstairs and confront Dad about his under-the-bed project, but when I got there he was drying a pan with a kitchen towel and whistling, having such a cheerful father moment, I couldn't stand the thought of breaking it. His T-shirt was loose over his jeans, and his hair had gone from polite to playful. He looked so happy I decided I didn't have the heart for a confrontation just yet. It would have to wait.

The next day I went to the movies with a couple of my friends, Sophie Birnbaum and Nat Frasier, Zebe and Brian Malo. Zebe's real name is Meggie Rawlinson, which sounds like some fifties cheerleader and doesn't fit her at all. We call her Zebe after her favorite zebra-stripe boots. We try to get together most weekends when there isn't a play, as everyone but me is in drama. Sophie and Brian usually are the leads and we give them crap because sometimes they have to kiss. They love each other like brother and sister, which apparently means they sometimes want to tear out each other's throats. Zebe does stage managing, and Nat is happy when he gets more than a couple of lines. Last year, every time we saw him, we'd say "This way, sir," after his Oscar-winning role as a waiter in *The Matchmaker*.

It was turning out to be Crappy Movie Weekend, as what we saw was basically one long boob joke. It was all girls in tight shirts with enormous buttlike cleavage and boys falling over their own tongues hanging out their mouths, the kind of thing that makes you wonder if there's any truth to evolution after all. Sophie got in a fight with Brian when he said that a little lighthearted movie with lots of tits was occasionally refreshing.

"We can help you hold him down," Zebe said.

"Hey, I don't want to touch him," I said. "Stupidity is a *disease*."

"I'll wash my hands afterward," Zebe said.

When I went back to Dad's, the house was quiet. It was so quiet that the refrigerator humming was the only noise, and I got that has-a-mass-murderer-been-here-and-now-he's-in-the-closet-just-waiting-to-jump-out-at-me feeling. Instead, I found that Nannie's coat was gone, taken back with her to Providence

Point, I guessed, and I noticed that a couple of pieces of toast had popped up from the toaster and had long ago grown cold. The coffeepot was on, with no coffee left in the pot, just a burning smear of brown. I always worried that this was how Dad really lived when I wasn't around, that the good cooking and orderly house were a show put on just for me and dropped the moment I left. I've come by unannounced before and saw unopened mail stacked six inches high, and egg yolk permanently wedded to the dishes it was on. That's the other prominent thing about divorce—you worry about your parents when they are supposed to be worrying about you.

I turned off the coffeepot and went upstairs. I found Dad on his bed, propped up not too differently than his mother the night before, with his glasses on and one toe trying to get a glimpse of the outside world from a hole in his sock. Those notes I had seen the night before were scattered all around him. Maybe it wasn't disinterest that had let the toast grow cold—maybe he was just excited to get back to his project.

"Knock, knock," I said.

"Oh, jeez." Dad startled, gathered up his papers. I'm surprised he didn't shove them under the pillow, stuff them in his mouth, and swallow them like they do in the spy movies.

"What time is it? You're early."

"Nope, right on time," I said.

"Wow," he said.

"So what're you doing?"

"Work."

"One, you look too guilty for work. Two, there's one of Dino's books open in front of you. Unless you got a new job I don't know about, that's not work. What's going on?"

My father sighed. He looked out the window, as if hoping the answer to my question would form in the clouds. *I see a giraffe! I see a pirate ship! I see that I'm nosing around on my ex-wife's new husband to try to catch him doing something horrible!*

I moved closer to the bed to see.

"No!" he said. He actually put one arm over his notes, same as those kids who make sure you don't cheat off them.

"Dad, God."

"All right," he said. "Okay! I just had a little feeling about something and I wanted to check it out."

"What kind of little feeling?"

"About Dino Cavalli."

"No shit," I said.

"Cassie, watch your mouth. Is that necessary? I was just thumbing through this book recently and something caught my eye that didn't add up."

"You mean you were hunting through it line by line for something that didn't add up," I said.

He ignored me, which meant I was right. "I found something. I mean, I think I found something, and I was just checking it out."

"What did you find?"

"I don't know if I want to say."

"What? He's actually a woman," I guessed. "A killer. A killer woman."

"A liar," my father said.

I sighed. "You should get a girlfriend, Dad. I mean it. It's been three years, and you haven't had a date."

"I've had dates. This isn't about dates. This is important. Your mother's life. Your life. If he's lied about one thing, he's lied about others, mark my words."

"Marissa what's her name. She seemed nice. A little Career Barbie but . . ."

"All right, listen to this," Dad said. He adjusted his glasses and began to read. "'My mother would make a simple lunch, gougere, some bread, and then I would practice.'"[7]

"Goo-zhair. Is that edible? I think our neighbor's cat had one of those caught in his throat once," I said.

"It's a lie."

"There's no such food?"

"No, it's a real food, but it's a recipe from 1969. He's claiming he ate it when he was eight or nine, and the man is older than I am. The recipe first appeared in a Moldavi wine recipe book, and the wine itself used in the recipe wasn't even made until 1968."

"God, Dad."

"I know," he said.

"No! I'm talking about you! What are you doing? So maybe the food wasn't around. Maybe he made a mistake. Maybe they got his age wrong. Maybe a thousand things. What does this prove? You've already got plenty of reason not to like him. Shit, in my opinion, *Mom* has plenty of reasons not to like him, and she still does."

---

7. *Dino Cavalli—The Early Years: An Oral History*. From Edward Reynolds, New York, N.Y. Aldine Press, 1999.

Dad got up, gathered his papers. He looked pissed at me. "It just may prove what I've always known. He's a fraud. You just wait."

It's tough to lip-synch violin playing, but I didn't say this. I turned and left the room, as I didn't want to fight with Dad. Anything I said would sound like a defense of Dino, and the Civil War began on less.

"That snake was fucking *strong*, man," Zach Rogers said. "A reptile's muscles you can't exactly see, you know, through that skin and everything, but I had two encyclopedias on the lid. Two, and he still pushed open the lid and got out. Here's the psychic-phenomenon-ESPN-shit part. One encyclopedia? It fell open to a page on *dinosaurs*. Tyrannosaurus rex. Biggest badass dude of reptiles in history. Now, that's almost *creepy*. What are the odds?"

I was walking home from school with Courtney Powelson, my neighbor, and Zach, though I don't even think he lived near us. He was just sort of migrating along with us, and I had the feeling he was soon going to look up and wonder where the hell he was. He either had a thing for Courtney or he was so used to seeing me that he forgot we were separate individuals. I had every class period with him, even lunch. It was one of those annoying twists of fate in a supposedly random universe. I've noticed that this kind of scheduling cruelty never happens with anyone you actually would want to spend all day, every day, with. No, I got Zach. Zach was weird. Entertaining, okay, but weird. He made me believe in alien life forms who come to live among us to steal our souls and our Hostess Cupcake recipes.

"A dinosaur isn't a reptile, it's an amphibian," Courtney said.

Zach ignored her, which was a good thing, since she was wrong, anyway. Courtney and I walked to school together often, but she usually pretended she didn't know me when she got there. She was one of the Popular Group, which meant two things: one, she could outfit a small town in Lithuania with the amount of clothes she had (picture innocent Lithuanian children in glittery HOT BABE T-shirts) and two, she was destined to marry some jock, have a zillion kids, and thereby assure herself a spot in front of a television forever. Queen of the American Dream. She didn't often walk home with me, as she was usually doing some after-school activity—the Sexy Dancing in Front of Male Sports Team club or the I Could Play a Sport Myself but Then I'd Have to Get Sweaty club. *Her mother should have named her MasterCard,* Zebe said once. Courtney and her two brothers bugged the hell out of Dino. "They have the glazed eyes of too much technology," he said once. "You look in their eyes and see Gillian Island reruns playing." *Gilligan,* he meant. Even though our houses were pretty far apart, you could often hear their TV blasting or the repetitive pounding of video game music. I still walked with her because, okay, I admit it, she was nice away from her friends, and because I was weak when it came to compromising my principles.

"I didn't even get to the best part yet," he said. "So the lamp I had shining on him? I stuck it down with duct tape. When this mother got out he climbed up the lamp, and when I found him, there was the snake, stuck on the duct tape, back of his head pinned like this." Zach threw back his head, did a really good stunned cobra impersonation.

"Hey, that was great," I said. "You could take that on the road."

"Eyuw," Courtney said. She shivered. I'm not kidding. Those kind of girls always shiver.

"I didn't even try to take it off. I was afraid I might skin him."

"Hey—perfect ad for the strength of duct tape," I said.

"Oh, my God," Courtney said.

"Had to take him to the vet. Luckily he was still alive," Zach said.

I pictured Zach putting his ear to the little chest to check for a heartbeat, a grateful tear coming to his eye. "How does a vet de-duct tape a snake?" I asked.

"Very carefully," he said. "Anyway, there's six encyclopedias on there now, to see if he can beat his record. He's my Bench-Press Baby."

"Well, here's our street."

I was right earlier, because Zach stopped and looked around. "Where the fuck am I?" he said. Then he shrugged his shoulders. "Cool."

Zach wandered off the direction we came, and I left Courtney to an evening of video fulfillment. At home I let Dog William in, went back out front to get the mail. Up the road came Dino's car. He parked in the driveway and got out. He had his suit on but wasn't wearing any shoes. No socks, shoes, nothing. It was *October. Way* too cold for simple, barefooted pleasure.

"Dino?" I said. "Hey, did you forget something? Or is this a new bohemian phase?"

Now, Dino was usually a pretty distracted guy. But this struck me as a bit beyond his usual absentmindedness. We're talking *shoes*. Not exactly something that tends to slip your mind.

This, my friends, is how quickly life can change.

A little kernel of unease planted itself inside my gut. "It doesn't matter," Dino said.

He slammed the car door and went inside. Something more was going on here; something was *not right*. I could feel this *wrongness* coming off him, just like you feel someone's anger or joy. I followed him, saw him discard his tie on the floor. He paced into the kitchen, and a moment later paced back out again. I was getting a seriously eerie feeling. An uneasiness that didn't have a name. It was his agitation. And he had this weird look in his eyes, like he was watching something I couldn't see.

"He always knows where I am, doesn't he?" Dino said. "He can see me wherever I am, that bastard."

Okay, shit. Something freaky was definitely going on. My body tensed in high alert. I wanted Mom home. Creepiness was doing this dance inside my skin.

Dino strode into his office, shut the door with a click. The house was quiet except for Dog William *huh, huh, huh*ing beside me. I was glad for his presence—at least I wasn't completely alone. I had one of those inexplicable moments where I looked at Dog William and he looked at me, and I decided that dogs really had superior knowledge to humans, held the secrets to the universe, only they couldn't speak. It's an idea you quickly discard after you see them chew underwear, but right then I felt better thinking one of us understood what the hell was going on.

And then suddenly the silence was shattered. Sorry for the

cliché, but that's what happened. Shattered, with the sudden frenzy of the violin, the sound of someone sawing open a tree and finding all of life and death pouring out.

"Wow," I said aloud. "Jesus."

He didn't tune first. That was what I realized. Not tuning was like a surgeon not snapping on his gloves. Like, well, going out without first putting on your shoes.

It was the first time he'd played in months and months. But this wasn't just playing. This was unzipping your skin and spilling out your soul. I had a selfish thought then. Actually, it was kind of a prayer to anyone who might be listening and interested. Please, I begged. Don't let Dino be crazy when Ian Waters comes.

Chapter Four

Here's the thing about dealing with people who are beginning the process of losing it. Your most overwhelming urge is to make sense of something that doesn't make sense. You try to make it fit, even if it doesn't really. You look at their crazy world from your sane world, and try to make your logical rules apply. As I stood in the hall with Dog William, I decided that there was a plausible story for Dino's behavior. Something rational. I was having trouble coming up with a story, but hey, there was one somewhere because there had to be. Maybe he got a letter from an old friend he wasn't so happy to hear from. And Italy—Italy was hot, right? How many times had I heard *that*? So you know, maybe he was homesick for his shoeless days in Italy. And what about Einstein? A genius, yeah, but he couldn't match his socks, so he gave up wearing them. Maybe this was something like Einstein. A shoeless, paranoid-ish genius thing. Of course, the deep inside piece of you that knows everything was saying this had nothing to do with Italy or Einstein or an old friend. That inside piece of you knows that your life is veering in a direction you have no desire to go. Basically, downhill.

That night I heard yelling. Dino just really going at it downstairs in his office. I'd heard him yell before, usually at his managers, but I couldn't imagine who he'd be yelling at now. Mom had gone to bed already, and the house had been silent. A moment later I heard Mom come out from their bedroom, her hurried steps down the stairs. The front door opened, slammed shut. I slipped out of bed, peeked out my front shades. Dino was on the front lawn in his bathrobe, his skin looking white in the moonlight. He stalked around a bit as if trying to decide what to do, then went behind the hydrangea bushes in the direction of the shed. I lost sight of him, then waited a while to see if he would reappear. Nothing. Finally I got back in bed, stayed on high alert. The house was quiet. I tried to go back to sleep, but when I finally started to doze I heard their voices downstairs. I couldn't make out their actual words, and though a part of me wanted to hear, a bigger part didn't. The uneasiness I felt that afternoon was appearing again, adding a new piece, and I wanted it *away*. But I could tell that my mother's voice was calm, a little pleading, and that Dino's was insistent.

The next morning I went down to get breakfast. I was exhausted from the night, feeling like shit and wondering how to define all the oddities of the day before. Mom sat at the kitchen table, drinking coffee. She looked tired too. She looked more than tired. She looked like someone had crumpled her up into a ball, thrown her in the trash, removed her, and tried to smooth her out again. I confess I had a Child of Divorce Reunion Fantasy Number One Thousand, where I for a moment imagined my father finding out that Dino really was a killer woman and that my parents would have to get back together. I saw them running through a meadow, hand in hand. Okay, maybe not a meadow. But I saw me having only one Christmas and one phone number and only my own father's shaved bristles in the bathroom sink. Having both of my own sane, well-rested parents in the kitchen in the morning. I didn't have these moments often, but the only time Mom ever seemed even mildly tired with Dad was when he had a bad bout of marathon snoring. Why she had brought Dino into our lives I'd never understand. I'd give her some excuse, but three years was a little long for temporary insanity.

"Well, that was fun," I said.

"You heard," she said. Mom pushed her bangs from her forehead, rubbed her temples. The gesture made me pissed off at Dino, at what he caused.

"I heard yelling. I didn't hear actual words. What was going on?"

"Dino was trying to write last night, and he swore he could hear the Powelson's television. It was bugging him. His ears— you know he can hear a leaf drop off a tree."

"I heard the door slam. I saw him outside."

"He went over there. To their house. He cut their cable wire with a pair of hedge clippers."

I almost laughed. I did. I mean, think of it—Dino creeping down the street in his bathrobe, aiming toward the glow of light in Courtney and gang's living room window. I could just picture him hunting around in the junipers for the cable, his gleeful discovery of the thick wire, the satisfactory snap. Then, the sudden extinguishing of the light to a pinpoint. The whole Powelson house with its television IV yanked. "It's almost kind of funny," I said.

"It's not funny, Cassie. Okay, it's a little funny. Oh, shit." She chuckled to herself. She shook her head, held her coffee mug in both hands.

I wanted to crack up, but the joke felt like a sick one, slightly morbid. If it had just been this, another Dino tantrum, I could have laughed. But there was also his shoeless display of weirdness yesterday. This wire cutting—it was more than excessive frustration. I knew that. "Something strange happened yesterday," I said.

"Oh?"

I told Mom about Dino. The shoes. His paranoia that someone always knew where he was. The way he played that violin. She just looked at me for a while. "He's off his medicine," she said finally.

"What do you mean, 'He's off his medicine'?"

"He's trying to write. He says it makes him too foggy. That he can't create when he takes it."

"I didn't even know he had medicine."

"For his depression."

Mom had first explained to me about Dino's depression early on in their marriage. No one I knew before had ever tromped off to see a psychiatrist every week. This seemed more than a tad overdramatic, and I said so to Mom. She went into this big discussion about what clinical depression was, as if I'd never heard those ads on the radio ("Do you have any of these symptoms? Change in eating or sleeping habits? Loss of interest in things that used to give you pleasure? Being critical and nasty to the people you live with?"). It apparently was not I'm-having-a-bad-day, but I'm-having-a-bad-life, with complications ranging from not being able to get out of bed to feeling like the world was out to get him. All things you want in a second husband.

Obviously, this depression also made him incapable of see-ing that he was luckier than 99 percent of the world's popula-tion. Okay, I know it sounds unsympathetic, and I know most of the time it's a chemical thing that happens to good people and can't be helped. But in Dino's case, so much of it sounded like a spoiled child who needed to be sent to his room. Really, did people who lived in third world countries with no running water or indoor toilets and that had to sew thousands of faux leather jackets in zillion-degree heat in order to eat get depressed and stay in bed? Could they not function without their psychiatrist connected to them like those sicko parents who put their kids on a leash? Call me cold, but his depression seemed like a luxury. I mean, I was depressed myself at having to live with the guy.

"Can't you make him take his medicine?" I said.

"Oh, sure," she said. She was right. It was a stupid thing to say. No one could make Dino do anything he didn't want to.

"I don't get this. What's going to happen here? Is he just going to keep getting worse? He's going to start thinking he's Jesus?"

She didn't answer. I guess she didn't know either. Great.

Terrific. What did this *mean*? "Cassie?" she said finally. "There's one more thing. I didn't want to tell you, but you'd probably see the truck." She was quiet for a moment.

"What?" I meant, *What now?*

"He cut our cable too."

"Are you kidding me? Why?" I didn't know what to think or feel. None of this seemed real. I guess I felt a little panicked. My voice was high and shrill.

"He said . . . he said he did it so no one could listen in on his work in progress."

"Oh, my God."

"I've got a call in to the doctor."

I felt a gathering in my chest, an on-alert tightness. Then, I knew what I felt. I was afraid.

That day at school, I looked at the people in my classes and thought about how different my yesterday must have been from any of theirs. No one in those rooms would have guessed what happened in my house last night. There was something about it that made me ashamed. And it was big. Too big to hold all by myself, even if it was embarrassing as hell. Zebe is the best listener in the world, even patiently hearing about your dreams in boring detail *(And then I turned into a fern. A talking fern, and then I got onto a bus heading to Miami, only it wasn't really Miami. It looked like the living room, and my second-grade teacher Mr. Bazinski, was wearing a kilt and sitting on an ottoman teaching long division . . .)*, so at lunch I tried a little of what happened on her. Not all of it. Just enough so I could handle the rest on my own. She had all of the basic facts—we'd been friends for a couple of years, and she knew my family.

"Dino's going nuts," I said.

"What? That cuddly, cutesy-wootsy teddy bear? I think you should write an essay and nominate him for Stepfather of the Year."

"Don't even call him that. My mother's husband. Okay? I don't even want *father* in the same sentence as Dino."

"I noticed you weren't acting like yourself," Zebe said. "Here. Have some Cheetos. Nothing like overly orange food to give you comfort. Think about it. Orange sherbert. Orange Jell-O. I'm going to dye my hair orange."

"Don't you dare." Zebe had this long, jet-black hair that was so shiny you could practically see your reflection in it. That day she was wearing fishnet stockings and a plaid skirt. She could wear anything and make it look cool.

"So what's Senõr Loco done now?" she asked.

"Dino's paranoid that someone can hear the new stuff he's writing," I said. "Through the television cable." I used my can-you-believe-how-stupid-he-is? voice. It was Zebe and I loved her, but this was as far as I was willing to go. I couldn't speak about how afraid it had made me. This craziness happening in *my family*, for God's sake. People might think it was catching.

Zebe twirled her finger by her head. "Oh, my God, what a freak! My dad got real paranoid when my parents got divorced. He climbed in a window of my mom's to steal her journals. He was sure she was going to post nasty stuff about him on the Web. She was even going to press charges, but decided it wasn't worth the hassle."

Zebe and I ate Cheetos. I thought about what she said. Really thought about what it must have meant to her. A ladder against a window. Your parent rooting around like an intruder. A police car in front of your house as the neighbors looked on. Maybe I was wrong when I thought no one at my school would believe what had happened to me. I looked around the cafeteria, the rows of tables jammed with people, scattered lunches, noise, crap on the floor. John Jorgenson grabbed some sophomore's baseball cap and threw it to his friend, and Danielle Rhone was trying to find something she dropped under a table, and three freshmen were huddled together over open books, doing their homework. Reese Lin shoved what looked like a full lunch bag in the garbage, and Todd Fleming brought three small pizza boxes to his table. Angela Aris and James what's-his-name leaned against the wall, making out. I wondered what went on behind the closed doors of these people's houses. A mother that drank too much, a father that hit. Parents that fought, or tried unsuccessfully to hide an affair, or who couldn't leave the house out of fear.

Maybe we all had our secrets.

I walked home alone from school that day, no Siang or Courtney. Zach and I had apparently had a successful operation to separate Siamese twins, at least for the moment. I was coming down our road, trying to ignore the fact that it was Tuesday, the day of Ian Waters's next lesson, and so of course was consumed by thoughts of nothing else. *Please let Dino act normal,* I said over and over in my head. *Please, please.* I had decided under no uncertain terms not to fall for Ian Waters, but I still didn't want him to think I lived in a nuthouse. Here was the thing—Ian was going to go away to school, and that was that. Letting myself fall for him was only going to lead to pain. I, for one, didn't need to jump headfirst into some overwhelming feeling that would lead to disaster. I could make a rational decision about where I was going to put my heart, or if I was going to put my heart anywhere at all.

I was what you would call Steeled with Resolve when this old Datsun, a horrible shade of banana yellow, drove up behind me on our road. It stopped in front of our house as I walked up, and this beefy, motorcycle type got out of the passenger's side, flipping up the seat to let Ian Waters and his violin out of the back. Rocket leaped out after him.

"Hey," Ian said when he saw me.

God, he had beautiful eyes. Gentle brown. Like deer fur, or those elbow patches on the jackets of college professors. A soft, comforting brown. I'd forgotten what effect the sight of him had on me. Goddamn it.

"Hey," I said eloquently.

"You've got to meet my brother and his best friend. Chuck, this is Cassie. Dino's daughter." I didn't bother to correct him with the real version of our twisted family tree right then, as huge Chuck was holding out this bear paw for me to shake, and the driver of the Datsun, a twin of the other guy, was turning around to see me. "And that's my brother, Bunny."

"Howdy." Bunny gave a wave.

Either Ian or his brother must have been conceived in a petri dish, because they were the unlikeliest brother combo you'd ever seen. Bunny was outfitted in a motorcyclist's black leather pants and a vest with a T-shirt underneath. He was older than Ian, by maybe seven or eight years. He had a wild bunch of dark brown hair, and was solid as the side of a mountain. You wouldn't dare point out the fact that he had the name of a cute fluffy animal. He looked like he could kill with his bare hands.

"Be good," Bunny said as Chuck got in and shut the door. Boy, I'd be good if he said that to me. I'd sit and embroider Bible verses, I'd be so good.

The car pulled away. I saw something that surprised me. They had a bumper sticker: TRUST THE PROCESS.

"We're twins," Ian said, and grinned.

"I could tell by your matching outfits," I said. Rocket had curled up on the lawn. I could hear Dog William whining on the other side of the fence.

"He's my stepbrother. He moved us out here when my stepfather died. He thinks it's his personal responsibility to look after us. He comes over and makes, like, six boxes of macaroni and cheese."

"Wow," I said. "I like his bumper sticker."

"Oh, man. Don't ever get him started on that stuff. I'm serious." We headed into the house. "Chuck and Bunny are into the whole metaphysical thing. They've been friends since they were, like, two. They go around to their motorcycle groups giving talks on The Wisdom of Your Inner Voice."

"Okay, this time you are kidding."

"I wish I was."

"That's hilarious. Metaphysical motorcyclists."

"It's worse. Neither of them has a motorcycle. Jeez." He shook his head and laughed. Okay, great. Ian Waters was nice, too. Beautiful, talented, *nice.*

"Shall we get started?" Dino said when we came in. I tried to check him out for any sign of irrational paranoia. His shoes were on. His eyes looked normal. I allowed myself the thought that maybe we'd all overreacted about yesterday. Or maybe Mom got Dino to take his medicine. This super-fast-acting medicine.

Dino grasped Ian's shoulder and squeezed it in warm greeting. It looked like the lesson was going to go okay, and I went upstairs. After a while I heard the music starting. God, if I could only explain it. You wanted to let it take up residence inside you. Let it flourish there, like a garden of wildflowers. You wanted to possess it, hold it, become a part of it. It wrapped around you like the cape of a wizard, full of magic color.

I wanted it. That music, him. I put my pillow over my head. That boy and his violin scared the crap out of me. My heart was beating so hard it felt like it was trying to make an escape attempt.

An eternity and an hour later, I heard the front door close as Ian left. Mom came home shortly after, and we shouted greetings to each other from different floors, something that never failed to piss off Dino. Soon, dinner smells rose up the stairs.

Dino's face was tight at the table, stern and rocky. The favorite game of temperamental people is Try to Guess Why I'm Ticked Off. *(Contestant number one, Why do YOU think he's pissed off? Why, I'm not sure, Bob, but I'm going to go with 'Because I Left the Faucet Dripping. BEEP. I'm sorry, that's incorrect. The correct answer is: 'Because You Happen to Exist.')* Even if I'm determined not to play, I get sucked in. My brain just does what it wants anyway, same as when I'm sitting in calculus, wondering if Mr. Firtz could possibly have a sex life, even though the thought is revolting. The brain can be a sicko, out-of-control thing sometimes, and at dinner I started wondering who did what wrong this time. Likely Dino was doing a Mount Rushmore imitation because we'd shouted at each other across the house. I put my money down on that one.

"How did the lesson go?" my mother asked Dino. She seemed more relaxed than she did that morning, in spite of Dino's obvious attitude. Like me, she was probably relieved to find Dino more "normal" again. Which meant, back to his old asshole-ish self.

"A beautiful lesson with the boy. Except for the fact that he was late. Cassie was entertaining him."

I never thought Dino was very attractive—if you've never seen a picture of him, his nose is chunky and his forehead is broad, and he's got full lips. He's pretty short, too, just a little taller than Mom unless she wears heels. His crowning glory was his headful of curly gray-black hair, but it's like the game you can play with the blond girls at school—imagine them without the hair and there's not much there. I'm not sure why women liked him so much. But right then, he was downright ugly. That's the thing with mean people. Eventually their spirit shows through like mold on cheese.

"Entertaining him? I talked to the guy for maybe a minute and a half," I said. I let the irritation show in my voice. I didn't care. I plunked a dollop of guacamole on my taco salad, took a forceful bite.

"The lesson started late."

So that's what his problem was. In forty years when he got Alzheimer's, he might forgive me.

"He needs to focus on his music. Nothing else."

"I said hello. He introduced me to his brother."

"Sounds harmless to me," Mom said. "She's not having a love affair with the guy, Dino. *Hello* won't kill his focus." She speared a tomato.

"This is not some high school boy, Daniella. We are attempting to train a genius. He has no room for kissy face."

"Darn, and I thought you didn't see my tongue down his throat," I said. I got up. Shoved back my chair. I wasn't hungry anymore. If there is something that can make you as angry as being unjustly accused, tell me. Or being disproportionately accused. You do well in school and you don't do drugs or have sex, but they get mad at you for not making your bed.

I went outside to the shed, got out my telescope. Swore under my breath at the psycho creep. It was late October and cold out, and I'd wished I'd interrupted my anger by getting a sweatshirt. Too late now. The clouds were doing this manic fleeing, in a hurry to get somewhere, and as they whipped past, they'd reveal these bursts of brilliantly clear sky. I hauled out my equipment and set up in the open grassy patch by the front of the house. It was the perfect viewing place—open sky, the garden ringed with hydrangeas and a view of the sound. The water smelled cold and deep and swampy in the darkness, the smell of thousands of years of whale secrets.

I sprang out the tripod legs of my telescope, swore at the fact that I only wore socks, which were now wet from dewy grass. Hey, cool. Now I could take them off and be a lunatic like Dino. Dog William whined for my company from behind the fence. If I was lucky I'd see Mars in between cloudbursts. It was more work than it seemed, looking through a telescope, as the Earth was continually moving and you had to move along with it. You don't realize how fast this actually happens, and it's kind of both creepy and wonderful when you stop to think about it. And it makes you realize there is absolutely no way to avoid change. You can sit there and cross your arms and refuse it, but underneath you, things are still spinning away.

Anyway, the telescope always made me feel better. I could go to a different place and didn't need chemicals or airfare to do it. I started hunting around for Mars when I heard tires on gravel. Bike tires. Oh, my God, bike tires. It was inky black out there, so all I could see was the white of his T-shirt underneath his black coat until he got closer. Ian Waters put his feet on the ground, balanced his bike with his hands. God, there he was, all of a sudden. Ian Waters.

"Hi," he said. His breath came out in a puff. That's how cold it was getting.

"Hi," I said. "What are you doing here?" I tried to breathe. My heart was doing this charming maraca number.

"Performance tape." He pulled a cassette from his pocket, lifted it up. "Mr. Cavalli wanted to hear one of my concerts. Can you see anything tonight?"

"Mars." I was trying to ignore the fact that his presence was charging up the night like an approaching lightning storm. I swear, my insides felt this surge of energy, a hyperawareness. I could smell his shampoo. I tried to breathe deeply. I mean, this was stupid. This was no big deal. I forced myself to sound casual. "Want to look? You've got to be quick, before a cloud comes."

Ian set his bike down on the grass, climbed over it. His coat was apparently a conductor of electricity, because when his sleeve touched my arm as he bent over beside me, I felt a jolt of current. I shivered.

"Cold?" he said, as he looked into the telescope where I had pointed it.

"I'm okay." Which was a lie. Some cruel person had invaded my body and was squeezing my lungs. I could barely breathe, so I'm not quite sure why I was suddenly worrying about my guacamole breath.

"No way," he said. "Is that it? Mars?"

"Big white ball? Yeah." Casual. No big deal.

"That's amazing. That's *Mars*? That's an actual planet? Man, that's hard to believe." He stood straight again. His eyes were shiny and happy. "We're looking at a *planet*."

"I know it. That's how I feel about it too."

"I've never seen inside a telescope before."

"Never?"

"No. You know, this is my usual method." He leaned his head back, looked up. "Wow. This isn't bad either."

He was right. I looked up with him and saw that the sky was showing off. The clouds had moved aside for a moment, and the blackness was deep, deep. The stars were both simple and magical, thousands of pinpoints of light. It was one of those moments you wonder how we could ever forget what was up there. There is that majesty, you are overcome by the wonder, and then the next day you're worrying about your math homework.

We just stared up there for a while, and then Ian sat down on the grass, on the tails of his coat. It occurred to me briefly to worry that Dino might see us, and about the trouble I'd be in then. I sat down on the grass beside Ian. Right there next to him, and I started imagining his arms around me. Eight months, I reminded myself. Eight months and he'd be gone and not looking back. I remembered how much it had hurt when I broke up with that asshole Adam Peterson, even when that had been my choice and he was a creep. I remembered my father's arm through the glass of his car when his heart was destroyed. I leaned down on my elbows. "This is the best way to see the stars this time of year, anyway," I said. "The telescope gets impossible. Shaky images. The atmosphere is more . . ." I looked for the word. Moved my hand in the air.

"Unstable?" he guessed.

"Turbulent."

I was sitting very close to him and he looked over at me, laid down on his side and propped on one elbow. He looked at me and I looked back, and he held my eyes for a while. I looked deeply inside of him, and he saw me too. Something passed between us right then. Some force, some connection, and, God, I wanted it so badly, him seeing me that way, me seeing him. I wanted more and more and more of it. I granted myself a concession. Friends. That's what I would do. I'd be Ian Waters's friend, and I could still have some piece of this without getting my heart broken.

I could do that. I was in charge of my feelings; they weren't in charge of me.

Ian looked away from me, back toward the sky. "Wow," he said. He shook his head. Stood up. "Whew."

"Are you all right?"

"I've got to go."

"Okay."

He went to his bike, set it upright again. "You know, I'm jealous. You here, doing what you love."

"You do what you love," I said.

"I don't love the violin," he said.

"You're kidding."

"Sometimes I hate it."

"You do?"

"It runs my whole life. Then I try to remember that I'm lucky to have a talent for it."

"Talent?" I said. "You've got more than a *talent*."

"Mr. Cavalli thinks my playing lacks *passion*."

"Well, he's got too much of it. Way too much."

"That's what it takes to be great, he says."

"Then maybe it isn't such a good deal to be that great," I said. Passion—you had Dino on one side with way too much, and the Powelsons on the other with absolutely none. The cable truck had come and gone, and now their house glowed blue again from television light. There had to be a happy medium somewhere.

I was standing next to Ian and his bike. He picked up one of my cold hands. He rubbed it between his own to warm it. He let it go again. Friends could do that. Friends could wish that he didn't let go.

"Bye," he said. He smiled, pushed off hard on the pedals and set off down the road. I watched the back of him disappear.

I heard one of our upstairs windows slam shut. Angrily. Dino had been watching us, I realized. And then I realized something else—Ian had ridden off with the performance tape still in his pocket. Maybe the reason Ian came over had nothing to do with the tape after all.

"Ian Waters." I said his name into the darkness.

I rubbed my arms against the cold. The feeling I had gotten when our eyes met—I tried to shake it. Anyway, it was no big deal. Really. Because I had it all under control.

Chapter Five

People don't crack up in a linear, orderly fashion. A person on the brink can do something really wacky—believing he can be heard through his cable, for example—but then return to his regular old self for days afterward. It's a great way for you to convince yourself that things are okay enough. Then something happens again. And again. Until the creepy things are coming closer and closer together, and *regular* is farther and farther apart. It's an elevator ride—down, up. Down two floors again, and up seven. Up again to the highest floor, where the cable will snap and the car will drop in fast, mind-blowing destruction.

Dino was okay for most of the week after he cut our cable. Then on Friday night, Dino, Mom, and I decided to go out to dinner before I went over to Sophie Birnbaum's. During football season my friends and I sometimes go over to Sophie's in an informal ban of the display of caveman hormones going on at our school stadium. We play marathon Monopoly with our own system of money using M&M's, our reward for having to put up with cheerleaders flashing their asses at us during the afternoon assembly, and for being forced to clap for the football players with their D-plus grade averages.

We had dinner, and Dino was driving back. Mom and I were discussing whether I needed a ride home after Sophie's or not, when Dino spoke.

"I've ruined him, I'll guess," Dino said. "That's why he's stalking me."

Just like that, out of nowhere. The air in the car went cold.

"No one is stalking you," Mom said. "Quit that."

"He's jealous that I'm succeeding without him."

"Who?" I asked.

"You know who," Dino said.

Mom caught my eyes in the rearview mirror. Her eyes said, *I know. I heard the same thing you did.* They said, *Please, Cassie. Keep your mouth shut.*

"He's probably driving one of those outhouse trucks. What are they called. Porthole potties." Dino chuckled to himself. Porta-Potti, he meant, and it might have been funny. I might have laughed, imagining the poor sailor who would look out of a porthole potty. I might have cracked up at Dino being so hilarious about some guy stalking him, because of course it was a joke. But I didn't laugh. I was scared.

Insanity, see—it's hilarious until it's deadly serious.

Mom was scrambling eggs the next morning and talking

on the phone. She wasn't paying attention to them the way she should have. They were getting brown on the bottom.

"I've got to go, Alice." Alice was Alice Easton. Mom's good friend and a clarinet player in their orchestra. They often carpooled together. Alice was the warm kind of person who baked a lot. We were always getting things from her like banana bread and cookies and muffins. Good kind of friend to have. "I'll try. Okay. Bye," Mom said, and hung up. One of those kind of hang-ups that happen because you are suddenly in the room.

"I thought you were going to make him take his medicine," I said. Here was my message: *Fix this,* I was saying.

"I never said that. I said I was going to talk to the doctor. Which I've done. No one can *make* him, Cassie. The doctor says we'll just have to wait and see what happens."

"Terrific. What's next? The CIA is going to talk to him through the television? Who does he think is stalking him?"

"William Tiero. Look, it's pointless to try to make sense of this."

"William Tiero? Why William Tiero?"

"I don't know, Cassie. They've had a long history together. One of those love-hate things. Epic drama of good intentions and bad blood. I don't want to talk about this now, okay? I'm exhausted. Just . . . I can handle him. Try not to worry."

"I don't really see how that's possible."

"Let me worry. The good thing is . . . well, he's writing," she said. "He'll finish his writing, and things will get better. I promise."

When you think of Hemingway and William Styron and

Virginia Woolf and Robert Lowell and Mozart, think too of the people around them. The brothers and friends and wives and nieces and daughters. Think of all of the people who had to be normal in crazy conditions. Who had to pay bills and figure out what to have for dinner. Who worried, and tried to understand, and called doctors, and placated in their attempt to define and control what wasn't even of this world. Who acted as the stabilizing force, the pull of the moon on a wobbly earth, calming its own natural impulse to spin out of control. And think of those who couldn't hold on to their own sanity while being pulled down by others. Liszt, who went mad himself dealing with his crazy family, including his daughter with three kids out of wedlock with Wagner; and poor Robert Frost, with his nervous breakdown after trying to pay for all of his family members in insane asylums. And Theo van Gogh, devoted caretaker, who died six months after his mad brother. Sometimes, the job would have been too much.

I decided to get out of there. It wasn't just the night sky that was tumultuous, filled with smashing air currents and forces of nature at their most raw and untamed. My house felt that way too. Depression is a force, paranoia is a force, huge moving masses that affect everything in their way, same as continents colliding. And just like looking through a telescope when the weather gets cold, the instability in the air makes the images blurred and confused. I wanted to be in a place where I could count on things being calm and making sense.

I walked to Dad's. I had to pass Ian Waters's house, the

small cottage near town that now had a new coat of paint and some flowers out front since he'd moved in. I felt a little surge of glee seeing his tennis shoes on the front porch. I admit, I walked past kind of slowly, hoping he'd see me and come out, but the house looked quiet. It was probably a good thing. All week I'd been working hard to keep the thoughts of my new friend where they should be. I tried not to keep meeting his eyes in my mind. Eight months, I reminded myself, and he'd be off with his violin. I'd be lucky if he had time for a letter after he went to Curtis.

When I got to Dad's, I just hung out with him and helped him change the oil in his car. Afterward we drove over and picked up Nannie from Providence Point, and Dad made us all dinner. I didn't want to talk to him about what was happening at home—God knows how he'd take that and run with it. I just wanted to be with him. He made this great buttery pasta that probably had a gazillion calories, and then we played Crazy Eights and Nannie cheated. She beamed with victory and rode home with the most smug look you ever saw. It reminded me exactly of Zach Rogers earlier that day when we got back our math tests. He waved it over his head like an Olympic flag, in spite of the fact that he mysteriously got every one wrong that I did, and that during the test I could feel his eyes rolling around my paper, sure as marbles on tilted glass. Dad and I drove Nannie back home, and learned that we'd only gotten a glimpse of what was apparently a full-blown immersion into a life of crime. I dropped her purse on the way out to the car, and about five thousand restaurant sugar packets spilled out, along with two thousand little squares of jam and another several thousand tiny cream containers.

"Mom. What's this?" my father asked.

"What's what?" she said, scooping them back in with knobby fingers. "I don't see anything."

"Why do you need to do this? You take your coffee black. If you want jam, I can get you jam."

"I can't hear you," she said.

"The *jam*."

"I can't hear a thing he's saying." Which was a pretty great problem-solving technique, if you ask me.

"You got good taste," I said to Nannie. "They're all blackberry. My favorite."

"Don't encourage her," Dad said.

Before she went inside Providence Point, Nannie squeezed a five-dollar bill into my palm and a couple of jam packets. I kissed her cheek. "Go easy, Nannie," I said. "We don't want you convicted for condiment theft. You go to that prison, you'll meet big-time operators. Maple syrup stealers."

"I got catsup in my brown purse," she said.

On the way back home, Dad turned on the radio, hit his palm against the steering wheel to the rhythm of some eighties station. All eighties, all the time, lucky us. I was praying he wouldn't sing along, then wondered if God would punish me for only checking in with him during times of convenience: 1) when something monumentally awful was about to happen, 2) before a test, 3) when hoping something embarrassing would happen to the homecoming princesses riding around the school track up on the backseat of a convertible, and 4) when I sensed a parent was about to act in a manner that would make me wish for those paper bags they give you on airplanes.

"You're awfully happy tonight," I said. "Have you been drinking Optimism in a Cup?" That's what he called coffee.

"Nope. It's a natural high. Life is good."

"Hey, you're in love," I said. I pictured a female accountant version of Dad, and hoped she didn't have kids I'd have to deal with. Poor Zebe has a stepsister who actually goes to our school and is in her chemistry class. *She sits and files her nails and studies her split ends like they're about to discover a cure for cancer,* Zebe told me. *She carries a pink purse with her initials in rhinestones.*

"No, I'm not in love." It began to rain and Dad turned on the wipers. His eyes were as shiny as the wet pavement under the streetlights. "I'm just close to finding out something important."

"Oh yeah? The meaning of life? Why dogs roll around on dirty towels?"

"Better."

"If it's about Dino, Dad, I really don't want to know."

"Fine. I won't tell you."

"I think it's wacky you're snooping on him."

"I don't have to tell you a thing."

"Okay, fine. Tell me."

"Hand me an Altoid."

"Jesus, Dad, okay, I said tell me."

It started to really pour, the way it can in the Northwest. Dump, is more like it. It's the kind of rain that makes you wonder if a monsoon could really be much worse. The kind of rain that can make even a gas station minimart with a creepy cashier look cozy and inviting. Dad switched his wipers to manic mode.

"'Bermuda, Bahamas, come on, pretty Mama,'" Dad sang. "'Key Largo, Montego, ooh, I want to take you . . .'"

I folded my arms, stared out the window. Some poor dweeb got stuck walking his dog in the rain—if he lifted his head, he might drown like a turkey. "You know, for a parent, you're really pretty childish."

"Okay, okay," Dad said. "I'm having a little trouble locating Mr. Cavalli's birth certificate." Dad raised his eyebrows and smiled. His teeth looked really white in the darkness.

"So what. The guy's old. Foreign country. Some ancient hill town, for God's sake. People with no teeth. Women with mustaches."

"We'll see." He looked smug. Right then he looked just like his mother after she won at Crazy Eights.

Here's what I thought then. I was surrounded by lunatics. Dad was as bad as Dino. Okay, maybe not, but you know what I mean. It occurred to me then that there was very little in the world that wasn't ridiculous to the point that it made no sense. Putting on neckties was pretty weird, when you came to think of it. Ditto nylon stockings, and grown men using sticks to knock little white balls into cups, and government-access television stations. What the hell was normal, anyway? I mean, my God, something is strange with the world when pom-poms are a status symbol. Aliens would someday look at us with completely baffled expressions. Dogs already do.

I'd let my father have his lunacy, mostly because there wasn't anything I could do about it anyway. Control is easier to relinquish when you have no choice. Besides, I told myself, what he was doing was harmless, wasn't it?

Here was another funny but not funny thing. Remember the poor dweeb walking his dog in the rain? That poor dweeb was Dino, and that was Dog William, made unrecognizable by hair glued to his body with water and by his miserable expression. When I came home that night, Dino's wet wool coat was hung over the stair rail, smelling like a barn animal. His soaking socks were curled up in something that resembled embarrassment on the hall floor. He was walking around the kitchen in his bathrobe, his curly hair straight as a pencil, nothing like the simmering photo of him on the cover of his Paris journals. It struck me that Dino had aged. Maybe since the day before. Mom was drying Dog William in a towel. He looked cute for the first time in his life.

"Jeez. What happened here?" I said.

"Dino felt like a snack. Got caught in the rain," Mom said. She didn't seemed concerned. In fact, she seemed content, just drying off poor old Dog William.

"Hey," I said. "I saw you. I didn't know it was you."

"You could have given him a ride," Mom said. Yeah, I could have just invited him right on in the car with Dad. It'd be a nice, calm ride. Like when they transport violent criminals across state lines.

"I don't mind the rain," Dino said. "Good for the skin." He pinched one of his cheeks. He was pretty cheerful for someone who appeared recently shipwrecked. It must have been a good day—the weirdness of the car ride the night before had disappeared as quickly as it had come.

"He looks sweet," I said, pointing my chin toward Dog William.

Dino batted his eyelashes.

"Not you," I said. "The dog."

"My heart is broken," he said.

"How's this?" Mom put the towel around Dog William's face. It hung down his back, nun-style. "Sister Mary William."

"Dog with a bad habit," I said.

Dog William had enough of religion and took off like he was late for his bus. He was probably rolling around on the carpet, fluffing up and getting dog hair everywhere.

"I got us something," Dino said. He opened the brown bag that was on the counter. Really, it did this soggy tear, as the bag, too, was drenched. Dino held up a package of Hostess Cupcakes and a packet of Corn Nuts. Hey, good taste. Usually he won't put anything near his mouth that doesn't have some hyperculinary aspect to it. Sun-dried gorgonzola, rosemary cilantro crepes with raspberry sauce, that kind of crap.

He opened the cupcakes, even approached them the right way, by peeling off the icing and eating that first. I had a little surge of positive feeling. One of those maybe-everything-will-be-okay rushes of hope that usually only comes to me after a big swig of Zebe's espresso. Dino put his arms around Mom. He lifted up her hair, kissed her neck. She leaned into him, and I could see the chemistry between them. I hated to see it, but I did. I knew it explained some things about why Mom was with him.

Dino left the kitchen and went into his office in his bath-robe. I heard him tuning and then the brief fits and starts of playing, which meant that Dino was writing. Mom made a cup of tea, sat down at the kitchen table, and warmed her hands around the mug. I had some too, even though it was the kind of tea that tasted like licking a grass welcome mat. Mom tilted her head and we both listened to Dino create, as Mom's own cello leaned in the corner like a bad drunk. She looked pretty. She took a barrette from her pocket, pulled her hair back. Her face was peaceful. She smiled. "He had a good day of writing. An awesome day," she said.

"He seems really happy," I said. She did too.

"He said that for the first time in his life, it's coming easily. Maybe I was worried for nothing."

"That's great, Mom."

"We may make it to March after all," she said.

"You don't have to lurk back there," I said to Siang Chibo the next day after we got to my house. "Just walk with us, for God's sake. The stalking has got to go. You make me feel like I'm in one of those horror movies where you know something awful's gonna happen and the girl's car never starts."

"I can't walk with her. She makes me nervous."

"Who, Courtney? Just pretend you're watching bad TV. That's how I get through most of the school day."

"She makes me feel like a loser."

"Don't ever feel that way. You are not a loser. You are so smart. Courtney could only fantasize about being so smart. You know how some people laugh at their own jokes? Courtney can't. She doesn't *get* her own jokes."

Siang smiled. "Is Mr. Cavalli here today?"

"No. He's at the dentist getting his teeth cleaned. Gingivitis." Lie. But I tried to toss Siang some reality every now and then. Just to keep the adoration at manageable levels.

Disgusting gum disease didn't dampen Siang's enthusiasm one bit. "Let's go in his office."

"Ooh, okay. That'll be a memory I can put in my scrapbook. You can't touch anything, though, because he's been writing. If you mess anything up in there, I'm dead."

I knew I'd made a mistake the second I opened the door. At first I only saw the mess of papers, empty pages, all empty white sheets strewn around on the desk and the chair and the floor and around by the windows. It was easy for your eye to be drawn to the one page that wasn't blank, the one that was smeared with blood. It was crumpled up, as if it had been used as a towel to clean up some bleeding, and that's probably just what had happened. It lay among some shards of glass, a pile of crystally chunks, the remnants of the frame that had held William Tiero's picture that had obviously been thrown against the wall, same as that wineglass. The force had knocked the print that hung above his desk, those yellowy flowers, askew. It was barely hanging there, threatening to crash to the floor.

Siang gasped.

I tried to take in what I was seeing, but it didn't seem real. Some awful feeling filled my heart—horror, shock. I felt like the ground was suddenly pulled from underneath me, and that things were falling, falling. He was writing, so everything was going to be okay. And here it was. All of those empty pages. All of that frightening white.

"I'm not sure what's happened," I said.

"Oh, my God," Siang whispered.

I wanted to shut the door. I wanted this out of my sight. Those pages, that gash of blood, sucked the air right from me. I felt a wave of shame, too, a sense of letting Siang down in an important way. I reached for the knob, but Siang put her hand on my arm.

"Wait," she said. Siang stepped into the office, did something I would respect her for forever. She walked over to that painting above his desk and she straightened it. She made sure it wouldn't fall.

Tears gathered tight and hot in my throat. I just kept seeing Mom the other night with her tea and her happiness. I kept thinking about our hope.

"It's okay," Siang said. She actually put her thin arm around my shoulders. "Come on."

I closed the door behind Siang and me. The latch clicked. I felt like I was trying to shut a monster into a room. A monster that would not be held back for long by something so simple as a lock.

I brought Mom to Dino's office when she came home. I had to confess to her that I'd gone in there with Siang. Mom just stood in the doorway where I had, held her hand to her mouth. *Oh, dear God,* she had said. *No.*

That night, I didn't know where Dino was. His car was gone.

I knew where Mom was, though. I found her in their bathroom, the pills from Dino's medicine bottles laid out along the counter so that she could count them. The white pages sat in a stack on their bed. What you learn is, stability is a moving target. What you learn is, destroyed hope is the most profound loss of all.

I went outside, took out my telescope. I was out there a long time, and I was looking at the moon. Thinking how many people looked at that very same moon. Wondering if maybe Ian was looking at that same moon now, too. And it was like I had almost called him to me, when I heard those bike tires. I thought I imagined them. I actually walked to the edge of the lawn, because I couldn't believe my own hearing. But there it was—the sound was coming closer. It was him, all right, and suddenly all of the bad things just lifted up. They just rose and made room for Ian Waters as he rode, a bit wobbly, down that gravel street, as he laid his bike down on the grass. I needed something to take the place of the scary things in my life right then, and my heart surged with this ridiculous giddiness, went from bad to good with the simple sight of his coat.

Bright orange maple leaves from our trees had begun to cover the lawn over the last few days. When Ian walked toward me, his shoes and pant legs *shish-shish*ed through them.

"This is so weird. I was *just* thinking about you," I said. My heart filled with wonderful-fantastic.

"You were?"

"Just this minute."

"What were you thinking?" He stood close. Put his hands on my arms.

I forgot what friends could say and what friends couldn't. I forgot all about his leaving in eight months. It was so good to shove aside what was happening in that house behind me and have something else take that space. I would take five minutes of wonderful-fantastic, if that's all I could have. "I was thinking that maybe you were looking at the moon too."

"Can I?" He nodded toward the telescope.

"Sure."

He dropped his hands, moved to the telescope, and peered in. The wind blew in a gust, picked up an armful of the leaves, and tossed them around. A few made a run for it down the road, turning mad circles. Ian's hair blew around too. There was something about smelling his shampoo that made everything feel it was right where it should be.

"It looks like . . . the moon." He laughed. "It really looks like the moon."

"I know it."

Ian shoved his hands in his pockets. "Are you all right out here? It's getting cold," he said, and he was right. October had done that sneaky October thing, changed a season on you without you noticing it. Fall always came with a sudden realization.

"I'm great," I said. I had a nice little cozy bonfire going on inside. Warm, toasty happiness. His care made everything just fine. "I like the cold. It smells good out here. Can you believe it's almost Halloween already?" I said.

Ian looked up, surveyed the sky with those eyes of his. He didn't want to talk about Halloween. "Cassie," he said to the sky, and then looked at me. "I've been thinking a lot about you lately."

My heart avalanched. Raced my stomach to my feet.

"Me too," I said.

"I've never met anyone like you before. You're . . . real. I like that."

Ian reached up to my face, tucked a strand of my hair behind my ear.

"So pretty," he said. I closed my eyes. Listened to the leaves scratching along paved driveways and the road. I felt Ian's warm breath near my cheek, knew we were about to kiss. I felt as if I were being sucked in, taken captive. He could have asked anything of me and I would have followed, led along by this joy in his presence. I leaned into him. His coat smelled as good as the night—like coldness and fall and burning leaves.

We kissed. Soft lips, night breeze, drowning. Dangerous, willing drowning.

We had already pulled away from each other when the headlights shined up the street. Headlights, oh, shit—Dino. Instant fear reaction. Instant guilt at being caught, and the sudden remembrance that there were way too many reasons not to be doing what I was just doing.

I stepped away from Ian, and real life filled the space between us as Dino parked his car in the drive and just sat there in the driver's seat, watching us. This, Ian and me, it was something I couldn't do. I just couldn't. Not only because Dino would be pissed, and he certainly already seemed pissed, not only because our lives were fucked up enough already, but because of what would happen to me if I let myself feel this much, this deeply, this good. Ian was leaving, and when he did I would feel this much, this deeply, this destroyed. I'd already seen what happened when you let your passions have their way. There were plenty of images to choose from—take your pick. My mother counting pills lined up along the bathroom counter, round yellow pills like dress buttons. My Dad's haunted post-divorce eyes, the chaos in my mother's postdivorce house, bills and dishes and laundry, all the evidence of a life out of control. My father with the Cavalli books spread out over his bed. Broken and destroyed hearts. I was only seventeen. It was too soon to be part of a train wreck.

I broke away, ran into the house before Dino got out of his car. I left Ian Waters standing alone on the lawn. I saw his face, enough of it, anyway, to see that he was surprised and hurt, but I didn't care. I told myself I didn't care. What mattered was avoiding the train wreck. I ran upstairs to my room, shut the door. I shut it all out behind me. Shutting doors was the solution of the day. I tried not to imagine Ian standing there outside, making his way home to that house by the ferry terminal. I just said to myself *No.* I held that snow globe with the bear in it, turned him upside down. He was the more sensible one of us. Sure, he was floating aimlessly, but he would never leave that glass dome. He would stay inside that place, even if it snowed and snowed.

Chapter Six

"Cassie? I need to talk to you about something," Mom said to me in the morning. What a surprise. After last night I knew we would be having this conversation. She sure hadn't wasted any time—I was in the bathroom getting ready for school. I had just brushed my teeth and was doing a quick toothpaste survey, seeing if I'd ended up with a white toothpaste drip. I swear, every day I end up with a spot of toothpaste in a different location. It's like a game of Where's Waldo.

"What?" I said. I knew what.

"It's about Ian."

"What about him?" Defensiveness crept up my spine, settled somewhere in my throat.

"Look, I don't know what the situation is. . . ."

"There is no situation," I interrupted. Which was mostly true. There wasn't going to be a situation anymore.

"Okay, fine. If that's the case, great. There are just things you don't understand here, about this. If you were to get involved . . . okay, Cassie, stop with the face. Let's just say you were. It's not a simple thing. Not even for you."

"I know that. That's why I'm making my own decision about it. You don't have to tell me that." I was angry. I didn't feel like I was the prime concern here. "Tell me, though, because, you know, I just don't get it. I don't get why Dino should have such a problem with me and Ian, anyway. Can't Ian have friends? What, he'll be contaminated like the kid who lives in the bubble? Or does Dino just not want me to be happy?"

"Come on, quit it. It has nothing to do with Dino not wanting your happiness. He's got a responsibility to Ian. Ian's got to stay focused. Dino's got to stay focused too. It complicates things unnecessarily."

"For Dino."

"For Dino, for Ian. For Ian's family. Ian is coming here for training. Professional training. This is his life course we're talking about. He needs this scholarship. Think about him, too. Dino had to have a talk with him last night."

"Oh, great. Just great." Humiliation. Like we were a couple of kids caught playing doctor. Shit.

"He can't be coming over here with you on his mind when he needs to be dedicated to that violin right now. There's a lot at stake here. Yes, for Dino, too. The structure, the chance to help this kid succeed—it's a stabilizing force. It means a lot to him to have the chance to help Ian make it. Cassie, let's just . . . if we keep things . . . uncomplicated . . ."

"I already told you, I'm not going to get involved with him. You can tell Dino to relax. Ian's going away, I know that. It'd be stupid."

"Exactly. I don't want to see you get your heart broken, either."

"It'd be stupid," I said again. "Nobody has to talk to anybody anymore."

"Dino's record deal, this concert—it's all final. His three pieces have got to be finished by March. He's got to write. Ian's audition is right before that. Let's just get through those two things. Remember what's best for Ian, if you care about him. Help me out here."

"Mom, *okay*." Jesus. I got it. It was over. Finished. I'd decided that before she even opened her mouth. Before Dino ever opened his to Ian.

"Things will calm down after March."

"All right," I said.

"I love you, and I'm sorry things are crazy right now."

"I love you, too," I said.

"You got toothpaste there by your collar," she said.

I walked past their open bedroom door and could see Dino's figure in bed, the hunch of his bare shoulders. Even as he slept there you could feel the unease in his form. I resented the lack of peace he had brought my mother and me, resented the fact that you could look at that sleeping back and see a possible eruption, a mountain of problems rather than the quiet security that sleeping shoulders should make you feel. I wanted the safety of someone folding warm laundry, or plunking down a bag of capably chosen groceries, or fixing a broken lawn mower. But in that bed was the meteor we lived with instead, who brought unshaven torment and sheets of notes written in almost clichéd fury and shoved in the kitchen garbage along with the coffee grounds and crushed Cap'n Crunch box. It occurred to me then that all we want a good part of the time is to feel in safe hands.

If you've ever made a decision not to have something you really want, you'll know how I felt over the next few days. Sure, there were these moments of resolve, of Zen-like peace that lasted all of a few seconds. But mostly I was pissed off. At my mother and at Dino and at the world that didn't arrange things in a better way. At my own chickenshit self.

It wasn't the kind of pissed off that was raging and full of energy, but the variety that was flat and snappish and lethargic. I was going through life in a fog, an expression that was true in every sense. I felt like I was watching and not really participating, like my life source had called in sick and was wrapped up in a quilt somewhere, zonked on cold medicine. And the fog was a literal truth too—for those days it lay around in wispy streams, around the water and on the lawn in the morning, as if the clouds had pushed the wrong elevator button. That's what fog is anyway—lazy clouds. Clouds without ambition. The fog was eerie and beautiful, soft and thoughtful, and it usually lifted in the afternoon to an annoying display of sun that made the October orange colors so bright that they hurt your eyes. Everything glistened with dew, and it was vibrantly cold out. I didn't want that, the cold that made you want to put on a big coat and do something useful and happy, like rake leaves. I wanted the rain again, or just the fog, looking miserable and spooky.

I went through the motions at school, caring even less than usual about the fact that Kileigh Jensen highlighted her hair or that rumors were flying about what Courtney did with Trevor Woodhouse, which everyone knew anyway by taking one look at them. The things that I might have laughed at, the fact that Sarah Frazier wore enough makeup for her and two of her closest friends, for example, or the coincidence that Hailey Barton's bra size doubled right about the same time that two Chihuahuas disappeared from the area, didn't even seem very funny.

My emotions were manic-hormonal, and when Jeremy Libitski got up and turned in his math test after, I swear, five minutes, I started to get all panicky. By this time you *know* better. You *know* there's some kid who always turns in his test after five minutes and you have that oh-shit moment of realization that you're still on the second question. You know to tell yourself that he's either some super-smug genius or just went along answering B to everything. But I panicked, and even the easy stuff seemed suddenly complex to the point of total confusion—*Name:*, for example. This is how messed up I was.

On Friday it was Halloween, and I decided to go to Brian Malo's party even if I wasn't really in the mood. I thought that maybe being with my friends would help me remember where I was before I even met Ian Waters, and remember that I existed fine without him before. It's strange, but you can feel excitement in the air on Halloween night, even if you're staying home, as if all the energy of those little kids too jazzed to eat dinner is just zipping around the atmosphere. We carved pumpkins the night before, and I Just Said No to those intricate designs that take three days without food or sleep to carve—haunted houses and cat faces and Leonardo da Vinci's *The Last Supper* done in gourd. I did two triangle eyes and a frown and tried to put a tooth in there, but it fell out and I had to stick it back in with a toothpick. Mom, who for the last few days had been talking to her friend Alice a lot on the phone and walking around Dino as if she were carrying a feather in cupped hands, carved the same thing she did every year, a music note. Dino came out of his study and watched us light the candles and sat there in the dark with us, which is probably a metaphor, come to think of it. Since Mom confronted him with the blank pages, he'd been defensive, then well behaved. It reminded me of Mom (a leadfoot) when she gets a speeding ticket. First, she's ticked off at the cop. Then, for three days running, she won't go a notch over the speed limit. After that, she's back to her old extreme and dangerous ways.

When I left, Mom and Dino were doing something they never did—just sitting on the couch and watching a movie. Very regular couple. Very non-genius of Dino. His arm was around my mother, sucking up. This was what his illness was like. A crash. Then enough quiet to make you think it might be getting better. Then an earthquake. And Mom would just buy into it. That's how bad she wanted things to be okay.

I walked to Brian's, because I liked to see the little kids with their costumes flowing out behind them as they ran, their parents calling *Thank you!* to open doorways, the miniature ghouls and power guys and gypsy girls. I remembered sweating like a sumo under rubber masks, and as a kindergartener, parading around the classes of big kids. I remember pouring out my candy on the floor when I got home from trick-or-treating, picking out the Butterfingers and separating similar things into piles. I remember my mom wearing a witch hat to answer the door, and my dad holding my hand when we crossed the street, and me sleeping in my bride costume when I was six. Yes, okay, I had a bride costume, so don't give me any crap about it. That night, the streets were full of the sound of tennis shoes running on pavement and of the spooky music some people played when they answered their doors. The air smelled like singed pumpkin lids and the beams of flashlights bounced around the darkness, and for some reason it all made me want to burst into tears.

Brian's party was noncostume, but a few people were there anyway in bloody and gory wounds and cat ears and the like. Michael Worthman, who I had a crush on last year, came as Minnie Mouse, which doused any lingering sexual chemistry. Beth Atkins, a girl who made costumes for drama, came dressed as a cow, demonstrating that it takes guts to wear an udder. Jeff Payley wore a dog costume, and went around shaking his butt and saying, "Look, I can wag my tail!" I ate pumpkin seeds and wondered why, as the experience is vaguely like munching on toenails. I talked to Zebe, who was wearing fishnet stockings and glow-in-the-dark fangs that she had to take out in a rather drooly fashion whenever it was her turn to answer.

"Michael Worthman's been checking you out all night," Zebe said.

"He's wearing a dress. With polka dots," I said.

"Hey, his legs look great in it," she said, raised her eyebrows up and down, and popped in her fangs again.

I left after a couple of hours, telling everyone I had a sore throat and wanted to go home to bed. I didn't talk to Zebe about Ian and me, because for starters, nothing existed between us. I was still out of sorts, and all of the cheer around me was just making me feel crappier. Only a few boys who were too big for trick-or-treating were still on the street, and Mom had blown out the pumpkin candles. When I came in, Mom and Dino had already gone to bed and there were only a handful of Sweet Tarts packs and boxes of Dots left in the candy bowl. Mom's taste in candy stank—she always went for the low-fat stuff in case we had any left and she was tempted to eat it. Dots were as far down on the evolutionary candy scale as you go, but I took a few anyway, which only goes to show the level of my general dissatisfaction. I went upstairs and got in bed, ate Sweet Tarts and disgusting cherry Dots in the dark. I tried to fend off images of Ian coming down my street that first time I saw him, of his face when I left him that night. That kiss. God, that kiss. I tried to get rid of overly sentimental pictures of my mother handing my father a cup of hot cider after we would come back home with our candy on Halloween nights. It occurred to me that if you loved it sucked, and if you didn't love it sucked, so either way you were screwed. Maybe love was better. At least sometimes you got chocolates.

My resolve was weak, so I was glad I didn't know Ian's phone number. I reminded myself for the zillionth time that I had to do what was best for Ian, too. I felt on the edge of tears, as if I could have cried at the sight of a drooping plant. Some kind of grieving was working around inside of me, and I didn't want any part of it. I got up to pee, and went downstairs for more candy or a glass of milk or a miracle cure. For some reason, I can't even tell you why, I went into Dino's study and pulled the Cavalli biography from the shelf. I sat right there on the floor, with the open book on my lap.

Lutitia Bissola, neighbor: The boy had his first concert for us, in the piazza. Anyone doing their shopping stopped to watch. His mother and father held hands and listened, and Mrs. Mueller, I think it was Mrs. Mueller who started it, put the bouquet of flowers at the child's feet when he was finished.

Francesca Bissola, neighbor: It wasn't Mrs. Mueller. It was Honoria Maretta. But after she put the flowers down, everyone else began laying down objects.

Honoria Maretta, grade-school teacher: I put the flowers down, yes. He was my student, my boy. He was like a son to me. He would come to my house to see my cat sometimes, and I would give him books and pizzelles. They were his favorite. I would bake them on a Sunday, when he might come over. My only little child, among all my students.

Francesca Bissola: Alberto what's-his-name put a loaf of French bread by the flowers.

Lutitia Bissola: Alberto Terreto. He put the bread down. And then there were other things. A zucchini. A melon. A lemon branch. Little offerings, laid at the boy's feet. Even Father Minelli had opened the doors of the church with the sound of the playing and stood there listening, his face turning red from the sun.

Francesca Bissola: His face was red from too much wine. The sun had nothing to do with it. He was a boozer, God rest his soul.[8]

---

8. *Dino Cavalli—The Early Years: An Oral History.* From Edward Reynolds, New York, N.Y. Aldine Press, 1999.

I smiled. In spite of myself, and in spite of the Dino-hero-worship, those people from Sabbotino Grappa could get to you. The words brought you to another time and place. Escapism was a nice thing sometimes. Personally, I don't see the problem with escapism and denial, those friendly twin coping mechanisms. I carried the book back to my room, read some more until the hot sun of Italy made me sleepy enough to turn out the light.

The next time Ian came for a lesson, I waited in my room until he was safely inside Dino's office, then I hightailed it out of there before they even started tuning. In my current state, I didn't even dare listen to Ian play. I didn't trust myself not to do something humiliating and out of control, same as you fear shouting out some swear word while you're at a church service. I could just see myself flinging open the door and throwing myself in his arms or something ridiculously schlocky. Or else I'd start weeping at the sound of that violin, picturing the notes drifting all the way to Italy, winding their way among the leaves of the olive trees.

Getting out, that was the main thing. Fall was still doing the cold, crispy thing, so I put on Mom's navy peacoat and borrowed Dino's lambskin gloves and hat that made him look like a bank robber. I stepped out the front door. Dog William had fallen firmly and steadfastly in love, and was looking happier than he'd ever looked in his life, lying on the grass with Rocket. His lips were curled up and his teeth showed, and anyone who says dogs don't smile is dead wrong. At least someone had their relationship life sorted out. He even looked kind of cute again. Rocket was sprawled out, looking serene and sphinxlike, and you could already tell who was the boss of the couple. I kicked through the leaves on our road, passed old Mr. and Mrs. Billings' house. Their pumpkins, out on their porch, now looked a bit caved in, same as Mr. Billings's mouth without his dentures.

Something about Dog William's happiness pissed me off, and I took my sour mood down the road and kicked at leaves. Goddamn, I mean, even a dog handled his life better than I did. I looked up, and saw that banana yellow Datsun stuck in the road. There was Bunny, Ian's brother, and Chuck, Bunny's friend—the metaphysical nonmotorcyclists—standing there beside it.

"Get the jack," Bunny said.

"What jack? Monterey Jack?" Chuck chuckled. "Jack-in-the-box?"

"You don't know jack shit," Bunny said. "In the trunk. And the lug wrench."

"What's it look like?" Chuck was as big as a dump truck and was wearing a fringe vest with beads. He had a lovely braid, I don't know, maybe two inches long.

"You know what it looks like. A big cross. With knobs. Quit stalling. Jesus."

"Do you guys need some help?" I asked. "I'm about two seconds from a phone."

"Hey. The teacher's kid," Chuck said.

"Ian's friend," Bunny said.

"Whoo hoo. You saved me." Chuck raised one arm, did a little victory dance. It reminded me of when you set a big bowl of Jell-O on a hard surface. "Rescue chick."

"No problem," I said. "Should I call a tow truck?"

"Tow truck, my ass," Bunny said. "It's a flat tire. Get back there and find the jack," he said to Chuck. Bunny shook his head. "Sheesh. He's never changed a flat before. We could be here all day."

"You know, my house is right there. I could call someone for you."

"I've changed thousands of tires," Bunny said. "It's him that hasn't. This is a learning experience."

"I hate learning experiences," Chuck said.

"Learning experiences suck," I agreed. "Anything that's called a learning experience, you know, run for your life."

"What a couple of whiners," Bunny said.

Chuck had the trunk open and was fishing around inside. "Is this the lug wrench?" He held up a hat with ear flaps.

"I hope neither of you has worn that thing," I said. "Very Elmer Fudd." Chuck tossed it to me and I yanked off Dino's burglar hat, put it on. "Cozy," I said.

"Oh, man, you two are a handful," Bunny said. I was starting to have a really good time. "You two will try my abundant patience."

"Okay, okay. The lug wrench," Chuck said. He took it out, held it up in one hand as if it had the weight of a toothpick.

"You blocked the tires already? Good. Now loosen the bolts while the car's still on the ground." Bunny folded his arms, watched Chuck sit down on the asphalt.

"Cold ass." Chuck rubbed his huge butt. He stuck the lug wrench on one of the bolts. "Knee bone connected to the shinbone." He gave it a crank. It freed easily, a knife through warm butter. "Big friggin' deal," Chuck said. He sure looked pleased with himself.

"Don't congratulate yourself until the job is done. You can't change a tire and pat yourself on the back at the same time. Not enough hands," Bunny said.

Chuck whipped through the second bolt, but the third stuck. I learned a whole bunch of cool new swear words, in inventive combinations. Sweat gathered at his temple and in the nooks and crannies of his shirt. I could smell the sour odor of underarms under stress.

"Never count your chickens before they hatch," Bunny said.

"Shut the F up, Bun," Chuck said, and let loose a stream-of-consciousness array of nasty terms in Bunny's direction.

"So why are you letting him make you do this?" I asked. Maybe it wasn't such a good time to bring it up. Chuck was grunting like a pig stuck under a fence.

"Learning. Experience." He exhaled. "Personal. Growth."

I wanted to laugh. Picture again what I was seeing. This motorcycle guy in a fringe vest with a two-inch braid, wrestling a tire and sweating bullets and gasping about personal growth as his buddy watched over him with the folded arms of a sadistic PE teacher.

"You got to do what you fear," Bunny said. "Embrace the unknown. You keep yourself sheltered, you overprotect yourself, you might as well stay home and become an agraphobic."

"Agoraphobic," Chuck grunted.

"Agraphobic probably means you fear farmland," I said.

Bunny ignored us. "Growth is in the feared places."

"Did you steal that from a *Star Trek* movie?" I said. "It sounds slightly ominous."

"There!" Chuck said. "Hot damn."

"Excellent. Step two."

"Shit, there's more?"

I watched Bunny instruct Chuck to jack up the car and remove the tire. Kyle and Derek, Courtney's two little brothers, got off the school bus and came over, slung their backpacks to the ground and watched.

"I saw this guy get crushed by his own car on *True Traffic Tragedies*," Kyle said. Kyle was twelve and wore slouchy pants. Derek was a year younger, but was bigger than his brother.

"Gee, thanks for sharing," I said.

"If we had our video camera, we could film this and win a thousand bucks."

"I saw this other guy get his leg pinned on *Road Rescuers*."

"That looked so fake," Derek said.

"No blood," Kyle agreed.

"Hey, guys, there's back-to-back episodes of *Fat People on Bikes* this afternoon." Bunny looked at his watch. "Starting now."

"Oh, cool," Derek said.

They picked up their backpacks, headed off. "*Fat People on Bikes?*" Chuck said.

"Hey, they believed me, that's all I care. Little television monsters." I guess he and Dino had one thing in common, which would have made Dino shudder.

"That's all they do. All day, every day," I said.

"I hate it when kids don't *participate*," Bunny said. "They could be outside playing ball. Collecting bugs."

"Hanging out at ye old swimmin' hole," Chuck said.

"Shut the F up, Chuck. If you don't participate, you're just taking up oxygen."

"Life is a banquet. Approach it with hunger," Chuck said. "Hey, I'm done, right?"

"Wow, it looks great. I just hope it doesn't fall off when you're driving," I said.

"I saw that on *Terrible Traffic Traumas*," Chuck said. I smiled. I really liked those guys.

"Now you've had your learning experience," I said.

"Congratulations, Chuck, you big idiot," Bunny said.

"Thanks, man," Chuck said. "Sorry about all the things I called you back at the lug nuts."

"No problem. I'll consider us equal for what I said to you when you made me call Sonja for a date."

"You should've heard him," Chuck said to me.

"I hope this Sonja said yes," I said.

"With my good looks? What do you expect."

"He was trembling like a baby bird," Chuck said.

"Anyway," Bunny said, in a lame effort to change the subject. "We better get going. Hey, Lassie, thanks for your help. It was great hanging out with you."

I laughed. "Cassie," I said.

"Cassie? Man, I could've sworn he said Lassie."

"Woof," I said. "*Lassie?*"

"I don't know. I thought maybe your folks were real animal lovers."

"Bunny, you F-ing fool," Chuck said.

"You thought it was Lassie too," Bunny said.

They climbed into the car. The small spare tire looked shy and inadequate on the Datsun.

"Jesus, you stink," Bunny said to Chuck.

Chuck yanked the paper Christmas tree deodorizer off of the rearview mirror, thrust it under his shirt, and gave it a swipe under each arm. "Smellin' like a rose," he said. Then he started the engine, gave a wave, and drove off.

After Mom confronted Dino about the blank pages and his lies, Dino did appear to get down to real work. Supposedly this was what we were wanting, but I didn't know why. The pressure of having to create and the creation itself were what led him to a disturbing restlessness and increasingly odd acts. Several times I heard him awake in the night, creaking down the stairs, performing in his office, and then clapping for himself when it was over. During the day his usual perfectionism was in high gear—he would remake a bed Mom made, rewash the dishes, pour out coffee that was made for him and make it again "properly." His testiness increased. He would turn every innocent remark into a perceived criticism of him. *It's a nice day,* you would say. And he would snap in reply, *Did I say it wasn't a nice day? Just because it's a nice day and I don't remark upon it doesn't mean I'm a pessimist.* He bit Mom's head off for giving him the wrong size spoon, yelled at me for walking too heavily down the stairs, leading me to have Brief Fantasy Number

One Thousand and Twelve, whereby I borrowed Nannie's old bowling ball and sent it crashing down two flights.

I was living with a bolt of lightning, never knowing when or where he might strike. I spent a lot of time in my room, ate dinner as fast as possible. Headphones are great when you live in a disturbed home—I started wearing them at night, so I could pretend a peace that didn't exist. Worst of all, though, Dino started up his freaky obsession with William Tiero again.

The newspaper is gone, Dino said one morning.

Probably late, my mother replied.

Maybe he wants my paper, Dino said. *He wants me to wonder where it went, to wonder if he has been here to take it. He is messing with me.*

God, it gave me the creeps. There was this feeling of horrible anticipation, of knowing that things would not keep going this wrongly and suddenly right themselves. No, wrong like that would keep building. Wrong always seemed to double and grow like cells under a microscope. Right could be steady, but wrong fed upon itself. Sometimes I wished "it" would just go ahead and happen, whatever "it" was.

Mom looked like she was losing weight, in spite of the fact that Alice's loaves of banana bread were increasing. Dino's working, the writing—it seemed to pour a life-giving liquid onto old, sleeping torments of his. He started smoking, too, a habit he'd given up years ago. One cigarette after the other he smoked, horrible bursts of nicotine poison filling not only his lungs but mine and Mom's and Dog William's, getting into the strands of our clothing and even making the bread left out on the counter taste bad. You'd find snakey bits of ash all over—in coffee cups and saucers, and once in Mom's potted ficus plant. I hated those cigarettes. They were a visual reminder of a growing disease.

"I don't understand something," I said to my mother one afternoon. We were having a domestic mother-daughter moment, folding laundry together, which was a rarity in our house. When you've got a working mother, I've noticed, you learn to live with dirty clothes, talking yourself into the fact that no one will really notice the blotch of yogurt spilled on the leg of your jeans, or you learn to do laundry yourself, or else you learn to root through stacks of clean/nonclean clothes for a pair of socks, with the skill and speed of a pig hunting for truffles. Zebe's mother is a graphic designer, and Zebe has used adaptation number two. She is so good at the laundry she could do the presidential under-wear. Everything in her closet is folded and organized by color, but I still love her anyway. At our house we usually do the root-and-find method, although Dino's clothes always manage to get done. Something about seeing my mother iron his shirts really pisses me off. I know she hates to iron. I know she would rather go out in sweats than get the wrinkles out of cotton, yet there she is, starching and pressing Dino's clothes. Fast forward to Brief Fantasy Number One Thousand Five Hundred—two big steaming iron-shaped holes over the boobs of each of Dino's shirts.

Anyway, we were folding clothes. "I don't understand something," I said, which I think I already mentioned. "If composing causes Dino this much pain, why doesn't he quit? Why doesn't he take up fishing or something? Embroidery? A low-stress occupation like forest ranger?"

Mom held one matchless sock in her hand. She thought about this. "Because quitting would cause him more pain," she said finally.

"I don't get that. If something causes pain, then bam, get rid of it," I said. I was thinking of Ian. Okay, I thought about him endlessly. Okay, I had daily arguments with myself over my desire to just give in to my feelings and to say to hell with what Dino might think. But I was mostly holding all of that at bay. Fear can give you more strength and resolve than anything else I can think of.

"Oh, Cassie, nothing's that simple. Very few things are that black-and-white. I wish they were. Nothing's a hundred percent good. Nothing's a hundred percent bad."

"Okay, eighty-nine percent. If it's that bad, get rid of it. Eighty-nine percent is enough."

"You're talking like a scientist," she said. "Some things can't be measured. Let's say you love astronomy. But let's say it causes you some problems. Back pain, eye strain, I don't know."

"We're talking mental anguish. Astronomy doesn't cause that."

"What if it did? What if, say, I don't know. Maybe this isn't a good comparison. Say you couldn't get into a school to study it. Say your math skills weren't good enough. Say you really had to struggle or something. What would you do?"

"Give it up."

"But you *love* it."

"It depends how much I love it versus how much pain," I said.

"Love is not something that can be measured, Cassie. Sometimes love just *is*. Sometimes it's a force with its own reasons. Reasons we don't necessarily understand, but with a power that is undeniable."

"You sound like an After School Special."

Mom sighed. "Fine. Never mind. Sometimes you can cattle rope your heart and sometimes you can't, is all."

"Now you sound like a country-western song."

"I'm shutting up with my motherly wisdom. You're on your own."

"He's giving us all cancer. He's giving the *ficus* cancer."

"I'm going to make him smoke outside," she said, though we had already agreed about her ability to make him do anything.

"I think he should become a bank manager," I said.

"Without his music, Dino wouldn't know who to be."

Two nights later I went to a school music concert. I usually didn't go to these things, but Siang had told me that she was doing a solo and hinted around that she'd like me to come. I wanted to do something nice for her after her kindness that day in Dino's office. Usually once I got home on a cold night, any good plan I made didn't seem as good as staying inside and warm, especially a plan like listening to classical music, which I got more than enough of anyway.

But I didn't change my mind—I went out into the cold night and fought the cars jamming the parking lot, and found a seat with Sophie Birnbaum and her parents. Sophie's little brother played the viola and was in the concert too. His group played first, and Sophie and I grimaced at each other at the squeaky parts and made fun of some of the names in the program, like Harry Chin.

I was having a grand old cultural time when Siang's group came on. She looked so thin and scared when she walked up to the microphone in her long black skirt and white blouse, her hair straight and shiny black, almost blue, under the lights. I could see her hands shake, and all I could think of was the time Marna Pines puked right on stage during the second-grade play and how no one ever forgot it. Poor Marna would always be remembered as the girl who threw up right during her solo, stopping the show cold until the janitor could come out and deal with the whole matter with his mop and sawdust. Forever after she would be Pukey Pines, or one notch up on the cruelty ladder, Upchuck Woodchuck, due to her slight overbite. I didn't want anything like that for Siang. Sure, her Dino hero worship drove me nuts, but there was something more than fandom at work in the way she tilted Dino's painting straight again. Siang was a good person.

The orchestra had a false start, causing some of the audience to snicker. Then the orchestra began again, and Siang came in with a forceful stroke of bow against violin, her chin down, her fingers flying. Jesus, there was Siang with her little *Indiana Jones* Boy Sidekick voice and her annoying habits, just taking control of the whole situation and kicking the shit out of that violin, which I know isn't exactly an appropriate musical critique but true anyway. The audience didn't move. She just had them there right with her. My heart just got all full. I was so proud of her.

After the concert I waited for Siang and told her how great she was. Her parents told me about eight times that it was good to meet me, beaming at me as if I had just given them one of those huge Publisher's Clearinghouse checks for a million dollars. I found the frosted sugar cookies at the cookie table and brought back one on a napkin for Siang and then headed back outside, feeling satisfied and happy and hopeful, though I'm not exactly sure why. I got out of the school parking lot, and instead of going home, I was overcome with a strange urge, which was to drive down to the ferry terminal, near the little house on the corner where Ian now lived.

Maybe it was Siang's bravery that made me do it, frail and breakable Siang showing so much power in front of that audience, or maybe what was really knocking around inside my brain was what the metaphysical motorcyclists without motorcycles had been saying about fear. Mom's voice was there too, I think (although she would not have been happy to be a motivating factor), talking about love as a force with its own reasons. Maybe all three things collided together and formed something new, some philosophical Big Bang in my brain, I don't know. What I do know is that I parked across the street from Ian's house. My body was cruising along without my permission—it got right out of the car and walked to the door, and it was only after I knocked that my brain caught up and I realized what the hell I had actually just done. The optimistic energy I'd been infused with after the concert had evaporated instantly, reminding me of my other failed surges of *Yes!* like the time I decided to redecorate my room with some leftover paint we had in the garage and got as far as the door frame before I realized I was tired, far from finished, making a mess, and running out of orange.

Now I just stood by Ian's door, looking at this mosquito with its dangly legs all caught up in this spider's web by their porch light, and thinking a panicky *Shit! Oh, shit!* I heard footsteps and a dog barking, Rocket, no doubt, and I had the urge to jump into the huge juniper plant, the same way as when we used to play Ding Dong Ditch when we were kids.

The door opened. Ian's mom stood in the doorway, with Rocket peering around her legs like a shy toddler, and I wished I had something to hand her—one of those peanut butter cookies I was going to stick in my pocket back at the cookie table, a pamphlet about a politician, or a trick-or-treat bag (weeks late, but still).

"Mrs. Waters?"

"Yes?"

She had Ian's eyes, but they looked different on her, wrinkled at the edges, like they knew things that had made her tired. She was wearing a T-shirt with some metal rock group on it, which surprised me. Golden wings spread out with a skull between them, and pictures of scary-looking guys. She was holding a towel, drying her hands, and I could smell something warm and buttery cooking inside. She opened the screen door and held it open with her foot. Her hair was pulled back, and her forehead was broad and sturdy. Ian's *mother*. The one who taught him how to be in the world and who told him to clean his room and to get in the car because they were late.

"Can I help you?"

"I'm . . ." Okay, real functioning words were required, and if it says anything about my character, the first ones that sprang to mind were a lie. A bad one, too. The name that first popped into my consciousness was not my own but *Harriet Chin*. "Cassie Morgan. A friend of Ian's." I put my hand out for Rocket to sniff. She put her black nose against my palm and licked my fingers.

"Oh!" Ian's mom said.

"Ian studies with my stepfather, Dino Cavalli." What a shameless name-dropper I was.

"Cassie. Come in! I'm Janet. Ian's mom. Ian's not here, but please. I know this sounds very fifties housewife, but I was just making cookies. I had this incredible craving for fat and sugar."

I liked her already. Her toenail polish was chipped. And anyone who has a craving for fat and sugar and gives in to it is okay by me. "No, thanks. I better get home. I just stopped by to say hi because I hadn't seen him in a while. I'm always gone when he's around lately." I peered around her, into the house. Ian's home. It was very sparsely furnished; well, pretty empty, actually. Trés minimalist.

"Well, I'll tell him you came by. Are you sure about coming in? I gorged on dough, and now there are warm cookies. I'm going to make myself sick if someone doesn't stop me. Hormonal chocolate frenzy."

"What is it with that?"

"I have no idea, but I'm worse than the lions with the zebra carcass on Animal Planet."

"Well, good luck. I wish you cold milk and the ability to fit in your jeans tomorrow."

"Amen. I'll tell Ian you came by."

I crossed back over the street, got in the car that had already grown cold. Okay, so his mother was cool too. I turned the key, just watched the dashboard lights glow for a minute. I looked over at Ian's house, at the yellow light in the windows, at the lawn growing frosty-tipped in the cold night, sparkly by streetlamp.

Small house, with a porch that needed painting, same as his mom's toenails, and what I guessed was one of Rocket's tennis balls in the driveway gutter. This didn't have to be as large as I was making it out to be, or as scary. This was a houseful of normal, faulty people leading normal, faulty lives, and Ian was one of them. I liked the people in his world. And he did not, I realized, hold the secrets of the universe or the power to destroy. He was just himself, with a spirit and a talent who also lied to the dental hygienist about flossing every day, just like the rest of us.

I sat there, and my heart opened up, just a little. Go where you fear, Chuck and Bunny said. Participate. I could hear my heart make room. *Maybe,* is what it said.

Chapter Seven

It is one of those Murphy's Law things that if you have a group project at school, the more important it is to your grade, the more likely you are to get stuck with partners whose safest contribution is to color the map. Even that makes you nervous. The project in question was a report on the economic system of a Pacific Rim country.

Partner number one, Jason Menyard, studied the list of choices. "Let's do Honduras," he said. "My parents went there on vacation."

"Honolulu. They went to Honolulu, you idiot." Partner number two, Nicole Hower. Nickname, Whore, because if you said her last name fast, this is what it sounded like for one, and for two, because her clothes gave the impression that she wanted to share her boobs with mankind, some goodwill mission like those people who go to third world countries to spread knowledge of how to keep their drinking water clean and improve their educational systems. Jason's eyes were already so glued to her exposed chest you would have thought a good movie was playing there. Pass the popcorn.

"How do you know?" Jason said to Nicole's boobs.

"Your parents brought mine back a present. Macadamia nuts. You don't even know where your own parents went. God," she said.

"Show some respect," Jason said. "'R-E-S-P-E-C-T,'" he sang. "'That is what you mean to me. Ooh, just a little bit.'" Jason snapped his fingers.

"Hey, he actually does a good Urethra Franklin," Nicole said to me.

Right about this time I was working on dual theories: that Nicole's parents were first cousins, and that Jason's brain and a jockstrap had much in common. Basically made of holes and not holding anything too important. I was also coming to the quick realization that I'd have to go to the library after school that day, since I'd basically be doing all the work here. This meant I'd miss the chance to see Ian before his lesson. I'd been holding on to that little open feeling, preparing myself to take a step in his direction whether Dino liked it or not, and I was going to do it that day. I, for one, would let Ian decide what was good for him. This glitch in the plan filled me with the low-level annoyance that is actually rageful, crazed fury held in a straitjacket.

At the library I grabbed everything I could on Honduras and bolted out of there. Finally, I headed home. I breathed a grateful sigh of relief when I saw Rocket on the front lawn entertaining a gloriously happy Dog William. Call me a pessimist, but I started having the creeping fear that now that I had finally gotten the courage to make a move, Ian would not be there that day, so I was glad to see that I was wrong. I dropped fifty pounds' worth of Honduras books on the table and looked in the fridge for something to quench my weight-lifting thirst. I could hear the rumblings of Dino's voice in his office, intense, making a point.

I closed the fridge door, stepped back into the hall to eavesdrop. I would have put my ear to the door, just like they do in the movies, had it been necessary, but it wasn't. In fact, Dino's voice got louder and louder over Ian's playing.

"Bam, bam, bam. You need to hit it." I could hear something being smacked against a table, a book maybe. Ian continued to play. "Again," Dino barked.

Ian stopped, started again. I don't know what he was playing, something frenzied and fast.

"Bam, bam, bam," Dino said again. The book cracked against the table three more times. The sound made me flinch. "Don't you hear me?"

"I'm sorry," Ian said.

"Don't stop. Pick it up and do it again. It is forceful. Fast. One-two-three. Not one. Two. Three. You have no command."

"I'm sorry," Ian said again.

"What is sorry? Sorry has nothing to do with anything. I don't give a fuck about sorry. I give a fuck about you doing it right. What is the matter with you?"

"I don't know," Ian said.

Something crawled up along my backbone. Shame. I'm not sure why—shame at Dino's behavior, shame for Ian. I felt sick.

"I thought you were supposed to be such a talent."

"I'm sorry," Ian said again.

"Do it again. Show me that what everyone says about you is true, because it is not what I see."

I held my breath. Prayed that my feet would stay where they were and not burst in to interrupt this cruelty. The prayers were unnecessary, though, if I were telling the truth. I knew I couldn't go in there. It was nowhere I belonged, and something I didn't understand.

"Maybe it's not true," Ian said. "Maybe I wasn't born with some gift."

"Nobody is born with that gift. It's not about *gift*. It's about *need*. A deep, ugly seed of need," Dino said. "What is your need, Ian? In what need does greatness lie?"

"I don't have a need. I play because I choose to."

Dino laughed. Mocking. "What bullshit."

"And when I choose not to, I'll stop."

"You know that's a lie. Choice has nothing to do with it. There is no choice."

"Maybe not for you."

"Need. Ugly need. You're no different."

"How do you know?"

"You have no choice. You must save your mama, Ian. You must save her from despair. That is your need. You are the savior." What the hell was he talking about?

"You don't know anything about it," Ian said. His voice was angry, full of tears.

"I know all about it. Play to save your mama, boy."

"No."

"Play! Bam, bam, bam. Play it."

Silence.

"You think I'm hateful, don't you? You think I'm a bastard. But you also think I'm right. I know you."

"You don't know anything about me."

"I *know* you. Play, God damn it. The need will speak."

More silence.

"Stupid boy."

And then, the beginning notes of the song. So tender, you pictured them floating in midair and then breaking in two. The music rose, gathered intensity. I recognized the part they had been practicing. It came, forceful. Building. Bam, bam, bam. I heard it; I knew nothing about this shit, but I heard it. One, two, three—driving into me, hard, so hard.

He stopped then, and the silence was abrupt. The kind of sudden, sharp silence that comes after a slap. And then Dino began to applaud. "Bravo!" he said. "Bravo, boy!"

I stood there, stunned. My heart hurt. My soul and insides felt wrung out, perched on the desire to sob. Oh, how I hated Dino right then. The office door opened and Ian ran from it. His coat was over his arm, and he shoved past me. He slammed out the front door, hard enough to rattle the windows.

Dino came out from the office. He looked at the shut door, shook his head.

"Bastard isn't the half of it," I said to him.

"You're a child," he said to me. "Silly child."

Erik Satie, contemporary composer, wouldn't wash with soap, and became so suspiciously obsessed with umbrellas (yep, I said umbrellas) that he had more than two hundred of them when he died. Tchaikovsky, of *Nutcracker* fame, killed himself with arsenic, and Schumann spent the last years of his life in an asylum. Beethoven was a Peeping Tom. When he was arrested, it is said that he yelled, "You can't arrest me, for I am the immortal Beethoven!" Police later found that he had spread feces over a wall of his house. Crappy taste in decorating, if you ask me.

And since what happened next happened on Thanksgiving, let me tell you a few food-related wacky-genius stories. Poet Elizabeth Barrett Browning was an anorexic, due to her brother's death and her father's inability to let his children leave the nest (he disinherited any of them who dared to marry). Lord Byron was a bulimic, dieting and exercising down to the skeletal, and believed that if you ate a cow, you'd endanger the appetite of all cows. Charlotte Brontë basically threw up to death while she was pregnant because she was too whacked out to handle it. Vincent van Gogh ate his own paints. Yum.

Let's also not forget that more people commit violent crimes on Thanksgiving than on any other day of the year. This is not just by people forced to eat Brussels sprouts, which would make the statistic understandable. Thanksgiving can be torture, and I don't just mean the times when some well-intentioned person suggests, "Let's all say something we're thankful for," and you want to drop through a hole in the floor. I mean that for some people life is already stressful enough without multiplying human relationships by five or ten or by however many napkin rings you happen to have.

Every year for the past three, my mother and Dino hosted a Thanksgiving party for certain members of the Seattle Symphony board of trustees, high-end givers, major players in the music arena, and Dino's associates—his manager and agents and anyone from his recording companies and publishers who wanted to travel in for the occasion. I believe that he chose Thanksgiving in the hopes that most people would be with their own families—he'd be able to extend an invitation and get social credit for that, without having to have total follow-through. A good plan, really, but it never ended up that way. A gazillion people answered the formal invitations, mailing back tiny envelopes of RSVP.

Mom had the event catered, thank God. She can get flustered when the phone rings and she's making a grilled cheese sandwich. This year it seemed like there were more people than ever in our kitchen, more trays of food, more waiters carrying hors d'oeuvres and canapés. The house looked beautiful and different than our regular house with the cereal box left out on the counter. You wouldn't believe how good it looked. We're not talking decorations of turkeys with accordion-paper stomachs like we used to have when Mom and Dad were married and had Nannie and Aunt Nancy and Uncle Greg over. No, we're talking cinnamon-smelling candles in hurricane glass on every surface, and evergreen boughs, and cranberry-colored vases of white roses. Linen napkins, and china with boughs of fruit around the edges. We're talking a turkey the size of a brown bear, and the dining room draped with gauzy curtains and burgundy ribbons. There was enough food to feed a small town, all of it steaming and glossy and colorful. Mom wore velvet and I wore my beaded vintage dress, and Dino's dark suit and restrained curls made him look like the man on the *Paris Diaries* cover, whose sex life was the talk of the town when he was younger.

I was glad my dad couldn't see us now. This was the good news, the everything-is-working-out-beautifully that you want to hide from the other parent. Their worst nightmare of their former spouse having a better life after all, as they passed the yams back at home. We all smelled soapy and perfumed, and the doorbell kept ringing and ringing, and the house got so stuffed, people went outside to cool off. You wondered if all of these people didn't have family to be with, or if the chance to be with a world-famous composer and violinist was enough to make them ditch their own grannies.

Andrew Wilkowski, Dino's new agent, had apparently solved this conflict by bringing the whole gang along. He had brought his quiet wife, thin as a file folder, and his twin seven-year-old boys, who wore ties and ran around like crazed, midget businessmen, popping olives and caviar. I don't know why they liked the stuff—fish eggs as a delicacy was always a hard one to understand—but I swear they ate half of the mountain of it, in spite of the fact that their mother told them repeatedly to stop. I caught her grasping each of their arms fiercely and hissing in their ears, showing her less passive side. Andrew Wilkowski also brought his aging parents, who looked at the thin wife and caviar-sucking children as if they were characters in a horror flick.

Meanwhile, Andrew himself was glued to Dino, filling his plate and wineglass and doing the most shameless ass kissing I'd seen since Katie Simpson brought our sixth-grade teacher a dozen roses and a box of chocolates on her birthday.

I played good daughter at the party, and tried not to miss the old days of Dad's overcooked turkey and Mom's pies and watching the Macy's parade on television. I talked to lots of old people with white hair who probably each had a gazillion dollars, ate way too many little chocolate tarts, and tried to figure out if there was something going on in the romance department between these two waiters. I saw that Dino had broken free from Andrew, and for a moment I was sincerely happy for him that he managed to cut loose from the weasely brownnoser.

But then I noticed that Dino was striding with a sense of purpose to the dining room windows. He peeled back the curtains, cupped his hand to the glass, and looked out. There was something about the way he walked—too much purpose, obsession, fury—that I recognized from that night I saw him on the lawn when he cut the cable. Oh, God. Not now. No.

I immediately scanned the room and looked for Mom. Instead of chatting amiably with the orchestra creative director or with one of the donors, I saw that Andrew Wilkowski had taken her elbow and was heading out of the room, as if to talk to her in private. Great. Terrific. Something was definitely wrong.

Dino apparently had not found what he was looking for. He moved toward the hallway and the front door. I thought I'd better follow him, though what the hell I'd do if he freaked out while I was with him I hadn't quite figured out yet. Dino opened the door and I stepped out after him. I did not want to step out after him. I wanted to go someplace else, where I was completely alone and where no one could find me. I wanted to tuck my quilt around my head, disappear. I did not want right here and right now.

Outside, the night was amazingly quiet, with the noise of the party behind us, inside the house. It was November cold, and the air was dewy and full of rain not yet fallen. Thick, wet clouds filled the sky. A couple of people were standing and talking by the long line of parked cars. I heard a trunk slam, and a man and a woman with instrument cases walked back up the street to our house. Dino looked up and down the street, and headed toward the box hedge at the perimeter of the yard.

"Dino?" I said.

"William," he called. "Wil-yum."

A bit of hope. "Did we lose the dog?" I asked.

"No, not the *dog*. William Tiero, the leach. I know you're here."

Shit, I thought. *Oh, shit!* I wanted to call for Mom, to find her, but I didn't think I should leave him. I didn't know what to do. I just had no idea.

Dino crouched over, looked under the hedge. I was glad that the people with the instrument cases had gone inside. I decided to be calm. If I used a really calm voice, then he'd be calm, and I could go and find Mom.

"You're getting your pants all wet," I said. "Let's go in."

"I knew he couldn't stay away."

"William Tiero is not here, Dino," I said. My voice sounded high, like it might break. I was fighting a weird sense of unreality.

I didn't even feel like me, talking calmly to this man I lived with, who was looking in the hedge for someone who wasn't there. I felt like I had gone into someplace past fear. Someplace way farther than that, where you cut off from what's happening in order to function. I was watching this poor girl with this crouched-over man who was losing it. I looked down and saw my own hands, and they seemed familiar but not.

"You don't know what you're talking about. That prick will never let me out of his life."

"No one's in the hedge, Dino," I said.

"You're right."

Dino came out of the hedge, hair messed, bits of leaves on the arms of his jacket. I don't know how to describe his eyes except to say that they were not unfocused or bleary like someone who's been drinking. In fact, they were the opposite—hyper focused. He stood still, listening. It was as if his senses were broken open—his hearing more acute, his gaze taking in things no one else could see.

"Why don't we go inside now," I said.

"He's not in the hedge. I'll check the back. You check the cars," he said.

"Please, Dino." I wasn't doing well with calm. My voice was pleading and anxious. I was climbing the slope of panic right alongside of him. Where was my mother? Where was someone who knew what to do?

"Check the cars before he drives off. He called and hung up just now. He can't stand it, that this is happening without him."

"William Tiero isn't here, Dino." Okay, the calm was gone completely. *I don't want to do this! I can't!* I felt like crying.

"Of course he's here. I know he's here." He pulled his cell phone from his jacket pocket, showed me the display. It was true that someone had called. The ID read UNIDENTIFIED CALLER. The letters glowed in the gathering darkness. The two people who were talking by the car were carrying large instruments into the house now, also. A bass and a cello, by the looks of it.

"Is everything all right?" one man asked.

I wanted to cry out. *Help me,* I wanted to say, but I didn't. "Fine," I said. "The dog is missing."

"Pets," the man said. He hauled his instrument through the door, a loud gust of party sounds escaping as he went through.

"Dino," I said. "Unidentified caller. That could be anyone. William Tiero is not out here in the bushes. Or anywhere." *Please,* I begged him with my voice. But you can't reason with insanity, or plead with it. It's the frightening tyrant, the boss, the kidnapper.

"He did this last year. I smelled his cologne. I saw him looking in the window. I'm going to catch the dirty little bastard. I'm going to check the back."

I changed my tactics. "Let me check the back. I'll make sure I find the dirty little bastard," I said. "You go inside."

"He couldn't let me free. Obsessed."

"Come on."

"He'd rather have me dead than free of him."

I took Dino's arm. His unreason made him seem capable of anything, and I didn't even want to touch him. But I did—I pointed him toward the house. I tried to keep from letting the tears come, from letting out my own desperation. I looked around for Mom.

Inside, people were gathering in the living room. The quartet of musicians had set up an impromptu concert, began to tune for the crowd. I wondered if they were expecting Dino to join them. Some woman was ushering everyone out of the dining room for the concert—they were squeezing out of the doorway and packing into the living room. Dino stalked into the dining room, empty of people now. He looked back out through the drapes again.

"I see movement," he said. "Turn off the lights so that I can see."

"Dino, no. He's not there." I felt the tears working away at my throat. Where the hell was Mom?

"Turn out the lights!"

His voice was loud, and I flinched. I knew that my job right then was to hide the mess, make sure none of these people noticed anything. To keep the secret. So I went to the switch and turned off the lights to keep him quiet. Thankfully, everyone was either jammed in the other room or overflowing out into the hall, happy to be in an important house of an important man, spilling drinks and talking and eating tiny, fancy desserts on glass plates.

Only the candles flickered in the room. I could see their flames reflected in the glass that Dino was peering through. "Shh," he said, even though I wasn't saying anything. "Come here."

I went. I hated standing beside him. His breath was fogging up the glass. His coat was hanging dangerously over the candles on the table under the window.

"Be careful, Dino," I said. I watched his sleeve dangle by the flame. "Jesus."

"Holy shit, look!" Dino said.

I looked outside, where he was pointing. "Oh, God," I breathed.

He was right.

He was right, there was a figure outside, a dark figure in a big coat.

I jumped my ship of sanity, got into Dino's boat, because he was right. And if Dino was right about this, maybe William Tiero really did have evil plans for us. Maybe Dino really was in danger. The quartet began playing in the other room. All four instruments, a sudden, thunderous sound of frantic motion.

"Get the gun," Dino hissed.

"Don't be crazy," I said, which is a rather stupid thing to say to a crazy person, but my own thoughts were out of control. My heart was thumping like mad, my hands shaking. A man in the bushes . . . "We don't have a gun."

"I said, get the gun!"

Right then, the figure came close to the glass, toward us. I let out a little scream at the same moment that I realized it was my mother standing before us, Andrew Wilkowski's navy wool coat draped over her shoulders. It was also at that same moment that Dino's elbow knocked over the glass hurricane candle and the flame began to lick up the fabric of the curtain.

Here is what I saw in my mind. The flame, gathering speed up the curtain, bursting into a ball of fire. Catching on to the other draperies, moving with the fury of some mythological god to the adjoining room full of people. I heard screams in my mind, the panic of sequined and silked guests, someone tripping on a velvety hem. Smoke suddenly everywhere, one doorway, glass breaking. Flames spinning up the stairwell, surprising a couple who were upstairs, looking for their coats. Fire trucks with twirling, dizzying lights on the dark street, and charred remnants of furniture and bodies, people crying on the front lawn, the house consumed and then disappearing under gusts of water from the hoses.

I watched as already the flame was beginning to lick its way up the curtain. I could see my mother through the glass, her mouth frozen in an O.

I grabbed the curtain with my hands. My bare hands, I just grabbed it and crumpled it up. It was the only thing I could think to do. No, let me say that again. I did not think at all, I just acted. I gathered up the fabric in a ball and extinguished the flame. The quartet kept playing in the other room.

Before I knew it, my mother was beside me. She was holding my hands in hers. There was ice in a towel. I didn't know what happened to Dino, but I guess Andrew Wilkowski had brought him to his room and calmed him down, telling guests he wasn't feeling well, implying he had had too much to drink, which was a sin forgiven with an amused smile. I couldn't stop shaking. My body just shook and trembled until I threw up. There was a call to a doctor, but my hands were okay. I was okay finally, and I stopped shaking after I was wrapped tightly in my blanket. The only thing that remained of the night was a small scar, which I still have. It sits in the curve between my thumb and forefinger, the place that looks like a small boat if you hold your hand up in the air.

I will never forget that night. The mark reminds me what fear can do to you, how fear can distort what is real to the point that the damage is permanent.

It was the same shape, come to think of it, as the scar on Dino's neck.

Chapter Eight

Zebe called the next morning, asking if I wanted to hang out with her and Sophie, but I told her I was going shopping with Mom. I didn't think I could stand acting normal and pretending that things were fine, and my other option, letting myself fall apart with them, sounded like it would take more energy than I could stand. I wanted to be *away*. It didn't matter where away was. The air was low on my own bike tires and I didn't want to stop and pump them up, so I grabbed Dino's bike, the one with the basket on the handlebars, and started to ride out to the ferry docks. The burned curtain lay in a heap on the floor after Mom took it down, and the whole house looked hungover from the party. On top of everything else, the caterers had done a crappy job of cleaning up and there were cups set in odd places—the potted plant, behind the toilet—and bits of food on napkins. Two people had forgotten their coats. Dino had still been sleeping when I got up, but Mom looked haunted and stressed and she snapped first at me when I dropped my toast on the floor and then at Dog William when he lunged at it with greedy opportunism. God knows what she'd be like when Dino woke up, or what would happen then.

My hands were freezing on the handlebars and my legs were cold even through my jeans, but I didn't care. The fresh air felt good. The atmosphere inside that house felt doomed. It felt fatal.

It's mostly downhill to the water, and the ferry dock is the end point of the bay. I had Brief Fantasy Number Four Thousand Twelve, of sailing straight down that hill and flying off the end of the dock, destructo-movie style. I like those kinds of movies. Things blowing up and strong, definite action. Zebe and I go together because we can't stand the frilly-ass movies of girls fighting their way to the big cheerleading final, or some such dance-movie-drama crap. We both like the certainty of action movies.

I sped past the bakery, warm smells catching up to me a block later, and the haircutting place and the bookstore. I passed the new Thai restaurant, with the surprising name of Phuket. We couldn't believe it when they put the sign up. Even Dino laughed. Brian Malo told us he called the place a few times, just to hear them answer the phone. I have no idea if this was bold humor on the restaurant owners' part, or if these poor people had no idea they're telling the nice folks of Seabeck to Fuck It.

I set the bike down on its side. I was so cold my nose felt like it could break off, making me one of those Roman statues you see in the museum. I sat on one of the benches on the dock, shoved my hands into my pockets. There were a few fishing boats tied up, though what you'd fish for that time of year, I have no idea.

My fish knowledge is on the slim side. It smelled like *green* out there, murky. The smell of fish/seaweed/cold depths. Seagulls were walking around with the aimless air of those with nothing better to do, or were perched on pilings, wearing the cool, unaffected looks of those secretly sure they are being admired. Kind of like the jocks in the cafeteria at lunch.

I watched a ferryboat come in, knocking into the dock, reminding me of my stint during driver's ed when I backed into the side of the garage. The boat unloaded and reloaded, glided away again. There was something about watching the ferryboats come and go that was calming—the rhythm of the departure and arrival. I was wondering how many people on that boat led simple lives where they ate meatloaf and worried about their lawn having weeds and their bathrooms being shiny. That's how it was *supposed to be*, wasn't it? But maybe *supposed to be* was what was wrong. Maybe *supposed to be* was like a child's drawing of a night sky—stars all alike, a yellow moon—simple and pretty and nothing to do with reality. It seemed cruel to feel all this shame because we had more than weeds to worry about.

I was deep in my own profound (ha) line of thought when I saw Rocket trotting down the dock. I was surprised and so glad to see her. I was just so happy to see a creature who was so nice and simple and cheerful. I patted my leg, and she came to me. She set her chin on my knee, and I gave her a good scruffing under her ears, all the while looking around for Ian. My stomach was lurching around like crazy with sudden nerves-slash-excitement. I couldn't see him anywhere, though, and wondered if Rocket just regularly went off on these small, independent adventures.

I was already planning my return of Rocket to her home—
I thought she might be lost—when I saw Ian walking up the dock.
I almost didn't recognize him—he wasn't wearing his long black
coat, but instead had some puffy ski jacket on. It was good to see
him. God, it was so good. Happiness was spilling over.

"I saw you ride down here," Ian said.

"Fly down here," I said. It was so freezing out there that when
I spoke I felt like a member of those African tribes you see in
National Geographic, with the discs in their lips. I sounded the
way you do when you get back from the dentist.

"You can see this whole area from the bedrooms upstairs,"
Ian said.

"Wow."

"It makes up for the fact that the rooms are midget-size. I
heard you came by."

"I just . . . I don't know. Something possessed me."

"Hey, I'm glad. I'm glad you didn't go in too."

"Why? Your mom seemed great."

"She is great. The house, you know, we're still moving in."

"Trés Zen. Feng shui."

"We might've had that for dinner last night," he said. God, I
liked him.

"My lips are so cold I can barely talk," I said.

Ian reached out his fingertips, set them on my mouth, the way
you would shush someone you loved. That gentle. Then he moved
his hand to the tip of my nose. "Your nose is cold too."

I took hold of his fingers, held them in my hand. We were
just standing there on the dock, me holding Ian's hand, and

Rocket looking on to see what might happen next. We were both smiling away at each other.

"I haven't seen you in a while," I said. I hadn't really *seen* him since we kissed. Except for when he was at my house last, when he left in a rush after that horrible, humiliating lesson.

"I'm quitting."

"What? What do you mean? Don't let him do that to you. If this is what you want, don't give in because he's an asshole. . . ."

"He's an amazing player. Amazing, God." Ian shook his head. He settled his hand more comfortably in mine. "Amazing doesn't even touch how he plays."

"But he sucks as a human being."

"I don't know how you take it. I don't think I can. Is he always like that?"

"Domineering?" I asked. "Critical? Mean?" I didn't say *crazy*. The other things were bad enough. "Yeah, pretty much. He's got a few really likeable moments, and that's about it. I don't know how I take it. I've been thinking about moving in with my dad." I didn't know I'd been thinking that—it just came out. One of those times the subconscious is clicking along doing its own thing, like when you're walking home and realize you're there but don't even remember the trip.

"What about your mom? She needs you."

"Maybe." I thought about the lesson I'd overheard. *You must save your mama, Ian. . . .* What had Dino meant? There was something about this comment that seemed unapproachable, but I wanted to approach it anyway. I decided to tread carefully, to give Ian an open door in case he wanted to go in. "My mom can take care of herself, though. I mean, doesn't yours?"

"Sure, she does," he said. He ignored my open door. Maybe the comment was more of Dino's usual craziness. "I just thought you'd worry about hurting your mom's feelings by moving out."

"You're right. It's the only thing that's keeping me from getting out of there." I cared about Mom. Too much to let her think she failed me.

"Rocket!" Ian yelled. The dog had trotted off and was smelling a net that a fisherman had thrown onto the dock. "Come on, girl."

Rocket looked up to see if Ian was sure, and when he clapped his hands, letting mine go, Rocket came reluctantly back. Ian sat down on the bench, and I sat beside him. He told me about Thanksgiving, how Chuck and Bunny made lasagna and garlic bread. Bunny had brought over some incense and it stank so bad Ian's mom had to open the windows and they all had to wear their coats as they ate. I told him about mine, but left off everything about Dino's behavior. I only told him about the food, and the guests, and the two waiters on the brink of a passionate affair.

"See everything you'll miss if you quit?" I said. I don't know why I was encouraging him. His continuing meant one thing—that Dino would do whatever he could to help get him into Curtis. That Ian would move a zillion miles away. Still, I'd rather have him go away than quit what he loved because of Dino.

"Everything I'll miss? Everything I'll be free of, is more like it," Ian said. "Pretentious people."

"Endless practicing?" I offered.

"Nothing but music. I'm so goddamned sick of it. I want

other things in my life." He looked at me then, and a jolt passed between us. At least, I felt it. He took a strand of my hair, wound it around one finger. My hair had never been so happy.

"Free of Dino's nastiness," I said.

"That accent." Ian shook his head. "I hear it in my sleep."

"And all of the endless stories about Italy. God, I get sick of that."

"He tells me them too."

"His mother teaching him to play the piano, which he couldn't do, but when they brought out his father's old violin . . ."

"He played some song like he learned it in the womb," Ian interrupted.

"I hate when he gets to the 'in the womb' part. *Womb* is a creepy word anyway, but when he says it . . ."

"Wuuum," Ian tried out an Italian accent.

"And the bicycles," I said.

"In the canals," Ian said.

"I've heard it five thousand times."

"I never understood why they threw them in," Ian said.

"'We were hooligans.'" I tried out my Italian accent. Mine was better.

At that moment, that very second, we both looked at Dino's bike, lying on its side there on the dock.

"That's his bike, isn't it?" Ian asked.

"Mmm hmmm."

"It had to be."

I turned to Ian. "Are you thinking what I'm thinking?"

"Are *you* thinking what *I'm* thinking?"

"Let's do it."

"Ve are zuch hooligans," Ian said. He sounded kind of German.

I picked up my end of the bike by the handlebars; Ian lifted the back tire. I was giggling away like mad. "Ze bicycles in ze canal," Ian said. "Is ze serious matter." He was more German by the second.

We lugged the bike to the end of the dock. Rocket was looking on, giving us the *Those wacky humans* dog look.

"Hold ze bicycle in ze air," Ian said. His hair was in his eyes.

"A moment of victory," I said.

I tried my best, but it was heavy. My end was drooping during that part of the ceremony.

We counted. One, two, three. We heaved it as far as we could, which was maybe a few feet. It landed in the water with a splat more than a splash, and lay on the top for a minute before the back wheel started heading down.

We started to clap. I was filled with a surge of joy. Water rushed through the wire basket.

"We are ze king and ze queen of bicycle tossing," Ian said.

"Conquerors and champions," I said.

Ian took a pinch of my sleeve, brought me in to him in a hug. I could smell his coat, nylon left outside; his hair, some kind of clean vanilla.

"I'm quitting lessons, Cassie," Ian said.

"Don't do it if it's just because of Dino. Don't let him have that kind of power."

"It's not just Dino. Cassie? I don't want the violin running my life. I want more."

"Okay, then. All right," I said.

"And I don't want to go away to Curtis," he said. I set my cheek against him, let the hope fill me. I could hear his heart, even through his puffy coat. It was beating pretty wildly in there.

"Then you won't go," I said.

We pulled apart. Here's what I felt—our eyes, they made a pact. To be away from the music, the all-encompassing enemy, to be safe with each other. It was settled. No more violin, no more frenzied, singular visions. Ian would be the place where everything was okay.

Ian leaned in, kissed me. Warm, so warm, soft. A long, slow kiss. I didn't pull away, and I didn't run. He swallowed me up and brought me in.

When we pulled apart again, we just looked at each other. Because of course, everything had changed.

I started seeing Ian every day after school. He hadn't told his mom that he'd stopped going to lessons, so he'd pretend to leave at the same time each day and we'd meet somewhere. Sometimes we'd go to the ferry dock, and sometimes we'd go to the planetarium, because Dave, the guy that works there, always lets me in for free. We'd sit in the plush seats, and I'd point things out to Ian and he'd interrupt me with questions. Every now and then Ian would have Bunny's car, and we'd park somewhere and kiss and steam up the windows and go to the edge of want. Or we'd sit in the chairs in the back part of the library and talk, and once we listened to classical music on the big, puffy library headphones, those old kind from when headphones were first invented. He explained to

Deb Caletti

me the difference between legato and staccato, and for the first
time in my life I actually cared. About the music, about someone
else. Cared—love. My God, love. Here it was, and it was fantastic.
Everything felt larger. I felt like things made sense. I was myself,
and more than I ever knew I could be. I wanted to be so close to
him that I was *of* him. I wanted to be in his mind, in his arms. I
loved the way his hair fell in his eyes, his gangly limbs, the way I
had to stand on my toes to reach him. I loved his sudden laugh,
the way he thought about things, his intelligence. I started wearing his coat around when we were together. I would have worn it
when we were apart, if I could. And Ian was a harbor. A place to
hide from what was happening at home. A gazebo to run to and
take shelter in during a thunderstorm. If you think that all of this
is corny, tough shit. That's the way it was.

I explained away my absences with my handy Honduras project. It was the biggest project in the history of projects. It was the
longest, too, even though we'd given the oral report on it weeks
ago, Nicole holding and gesturing to the visual aids like a game
show hostess, and Jason sulking and not saying anything because
we'd rejected his idea of playing music in the background while
we spoke. He'd brought in a tape recorder and a compilation of
Hawaiian favorites. He perked up when we let him pass out the
information sheets to the class, though. Of course, all three of us
got an A, even though the only thing those two really contributed
to was my understanding of homicidal behavior.

I kept different pieces of my life in different places. I was
overcome with this bizarre need to talk about Ian, to bring him to
me with words, but I only gave in and did this with my bonded

twin, Zach Rogers, the talented duct-taped snake impersonator. I chose Zach to mention Ian to because one, he had every class with me, and two, because he had the memory of a goldfish. I didn't tell any of my friends about Ian, even Zebe.

"What is with you?" she asked me at lunch one day. "You aren't yourself. I feel like I'm talking to my Coke can. No, wait. It's more responsive." She held the can up to her ear. "Yeah, uh huh, I know," she said to the can. "God, Cassie. You've been acting weird for over a week now."

"No, I haven't. I'm fine."

"Shit, you know? I thought I was your friend."

"I'm sorry. There's really nothing . . ." I thought quickly. "Things are messed up at home. More than usual. I'm thinking of moving in with my dad. It's just really been on my mind a lot."

"You can't talk to me about that?" Zebe said. "Man, oh, man, you gotta share this stuff or it kills you. I was going to tell the counselor you had an eating disorder just so she'd call you into her office."

I still got together with everyone on most weekends, but inside I was rushing through those times and others. I had an ever-present inner *hurry up!* until I could be with Ian again. So that I could be free in the afternoons with the ease of one all-encompassing lie, I told my friends and even Siang that Mom got me a job helping with symphony correspondence.

I'm not sure why it felt so necessary to keep Ian a secret. I guess I wanted what we had all for myself, to protect it. I didn't want what was happening between Ian and me to become the usual thing, where you date for a few weeks and everyone talks about it like it's a ridiculously moronic soap opera, and your friends call his friends and his friends call you and it all becomes stupid and shallow. It was too special to have as the news of the day. It was too deep to be about other people.

I also didn't tell my parents about Ian for obvious reasons, and though I did tell Ian about my parents, I didn't talk about Dino. I didn't tell him that since Thanksgiving, Dino was up and down and paranoid and rational. I was sure it was too bizarre for him to handle. It was too bizarre for *me* to handle. Let's face it. Mental illness is embarrassing. In a perfect world, we wouldn't look down on people too ill to hold it together, who cry while looking out the window and don't bother getting fully dressed before going out. We'd be patient and understanding, instead of letting out our fear and uneasiness with the same kind of jokes we make about funeral directors. But it does make you uneasy. You do want to hold it away from you by saying his tie would match his straitjacket, even if that's not nice. This is not me, this is not mine. My mom makes cookies, too.

I couldn't show Ian that part of my life. It was something I wanted to run from, so why wouldn't he? And there was another thing, too. Ian was a part of the situation in a way a stranger wouldn't be. I can honestly say that I lost track of who I was protecting, and why.

"He didn't show up for his lesson again," Dino said one night as we were all in the car going out for dinner. "Two times, now. Two times!"

"I told you, just let him sort it out on his own. He's obviously struggling with the music just now."

"I'm going to call his mother. You want me to wait until it happens a third time?"

"Third, fourth. Let him have a rest. You know how the pressure can get to you," Mom said. "Let him decide he wants this. Be calm, Dino."

"We're losing precious time, Daniella," Dino said. "Don't you see? We've only got three and a half months before his tape must be in."

"Why is this so important to you anyway?" I asked. I never did get that. I mean, why not let Ian *be*?

"How can you understand? I can make a difference in his life. I can save him the struggle I had," Dino said. His eyes in the rearview mirror looked disgusted at my question.

"You see yourself in him," Mom said.

"Youth, need, talent . . ." Dino said. "But how can I help him if he doesn't help himself? It's a waste, and I detest waste. He will lose his chance if he doesn't stop these foolish games."

"Maybe he quit," I said. I couldn't help myself. I was a little smug at having the inside information. I also wanted to help Ian out. He was so happy about not playing anymore that the sooner Dino got it through his head, the better. Dino's pride at not having succeeded with his first student would just have to hurt a little. Or a lot. The Curtis School a zillion miles away would just have to do without Ian. If you're thinking here that my motivations were selfish, you're right about that too. Sure, I was glad he quit. If it meant he wouldn't leave, I'd have been happy if he decided to become a ferryboat driver and live here forever.

"Ha," Dino said. "He'll never quit."

A little flame of anger rose up. "What makes you so sure?"

"I know. He will never quit. He'll be back."

"You can't know," I said. "You can't know for sure what someone will or won't do." I hated the look of the back of his neck, that curly hair he was so proud of. What I'd have given for a pair of scissors.

"Don't be ridiculous. He'll be back. I'll call his mother in the morning," Dino said.

"No, Dino. It will be better if he comes back here on his own," my mother said. "You know how it gets sometimes. You think you never want to see a sheet of music again."

We pulled up to the restaurant. I didn't feel like eating. I didn't want to sit across from Dino and see him get salad dressing in the corners of his mouth. Hatred and nourishment didn't go together.

"His mother will do what I tell her to do. They always do. That idiot Andrew Wilkowski would jump off a bridge if I told him to," Dino said.

"Wearing his music-note tie," my mother said.

"Tacky man. William Tiero, that prick. He was the only one who wouldn't. He told me what to do, and I hated it. How many years, I followed like a lamb."

"All right, love. Let's not think about that now," Mom said. She opened her car door.

"They would all jump off a bridge if I told them to." Dino snapped his fingers in the air. *Just like that,* those fingers said.

Christmas came. A big tree was brought into the house, delivered already decorated, a present from Andrew Wilkowski, who probably had just gotten his first commission check for the deal he set up for Dino, the CD currently titled, *Then and Now,* a mix of his old stuff and the new pieces, a way of putting out a new album without a full set of fresh material. You should have seen this tree—it was the kind of thing that you see in department stores, with miniature packages wrapped in gold paper and gaudy, huge ornaments and sparkly pears and doves. It was either gorgeous or horrid. Either way it didn't exactly give you what you would call a warm, Chestnuts Over the Open Fire kind of feeling. More, Nordstrom's Holiday Home Sale. When it was being delivered, Courtney and her media-monster brothers practically wet themselves with excitement. They stood in the street and watched the tree—and the two delivery guys it took to carry it—disappear into the house. Mom said Courtney actually brought her parents by later to gawk. This wasn't hard to do. You could be three miles away from the front window and still see it. Thank God there were no lights on it, or the Coast Guard would think there was a ship in distress.

In spite of the tree, there were bits of evidence of the way Christmas used to be too, when it was just Mom and Dad and me. There was this decrepit gingerbread house we'd made years ago, the candy so ancient that it was pale and drippy and would kill you if you ate it, and our old Nativity scene. Mom and I still liked to have fun with it by moving the figures around in what you could politely call "nontraditional positions." Mom's not very religious in any regular way. She called the Nativity "Christmas Town," as in *What's happening in Christmas Town today?* I'd wake up to find the camel in the manger, say, with Joseph chipping in with parenting duties out front, and then I'd move them around to surprise her the next day with everyone standing in a circle around the donkey. Several years ago, the scene acquired a large plastic dinosaur, and later, a miniature replica of the Statue of Liberty that Mom got when she played a festival in New York. The poor folks of Christmas Town ran from Godzilla one day, and the Statue of Liberty got to be a fourth wise man. I remember that my dad used to get a little ticked at us for this, as Christmas Town had been a gift from Nannie, and he disapproved of our sacrilege. I remember Mom sticking out her tongue at him, and him swatting her butt. I don't think Dino even noticed Christmas Town. I'm not sure Dino even noticed the Christmas tree that had invaded the living room.

I spent Christmas Eve with my dad. There was no talk of his Dino detective work right then, thankfully, but I saw that the books and notepads were still in his room, stacked neatly beside his bed. Dad had brought Nannie and two other old ladies home with him for the holiday, and he made a fantastic dinner that all the old ladies loved. One of them, Helen, drank too much wine and fell asleep before we had dessert, snoring away in Dad's favorite chair. We opened presents, and Nannie and the other old lady, Mary, got rambunctious.

"That would look lovely on Helen," Nannie said when she opened the nightgown from Dad. She placed it on top of the snoozing old lady.

"Put the necktie on her too," said Mary. So Helen got decorated with Dad's new tie, a car-washing mitt, and my new hat. Mary and Nannie were laughing so hard I thought we'd have to call the medics. Dad was trying to get Helen to hold the hand mixer I'd given him, when she snorted and flinched kind of violently, sending the car-washing mitt sailing and landing on the coffee table in a half-empty bowl of Dad's clam dip. Nannie was holding her stomach with laughter, and had to hurry off to the bathroom. I'd never seen her this loose.

"Jeez, what was in that wine?" I said to Dad. He was happy and relaxed, having a grand time too. When we got everyone packed in the car to go, Nannie had to come back in because she'd forgotten the slippers I'd given her. She was in there so long that it shouldn't have been a surprise that when we came home, we saw that her own Nativity scene had been moved to the dining room table, and the Christmas cards had been set upright along the mantel, just as they used to be when she'd lived there with Grandpa.

Christmas day I spent at home with Mom and Dino. If your parents are divorced, you know this is one of the side benefits of the whole deal, the time when all of the crap and the moving from house to house actually starts to pay off a little. Two or more Christmases, two or more birthdays. Zebe won the holiday lottery. She has five Christmases and one Chanukah. She has Christmases with her Mom, Dad, Grandpa, Grandma (they're divorced, too), and her other set of grandparents. Her stepmother is Jewish, so she gets Chanukah with them, too. Handing her the keys to a department store would be easier. Everyone wants to give you the holiday they remembered. You actually start to feel sorry for those kids whose parents are married to each other, poor deprived souls. Your social calendar becomes busier than the president's during election year, and keeping track of everything becomes akin to solving those annoying puzzles where you slide around the numbers and try to get them back in order. You never want to see another Christmas cookie or a turkey again in your life. You realize there are many stuffing variations, all pretty gross. You realize how truly *different* Mom's family is from Dad's family. But you've got a stocking in every house, and candy and love and presents rain down upon you, like the Red Cross flying overhead, dropping packages. All this because your parents sucked at being married to each other.

Dino had apparently done his shopping in no less than fifteen seconds total, and in the gift section of the men's department. He gave Mom a six-in-one flashlight, a gold pen, and a box of handkerchiefs. He gave me an executive desk dartboard and an executive stress-buster ball to squeeze in your hand. I was glad he passed on the golf ball–care kit and the six-pack of holiday boxers. The day was nice but uneventful, and after dinner, Dino went into his office to work. There were only three months left until the concert. Mom and I sat in the kitchen and ate a piece of apple pie, then took thin slices of what was left in the dish until we were thoroughly disgusted with ourselves. Dino emerged, his hair disheveled and tired-looking, his eyes with dark circles. Mom made him tea, rubbed his neck.

"We would have a pomegranate, this time of year," Dino said. "In Italy. No, a pomegranate every day."

"You must be exhausted," Mom said.

"Unspeakably."

Dino went to bed, and after I let Dog William outside for a last holiday pee, I headed for bed too.

Mom must have been feeling sentimental. She'd come in my room to kiss me good night. "Merry Christmas," I said to her.

"You too, my girl," she said. Her braid had swung over my face. Her own face looked thin and tired.

"I hope it's a really good year," I said.

Mom paused a beat. "I want that too," she said.

I woke up really early and happy the next morning, knowing that Ian and I were going to meet. Something about the morning seemed oddly still, too quiet, and when I peeked through my blind I saw why—it had snowed during the night, and it was a beautiful soft white everywhere. Snow is magical, and if you don't think so, you won't see magic anywhere. I got that excited feeling, like there'd be school closures, even though we were off school already. I went in Mom and Dino's room, shook Mom awake so she could see. She crept up so as not to disturb Dino, went out in the backyard in her nightgown and made a snowball to put in the freezer, like we always did. *I told you I thought it was going to snow. I could smell it in the air,* she said. She was always proud of her weather-predicting abilities, especially after no one believed her. There was no practice that day, so she went back to bed, and I got showered and dressed. I was too excited to go back to sleep.

I was hunting around the back of my closet for warm stuff when I heard a big *bamp* at my window. I swore at first, thinking it was Courtney's brothers, but when I looked out I saw Ian standing right outside, and bits of a snowball dribbling down my window. The street was still sleeping, and Ian's boots had made a path down the road. God, it was pretty out, and Ian had on his dark coat and held a slim white box. He was standing there in full view, really dangerous, and I urged him down the street with my hands, held up one finger to indicate I'd be right there.

I grabbed the slim white box in my own room, shoved on my mittens and my old boots, but got this in reverse order, since I couldn't work the laces. I flung off my mittens and tried again, pulled on my new snow hat from Nannie, and was happy/unhappy about it. Unhappy because it was scratchy, happy because the scratchiness reminded me of really great snowy days in uncomfortable hats. I tried not to clump down the stairs, and when I stepped outside, the only thing the cold hit was my face. I had on layers of clothes and so I could barely move, just the way it should be. Ian was down the street, clapping his mittened hands for me to hurry.

I clomped and sloshed down the street. I picked a clean patch so that I could make my own footprints. Something about marring smooth sand or snow and making our mark must go back to our caveman days, because it is such a satisfying feeling. I was hot already and pulled off my hat, making my hair look superb, I'm sure. Otis, the neighbor's cat, was picking his way across the snow with tenderly raised paws and a great deal of caution.

I tossed a snowball in Ian's direction. "That's for the one at my window," I said. My aim sucked and I hit the Fredericis' mailbox.

"You better watch it," he warned. If my hair had gone all

undersea creature on me, Ian didn't seem to care. He grabbed me up in his arms and lifted me up and set me down again.

"Snow," he said. His breath came out in a puff.

"I love it," I said. "This is the best."

"Let's go to the riding trail, then we can do the presents," he said.

"Okay."

We walked hand in hand, or rather, mitten in mitten, which is about the coziest and Everything All Right with the World feeling you can get. We walked toward the school, the center part of the island, where there is a perimeter of forested riding and walking trails. We walked past the trail marker, and I slid the snow off its top into a heap. The trail didn't look real. It was a postcard day. The branches of the trees were heavy and drooping with white thickness, and the ground was a soft and sparkly carpet.

"So beautiful," I said.

"You too," Ian said. He took hold of one strand of my hair, looked at the color of it against his mitten. He looked at my face. "Brown hair, dark eyes, white snow."

We walked a bit, just listening to silence. Snowy quiet is more quiet than regular quiet. It's like the world is holding its breath.

After a while, Ian stopped. "Presents?"

"Sure," I said.

We both knew what we were getting each other. We agreed to get each other the same thing, only we'd choose which kind. Eliminate all gift-giving hassle and anxiety. We swapped boxes. I bit the fingertips of my mittens and pulled them off, tossed them to the ground so that I could open the package.

"Ready?" I said, and we both pulled the scarves from the boxes. Mine was red, amazingly soft, fuzzy. The one I'd chosen for Ian was blue, with thick, wide stitches.

"Let me," Ian said. He wrapped the scarf around my neck.

"I love it," I said, and wrapped his around his neck, tucking the ends inside his coat.

"Me too," he said.

We hugged for a while, stood together, and I had that feeling you get in nature that you are small against its grandness, same as when you used to see the tiny figure of a person against the Latitude Drive-In Movie screen, before they tore it down to put a strip mall there. Ian put my mittens back on my hands, and we walked a little, boots crunching.

"Fir, cedar, evergreens," Ian pointed. "Spruce. Poplar. Deciduous. Water can go up hundreds of feet, to the tiniest branches up there. Just travels up, molecule by molecule."

"I didn't know you knew about these things."

"I like to study trees." He looked upward, and his dark hair fell away from his eyes. "They're quiet. They're solid. Sure of where they are."

"You must get tired of sound."

"God, really."

"You could study trees instead."

Ian laughed.

"You could."

"I'd love that. I would so love that."

He stopped on the trail then, and we kissed in the snow, in our new scarves. It was one of life's perfect moments, where you look around and think *I want to remember this.* You try to etch it in your brain so that when you are Nannie's age and are living at Providence Point, you will look out the window and see red and blue scarves against a white background, Ian's breath against the backdrop of trees, new snow beginning to fall; at first, small diamonds, and then huge fat flakes that sat on the shoulders of Ian's dark coat and fell upon his hair. You will remember the soft flakes against your upturned face, the way they fell upon your tongue, and Ian telling you he loved you into your hair. You would remember all of it, and feel that sense that you had everything you ever wanted in the world.

We walked back home, stopped at the beginning of my street. The media-monster boys didn't even have their sleds out, and there were no forts or snowball fights or snowmen and women, but the blue light from the television shone from the living room windows. Mr. Frederici was shoveling his walk, even though the snow would likely turn to rain by night, and the snow would be mostly gone except for a few lingering patches by tomorrow. That's how the snow was around here. A day or two of thrill and traffic all messed up, and then you had to wait another year for it to happen again.

Ian put his mittened hands against my cheeks and kissed me, his mouth cold, and then warm again. His dark hair was wet from the snow. I'm sure I had mascara all over my face, but he looked at me like he loved me. Then Ian gazed down my street, at our house.

"My mother was playing one of his recordings yesterday," Ian said.

I was silent. We both just stood and looked at my house. Unease was starting at my toes, creeping up. The day had been so perfect.

"What his music does to you—there aren't even words."

Perfect, and fleeting.

Ian returned to his lessons, of course.

He didn't even tell me. I just heard his voice in the house a few days later and I knew what had happened. God damn it, it made me mad. I wasn't sure who I was so mad at. Dino, for being right. Ian, for giving himself up. He had broken our pact. It was *settled*. At least that's how I saw it.

"Ian!" I called, after he left on his bike. He put on his brakes, had his head down. Like Dog William when he peed on the carpet. I ran to catch up to him. Fury, confusion, and hurt all mixed together so I didn't know which was which.

"You didn't tell me."

"I'm sorry. I don't know. I couldn't."

"Why? And why are you doing this? You don't even want this. Why? Please. I just don't get it."

"Look at you. I knew you'd be hurt. I didn't want to hurt you. I just couldn't do it." He reached over, picked up my hand. He rubbed the top of it with his thumb.

"What happened, Ian?"

"My mom found out I quit lessons, and flipped. I told her about us. She doesn't even want me to see you anymore. Cassie, I don't want that."

Great. Nice Janet with the chipped toenail polish. Anger

bubbled up. Love meant nothing, I guess. Not compared to what that violin meant. I turned my head away. I stared at the Fredericis' house. I didn't even want to look at him.

"I don't want that," he said. "Do you hear me? Cassie."

"I don't see what the point is. You're going away. You're going away, right?" I said to the Fredericis' house. I didn't understand. I didn't get how things could change from that perfect day in the woods to where they were now.

"Cassie, look at me." He took my chin. Brought my eyes to his. "You know I love you."

"You sold yourself out. You're going away, right?"

His eyes were wet, from cold maybe. Maybe he was about to cry. "Yes."

"Leave me alone," I said. I broke away from him. Hurt, the winning emotion, was rushing forward, gathering up my insides and holding them too tight. Hurt squeezed my heart, and I ran. He betrayed himself, so he'd betrayed me.

Chapter Nine

I knew Ian came early to lessons to see me. I knew he stayed late, hanging around the front lawn. He even threw something at my window once, which I ignored.

"The boy is back," Dino had said that first day, with this horrible glee in his voice. How I didn't throw my water glass at him, I'll never know.

"So it all works out," my mother said.

I hated everyone. Dino. Even Mom sometimes. Dog William for being happier than ever, having Rocket back in his life. I fantasized about funding my father's sabotaging-Dino efforts, the way one government secretly funds the destruction of another. Okay, the way *our* government does that. I hated school and almost everyone in it. They changed the seating chart in World History, and I ended up sitting next to these two girls who I always thought looked like those monkeys from *Planet of the Apes*.

In science we started labs. My partners were Orlando, who didn't yet know he was gay, and this girl, Julia, who already knew she was. So during one class it was the Bad Primate Movie film-fest, and the next it was the Rainbow Pride Hour, with Orlando using words like *exquisite*, and Julia showing us pictures of her and Allison Lorey at homecoming. Zach, of duct-taped-snake fame, had suddenly moved after his dad got a new job. I felt a sadness and inexplicable loss. Twins separated, phantom-limb stuff. I actually missed him. Worse, we were into that long spell where there were no vacations until Spring Break, unless you count that perennial holiday favorite, President's Day. Such a time of revelry and celebration, where the whole country stops in joyful remembrance of William Howard Taft and Grover Cleveland. Party on.

The next time Ian had a lesson, I stayed in my room. Chuck and Bunny had given him a ride; I heard their car and Bunny's deep voice calling out a good-bye. No Rocket that day—Dog William would have his heart broken. Good.

I held the snow globe, turned it upside down enough times to make the bear truly pissed off, if he could get pissed off. I thought maybe I should name him. I wondered what a good name for an unanchored bear would be. Bingo? Dave? Timmy? I ignored the goddamn beautiful sounds coming from downstairs. I wondered how Sabbotino Grappa, full of lemon trees and curved, cobbled streets could produce a man with a stone heart.

"Cassie!"

A knock at my door. Shit, a knock. I dropped the bear on my bed. I guess the music downstairs had stopped some time ago. It was Ian. At my bedroom door.

"Are you crazy?" I said to the door. "Dino will kill you."

"Open up. Come on. Cassie, come *on!*"

"Ian, what are you doing?" I said through the closed door. "He's right downstairs."

"I don't care."

"Go away."

"I'm not leaving until you talk to me."

"Jesus," I said. I opened the door. "Get in here before he sees you." I yanked his sleeve, shut the door behind him. "What are you thinking?"

"I'm thinking I'm in love with you. I'm thinking I miss you and I'm sorry you feel I've let you down."

His brown eyes were soft. I wanted to put my hands in his hair, inside his coat, around his waist. *Pain versus happiness,* I'd told my mother. There must be a simple mathematical solution to figure it out.

Some strange memory came to me then. A story from when I was little, told again and again by my parents. I was climbing the attic stairs as my mother stood behind me. *Are you afraid of the stairs?* My mother had asked. *No,* I had said. *I'm just afraid of falling.*

"Hey," Ian said. "I'm in your room. I've never seen your room."

He looked around at my lamps and my hula dancer dash-board guy, and at my Einstein Action Figure. He picked up the tiny plastic television on my dresser, looked inside the peephole and clicked through the pictures of Dogs on TV—tacky dogs in tacky costumes. He stared at the star chart on the back of my door.

"You've got to get out of here," I said.

"Not yet." Ian took his sweet time looking around. He read the quotes stuck up along near my bed, picked up my snow globe, which I'd ditched quickly on the mattress. He gave the bear a spin, watched him swirl.

"I've had him since I was a kid," I said. "He used to be glued down."

"I like him like this," Ian said. "He looks happy. Free. He's just cruising around." Ian gave him another spin.

"He's totally unanchored. Lost in space."

"He's *smiling*. Look, miniature painted lips. Smiling." He held the globe above us, pointed out the tiny red line on the bear's face. "Cassie, what are you so afraid of?" Ian said. He handed the globe back to me.

"It's obvious."

"No."

"Losing you. Having you go away. Feeling too much. It doesn't seem to lead to good things."

"It's like . . . you're on vacation. But instead of enjoying the sun and the palm trees, you're worrying the plane's gonna crash on the way home."

"You *are* leaving. I *will* lose you."

"I'm here right now. We don't know what the future will bring. Why don't we let that take care of itself."

I didn't say anything. Ian resumed his survey of my room. He saw my scarf, draped over my desk chair, ran it between his fingers. He picked up my pillow, held it to his face to smell my scent.

"I love the way you smell."

"Ian." I could barely speak.

"Cassie, *let go*."

I felt my throat close up with tears. Sometimes you build up these walls, you build and you build and you think they're so strong, but then someone can come along and tip them over with only his fingers, or the weight of his breath. I started to cry. Ian came and put his arms around me, and I tried to think tough things because I hate to cry. I told myself not to act like I'd been abducted and brainwashed by evil Hallmark robots, but it was no good. He held me, and I tried not to think about what was really on my mind—all the times that people came together and really loved each other, all the times that meant they'd have to lose each other too.

"I'm sorry," I said.

"What are you sorry for? Don't be sorry."

"Just, how I handled things."

"I've hated disappointing you," Ian said.

I got myself together. Unburied my face from his shirt. I probably got makeup on his dark coat. I'm sure my eyes looked trés Ringling Brothers.

"God, Ian. What are we thinking? You've got to get out of here. Dino's going to know you're here. He's like a hawk. A hawk with ESP. He notices everything. He catches every *thought* someone has that's against him. He catches every thought about maybe having a thought someone has that's against him."

"I don't care. I'll do the audition, but I want a life, too. I told my mother the same thing. Dino's going to have to accept it too."

"It's supposed to affect your focus. Spending time with me means you're not giving everything to your music the way you need to. You only have two more months until your audition."

"I can handle it fine. There's no reason I can't do both," Ian said. "I don't care if Dino knows. I don't want to hide anymore."

I felt a surge of brave glee. It felt good. No, it felt *great*. "I hope you know what you're doing," I said.

"I've never been more sure."

"Oh, God. He's going to kill me." More glee in this, the anticipation of good conquering evil. Some sicko part of me was thrilled at the idea of the shit hitting the fan. It was very Romeo and Juliet, only we know what happened to them.

"Kiss me. Then walk me down."

"Man, you are asking for it."

"He's going to have to understand."

I knew when he said this that he didn't understand Dino very well. We stepped out my door, walked down the stairs. Of course, Dino was coming out of his office when we reached the landing. I'm sure he knew where Ian was the entire time, and was keeping track of the passing minutes on his watch.

"Ian needs a ride home," I said. "He came to ask me." So much for conquering evil. I was already descending into fear-induced excuses and barely concealed panic. I realized that I'd have to make good on my quick thinking, was relieved to remember that Mom carpooled that morning, as she often did to save on ferry passage.

"Thanks for the lesson, Mr. Cavalli," Ian said. And then he picked up my hand, laced my fingers in his.

"Good-bye, Boy Wonder," Dino said.

I drove Ian home, my heart leaping around with Oh, Shit, What Have We Done jubilation and anxiety. And at just plain happiness at being with Ian again. You know what I'd missed? The smell of him, how he always smelled like he'd just come in from the cold, and like that vanilla shampoo. And now I could smell him there in the car beside me and it made me so happy. I felt like I could just drive around for the next twenty years and be perfectly content, there in Mom's Subaru, with her half-eaten roll of butterscotch Life Savers in the ashtray, paper coffee cup crinkled on the floor, and *Seattle Weekly* in tossed disarray on the backseat.

I turned the radio up loud. Some old rock song. Something very un-classical. I guess even Mom needed a break from it too, while she was driving. Ian patted his thigh with his palm to the beat. We arrived at his house and kissed in the car for a while. Man, did I like kissing Ian Waters.

We steamed up the windows until Ian had to go. I hated to see him leave. Kissing him in the car made me want to never have to see the back of his coat going away from me. He walked up the steps to his house, and I watched him. He turned and waved good-bye.

It wasn't until I'd gotten home that I realized he'd forgotten all about his violin in the backseat.

The bizarre thing was, Dino didn't say a word about Ian and me all that night, or the next day even. He was only his usual depressed self, this morose person who was becoming our usual household companion, this man on a constant hunt for the ways he was sure he was being harmed. I wondered if he'd given up on the theory that he could feel more in control of his own life by controlling someone else's, or if he just didn't care anymore. What I really thought, though, was that it was all building up inside of him—his anger, his disease. The vicious mix was simmering.

Dino must not have even told Mom about Ian and me. She didn't mention anything, or even seem annoyed with me. Dino stayed holed up in his office, then went to bed early. He just stayed disconnected from me. But then again, he'd never truly connected with me in the first place. I was like the dishwasher, or the coffeepot, and always had been. I just came with the package, and as long as I was doing what I was supposed to do and kept quiet, fine. Sometimes, in a step-situation you've got all the pieces, but it just doesn't make a family. Everyone is trying to make believe that it is, but you can tell the difference. No divorce book is going to help, no "new traditions" are going to help, and God, no family vacations are going to help (unless purposely staying behind at the rest stop and making a new life there fixes things), because it just doesn't feel right. Your parent makes a choice, based on who knows what, and you're forced to live with that choice. That's the reality. "Family" is not the reality. Zebe had a stepsister who's supposed to be a sister, and I had a stepfather who's supposed to be a father, and we're all just faking it, and not very well, either. There's an aversion to the Required Relationship, same as I have an aversion to those miniature, creepy corns. They look unnatural to me, but I'll eat them if I have to. Let's just be honest. Sometimes there's love there, and it all works great. But sometimes there isn't. A lot of times there isn't. These people are just strangers who live with you and take on assumed family-like names. And even the tolerance that usually comes with blood relatives isn't there. It's all painfully staged. It's a bad play, that you sit in your seat and squirm during with awkward anxiety; it's a pair of shoes that *just don't fit* that you jam your feet into anyway. It's not home. It's people in a house.

Anyway, he didn't say anything. I called Ian for the first time.

"Check it out," I said. "I'm calling you at home."

"Say something more so I can hear how you sound on the phone," he said. "Just talk."

"Four score and seven years ago," I orated. "This country brought forth a new nation. Really important things started happening, and men who weren't even gay started wearing white wigs and frilly coats. They looked lovely, but even more importantly they . . ."

"I like your voice on the phone," Ian interrupted. I was just getting warmed up too.

"I better not stay on long. I just wanted to tell you that he's been silent. No screams. This is actually me talking, and not my murdered ghost."

"See? We didn't need to worry. He probably just accepts that there's nothing he can do."

"Ha. Calm before the storm," I said.

And I was right. The next day I felt the tension, more than saw actual evidence of it. The air was thin and nervous, electric.

Being in the same room with him was unbearable—you could feel that pebble that had just snapped into the windshield, the breakage line snaking up, the knowledge of an inevitable shatter. We bumped elbows in the kitchen the next day, as Dino went for the refrigerator and I went for the cereal bowls, and I could actually feel him flinch. Mom was making coffee and obviously talking Chinese, because I couldn't understand anything she was saying. I got the hell out of there, fast. I thought maybe I should live at school. I could borrow the janitor's room, that snug, weird place of mops in buckets and detergents, and a calendar with sports cars on it that was still showing September. I even made small talk with Courtney on the walk home, even though every talk with Courtney is small talk, if you know what I mean. We talked about nail polish, for God's sake. She told me about a hair removal kit she got on the Home Shopping Network with her mother's credit card. I fed her more topics—hairstyles, breast implants, the love life of Toby Glassar, this muscle-choked senior guy all the blond girls liked—until she looked at me as if we had really bonded. *Thanks for the great talk,* she said, and then told me she had to leave to go watch the soap *All My Sex Partners.* Okay, it wasn't really called that, but you get my drift.

I stayed in my room until Mom came home and it was dinnertime. If there's ever a time you feel the stepfamily disconnect, it's at the dinner table. You've got to sit there and look at your differences until you've downed your lasagna as fast as possible. You learn that every planet teaches manners differently, and the one your new alien family members came from probably either didn't teach them at all (making dinner a revolting nightly replay of a pie-eating contest), or taught them too well (making dinner a new Olympic sport called Every Food Has a Rule). That night, the tension was lying between us, sharp and thread-like. No one was talking, and the sounds of silverware on glass plates were painfully loud, seemingly capable of breaking apart what was holding us all together. You could hear Dino's chewing (you could always hear Dino's chewing), and he was drinking wine. Too much wine, I could tell, from the way my mother kept eyeing his glass as he refilled it. She was obviously on the wrong page; her own tension stemmed from the surplus Burgundy and not from what was going on between Dino and me right under her nose.

"My bike is gone," Dino said finally.

I swallowed hard. It was either that, or blast out a mouthful of lasagna. I practically burst out laughing from nerves and surprise. His bike. Thrown in ze "canal" by ze two hooligans. I'd almost forgotten about it.

"What do you mean?" my mom said.

"Gone. Stolen."

"Who would steal *that* bike?" Mom said. She actually laughed. I felt like busting up too. I took a drink of milk. Trained my thoughts—*death, destruction, devastation*—so that I wouldn't bust up and explode it out my nose.

"It's gone," he said. He chewed a chunk of bread. You saw it in there, being swirled and mashed to death. "I wonder if you know anything about this?" he asked me. "You are the one who rides it."

"I don't know what happened to it." Lie. "I haven't ridden it in weeks." Truth. *Couldn't* ride it since it was at the bottom of the sound.

"I went into the garage and noticed it wasn't there."

"I wonder who might have done something like that," I said. "You never know." I mean, where was his paranoia now? Why couldn't William Tiero have done *this*? He'd supposedly followed us, tried to ruin Dino's career, sent us annoying junk mail, called repeatedly, and done a thousand other things. He should have at least been in the lineup.

"I spoke with Ian's mother," Dino said. "This afternoon."

"Why?" Mom asked.

"About the budding lovers," Dino said.

There it was. The beginning, and I was already lost. I was already gone to anger; he'd already won.

"We're not lovers," I said.

"Shall we count our blessings for that?" he said.

"Not yet, anyway," I said. I wanted to put the knife in. I wanted to twist.

"You are such a silly child. Your immaturity is astounding."

"I'm supposed to be immature. I'm the kid. What's your excuse?"

"Wait a minute. What is going on?" Mom said. Her face was flushing red.

"You have no idea what you're doing. No idea of the harm you can cause."

"You have no idea what *you're* doing," I said to him. "You're going to kill any desire he has to play that stupid fucking violin."

"Listen to this tramp, Daniella," Dino said to my mother. "Look at her. Listen to her mouth."

"Hold on a moment here," my mother said. "You just hold on. I don't want to hear that kind of talk from you, Dino. Or you, Cassie."

"She is ruining everything. Don't you understand that?"

"What is going on?" my mother asked.

"Ian," was all I could say. "Ian and me."

"He's got less than two months. Seven weeks, and he's not ready. Even the *Chaconne* is rough. How can I help him? How can I make it turn out all right for him when he is running around in airy-fairy land with her? This child could destroy everything he's worked for."

"Ian has some say in this too. I am not some evil sorceress making him do things against his will."

"Jesus, Cassie! What's been going on? I thought we agreed. . . ."

"The boy must be managed. His career must be handled. He's not to be trusted to know what he needs," Dino said.

"Sometimes love just *is*," I threw her words back at her. "Sometimes it's a force with its own reasons."

"Where did you get such idiocy?" Dino said. "This is a practical matter. Someone's life is in your hands. He fucks up this audition, and his future is shit."

"Maybe he doesn't want to play. Maybe you should let him be. His life has nothing to do with you." I pushed my plate away.

"Cassie," Mom said.

"I'm his teacher. He is my responsibility. I can change his life. I have a chance to make things go right for him. You think you understand him? You don't. You don't know the first thing about him."

"Oh, you don't think so," I said. I hated him saying that, I really did.

"*I* understand him."

"Come on, you guys. Let's all just calm . . ."

"You can't possibly understand him. You're making him do things he doesn't want to."

"I know him. I know his life."

"Maybe he doesn't want to turn out like you. Maybe he doesn't want your life." I couldn't help the words falling from my mouth. They had a will of their own, the same as thunder does. The same as some storm that needs to be released. "Maybe he doesn't want to be depressed and crazed and making everyone unhappy because his beloved music has made him nuts."

"God damn it, Cassie, that's enough," Mom said.

"Maybe the tortured-genius thing just doesn't look too appealing."

"You've raised an imbecile, Daniella," Dino said.

Mom stood up. "I said that's enough. Both of you."

"I have that book by my bed. I've read it. All about Sabbotino Grappa, all about your beautiful parents. I feel sorry for them. Your mother must have been ashamed that she raised such a nasty person."

Dino shoved out from the table, knocking over his wineglass. His hands were flat on the table, and I could see them shaking. "Shut this child up," he said through his clenched teeth.

"People . . ." Mom said.

"Shut this child up about my mother!"

I had gone too far. I knew it even before he picked up the chair with one hand and threw it. It crashed to the ground, a horrendous clatter. I shut my eyes against the sound, against the scene. When I opened them again, I could see that Dino was leaving the room, and that my mother had covered her face with her hands and just held her head there, as if trying to hold the pieces of herself together.

"Mom?" I was afraid to talk. I had already done too much of that. "Mom, I'm sorry."

My mother raised her head. She sighed. "You know, Cassie, I'm sorry too."

"I hope you're okay," I said.

"And I hope you're okay."

We sat in silence.

"I guess none of this is all right," she said finally.

You know what I was most sorry for then? I was sorry for her. That things had turned out like this for her. That she had made a leap and ended up crashing onto concrete.

"Probably not."

"Life's messed up at the moment."

"Yeah," I said.

"If you're fine just now, I'm going to go talk to Dino."

I nodded.

Every circus needs a ringmaster, and ours gave my shoulders a squeeze and disappeared out of the room.

Dino found a way to solve his problem with Ian, which was that he would allow Ian to have a private life, only he would give him no time in which to have it. His requirements for continuing to help Ian were that Ian must commit to daily lessons with him and to evening practice at home. Dino and Ian's mother had had a meeting. *They'd jump off a bridge if I told them to,* Dino had said. Ian's mother had a talk with Ian. He had no choice, Ian told me. Curtis was the single scholarship-only college in the country. Affording even a small part of a partial scholarship was out of the question, paying living expenses was out of the question, and a degree from Curtis would ensure his best shot at a job and performance contracts.

What about trees? I had asked.

I can't do trees, Ian had said. *I just . . . I can't explain. I've got to make his happen.*

I don't get it. It's your life.

It's an opportunity I can't pass up.

I had the sick feeling that Dino had been right about one thing. He understood Ian in this way that I didn't. There were things I couldn't see or know. I didn't realize then that everyone had their secrets.

I didn't see much of Ian, which was obviously part of the plan. He studied in the morning at home to finish his requirements for school, came over in the afternoons for lessons, and had to leave quickly in order to get his practice time in. We only had a moment for a quick hello and good-bye, and the times I saw him he was tired and strung out. The only real piece I had of Ian was his music, traveling up the stairs during his practices, or coming through the door as I sat my back down against it and listened to what was happening inside that office. I savored what

I had. I'd close my eyes and let the music lift me up and hold me. *Yes, yes, good. Very good,* Dino would say. I would imagine lemon trees and cobbled streets made warm by the sun, orange-colored buildings and baskets of figs. I would imagine us sharing a cup of coffee at a small iron table, sneaking into an old church to gulp cool air. A life together of simple, good things. I imagined bicycles in canals, Sabbotino Grappa at sunset.

After practices, Dino himself would disappear into his office and his own place of creation. If he was paranoid then, I didn't know it. I never saw him. But my mother was dealing with things I had no idea about. I heard her on the phone a lot with Alice, and Mom would hang up quickly when I came in. I would hear her crying, and when I would investigate, she'd wipe her face and lie and say she wasn't.

It was as if Dino and Ian had both descended into some other dark world, where all thoughts and all moments were music, music, music. Frenzied playing, lost men. Italian phrases— *sforzando, con calore, adagietto,* a land with its own language, even. The repetition of passages; frustration at not getting it right, try again. Try again until it is perfect, the perfect translation of all of love and sorrow, of struggle and triumph. It wasn't notes they were playing, not really. It was not songs. They were playing all the passion and drama of life, nothing less. Expressing the questions, searching for the answers. At least they were able to do this through their music. I had questions, questions that seemed to multiply like bad news multiplies. Even the vastness of the universe, looking through my telescope, did not put those questions into perspective.

Siang came over one afternoon, when they were at their

height of joint possession, Dino with his composing, Ian with his practicing. I was worried about her being there, tried to get her to go home, as I was afraid of what she might see. The day before I'd experienced the first sign in a while that Dino was still in the throws of his illness. I had come home to the stereo blasting, and when I turned it down Dino stormed from his office. *What are you doing?* he had said. *I need that on. If that prick is listening somehow, he won't hear a thing.*

Siang had practically begged to come in. When we finally went inside, I wished right away I had held my ground. The kitchen was a mess—filled with clutter and disgusting cigarette butts. Their snakey stink was everywhere—in coffee cups, on the newspaper, in the sink. I cleaned up as Siang either didn't notice or pretended not to. She had slung her backpack to our kitchen floor, unzipped it and rifled through.

"I want to show you something," she had said. "Something I found out."

"I don't want to hear obscure facts of Dino's life, okay? I don't give a shit how old he was when he first rolled over." I clanked a coffee cup against the side of the garbage can to dump the ashes, saved it from getting cancer.

"It's not that," she said into her open backpack.

"I don't give a shit when he first said goo goo."

"Just wait," she said.

"He got his first chest hair at sixteen. Whoopee."

Finally, Siang pulled a folded sheet of paper from her backpack. She carefully flattened it out, smoothed out the creases with her palm. "That painting. In his office. The one over his desk."

I looked at the image. Sure enough, it was the painting of the flowers that Dino had there, the one Siang had straightened so carefully that day we had seen the blank pages.

"So?" I said.

"And this," Siang said. She fished around in her backpack some more, pulled out *Strings Magazine*. She folded back the cover to an interview that Dino had given, and began to read.

"'Question,'" Siang squeaked. "'Who or what was your greatest influence?' 'Answer: Well, naturally it was my mother. She was a rose. A wild rose. Beautiful because she was wild. Wild because the world gave her too much beauty. More than could be tamed.' 'Question: Is that a good description of you too? Beauty that cannot be tamed?' 'Answer: I wish it weren't so. Then I could be at peace. Wearing my slippers and smoking a pipe.'"[9]

"What's your point?" I asked.

"That's the name of the painting. It's called *Wild Roses*. It was done by van Gogh."

"I think it should be called *Ugly Flowers on Bland Canvas*," I said.

"I think it is especially beautiful."

"Jeez, Siang. Maybe if you cross your eyes. Maybe if you're color-blind. Or asleep."

"It's beautiful because it was one of his last paintings. It was done when he was at Daubigny's garden, experiencing his most intensely creative period. Right before his suicide."

The word hung there between us. *Suicide*. This word that is

---

9. From Sylvie Partowski, "Master's Chat: Dino Cavalli." *Strings Magazine* (August 2002): 56–60.

usually so far away from you as to have a sense of unreality. Right then, spoken aloud, it became as real as those ashes, as Dino's eyes searching for villains, as my mother's hushed calls to the doctor.

Siang was trying to tell me something, I knew. Her urgency, these clippings, were both a warning and an attempt to get me to understand something important. I'm sorry, but it wasn't anything I cared to hear.

I gathered the clippings, put them back inside her pack, and zipped it closed. "It's just a stupid painting, Siang," I said.

Chapter Ten

You should have seen Ian's eyes. Dark, smeary circles underneath, like someone had set a pair of coffee cups thoughtlessly there without a coaster. I kissed him good-bye one day, and then put my hands in his coat pockets. The underside of his neck was a bright, angry red from the violin.

"Cassie, I've *got* to go." His tone was sharp. He'd never been short-tempered with me before. He was such a gentle person. I took my hands from his pockets, went inside. He called that night to apologize. *I'm just so tired. This schedule is killing me.*

He wasn't the only one looking like hell. Dino's concert was a few weeks away, and rehearsals were scheduled to begin. According to Mom, he had two of the three pieces finished, but was still writing the last one. Worse yet, he'd heard that William Tiero had taken on a new client, the acclaimed female violinist Anna Zartarski. She'd been asked to do the Great Performers

Series at Lincoln Center in New York, which would then be shown as a PBS television special. Dino walked around in a perpetual state of anguish. His body was there, his eyes would even look at you, but his replies were random. He went through those horrible cigarettes like Zebe can go through a bag of Cheetos. His paranoia was increasing, though it came in waves. I saw him checking the caller ID repeatedly, and he asked daily about the numbers that appeared there. *That's Zebe's number,* I'd say for the thousandth time. *That's Sophie's.* He pelted my mother with questions about when she went out. If she'd seen anyone hanging around. If she'd heard anything from various people who knew William Tiero. Even if she were meeting with him herself. He looked in the paper twice a day, the same paper, for mention of Anna Zartarski, I guess. We were living with an astrological phenomenon—something like the comets the size of a house that every few seconds break up in the atmosphere as they approach Earth. Daily explosions, not quite disasters.

Irritability was going around like the flu. It seemed like it was just as contagious. My mother had to practice now too, as performances were coming up for the theater she was contracted with. She'd set up in the dining room, but suddenly our house was too small. She couldn't practice when Dino was working, so she waited until the evenings, after he'd holed himself in their bedroom. The low tones of the cello were soothing after the manic, high-strung violins I'd been hearing for weeks. The cello sounds like a kind grandfather, while the violin is the ultimate PMS instrument.

One afternoon, I listened to Mom play for a while as I did my homework in my room. World History had given me the sudden craving for food that boredom can bring, and I had just gotten up to head down to the kitchen when I heard the *thud thud thud* of feet on the stairs, then in the hallway, heading for the dining room. The cello stopped.

"Am I disturbing you?" Mom asked.

"Your playing is grating on my nerves," Dino barked. "I am trying to *rest.*"

"You know I have to practice too." I could tell she was on the edge of being really pissed off. Her voice gets this sound of having walls around it.

"That is abundantly obvious," he said.

What came next wasn't exactly silence, because although it was quiet, a thousand things were being said. I hated that part about an unhappy household—that feeling of being perched and listening, the way an animal must feel at night in the dark, assessing danger. Dino must have decided to leave then, because I heard the front door open and close. His car started up in the driveway. My heart felt sick for my mother at the blow he'd dealt. I had Brief Fantasy Number Twelve Thousand and Four, Dino wrapped in the heavy, partly singed dining room curtains. Rolled up like those foil-wrapped candies, twist-tied at the end. After a few moments I went downstairs and into the dining room where my mother stood, holding up Grandfather Cello as if she'd just helped him to the bathroom. She sat back down again in front of her stand, looked at me, and then groaned out a few notes with her bow.

"Damn it," she said.

"That was real nice of him."

"I shouldn't say this, but you know, sometimes he's really an asshole."

"News flash," I said.

"I keep trying to tell myself he's a sick man."

"Yeah, but maybe if he wasn't sick, he'd just be a healthy asshole."

"I'm tired, you know that? I'm going to become a nun."

"Then you'd be married to Christ and he probably wouldn't pick up his socks, either," I said.

"Really." She sighed. "A few more weeks. Four," she said. "He promised he'd go back on the medicine right after the performance."

"If he doesn't crack up before then."

"Please, Cassie. You know? Let's not do this just now. I've got more than I can take as it is."

As I said, irritability was everywhere.

I heard violins in my sleep. I'd actually be dreaming and they'd be playing in the background, or they'd be the focus of the dream, my math class playing them, say, or me performing in front of an audience but forgetting my music. Mostly I dreamed of violins destroyed. People bashing them, violins falling from the sky, or floating on the water. Thrown into the water and sinking. We were a month away from that horrible concert. Just two weeks from Ian's audition.

I began to shut out the sound of those violins whenever they were practicing. Even Ian. What was my only connection to him became a hated sound. The violin was the object of his possession, in the way a bottle of wine possesses an alcoholic before it destroys him. I put on earphones, or got into the car and drove when I would hear the instrument. I would stand out with my telescope under a sky too clouded to see a thing. I would slam the door before I left so that my mother would know how angry I was at where our lives had gone. I felt sorry for her and her obvious unhappiness, but then my pity would just flee the scene and I'd get pissed. I blamed her for bringing us there, for being taken in by genius and fame and some twisted form of love, blinded, so that her own well-being and my well-being had been drowned out by the sound of that music. So, slam—that's how I felt about it all. Let the windows rattle with my fury.

The next time Ian came for his lesson he was wearing his dark coat and his scarf. When he came inside I saw that the scarf had slipped down so that one side was falling down the back of his coat, prevented from hitting the ground only by one small end piece that was doing its desperate best to hang on. It was just luck that kept it from dropping away from him on the way over, lost in a juniper bush somewhere, carted off by some neighborhood dog, dropped on the muddy street and run over by the tires of a telephone company truck. Okay, if I'm sounding a bit dramatic here, it's because I was feeling a bit dramatic. It was symbolic to me, that scarf I gave him slipping and falling, the carelessness he showed in letting it happen. The way it could be lost without him noticing.

He was already in practice mode, so I doubted he even realized that when I pushed past him that day and went outside it was with the same kind of fury and helplessness I slammed doors with. No one was *paying attention*. No one was *seeing*. Our lives were careening downhill, gaining the momentum that only self-destruction has, and no one was even trying to hold on.

My scarf anger turned to surprise when I saw Chuck and Bunny in the Datsun parked at the curb. For some reason I pictured Ian on his bike, the scarf dropping off behind him as he rode on, oblivious to the near miss of it getting caught in the spokes. I hadn't pictured it slipping off in Chuck's backseat, lying there for a nice ride around town amid a couple of old coffee cups, a pair of muddy tennis shoes, a two-disc compilation of Donna Summer hits and some library book titled *Planning the English Garden*.

I poked my head in the open window of the car. "Don't you guys ever work?" I asked.

"Hey, Lassie," Chuck said.

"There's a strike at the Dairigold plant," Bunny said. He was unwrapping the foil from a cheeseburger. "That's where we work. Anyway, I got some money tucked aside."

"We both got our massage therapist licenses, but there're not many openings here," Chuck said. "Jesus, Bun, eat over your napkin. You see why I don't let him eat and drive? It's a hazard."

"These aren't my clean jeans," Bunny said with his mouth full. He plucked the spilled bit of pickle and lettuce from his lap and popped that in too.

"Massage therapists? You're kidding." That could scare the crap out of you, lying there on some table with only terry cloth for protection and seeing one of them walk in. You'd scream with fear that you were about to be taken hostage and made to wear leather pants and a shirt with some biker chick on it that said BUILT TO RIDE.

"The healing power of touch can work miracles," said Bunny through the cheeseburger. At least I think that's what he said. It could have been "The strength in my hands could break you in half." Or maybe "I should never be allowed to touch anyone because the back of my Harley-Davidson T-shirt says IF YOU CAN READ THIS, THE BITCH FELL OFF."

"Wow," I said, mostly to be on the safe side.

"It is a great release of negative energy," Chuck said. "Flows through your fingers and disperses into the universe, floating away with your cares." He was sounding like a bubble bath commercial.

"Speaking of negative energy," Bunny said. He slurped his drink. He held it between his knees. Hey, Mom had that kind of cup holder in her car too.

"Have you noticed that Mozart's been a little uptight?" Chuck said.

"Just a little?" I didn't correct him on the fact that Mozart never played the violin—we both knew who he was referring to.

"Frankly I'm getting a little concerned about him," Bunny said.

"His chakras are all blown to shit," Chuck said.

My heart rose a little. I didn't know my chakra from a hole in the ground, as the saying sort of goes. It sounded like something you had in a Greek restaurant with a side of yogurt sauce, but who cared? Someone else was on my side in this, this feeling that things were getting out of control. I felt a surge of energy; the relief of someone helping you pick up the other end of something heavy.

"He looks horrible," I said. "He looks so tired."

"He left the dog out all night."

"He needs a day off, only his mother doesn't see it," Bunny said. "I love her to death, but she can't see the forest for the sea where that violin's concerned."

"Trees," Chuck said. "You moron. Forest for the trees."

"Trees? That don't make any sense. Of course you see trees in a forest."

"That's not what it means," Chuck said.

"I don't care, all right? You know what I'm saying."

"I agree," I said. "He needs a rest."

"Sea." Chuck chuckled. "Heh, heh, heh. Forest for the sea."

"Shut the hell up, Chuck. I heard you sing the 'Twelve Days of Christmas.'"

"So what?"

"Three French men, two turtle doves."

"No one knows all those words. It's a fucking long song."

"Three French men? Wee wee, monsieur. Jacques, Pierre, and Luc," Bunny said.

"It's the stupidest and most boring song in history. I was only trying to jazz it up."

"I don't know if there's anything we can do," I said. "About Ian." I was trying to get them back on track. Something about this reminded me of the time I dropped our old thermometer and mercury bounced crazily all over the bathroom floor.

"Why don't you sit down here in the back for a minute and

we'll make a plan," Chuck said. "Crouching over in the window like that's gonna strain your lattisimus dorsi."

"Hey, he's my favorite *Star Wars* character," I said. "I even had the action figure." I got in the back, shoved over Donna Summer. "Groovy music. Boogie down." I waved the CD around between them.

"Record club. I forgot to send in my coupon."

"Same with this?" I held up the book.

"Literary Guild," Bunny said.

"If you don't mind, I'm leaving the window open," Chuck said. "Nothing worse than the smell of french fry grease when you're not hungry."

"How about we take Ian on a trip?" Bunny said.

"A trip? What kind of trip?" I asked.

"It doesn't even matter. We just stick him in the car and go. Make him relax. The kid's gonna break."

"He's flying out for his audition in two weeks," I said. "We can't really take him on a trip."

"Okay, for the day then," Bunny said. He was folding up the foil wrap from his hamburger into a decisive triangle.

"A day of rest and rejuvenation," Chuck said. "One day off of practice is not gonna kill him. He keeps up like this . . ."

"We'll put him in the car. Pick you up," Bunny said. Something about the three of us plotting there in the parked car made me think of a bad movie with gangsters. "Tomorrow. Do you have school?"

"I'm suddenly feeling a sore throat coming on," I said. "Eck, eck." I coughed.

"We don't want you getting into trouble," Chuck said.

"I haven't missed a day yet this year," I said. I was getting excited. Common sense hadn't quite caught up yet. It was just one of those times where you're so happy to have an idea that you don't quite stop to figure out if it's a good one.

"Mental health day," Chuck said. "I saw it on my calendar."

"Where will we take him?" I asked.

"Just get in the car and go," Bunny said.

"We'll figure something out," Chuck said.

We decided on ten o'clock. I hopped out of the car, feeling like I'd done a good thing. I actually thought I was helping. That night I stayed in my room, afraid that my face would give away my secret. I didn't sleep well, but only because I was excited and hopeful. Let's just make it clear that my lack of sleep had nothing to do with premonition of disaster.

Every person above the age of seven knows how to do it—you sag your face down so that your eyes look lifeless, and then slump in a chair like a sweatshirt tossed there by someone with bad aim. You've got to hang over the chair a bit, your head on your arm, too heavy to hold up.

"I feel like crap," I said to Mom. I lowered my eyes, held my hand to my throat. "Hurts."

"I thought we were doing too well this year with no one getting sick," she said. She was hurrying around to catch her carpool, shoving random things in a brown bag for lunch. Someone needed to go to the store. You opened the fridge door, and you could see your own reflection. "Do you need to stay home?"

"I've got a test," I said. "I can't." Utter brilliance. Applause, bow.

"If you're sick, you're sick," she said. "You know how I feel about that."

"I know," I said. Yep, I knew.

She put her hand on my forehead, cold from the fridge. "You *are* warm," she said. And in case this gives the impression that Mom wasn't too smart, I'd better correct that right here. She was hugely smart, read all the time and knew something about everything. But she was someone who tended to get absentminded when she had a lot on her mind. The week before she'd walked into my math class while it was in session because she was a week early for conferences, and a couple of days before that, she left the water running in the bathroom while hand washing a sweater. I found water spilling over the counter and soaking the rug.

"I'll call the school," she said. "Back to bed." Which would have been the three most fantastic words in the human language if I didn't have better things to do. You may be wondering if I felt the least bit bad about deceiving my mother right then. Or at least maybe I'm wondering it, looking back. And the answer is no, I didn't feel one bit bad. Or at least the parts of me that might have felt bad were silenced by the importance of what I was doing. Sometimes rightness was bigger than lies. And if Mom did get mad over what I did for love, well, hey—what I was doing seemed pretty mild compared to throwing away a home and a man and a family and a shared toaster and vacation photos and a sock drawer with intermingled socks, for the possibility (impossibility) of forever, tortured romance with the Prozac poster boy, *People* magazine's Most Fucked-Up Man Alive.

I went back to bed for a while, and lay there with my eyes wide open and my heart racing, like a kid on Christmas Eve. Mom came up and kissed me on the cheek and reminded me to stay quiet for Dino, as he'd be home working. No problem, I said. I'd be so quiet, it'd be like I wasn't even there.

I watched out my window for the Datsun, and grabbed my coat and went outside when I saw it come up the street. I opened the back door and climbed in beside Ian. There was a handker-chief lying beside him, as if they had tried to blindfold him or something. It really was like a bad gangster movie. There was even a violin case on the seat.

"So you're in on this, too, huh?" he said.

"Mission accomplished!" Bunny said.

"Partners in crime," I said. "We were worried about you," I said to Ian.

"As long as I'm back before practice," Ian said. "You guys know I've got to get ready." I checked Ian's face for signs that he was pissed off, and saw only the tight, tired face I'd gotten used to.

"Oh, we know you've got to get ready. Yes, sir," Bunny said.

"I mean it, Bun. Two-thirty max."

"Full tank of gas and a road atlas. We'll make it to Malibu by sundown."

"Not funny," Ian said.

"Where we headed?" I said.

"It's a surprise," Chuck said. "You got enough room, or should I move up my seat?"

"Perfect," I said.

And it was. Just being there in the backseat with Ian in his long coat that smelled of coffee and cinnamon, knees touching. Riding down my street with that delicious feeling of everyone else being in their normal routine, poor suckers, while you were having a new day. It was cold but bright out, a nice show of sun that added a couple of notches to the cheer level. I picked up Ian's hand. It was dry and chapped from the cold, as if the last weeks were slowly sucking the moisture from him.

We drove through town, past the Chinese restaurant with its plastic-covered menus, and the real estate office with its pictures of Seabeck homes in the windows. We didn't have many tourists this time of year, so the Gift Gallery, selling wind chimes with ferryboats and tacky sweatshirts with plastic whale decals, was quiet, as was the hemp clothing store (run by the perpetually stoned Mrs. Ramadon), and the bookstore/coffeehouse, which had the best coffee cake of anywhere in the universe. We headed down to the ferry docks, past Ian's house, and Bunny bought a ticket from Evan Malloney's dad in the ticket booth. I wondered if Evan Malloney's dad knew what we all knew about Evan Malloney—that he was already a drunk. The kind that made people so uneasy they steered clear of them. Like anyone whose future you could see (the terminally ill, ninety-year-olds, girls who slept around) it was too much reality to want to look at.

"If we're getting on the ferry, we've got to watch the sailing times," Ian said.

"Would you relax, for Christ's sake?" Bunny said. "That is the whole point of this journey. I'm going to make you do some relaxation exercises."

"Oh, God. Anything but that," Ian said. "I'm relaxed, okay?"

He shook his hands and turned his neck in a circle, the way Mom did whenever she was getting a headache. "Mellowness has come." This was the Ian I loved.

We parked in the loading lane behind a camper. Its license plate read CAPTAIN ED. He had a bumper sticker that said HOME OF THE BIG REDWOODS.

"Just do it. Picture yourself somewhere you want to be," Bunny said. "A beach. A mountain cabin."

"Very original ideas, Bun," Ian said.

"What you want me to say, a Taco Time? A Jiffy Lube?"

"I'm in a boat on a lake," Chuck said.

His head was resting back against the seat. I could see in the window reflection that his eyes were closed.

"Cassie, you too. Close your eyes."

I closed my eyes. Snored loudly. Ian cracked up.

"Find your place of inner peace," Bunny said.

"It's sunny on the boat," Chuck said. "There aren't even any waves. I just had a big roast beef sandwich. I'm thinking I should have remembered sun lotion. Damn, I wish I had a beer."

"Would you shut the hell up, Chuck, I'm trying to relax these people."

"Okay, go ahead. Move along, Bun. I've got my quiet place." Ian poked my leg. He mouthed *bowling alley*.

"School cafeteria," I whispered.

"Airport runway," he whispered back.

"I hear a splash," Chuck said. "I look up. Some asshole in another boat just tossed in an empty can of Mr. Pibb. Man, that pisses me off. I hate litterers."

"Now, start at your toes. You feel them getting heavy. They are totally relaxed. Your foot is relaxed."

I held up one shoe, swirled it around. Ian put a finger through the lace and dangled my foot from it.

"Now your calf is relaxed. Now your shin. Your lower legs have never felt so relaxed." Something about this wasn't right. Maybe I didn't know about these things, but it seemed pretty damn impossible to relax a bone.

"Not the shin," Chuck said, reading my mind. "You don't relax the shin."

"Okay, the leg. The leg. Your leg is relaxed, all right? Go back to the lake, Chuck, Jesus, and let me do my work." He reached for the pack of gum on the dashboard, pulled the little red plastic thread and picked out a stick. He popped it into his mouth, and crinkled up the foil into a little ball and tossed it at Chuck.

"It's like telling you to relax your collarbone," Chuck said. His eyes were still closed. He didn't even notice the foil ball tap his massive arm.

"Meanwhile, back at the legs," I said. I was peeking. Ian was peeking too. It reminded me of the times when my parents were still married and Dad made us go to church. Everyone else would just be praying away while Mom and I were peeking at everyone.

"Legs like Jell-O," Bunny said.

"Lime. Yum, my favorite," Chuck said.

Bunny ignored him. "And then your thighs. Warm and heavy and relaxed. They've never been so relaxed. The warmth spreads to your buttocks. . . ."

This was getting a little embarrassing. In one of my heights of emotional maturity, I started to laugh. It made me think of Aaron Mills, during this science lesson. Mr. Robelard had told the class that the cut of a rock was called a cleavage. After a few snickers, he paused and then sternly told everyone that they had better just get all of their laughs out right then. The class was dead silent, except for Aaron, who just sat in his seat busting up, holding his stomach, he was laughing so hard.

Right then after the warm buttocks, car engines began to spring to life around us, thank God. The ferry was loading, and so I'd never get to find out how Bunny was going to handle what we were going to relax next.

Chuck shook himself as if he had really fallen asleep and was awakening back into the world. "Whew," he said. "Wow. Rejuvenation." He seemed to really mean it. Bunny started the car, followed Captain Ed onto the ferry, squeezing tight behind him. I was hoping we'd be able to see what Captain Ed looked like, but no one got out and the windows were tinted, and Bunny was already zipping up his coat and readying to leave our car.

I could see the couple in the BMW next to us staring at Chuck and Bunny as if they'd better lie low and pretend to be really nice people until Chuck and Bunny got on the ferry, in spite of the fact that Chuck's big butt bumped their side mirror as he tried to squeeze around the Datsun to the ferry door. Already, the noise of the boat filled your ears to the point of bursting, a thunderous roar that appeared to make the brain cells expand to the outer edges of their living quarters. Chuck shouted something that no one could hear, and then pretended to do sign language, moving his fingers in a way that was hugely unpolitically correct and a nice lawsuit for the attorney for the Deaf People Of America who was probably sitting in the BMW whose mirror Chuck had just knocked askew with his ass.

We walked sideways until we got to the ferry door, which Bunny opened with no problem at all in spite of the fact that those doors usually weighed a thousand pounds. We were suctioned into the quiet of the ferry stairwell.

"You going to be warm enough?" Ian said.

"No problem." I was wearing my wool peacoat from the army-navy surplus store, and you could be in an arctic blizzard in that thing and feel toasty.

The ferry crossing from Seabeck to Seattle is short, thirty minutes tops. Just long enough to have all of the ferry fun without the ferry boredom. Chuck and Bunny sat in the restaurant and ate cheese dogs while Ian and I made a tour of the decks and stood outside in the blasting wind. We stepped out to the farthermost edge of the deck, just watching the water rush at us from below. The land looked as if it was being brought to us, per our instructions. We went inside again to get warm, and bumped into Chuck and Bunny heading our way.

"You got to be outside when the ferry docks," Chuck said. "No matter how cold it is."

"It's like, you've got to take your shoes off at the beach, no matter what. Same kind of law," Bunny said.

"Your guys' hair looks hilarious," Chuck said.

I socked his arm. We walked out with them, though, because they were right about the "laws." I'd add a few to theirs—you had to roll the window down a little bit in the car wash, just to freak out your passenger, and you had to yell wherever your voice would echo. Ian took my hand and put both of ours in his coat pocket. We ducked our heads against the rush of wind that attacked us as we opened the door, walked like Polar explorers to the edge of the deck once more.

Ian put his arms around me from behind, and set his chin by my neck. I let myself forget my drippy nose and the wind that was blasting my face. I just let this good feeling, love, the amazing beauty around us, overtake me. A red carpet of feeling began at my toes and unrolled and filled my heart. I'd been so scared to hand myself over to someone like this, but I'd gone ahead and done it. Love, this letting go, had snuck past the guards and the attack dogs, and now here I was. I was certain that the experience would be akin to putting on nylons (which, if you have any sense, you don't ever do), in the way that when you first stick your foot in, they are going along fine, lying pretty straight, but by the time they're pulled up, they're twisting around hopelessly in some form of leg strangulation. But love hadn't turned out like that. Standing there in the icy wind with Ian wasn't one bit that way. Here was the feeling: delicious and exhilarating. Full to the tiniest pieces.

Bunny was a hypocrite to talk about our hair. You should have seen his. I pointed and laughed, another law. You must always point and laugh when someone you really like's hair looks particularly funny, or when they've spilled food in an embarrassing location on their clothes. "Hey, Bozo the Clown," I said.

"Hey, chick Einstein," he said back at me. Okay, so, my hair was like something you pulled out of a clogged drain.

"Is this amazing or what?" Chuck spread his arm out over the waters of the sound like a game show host displaying the washer-dryer combo.

"Group hug," Bunny said, although I suspect he was just freezing and wanted warmth. He came over to us, wrapped his bear-size paws around Ian and me. Chuck came around the other side and did the same. It *was* nice and warm in there. My nose was smushed up against Ian's chest, and his breath was warm in my hair. I still had a view of the city fast approaching. It was a display of building blocks set up by a genius child, or maybe by his parent after he'd gone to bed. They seemed like they had just been plunked down, rectangles and triangles and squares. It was bright and shiny, the sun hitting glass. We were being delivered to the door, like Dorothy and gang at the gates of the Emerald City.

"Tell me how life gets any better than this," Bunny said. "What could you do to improve this moment?"

And he was right. In spite of the fact that I was squeezed and frozen and had to use the bathroom, he was 100 percent right. I couldn't believe it. I loved my mother and I loved my father, but there in that circle I felt something I hadn't for a long time. It was that something I'd been missing, that I'd been longing for without even realizing it. It was a sense of family. That's what it was. My throat closed up, got so tight I felt like I might cry. You just get to missing that so much, that feeling of everything in its right place. You just feel that loss so deeply that you don't ever give it a name. A hot tear rolled down my cheek. I couldn't believe I was crying, but I just let the tears come. There was so much unexpected emotion that it needed somewhere to go. So much

love and pain and absence and cut, living roots. And here, unexpectedly, something to fill that space. You just never knew where
you might find your kindred ones. Usually you just walk and walk
among people who are not of your tribe, and then suddenly, there
you are, in a place that feels familiar and known.

I took my arms out from the middle and reached around this
wide group. I hugged back, patted a tattoo.

Chapter Eleven

Ian stuck a ferry schedule from one of the racks into his pocket on the way back to the car. Everyone squeezed in their vehicles and the guys in the orange vests unhooked the chains so that the cars could *ba-bamp, ba-bamp* off of the ferry. Captain Ed headed off in the direction opposite us. Ian's mind was obviously still on his lessons, and as we drove through the city and headed onto the freeways toward the mountain passes, I could see him looking at the time, watching for the point we'd have to turn back around before he'd be late.

"It's still early," I said.

"If I miss, Dino'll kill me, is all."

"Aren't you ready enough? You've been practicing nonstop for weeks. How much better can your pieces get?"

"Ix-nay on the violin-talk-say," Bunny said. And I thought I was the only one who could never get the hang of pig Latin.

"Dino says I'm uneven. I go from brilliant to shit, in his words. My partita is weak." Bach's *Partita No. 3 in E Major*. One of his hardest audition pieces, far as I could understand. He explained to me that his performance was supposed to demonstrate that he could handle different styles from different time periods, multi-movement pieces, and technically difficult ones. The Bach was in the last category.

"Dino will kill you in the process," I said.

"He's halfway there, if you ask me," Chuck said. "Anyone else hungry? I got Corn Nuts."

"This is a day off from violins," I said. "What have you got, barbeque or ranch?"

"Both," Chuck said.

"Yum," I said. I popped my hand over the seat when the foil bag appeared, and Chuck shook some into my palm.

"There can't be days off until after the audition." Ian watched the speeding scenery. We had driven over one of Lake Washington's floating bridges, long concrete air mattresses that connected Seattle to its suburbs. Then we had passed the wide expanse of Lake Sammamish, which sat to our left, the second lake in five minutes. Mount Rainier was on our right. It looked as if it had been plunked down in the middle of civilization, and not the other way around. That's how we talk about it too. On sunny days when it's visible we say, "The mountain is out," as if a crew of burly guys haul it out only on occasion.

The speed limit had started to increase, and so did the amount of trucks, most of which were piled high with loads of huge, bound tree trunks. We passed the point where humans had sprawled, which meant you started to see only towns with one gas station and a cemetery, bringing to mind the obvious question of where the latter got its customers. Maybe you'd see one or two houses every zillion miles, and you wonder what they do when they run out of milk, and what they do for fun. Watch the rust grow on the broken tractor? Stir up some excitement with another UFO report?

"So when *do* you get a day off?" Bunny asked. "When you're the best in your class? When you win more awards? When you—"

"Quit it," Ian interrupted. "Why are you making me wrong, here?"

"I'm not making you wrong," Bunny said. "I'm making your mother wrong."

"I don't think that's fair," Ian said. "And you know it's not." There was a bite to his voice. Dino's own words flashed in my mind. *Shut this child up about my mother!* Was this the secret to genius violin playing? Unresolved mother issues?

"I don't know it," Bunny said. "Everyone's got their own journey. This is about her pride."

"What? What's going on?" I asked. "Is your mother a frustrated musician?"

"She doesn't even know?" Bunny said.

"Shut up, Bun."

"You don't share these details with your girlfriend?" Bunny said.

"I said, shut up."

"What's going on?"

"I like the ranch better than the barbeque," Chuck said, crunching.

"What, are you ashamed?" Bunny said.

"What?" I said. I took Ian's hand.

"It's just, my family's situation."

"Your mother's situation," Bunny said. "She's broke. Way beyond broke. Seventy thousand dollars in debt."

"God damn it, Bunny. Shit."

"She should at least know what this is all about. Don't you know anything about communication?"

"The biggest stumbling block to a healthy relationship. Next to sex," Chuck said.

"Why didn't you tell me?" I said.

"They lived in their car for a few weeks in California before I heard about it," Bunny said.

"Enough, okay?" Ian said. "Enough." His face was red. He had let go of my hand and was combing his fingers through his hair.

"And child raising," Chuck said. "Communication, number one. Sex, number two. Child raising, number three."

"They were kicked out of their apartment. They used the bathrooms in fast food places."

Ian covered his eyes with one hand. "Shit, Bunny," he said. I thought he might cry. I took his hand. The car got quiet. The kind of quiet that hurt.

"I'm so sorry," I whispered. "You could have told me." The words caught in my throat in the way a lie does. I thought about Dino's craziness. All the things I never could say out loud. I thought about saying it right then, but something stopped me. Being poor was one thing. Creeping around in bushes because you think you're being followed and almost setting the house on fire is another.

"It's just . . . I don't know. Not exactly the way to start things out with you. 'Hi, I'm Ian. My stepfather had a long illness and didn't have insurance, and when he died he left us destitute for my mother's lifetime unless I can do something about it. Oh, and by the way, the only reason we've got a roof is my stepbrother's charity. So would you like to go for a walk, because I haven't gone to the movies in three years and couldn't buy the popcorn.'"

"Oh, Ian. Oh, I'm so sorry." I pictured again Ian's mother with her chipped toenail polish. A man in a hospital bed with tubes in his nose and arms. Sleeping in a car. *Living* in a *car*. The Ian that I loved. The hurt of that squeezed my heart. My stomach felt sick. "It's you I care about."

"Okay. Here it is. If I don't get into Curtis, we don't have a chance of getting out of this mess. Number one, it's a full scholarship. Number two, going there would give me what I need to get some good paying performances. *Good* paying performances. Recording deals, eventually. The works. We lived on my performance money when my stepdad was sick, but now that I'm older I've got to be much better. I can't be just a cute kid playing the violin."

"Oh, God, Ian." For the first time I clearly saw the choice that sat in front of him. I didn't know what the answer was. I could only sit there in that car, my body filled with the pain of his decision.

"Giving up what you really want—it's not your only option, is all I'm saying," Bunny said. "It's not your job to solve the problem. You don't need to, you know, give up your whole life to do that," Bunny said.

"So what are the other choices? She has her wages garnished for the rest of her life? You feed us, and we live in your house forever?"

"She can stay there till she's eighty, for all I care," Bunny said.

"The average life expectancy is eighty-four," Chuck said.

"Ninety. A hundred. Her job is going well. We deal with the hospital somehow. I don't know. The net will appear. The net always appears if you leap," Bunny said.

"The charity hurts," Ian said. He was looking out the window, his whole body turned away from me.

"Charity, bullshit. She took such good care of my dad. This is family. That's what families do."

"You got it. Exactly. That's why I've got to get into Curtis," Ian said.

"God damn it," Bunny said. "He's obstinate. Hand me some Corn Nuts, Chuck, the kid is stressing me out."

"I'd try some deep relaxation for you, but you're driving," Chuck said.

I took Ian's hand. Brought it to my mouth and held it there. He couldn't even look at me. That was the worst thing about shame, I guess—its self-destructive power. The way it made you burn the bridges of anyone coming your way to help.

"I'm sorry," he whispered.

"I love you," I whispered back.

"Money, number four," Chuck said. "Communication, sex, child raising, and money."

"Ix-nay on the money-talk-fay," Bunny said.

The car climbed and rose around mountain bends. At first the snow was only scattered in the shady places, but gradually the whiteness grew until the road was buffeted by full-fledged snowbanks, glittery and bright in the sun. The tires crunched over sanded roads, though I could feel the wheels slip a bit on the ice, and Bunny slowed his speed. I was glad to see the summit and the lodge of Snoqualmie Pass, as the driving was getting a little nerve-racking. Bunny must have been glad too—he let out a big sigh of relief as he skidded sideways into a parking spot. The lot was nearly empty, except for a couple of cars with skis still attached to the tops, and an abandoned snowplow. It was weird. Usually at this time of year the pass would be crawling with people.

"Closed, I guess," Chuck said. "Shit, I've been thinking about hot chocolate and lunch the whole way."

"How can they close it? It's a beautiful day, and we need cheeseburgers," Bunny said. "Let's get out anyway."

"We can just look around," I said. "Eat lunch in the car on the way home." After our talk, I felt anxious to get Ian back to lessons on time. Either that, or have us both run away forever and never return home again.

"No reason we can't play a little," Bunny said. He leaned down, popped the trunk.

We got out of the car, stepped carefully onto the icy ground. The cold air felt great, stinging and fresh. I breathed deeply, as Chuck and Bunny pulled a pair of black inner tubes from the trunk.

"Guys, we got maybe twenty minutes, max," Ian said.

"Enough for a couple trips down the sledding hill," Chuck said. "Yee haw!" He gave the tube a shake over his head, his *yee haw* blowing in a huge puff of white from his mouth.

Bunny slammed the trunk. We walked flat-footed across the parking lot so as not to fall, then cut across the road past the lodge.

Walking was tough. If you trudged in the deeper snow you barely noticed the ice, but my pant legs were already getting soaked. We huffed behind Chuck and Bunny, who could sure haul themselves around for big guys. I was exhausted already, and realized why I'd never been a skier. Just the trip from the parking lot would make me ready to rest for the day by the fireplace in the lodge.

"I'm not sure this is such a great idea," Ian said. "There's no one around."

It *was* a little eerie, the lodge sitting solid and empty, and the lifts deserted and still. It was impossible, though, to really muster up any feeling of warning when the sun was so bright and cheery, and when the snow was glistening like fairy dust in some hokey Disney movie. We pulled ourselves up and up, walking in the deep snow, until I felt like I'd accomplished an amazing Tight Thighs in Ten Minutes. My legs hurt, my butt muscles hurt, my lungs were hot, and I didn't look up until we stopped at what must have been the top of a ski hill. I pictured myself on skis, looking down from this very spot, and realized I'd rather do a two-week punishing stint of math statistics than to throw myself down on a pair of matchsticks from where we stood. The hill was a sheet of ice going straight down, decorated with evergreens that were plunked in death-defying places. I changed my mind about the sledding right then and there.

"No way," I said.

"I agree," Ian said. "Too dangerous."

Bunny sighed through his nose, two straight shots of white locomotive steam. "I guess you guys are right. We'll go back to the baby sledding hill."

"Damn," Chuck said.

And right then, right at that moment before the word was even completely out of his mouth, his foot was yanked underneath him sure as if someone had pulled it. "Whaaa . . ." he cried, and Chuck was suddenly on the ground, a human toboggan, careening down the hill while still clutching his tube in one hand, the black ring skidding and turning as if having the happiest free ride of its little rubber life.

I grabbed Ian's coat sleeve. "Oh, shit!"

"Hang on, Chuck!" Bunny called.

The crazy thing was, there was nothing we could do. We just stood there, watched his limbs fly around until he landed at the bottom.

He was silent for a moment. And still. And then came his voice.

"Fuck," he said.

Bunny stepped forward to call out to him. "Don't worry, Chu—" His voice was lost as he crashed to the ground. Fell on his butt with a thud and whipped and whizzed down that hill like we'd just been shown an instant replay. Bunny held his tube too, but lost it about halfway when it skidded from his grasp, bounced off one of the trees, then bumped the rest of the way to the bottom until a part of it beaned Chuck on the skull and bounced off.

"Fuck," Chuck said again.

Bunny slid to a stop beside him. His arms and legs were all askew, a toy man tossed by a toddler.

"Bun! Bun! Are you all right?" Ian called.

He lay flat for a moment, unmoving.

"Ow," he said.

"Can you guys move?" Ian said.

Bunny shifted around. "Yeah, everything's working."

"Me too," Chuck said.

"Thank God," I said.

"Do you need us to get you some help?" Ian asked.

He was standing right beside me, right there, and then, *bam!* He was gone. Upright, talking, and then down on his back, his coat flying out behind him, riding down on the seat of his pants, sitting up as if he'd planned it that way. You really would have thought he meant to do it, if it weren't for the yelling he was doing along the way, if it weren't for the crash he had at the bottom, his crying out in pain.

"Oh, God," he cried. He was crying there, in the snow. "My arm. Jesus, my arm."

Chapter Twelve

Of course, I was still at the top of that hill. I was helpless, afraid to move. All we needed was for me to go down with the rest of them, and then we'd really be in deep shit. I decided I'd better go for some help, although the chances of finding anyone seemed nil after the looks of that empty lodge. I was holding the real disaster at bay in my mind—Ian's arm, maybe broken, certainly injured, the audition, the way we might have just changed the course of his and his mother's lives—and was trying to concentrate on the more immediate one, namely, how to get three guys, two the size of refrigerators, back into the car and safely home. I stepped back into the deep snow to anchor myself, called down to them.

"I'm going for help!" I yelled, and was glad to see that Chuck was attempting to get on his feet. I struggled back the way we came, a few steps at a time, wondering what the hell I was going to do when I got there. I was beginning to hate the sound of that crunching snow, hated the twinkling, beautiful white, when I heard a roaring sound, a loud zipping roar, like a chain saw almost. It turned out to be a snowmobile in the distance, and when the driver saw me, it quickly headed in my direction. I waved my arms around, which was unnecessary, as he had every intention of heading my way.

The guy was with the ski patrol and was pissed we were out there, wondering how we missed the signs that the place was closed. Apparently, in addition to the extremely icy conditions, there was also an avalanche warning in effect. So, hey, look at the bright side.

I put my arms around the shaking Ian when we were back in the car. I saw his wrist before the patrol guy wrapped it, the bone sticking against his skin as if trying to make a getaway, the color turning quickly to a dark purple. The patrol guy told us to get to a doctor right away and have an X-ray, but there was no doubt if you saw what I did that it was broken. The bone wasn't the only thing that had been shattered. I felt the devastation in his trembling; I listened to it in the silence on the car ride home.

If our lives had been losing stitches up until that point, they began a serious unraveling when we got home. I thought of the time when I was a kid and I had pulled one enticing loop from the afghan Nannie was crocheting. I knew I had done something awful and irrevocable, but the more I tried to hold it together, the more it kept coming undone, until the yarn sat in a wrinkled heap. Fragile things become undone at a frightening speed.

I waited in the emergency room with Chuck. Bunny, amazingly in one piece himself, went in with Ian to see the doctor. It
was evening before we got out of there. They dropped me off at
home, so I wasn't there for the moment that Ian walked into his
mother's house with a cast on his arm.

I had my own train wreck to deal with at my house.

"Where in God's name have you been?" my mother said as I
walked in. "I've been worried sick."

I walked past her, went up to my room, and shut the door.
So what? What was a little more trouble? I couldn't stand to face
anyone. After what I'd done to Ian's life, I wanted to drop into a
hole and disappear. My own shame made powerful punishment
seem certain—it was already withering my insides until I felt I
might throw up. I heard Dino in the kitchen. *It's that boy, I know
it.* I could hear the smirk in his voice.

I lay on my bed in my quilt. I wrapped it so tight around me.
I reached out for the bear in the snow globe. I wanted to throw
it against the wall, destroy it, but instead I put it under the quilt
with me, tucked it right inside that cocooned place.

"Cassie?"

Mom knocked, then came in. She sat down at the edge of my
bed. "Cass? What happened? Come on, talk to me."

"I can't."

"Talk to me."

"It's awful. It's terrible." I started to cry. Since I met Ian, I
was as bad as the faucet Mom left on when she was washing
her sweater. Someone had turned on the emotion and now it
wouldn't go off.

"What?" She sounded like she was afraid and trying not to be. "Nothing is that bad."

"Oh yes, it is." I sobbed, just let out these heaves of helplessness. Mom held me.

"I'm here, okay? Whatever it is. Are you pregnant?"

"Holy shit, Mom. No," I said through my crying. I swear, for parents it's always about sex and drugs. "I haven't been arrested for trafficking marijuana, either."

"Okay, Cass, I'm sorry. You know, what am I supposed to think?"

I curled up tight inside that blanket. The glass of the snow globe was cold, and I blew on it to warm it up.

"Should I call Ian's mom?"

"Oh, God, no," I said. "Please don't do that."

Mom sighed. I peeked at her, and saw her just sitting with her chin pointed to the ceiling. She looked so tired. Thin, too. She looked like she was losing too much weight.

"Ian broke his wrist. It was my fault."

"Oh, my God," she said.

"It was my fault."

"Oh, my God," she said again.

"I know."

"What happened?"

I told her the story. She put her arms around me. I could feel her hot breath through the quilt. "Oh, Cassie."

"I'm so sorry."

"You didn't cause it."

"That's not what Dino will think."

"That may be true, but it's not what I think."

I came out of the quilt, just a little. She brushed my hair away from my face. She bent down to kiss my forehead. "I'll always be here for you," she said. But she didn't need to say it. Right then, it was something I knew.

It started like a storm, low rumbling and then louder and louder still until the windows actually rattled and there was a crash of something being broken.

I told you she would ruin this! Did I not tell you she had to stay away from him?

And then my mother's voice, too low to be heard, the rhythms of calm explanation.

My God. It is over for him! I could have helped him. Things could have been different for him than they were for me. How can I help him now? How?

I heard my mother then, clearly. *His situation is different than yours,* my mother said. *He's a boy with options. It's not the same. You are not the same person.*

I could have made things turn out differently. Look what you people have done. You've wrecked him. You want to ruin me.

His voice was gaining emotion; my mother's turned pleading. *This is not about you. This is not about what happened in your life. I am stuck here in this nothing city because of you.*

Calm down, my mother said. She was trying not to get angry. She was saying those words to herself as much as him, I could tell that, too. *You made a choice to be here,* my mother said. *As much as I did.*

You are all the same. You and that bastard Tiero. You want to see that I am a failure. You want to see me fall.

I am not doing this, my mother said more loudly. *I am not talking to you about any of these things. And I will not accept this kind of behavior.*

Where are you going? He was shouting now. I wondered what I should do. If I should do something. It felt bad; I knew this was bad. Should I leave? Call someone?

I'm just going out for a while. So that you can calm down.

Fine! Leave! Run away, you coward.

I heard her coming up the stairs then. She called for me to come with her, and I did. As we went out the door, we heard the shatter from his office. He had slammed the door so hard that the print above his desk had come crashing to the floor, along with a paperweight and a coffee cup that it brought down with it. I made a strange little list in my head as I buckled my seat belt in Mom's car, as she turned the key with a shaking hand. All of the things that Dino had shattered. A wineglass. William Tiero's picture. The painting of *Wild Roses*. Our lives.

Chapter Thirteen

I spent a few days at my dad's house. That's where my mother drove us, to drop me off there. They had some conversation at the door, after she had told me to stay in the car. It was another one of those moments when I would have killed to hear what was said, but I also would have done anything not to hear it, ever. I was having a lot of those times lately, where what I wanted and what I didn't want were the same thing. I tried without success to keep Mom from going back home. She could stay with Alice, I suggested. Or we could go to a motel somewhere, the two of us, like the time she and I stayed at the Travel Lodge before Dino moved in, when we'd lost power. Yikes—unintentional double meaning, two points for me. The time we lost *electricity*. Losing power to Dino came later.

One of the things that had apparently been discussed during the porch powwow was my punishment for the Ian caper.

Apparently, I could not be disciplined for ruining his life and his mother's life and their chance to save their financial future, but they could make me pay for skipping school. They decided that my absence would go unexcused, which meant that I had to stay after school one day for a detention.

Zebe made fun of me all day after I told her I had to go. I told her I skipped school because I was just sick of being there, but that was all. I couldn't talk about it any more than I already had. It was one of those things that hurt so much that you needed to keep it safely contained in its little box in your gut, because who knew what might happen if it got out. I could see the awfulness spreading like some noxious gas in a sci-fi movie, poisoning a large city. Or at least, eating up my insides more than it had already. Ian's mother, Janet, had answered the phone when I had tried to call Ian to see how he was. *Hi, Janet, it's Cassie,* I had said. For a moment there was silence. And then, *Cassie? Please don't call here. There's been enough damage done already.* Then there was a click. A click and then silence.

I paid my dues in detention, sat amongst the coats that reeked of cigarettes and the notebooks with the Led Zeppelin stickers on them, and tried not to feel like I was a nerdy tourist in a Hawaiian shirt who had mistakenly wandered into the wrong part of town. The whole thing was pointless, because my real punishment was happening every moment, missing Ian, being away from him, feeling as if I'd ruined him. I'd gone ahead and loved him, and it destroyed him. At least, that's how I felt. I understood that they didn't want me around anymore, but it made life seem black-and-white, flat and one-dimensional. I craved the oxygen and color Ian brought. He had changed life, and now it just couldn't change back again.

That night Dad was cooking meatballs, rolling them around in the pan over the heat. He was wearing one of Nannie's old aprons that had a parade of smiling fruit on it. She sat on one of the kitchen chairs, arranging her collection of salt and pepper shakers that Dad had kept on the windowsill.

"I just can't believe the stoners are still listening to Zeppelin," he said, after I told him my story.

"They were hoodlums in my day," Nannie said. "If I missed a day of school, your grandpa would have beaten me silly," she said to my father. "Kids these days."

"Oh, he would not have," my father said to the meatballs. "He was the biggest softie. He never lifted a hand to you."

"Maybe not," she said.

"And from what they told me, they couldn't keep you in school if they tied you to the flag pole."

"Top of my class," she said.

"You barely graduated."

"Maybe not," she said. She took a pair of chefs with holes in the tops of their hats and paired them up with two glass Dutch girls.

"Anyway, I've done my time," I said.

"Let that be a lesson to you," my father said. "Though who am I to talk? I missed a college Spanish final and nearly flunked the course because your mother and I were having an argument on the front lawn of the foreign-language building. All that upset, and years later I can't even remember how to ask where the bathroom is."

"Quisiera el pollo." I'd like to have the chicken, is what it really means.

"See? That's why we had you."

"Top of my class in Spanish," Nannie said, and we both ignored her.

"You failed a final. You didn't wreck someone's future and their family's life."

"It wasn't your fault. Did you try to call Ian again? Get the dishes out; these are done."

"I'm afraid to call. After what his mom said? I went by his house, just to *apologize* if nothing else, but no one was there. He must hate me. I keep thinking he'll try to call, but Mom says he hasn't. God, it's just killing me." It was a relief, at least, to finally be able to talk to Dad about Ian. I went to the cupboard, took out three plates, and lined them up on the counter for Dad to dish out the steaming food.

"Why your mother is still in that house I do not understand," he said.

"I don't know, Dad. Dino's concert is coming up in only a few weeks. She thinks things will be okay then."

"Things were never okay. Things will never *be* okay. I don't care if he has the most triumphant concert in the history of concerts. She fell in love with an image."

"Well, she knows what he's like now."

"He's a lunatic. A bastard lunatic liar."

"Just like my father," Nannie said.

"Your father was a saint," Dad said to her.

"He was a sweetie," she said. "Such a softie."

"Anyway, if there is one more incident like that, I'm filing for sole custody and getting a restraining order."

"Make your feelings known, Dad. Jeez, come on. I'm a little old for a custody arrangement."

"It's my right as a father. I won't have you in that mess. She's not using her brain, and you're the one getting hurt. I won't stand for it."

"I don't want things to get worse, Dad. Can we not make this about your rights? Can it be about my needs? You and attorneys and all that crap again . . . no."

"Maybe there's another way to get that man out of your life," he said.

"Mafioso hit man," I said. "As much as the idea appeals to me . . ."

"Nah, prison food is supposed to be terrible. Something else is . . . happening. Something that may change the way your mother sees things. Grab some forks."

"What do you mean?" Okay, I'm sorry. I had brief Child of Divorce Reunion Fantasy Number Twelve Thousand. A meeting of the minds and hearts that occurred on the front porch step. Flash to Mom packing her bags. Flash to her lighting Dino's compositions on fire, which was maybe getting a little carried away on my part. It's a tad embarrassing to admit. The child of divorced parents is supposed to be over these things when you reach the age of eight. "Is this about you and Mom?"

"God, no. Nothing like that. Just, I'm doing what I can to reveal the bigger picture. I don't know if it's the right time to tell you. Things are upsetting enough for you right now with that wacko."

"Is this my recipe?" Nannie said when Dad placed the plate in front of her. She couldn't cook to save her life. Her favorite used to be creamed corn, which, I can say with some authority, looks like what a chicken might barf up. Nightmare flashback.

"I hate it when you do that, Dad. You drop these little hints of knowing and then, bam, clam up," I said.

"It's not very mature of me," he agreed. He sat down. "I try to do the right thing, but sometimes the wrong thing gets the better of me. The human condition."

"If you know something that has to do with my life, I'd appreciate you sharing it with me," I said.

He cut a piece of meatball, studied it a while. "It doesn't have to do with you. Just, I'm sorry, okay? I wish I could solve this mess, but there's only one person who can do that for you. And she's on a high wire without a net."

"Yeah, and you know she's not exactly the athletic type," I said.

"She's actually an excellent athlete," my father said.

"Thank you very much," Nannie said.

Dad and I stayed up late and watched an old *Die Hard* movie on what must have been a conservative station, because they'd eliminated any hint of swearing. Bombs would be dropping all over and Bruce Willis would face his enemy and say something like, *You rascals!* Of course, the voice that appeared at those times sounded nothing like his, and his lips were forming different words. Our favorite was when he barely escaped being killed by a landing airplane, and he stood up and remarked, *Holy shoot!*

I got ready for bed. I knew I shouldn't do it, but I tried to call Ian. I only let it ring twice before I hung up. I was missing a connection with him so much, that it helped just dialing that number. Maybe he'd hear the ring and know it was me. Maybe at least he'd know how much I cared. I tried to call Mom, too, but there was no answer.

"I'm worried about Mom," I said to Dad when he came into my room to say good night.

"She's strong, Cassie. I think she can handle things," he said.

"I know. But sometimes she doesn't . . . I don't know. *See.*"

"She is one of the most logical people I know," he said. "Even if she isn't showing it at the moment."

He was right about that. "She's logical, but then suddenly she gets carried away with a burst of passionate feeling," I said. I was thinking about her own cello playing, her methodical practicing, her sane musicianship. But then I would see her listening to Dino play, the way she closed her eyes and let him bring her to where she couldn't go herself. Like me, I realized. Great, like Ian and me.

"It'd be good if you could have passion without it having you," my father said. He was lost for a moment in his own thoughts. Memories, I'm sure, that he didn't want to share with me. And then one memory he did want to share. "Remember when Mom cut the bushes into the shapes of animals?"

"*Tried* to cut the bushes into the shapes of animals."

"Talk about getting carried away. She just had this sudden idea and whacked away at the poor plants. When I got home, they'd been massacred."

"One really did look like a rabbit."

"You've got to be kidding. A Picasso rabbit."

"And then this one time? She was teaching me to drive," I said. "We were in Seattle. She was doing really well. Not freaking out or anything. She sat there with her hands in her lap and only pushing her foot to the floor mat when she thought I needed to brake. Then we got onto the freeway. I'm trying to merge, right? And this big truck is coming."

"Oh, God." Dad laughed.

"She suddenly screams, 'Oh, shit, FLOOR IT!' Always good advice for the beginning driver."

"I think that's in the traffic-safety manual," he said.

"I practically wet my pants."

"Holy shoot!" Dad laughed. He shook his head, but it was a loving shake, not a critical one. It was strange to be talking like that about her, the two of us, but good, too. Nice. You got so used to keeping both parties separate, Mom here, Dad there, trying to be sensitive to everyone's feelings, that it sometimes got exhausting. No, it always got exhausting. Trying to keep track of the separate piles of emotions and what was to be kept where. Don't talk to Dad about this part of your life; don't mention to Mom about that. Dad will be hurt if he knew we had a good time. Mom will be hurt to know I tried something new when she wasn't there. Dad will be hurt at Mom's new car/vacation/home/baby/clothes/ guinea pig. Mom will be hurt at the things Dad's family said about her. Even if they told you a thousand times that there was nothing you needed to hide, that they were both okay about sharing all parts of your life (chapter three in the bestselling *Divorced Parenting for Dummies*), you could still see those brief flashes of feeling pass over their faces. A jealous look, a hurt one. And even if they were sometimes okay at hiding the snide comments, you could still see the feeling there, raw and exposed.

It was good right then, talking with Dad. Just having everything in one pile and it all being okay. Not having to walk the loyalty tightrope. Just for us all being able to love each other in the complicated ways of a family. For one moment we had that thing that I will go out on a limb and say that every divorced kid wants, this sense of family that is still family even if apart.

The possibility of it was sweet, but then it was gone. The human condition again.

"I worry about her too," my father said.

"I know you do."

"The thing I wouldn't tell you?"

"Yeah?"

"She doesn't even know the whole story."

"What?"

"About Dino."

I scooted up in bed. Again, I didn't want to know. A sick warning urge was creeping up my insides, but racing along with it was this adrenaline-fueled desire to hear what he was about to say. Maybe it was the same kind of desire little kids felt with the box of matches in their hands.

"What? Just tell me."

"I know now for sure. He's not who he says he is."

"Who is he then?"

"I don't know the whole story, but I know this. There was no Dino Cavalli born in or around Sabbotino Grappa, then or ever."

"No way. What about all of those people? They've all told their stories. You've read them."

"I don't know. Group hysteria. The desire to be part of the greatness. Reporters coming to this small town and livening things up. Maybe they've come to believe it themselves. Maybe the attention has just become too much fun to give up."

"No. The fig trees, his beautiful mother, the tossing him bread as he played . . ."

"Fiction. All fiction. Good fiction, a great story. But a lie."

"I can't believe it."

"Believe it. Cassie, there was no Cavalli family in Sabbotino Grappa."

Chapter Fourteen

I made him prove it to me, the things he said about Dino. I wanted to believe in Honoria Maretta, and the Bissola sisters, in lemon trees, and a small boy who made a tiny village happy with his playing.

And apparently the few people of Sabbotino Grappa wanted to believe it too. Whether it happened or not, they were pleased to go along. Same with Edward Reynolds, who must have found out the truth somewhere along the writing of his book. Because there was no Cavalli family in Sabbotino Grappa and there never had been. I didn't know yet what that information meant to me, or what I would do with it, but I did know one thing: My mother wasn't the only one who had fallen in love with an image.

I stayed with Dad long enough to get annoyed when he used up all the hot water when he took a shower and watched way too much of the History Channel at volumes loud enough to make you duck when the allied forces stormed in with guns firing. After the third day when he made my bed for me, I was actually longing for my old routine at Mom's. I missed my routine, even though I did not miss my mother's husband, the psycho liar, the evil stepfather, the Anti-Mr. Brady—Mike Brady with hair grown out and psychological issues and a cigarette. Which brings to mind another inane and mostly irrelevant side note, and that is that *The Brady Bunch* has got to beat out *Lord of the Rings* in terms of the best in sci-fi fantasy. I mean, the kids call their steps Mom and Dad, which we know you'd never do, unless you harbored a death wish or an all-out hatred for your own mother or father. They also never mention their missing parents. What about Carol Brady's first husband? Was he a drunk, a wife beater, or merely dead? And what about Greg, Peter, and Bobby's mother? Adulteress that ran off with Mr. Partridge Family? Decided she was a lesbian and started a new life? Career woman in another state? Also merely dead? And did no one long for their mom or dad? No photos by the bedside, visits to the cemetery, longings to be remembered at Christmas? For God's sake, no one has an attorney. No one even goes to a therapist!

Anyway. Things right then were fairly peaceful but irritating at Dad's. Add to the equation the fifty times a day that Dad said, "I think it's sad what your mother has done to her life," (meaning: what she'd done to his) or "Divorce is such a crime" (meaning: he had nothing to do with it) or "What did she expect?" (meaning: she got what she deserved). I hated the thought of being back with Dino, but I missed Mom and my room and my stuff. I missed the smell of my own pillow.

I talked to Mom on the phone, and she seemed really tired but okay. Okay enough that when she said she thought things were calm enough for me to come back, I went, in spite of Dad's protests. The concert was only a few short weeks away. And Dino had accepted the whole "Ian thing," according to her. It seemed amazing, miraculous, and completely doubtful, but I went home anyway. There was a piece of me too, that felt I could miss Ian better at home. I could miss him more thoroughly, being sur- rounded by places we had been together. I was beginning to feel that my missing him was all I had of him, and so I wanted it.

I went home the day before Ian had been scheduled to fly out to Philadelphia for his audition at Curtis. I called him again when I got home. His mother answered, and I hung up. I hurt without him. My heart felt like a cave, dug out, dark. I couldn't understand why he wouldn't call me, why we couldn't just *talk*. My fear was that he'd never forgive me, and I pictured him with his cast, hating me with the intensity I felt I deserved. I missed the feeling on the ferry, before it all turned bad that day. I missed the feeling of being where you belonged.

I avoided Dino as much as I could. He avoided me, or else was avoiding everything that wasn't music. He didn't eat, didn't appear to sleep, only built up the cigarette butts in coffee cups and saucers. He only said one thing to me all of that first day. *Turn the handle of the door when you shut it,* he had said. *It makes less noise.* I avoided Mom, too, but for a different reason. I was car- rying around this knowledge of Dino that Dad had given me, and it kept bumping between us. I was afraid that if I looked too long at Mom she might see it there in my eyes, or feel it between us in the room. I just lugged this secret around, and how she couldn't see it there, I don't know. It was huge and ugly and powerful. And I kept it close to me, my weapon. This stockpiled bomb that somewhere inside I was sure I would use when the enemy most threatened.

The days were hollow and vast as the sky that I saw through my telescope on those nights, though empty of any of the life that was also out there, stars dying and being born before your eyes, the life cycle taken to its outer edges of time and place. I had all of the vastness, none of the fire. Zebe and Sophie and Brian and Nat were all in rehearsal period for *Anything Goes,* which made things even lonelier. In English class, I sat for an hour as Aaron Urling read his poems aloud. Eleven haiku poems on Darth Vader. *Father and Son. Bonded by Blood. Eternal Destruction.* He had two light sabers in his belt as he read. *My visual aids,* he told the teacher. He snickered to his friends. He thought he was a real crack-up. In science we took a walk in the forest on school grounds to measure distances from trees, and Mr. Robelard called us back in with an elk call. I'm not kidding. It sounded like he was giving birth.

A week and a half until the concert. A week. No Ian. I didn't blame him for hating me.

Your own small universe moves on in surreal ways when you feel a crisis building, building. And when your sanctuary is gone. Walking home, I got stuck having a conversation with Courtney about split ends. Our neighbor, Mr. Frederici, left an angry message that Dog William, in an apparent act of outburst over the withdrawal of the object of his love, had gotten into the Frederici garbage can and spread litter all over his yard. The catsup bottle fell out of the fridge when I was getting some milk and spilled out in a blobby smear of goriness. Life just keeps ticking along.

I invited Siang over. I should have been trying harder than ever to keep her away. Dino's intensity was focused on his music, same as a kid focusing reflected sunrays from a mirror onto paper, hoping it will burst into flames. But it was comforting having Siang around. It reminded me of the simple days when Dino was merely a jerk and Siang would come over and steal his orange peels for her mini-tabletop shrine.

"My father said he's had to give up lattes for, like, six months to afford the concert tickets," Siang said. I had made brownies, hoping to drown my sorrows in three zillion fat calories, and we were taking chunks and eating them out of the pan. I had the feeling that Siang never did these kinds of things. First, she was thin as a sheet of foil, and second, she was going at them like she'd been lost at sea on a rubber dinghy for months.

"Slow down," I said to her. "If you choke, I'm not so hot at Heimlich. I was absent that day in health. I might dislodge something you need, you know, like a larynx. What concert?"

"Cassie! The world premiere of Mr. Cavalli's new work!"

"It was a *joke*. Six months with no lattes? That is so sad. That's like some fairy tale where some woman cuts her hair to buy bread. You should have told me. Maybe I could have helped."

"Those tickets have been sold out for almost a year," Siang said.

"I'm sure we could have done something."

"Wow. Do you know how many people would die to be in

your place? Or even mine, sitting in here in his kitchen, eating off his plate?"

"You're bypassing the plate, far as I can tell," I said.

"You probably didn't see the article in *Newsweek*. Or the *New York Times*? FAMED COMPOSER CHOOSES SMALLER VENUE TO UNVEIL NEW WORK?"

"Smaller venue? That's kind of insulting."

"The *New York Times*. Jeez, Cassie."

"As long as you're happy, Siang."

"Is he ready? There are rumors."

"What kind of rumors?" That he's losing it? That he thinks William Tiero is hiding under the table? That his stepdaughter ruined the career of his protégé and now he's cracked? That the only thing he seems to have ingested in a week is a box of truffles sent by his manager and twelve thousand pounds of nicotine?

"Just that the third piece isn't done."

"I'm sure it'll be done." I wasn't sure at all, but, Jesus, Siang seemed so worried, and now so happy with my words. She smiled, brownie in her teeth. "Go like this," I said to her, putting the edge of my fingernail to my tooth. Personally, I hate it when people don't tell you those things.

Siang removed the offending brownie. "I knew he'd be ready. He's a professional. An artist of the highest order."

Maybe we consider a piece of work to be genius in part because it goes places we cannot go. Maybe it is not so much that the geniuses are nuts, but that there is something in the nuts that is genius. That ability to get to not just the seed of emotion, but to the place that exists even before the seed is there. Maybe they live amid the raw materials of feeling before feeling becomes organized; maybe they work with the base elements, like the cosmos in formation. There seems, anyway, an ability to get to truth, the purest emotion, if you can see through the barbed wire of chaos that surrounds it. Maybe that's what we respond to in those works of genius—our own inability to be that emotionally unbound. An envy for the letting go of the tether and seeing what is beyond the frontier, the barrier of self-protection. Maybe the genius is only a letting go, in a way that most of us would be too frightened to. But maybe, too, the genius is just some wacky consolation prize for the pain of living out of this world.

I don't know. But I do know that the most honest, the deepest and purest forms of thought and creation appear to make their owners pay a price. The scientists with the world-changing ideas, the painters that change our vision, the musicians with the soul-altering music—they seem to blow a circuit in the process, or a circuit was blown beforehand that allowed the creation to happen. And sometimes, just before the final break, there is a huge outpouring of creativity. It's hard to know whether the outpouring of creativity causes the break or if the break that is coming causes the outpouring. Before her suicide, Sylvia Plath was writing a poem a day, working at four A.M. while her children slept, and Emily Dickinson cranked out her own poetry during her affair with a married clergyman, then collapsed in a nervous breakdown. And Vincent van Gogh. He had moved to Auvers, France, for peace and tranquility, and painted the flowers of Daubigny's garden, including his *Wild Roses*. He painted seventy canvasses in seventy-five days, and then shot himself in the chest.

I overheard my mother and Dino talking when I got home from school. It wouldn't have been hard to do. Courtney and her media-monster brothers could have overheard them talking, and it would have been better than anything on television.

"For God's sake, Dino, I'm going to call the doctor," my mother said.

"What does the doctor have to do with this? It has nothing to do with the doctor. This is between Tiero and me."

"You're worrying for nothing, okay? He won't be there."

"I know he will. He has never been able to stay away. He's like a fly on shit. I can feel him nearby. I've always known. He's always come."

"Dino, really. Stop it. If he's come before, it's only because he loves you."

"Love? You call that love? He tried to destroy me."

"Maybe he wanted to help you. Like I want to help you."

Dino had been right. When you turned the door handle, it did make less noise. I had crept up the stairs with my backpack and a box of crackers. I could still hear them. The conversation was giving me the creeps. I almost wanted to look for William Tiero under the bed.

"Maybe you want to destroy me too."

"Dino, no. Don't do this. I'm phoning the doctor."

"And you run to the doctor whenever I get too close to the truth. Just like he did."

Shit. Weren't these the kind of people who committed horrible crimes? Was my mother in danger? If anything, she was certainly kidding herself in thinking she could manage him. He was not manageable. This had gone way beyond a manageable situation.

"I think you'll feel better if you talk to the doctor a little."

"I'll feel better when Tiero lives his own life and stays the hell out of mine."

"Look, why don't we just have Andrew call him? We can tell him it's too upsetting for you to have him there."

"Andrew Wilkowski knows where Tiero is? They've talked on the phone?"

"No, they haven't talked on the phone. But it would be a simple thing to find him. Give you some reassurance that he'll stay away."

"He will never stay away. He can't. He vowed not to."

"It was a long time ago," my mother said. "He's done his job."

"His job will be finished when I die," Dino said.

"Dino, I think he would stay away if you just asked him to. If he understood how much his presence would upset you. He thinks you're just fighting about money."

"And you know what he thinks, don't you? You're two of a kind."

"No, Dino. No, please. I don't know how much more of this I can take." She sounded close to tears.

"You want to destroy me."

"I want you to be well. And that smoking isn't helping anything."

I heard the sound of inhaling, that black smoke curling up

inside of him, same as his poisonous thoughts. "If you call him, I will cut you out of my life forever."

Brief Fantasy Number Twenty-Five Thousand Two Hundred and Nine—handing her the phone with William Tiero's number already dialed. I didn't know how much more of this I could take, either. As soon as Dino was gone to rehearsals that night, my mom was on the phone. Dino's doctor. They reached some agreement, something about the doctor coming over. I thought about my mother's marriage to Dino Cavalli. They had run off to San Francisco together and had a judge do the honors at the courthouse. I thought about what my mother's dreams had been that day. Whatever she had imagined their future to be, I was sure it wasn't this.

Mom asked if I wanted to go for tacos. I was glad she was eating—she looked like hell lately, stress-thin. We left and picked up some food, and ate it in the car driving home. I love to eat in the car. There's something so satisfyingly efficient about the whole endeavor, taking care of two needs at the same time, and it's such a challenge of planning too. Where to put your Mexi-Fries (yeah, right—like we all don't know they're Tater Tots) and your hot sauce; how to balance your drink while keeping the insides of your taco from spilling out of their shell.

Mom negotiated an intersection while taking a sideways bite of her dinner. "I'm sure this goes without saying, but you know I'm expecting you to be at the performance on Friday," she said.

"What performance?" I said.

"Cassie!"

"Just kidding." Boy, that joke got a good reaction.

"You'll have to wear a dress."

"Cruel and unusual punishment," I said.

"The long one from the Thanksgiving party, how about. You won't even have to do pantyhose."

"Okay," I said.

"There'll be reporters and critics," she said.

"They won't even notice me, I'll behave so nicely." I knew why she wanted me there, but I didn't understand why Dino would. I said so.

"Of course he wants you there," she said. "We're family." I could hear the lie in her voice. "He really has taken the whole Ian thing well, after the initial blowup."

"He's been pretty quiet about that," I said. "But I heard you guys talking today."

"I know, but try not to worry. In two days this performance will be over, and he promised he'd get back on his medication. Dr. Milton is coming over tomorrow, just to help him through."

"You're not a lion tamer, Mom."

"But Dr. Milton is."

"It just seems like there's more than we can handle here. It's just . . . too much. You've been eating Tums and Maalox like candy."

"I'm walking around in someone else's life," she agreed.

Right then I thought about the secret weapon I held, this information that Dino's early life was a concoction, a lie. Everything that she'd already seen hadn't been enough to make Mom leave, so why would this? But maybe it would be enough to tip the scale. I opened my mouth to speak, then changed my mind.

"All this is almost over," my mom said.

She didn't know, neither of us knew, how right she was.

I'd set up my telescope over the past few nights, hoping and hoping that Ian would come as he had before. But he hadn't come. Still, it was better than being in the house, so after dinner that night I set up again. That night was clear and the sky was still in the hold of the midwinter turbulent atmosphere, the shakiness of the air blurring the images in the telescope, but making the stars twinkle. I gave up and just looked without an instrument, admired Sirius, the most scorching-hot star and the brightest thing in the sky next to a planet. It sparkled blue-white, dominated everything around it. I found Canis Major, the Big Dog, and Canis Minor, the Little Dog, though they looked more like spilled sugar than animals.

I was missing Ian something fierce right then, and I remembered our first touch, right there on that lawn. I packed up, put the telescope into the shed. I was heading up the steps to the front door when I heard his voice.

"Cassie?"

His dark figure came toward me, becoming clearer as he stepped forward, his face nearly white from the light of the sky. It was a dream, I was sure. This figure, approaching me slowly, appearing out of the darkness.

"Cassie?"

"Ian?"

"It's me." One sleeve of his coat hung limp by his side, and the lump of his cast was buttoned inside his coat. I couldn't believe it was him. I just couldn't believe it.

"You came."

"I've been trying and trying to call you."

"You have?"

"I swear, every time I do, Dino answers. I didn't want to make more problems for you, so I keep making up reasons why I'm phoning him," Ian said. "It's getting stupid. Where have you been, Cassie? What's going on? You haven't called or anything. I figured maybe you were under lock and key or something. Couldn't climb out your window like Rapunzel because your hair is too short. I came over one day and hid behind the neighbor's *car*, because Dino and your Mom were there in the driveway."

"I'm sorry . . ."

"I wanted to come over so bad, but I didn't want to risk getting you into more trouble. I figured it'd be safe now—Dino's got to be at the concert hall every night this week, right?"

"They rehearse in the day."

"Oh, shit—should I go?"

"No! No, Ian. I *have* been trying to call you. Over and over. Your mom told me not to call anymore. I didn't think you wanted to see me. . . ."

"You're kidding," Ian said. "Man, I had no idea. She . . . she's really upset. God, I worried maybe this wasn't worth it anymore to you. You had enough of all the crap . . ."

"No! I thought *you* . . . after your wrist, and what your mom said. . . . How could you ever even want to talk to me again?"

"I was really worried," he said.

I went to him, put my arms around him, the bulky cast between us. He felt so good. His mouth felt so good. All the pieces came together and made sense again. It wasn't happiness so much I felt, though that, too. There was just this profound relief. His cold mouth, warm breath filling me up again—just such relief.

"Whatever happens," he said. "Whatever, you've got to promise me you won't go away from me anymore."

I put my head against his shoulder. The worry and relief poured out together, lodged somewhere in my throat. My eyes welled up. "I am so sorry, Ian. I am just so, so sorry about your arm." I started to cry. He put his good arm around me.

"Hey," he said.

"I was selfish," I said. "You were working so hard. Please, if you could ever forgive me . . ."

"There's nothing to forgive," he said. "Look, fate decided things for itself. Cassie, look at me." He tilted my chin up from his coat. Kissed each of my eyes. "Look," he said.

I looked. He was right. His face was soft, relaxed.

"Oh, God, Ian. You're happy."

"Happy—I'm *ecstatic*. Worried as hell, but ecstatic."

"I'm so glad. I am so, so glad."

"I didn't have to make the choice. The choice was made for me," he said.

"What's going to happen?" I asked.

"I don't know. Financially . . . God, Cassie, things are such a mess. My mom's a wreck. I feel awful about it. But there's this piece of me in here. It's flying."

"You're frec."

"God, I'm free," he said.

Chapter Fifteen

Three days. Two.

One day and a bad night's sleep. A restless, tense household, my mother making tea at 3:00 A.M. Dino playing in his office at 4:00 A.M. The toilet flushing, doors opened and closed. Me turning my pillow endlessly to the cool side.

And then, the day of the concert.

It's funny about those monumental events that you wait and wait for, the ones that have the big buildup of a rocket launch. There's all the drama and the trauma and then the actual day comes in, soft as any other day, just appearing the way all of the other ones appear. Friday morning, the sun came up the same way it had for a zillion years. I tried to summon some feeling of importance, gather up a sense of the monumental, but instead I just felt cranky and overtired, got up, and went into the bathroom and checked my face for disaster, as I did every day. When I left for school, Dino was still in bed, and the only sign of an important night was catching Mom downing Maalox in the bathroom, and the newspaper on the kitchen table folded to the article CAVALLI TO PERFORM FIRST NEW MUSIC IN SIX YEARS.

The big thing that happened at school on Friday was that Mr. Robelard, the science teacher, caught on fire during an experiment in his second-period sophomore Life Science class. I was sitting in English class then, listening to Orlando, the gay guy from last trimester's World History class, recite his poetry about love. He flung his arms out dramatically, and everyone rolled their eyes when he described the female object of his desire. Yeah, right. *Her lips were pouting and red,* he panted embarrassingly, just as the door shot open and this sophomore girl ran in yelling, "The teacher's on fire! The teacher's on fire!" Some kid in the back of the class actually laughed until we saw Mr. Robelard run past, the back of his coat in flames. Apparently some alcohol they were using for an experiment got too close to a Bunsen burner, and poof. I wondered how this was going to affect his elk calls.

My own day may have seemed regularly irregular, but the outside music world was greeting it with anticipation. I got my first sense of this at lunch, when I felt a tap on my shoulder and turned to find Mr. King, the orchestra teacher, standing behind me with bright eyes.

"I just wanted to pass on my best wishes for this evening and my sincerest congratulations," he whispered. And then off he scurried, as if the performance had already begun and he was politely leaving the concert hall to use the men's room.

Siang was treating me in that delicate fashion too, telling

me after school that she would not be coming over today, as it seemed best. Some kid with a violin case slipped me a note: *I am a great admirer of yours,* apparently missing the point that the only thing I could do with a violin was make it into a decorative planter.

After school, I started to get a weird bout of nerves. My stomach was rolling and pitching, and I understood Mom's Maalox. I decided I needed something to calm me down. A huge sugar hit, some Twinkies or something. I got a ride from Zebe and she dropped me off at the Front Street Market in town. She took her neon yellow rabbit's foot off of her key chain and insisted I keep it with me for good luck tonight, even though it was creepy.

"People have had them for hundreds of years," Zebe said. "So they've got to be good for something."

"Not for the rabbit," I told her.

I perused the Hostess aisle happily, enjoying all of the beautiful possibilities. Momentarily, all would be joy. I was in the checkout aisle, purchasing more items than I care to tell about, when I heard some familiar voices over by that big ice compartment in the front of the store that you never see anyone near. You get to wondering if a dead body could be stored there, for all anyone ever opens it.

"Hey, Bunny! Chuck!" I said. I was glad to see them. We were bonded by our wonderful and terrible day together. Bonded by our love for Ian Waters.

"Look, I bought happiness," I said, and showed them what was in my bag.

"Whoa," Chuck said. "You won the chocolate lottery."

"Not all chocolate. Fruit pies, too," I said.

"We're just here for ice," Bunny said unnecessarily. The door was open, and big whiffs of white air were escaping the chest. If he stood there any longer, he'd start looking like that abominable snowguy in that geeky Christmas cartoon with the carpenter elf and the Land of the Misfit Toys. "My back is still hurting from that fall I took. You remember that fall I took."

"Vaguely," I said.

"He's sprained his lumbodorsal fascia, but he doesn't believe me," Chuck said.

"Ice, and deep-tissue massage," Bunny said.

"Maybe a chiropractor," Chuck said.

"Hey, get off my back, ha-ha," Bunny said.

"After the fiftieth time it's not funny anymore, Bun."

"I'm sorry you're still not feeling well," I said. "Would a couple of Ho Hos help things?"

"Waaay better than a chiropractor," Bunny said.

I shuffled around my loot, found the Ho Hos, and opened the package with my teeth.

"I guess you heard Ian's good news," Chuck said.

"That he's quitting," I said through the plastic. *At ee's kidding.*

"Quitting? No, that he got in," Chuck said.

I'd heard wrong, I guessed. I must have heard wrong.

"What do you mean, got in?"

"Maybe she hadn't heard yet. Shit," Bunny said. "God damn it, Chuck. You and your big mouth."

"What do you mean?" A sick feeling started in my stomach, some horrible dread. My face flushed red.

"He got in," Bunny said. "Curtis."

"How is that possible?" My voice sounded hoarse. I wanted to scream, and my voice sounded like I already had. "No! That's not possible! How is that possible?"

"Mr. Cavalli. He had a tape. He'd taped Ian before he broke his wrist. Cavalli sent it in. Talked to the school and arranged for the tape to be used as an audition."

"No," I whispered. "No."

"I thought maybe he should have asked Janet before he did that, but she's obviously beside herself with happiness," Bunny said.

"What about Ian?"

"I haven't seen Ian," Bunny said.

"No one asked Ian."

"Janet said he was happy. I don't know if this is the best thing for him or not," Bunny said. "All I know is, he's in. He's going to Curtis."

"I've got to go," I said.

"Hey, Cassie. I'm sorry if I said anything before Ian told you himself. I didn't know."

"I've got to go," I said.

I dropped the Hostess loot there on the floor and I got the hell out of there. I ran home. I ran so fast. Fury gave me this speed I didn't know I had. I wasn't myself. I didn't know who I was, but I wasn't me. Dino had taken Ian's life from him. No wonder he'd lost his outrage about Ian's arm. He'd already taken matters into his own hands. Well, now I would take them into mine.

I flung open the front door, slammed it behind me. How was that for turning the knob so it closed more quietly?

"Cassie?" Mom appeared in the kitchen doorway. "I'm glad you're home. We need to eat something before we go. God, what's wrong?"

"Where's Dino?"

"He's getting into his tux. You've got to hurry up and get dressed."

I ignored her, went upstairs.

"Knock, knock," I said to the closed bedroom door. I was trying not to shout. I was doing everything I could to keep those shouts inside. My heart was beating furiously. I was hot all over, from the running, from the anger.

"What is it?" Dino said. He opened the door. He stood there in the doorway in his tux, his tie loose.

"What did you do?" I breathed.

"I cannot handle your dramatics now. I've got to get ready," he said.

My mother arrived at the top of the stairs. "Cassie, come with me to your room," she said. "We'll handle whatever needs handling."

"Why did you do that? Why did you send that tape of Ian to Curtis?"

"So that's what the upset is this time. Always the boy, the boy, the boy. I saved his ass," Dino said. "Daniella, really. Would you kindly remove your daughter from our room?"

"He didn't want to go," I said. "He didn't want that."

"It's not always about what we want," Dino said. "If I had what I wanted, we wouldn't be having this conversation. I'd be in New York at this moment, preparing to go to Lincoln Center instead of

Benaroya Hall. And do you know why I am not in New York preparing to go to Lincoln Center?"

"Dino, that's not fair," my mother said.

"Because I married your mother, and your mother has you to think about."

"Dino. Stop," Mom said. "Come on, guys. We've got a big night ahead, and . . ."

"You." I breathed. "Are a horrible person. And a liar."

"You're wasting my time," Dino said.

"All of the stories about Italy and Sabbotino Grappa. Who are you, really?" I let the bomb drop from my hands. I let it slip to the floor, where it lay, ticking.

Everyone was silent for a moment. I could hear Dino breathing heavily.

"Because if you're really Dino Cavalli, your history is a lie. No perfect house and mother in a feathered hat. No lemon trees. Maybe not even any bicycles."

"Get her out of here, Daniella. I have a performance to prepare for."

"Cassie. Your room. Now."

"He's not who he says. What, did you pay those people to hide what you really are?"

He turned away from me. I couldn't see his face, which had become so hideous to me. If I could have seen his face, it probably would have been fallen and pale, I know now. Drained of cover and laid bare, just a human.

My mother took hold of my arm, led me out. "Cassie, what are you thinking? Do you know what you're doing? Jesus."

"There are things you don't know."

She closed my door with no small amount of anger. Her face was tight and her eyes flashed.

"I do know."

"No, you don't. Dino wasn't born in Sabbotino Grappa. All of those stories were made up. He never even lived there. What do you think of him now? You never even knew him. It's all a lie."

"I know that."

"What?" I sat down on the edge of my bed. My anger drained from me. Without it, I was suddenly exhausted. "What?" I wanted to cry. I was too tired for that, even.

"I know that. You're right. None of it was true. He made up the story when he was sixteen years old to cover the truth, and he's stuck with it ever since."

"That's crazy. That's absolutely wacko. You knew this? Just one more nutso thing. I cannot believe this."

"He was doing his first interview, and found the town in a book. He chose it because it wasn't a place likely to be visited, and too small to bump into anyone from there. He held a magnifying glass to the picture of the town square, the church, studied the tiny map. The rest . . . he just made up the rest."

"And all those people go along? Like you go along? I just don't understand."

"When Edward Reynolds did the oral history, William Tiero went to Sabbotino Grappa. He talked to the priest, who then spoke to the handful of villagers. They'd already read about themselves by then in a couple of articles. They thought they were famous. Most didn't need to be talked into anything. They didn't even have to be paid. They loved being part of things. They loved having this bit of excitement. It made them happy. Some of the old people—they started to believe they really did remember Dino Cavalli and his family living in the big house on Via D'Oro."

"I'm sorry, but that's fucking creepy. They all go along like they're in some kind of trance? Come on."

"It's not about a *trance*. It's a small village. It was fun for them, a thrill. They loved it. Some heard the stories so many times, they forgot what the truth was. This is not about *creepy*. This is about filling a boring life with something more interesting."

"You knew this. You knew and it didn't even matter to you. Someone just goes and makes up his whole *history* and this doesn't bother you?" Nothing would matter then, it seemed clear. This was my mother's life, and my life. Nothing was going to change if she didn't have limits of what she would tolerate. I would have to make some decisions. I grabbed my pillow and held it. Put my face down inside. Dad could turn down the heat of his house. Mom couldn't turn down the heat of hers.

"Honey." She sighed. She sat down next to me, just sat there in silence for a while. "Dino needed that history. *Needed* it. And it made those people *happy*. They're part of something bigger than the life they have there. I understood that."

"Why? Why would he need it so bad? Someone just needs to go and make himself up?"

"Dino was born Dino Tiero in the inner city of Milan."

"Tiero? They're *related*?"

"They're brothers. They were desperately poor. God, Cassie,

they were so poor that they once had to eat a rat that William caught. Can you imagine that?"

"No," I said. "It's still no reason to lie like that. Being poor . . ."

"His mother was a prostitute. They never knew their father. They saw their mother hanging on the shower rail when he was fifteen. Suicide. He and William found her."

"Oh, my God."

"A teacher, Giovanni Cavalli, had already given him his first violin a few years before. He taught Dino to play. Dino had a natural talent. That part was true. William got him jobs, and the playing kept them alive. Dino changed his name to honor the man who saved his life. William kept pushing, pushing Dino to greatness. They were always running from ghosts."

I was quiet. I felt horrible and cruel. Life could be so beautiful, and it could also be this mess of confusion and cruelty. I didn't know where to begin untangling things.

"I'm sorry," I said finally.

"Cassie, I'm not saying this excuses all his behavior. Just explains some of it."

"Why didn't you tell me before?"

"He didn't even tell me any of this. William did. Dino's doctor did. Dino fired William after he had Dino hospitalized. He thought he was ruining his ability to create."

"I just don't get it. People would understand. I would have understood. Maybe there would be more compassion for him. He didn't need to worry about the truth."

"I guess sometimes things seem too awful to say out loud." I guess she was right about that. I still hadn't told Ian the truth about what was happening at home. "I'm sorry I didn't tell you. I wanted to protect him; I wanted to protect you. He wanted to protect his mother. He didn't want the world to know her that way."

"I wanted to protect you," I said.

"Oh, Cassie." She looked so, so tired. She put her arms around me. "That's my job," she said. "To protect you. And I'm not doing it well enough."

I hugged her too. "All this has been hard," I said.

"How did you find out about Dino? We don't even know for sure if Edward Reynolds discovered the truth, though I think he had to have. Every magazine and newspaper reporter since has taken their information from that book."

"Dad found out."

"What? Dad?"

"He was worried about you."

"None of this is his business."

"Don't be mad at him. He did it out of love."

Mom sighed. Shook her head. "All the things," she said. "Done out of love."

Karl Lager: Well, then the concerts in the piazza started every Saturday morning. Do you understand what that did to my business? No one went into the store for an hour or more. They came to listen to that horrible child, not to buy peaches.

Father Tony Abrulla: I will confess I am glad he did not choose Sunday! I was just an assistant then, to Father Minelli. I close my eyes and still hear that music. It brought the people of Sabbotino Grappa together as one. For a few hours, this small boy kept Mrs. Salducci and Mrs. Latore from fighting. Even Frank Piccola came outside and stood to listen, and the threat of hell couldn't make him leave his house for mass on Sundays. Maybe he was depressed. We didn't have depression, then, of course, that we knew of.

Maria Lager Manzoni, grocer's daughter: Father finally gave me Saturdays off. Let me tell you a secret—that's when my Pia was conceived. Eli and I held hands through that child's sweet and tender playing, went home with passion. We barely closed the front door.

Honoria Maretta: No child was ever mine like he was. Like a son to me. I loved that boy.[10]

Here is what I remember about the rest of that night.

Dino puts a coat around my mother's shoulders. His own smells of cigarettes, like the boys in detention. I tell him I am sorry, but it is really more the sadness of his life I am expressing compassion for, rather than my anger at him earlier. There is too much between us for that. And too much that he's done that cannot be excused by the past. Still, I feel bad for the pain he felt. The pain he continues to feel. Maybe he chooses not to see me, as he has chosen to stop seeing other things in his life.

My mother drives. Dino sits in the passenger's seat. I see in the reflection of the glass that his fingers are moving in the air, on the strings of the violin that rides in its case in the trunk.

We take the ferry, stay in the car. I have seen Dino perform only once before, and Mom has seen him several times, but it was

---

10. *Dino Cavalli—The Early Years: An Oral History.* From Edward Reynolds, New York, N.Y. Aldine Press, 1999.

never like this. Never a release of new work after so many years, never so much riding on the outcome. Last time he was not nervous, but now his edginess infuses the atmosphere. Mom turns on the radio, but Dino switches it off. She helps him straighten the wings of his bow tie, then he flips the visor down and studies it in the mirror. Unsatisfied, he undoes it, ties it again. His hands tremble. I smooth the velvet of my dress again and again with my hands. I think about Ian, who in a few months will board an airplane for Philadelphia, but will tonight be somewhere in that audience. I think about how everyone is just a small person on a big earth in a bigger universe. I think about how everyone struggles to do the best they can in this imperfect place.

We arrive at the concert hall early, of course. We are backstage, where there is the chaos and noise of people and instruments and bright lights. My mother knows a few performers there, and I can see her watching Dino with sideways glances even as she speaks to them. Dino is using grand gestures and a big voice, but he is sipping water and once again I see his shaking hands. A violist asks me questions about school that I answer as I smile with a politeness that tries hard to hide my impatience. I feel likc I am talking to her forever, as she tells me what a shame it is that our schools do not make music programs a priority.

Mom rescues me. She whispers that she feels underfoot, that they want to practice a few measures. The conductor looks relaxed, laughs a lot. She tells me that he will be good for Dino, and that we can go get a coffee. I guess we could use some Optimism in a Cup right then.

We go out into the lobby, where it is mostly quiet still, and where there are huge posters of Dino staring out at us wherever I look. It reminds me of *The Great Gatsby*, which we read in English last year—something about that big sign that signifies death, or something or other that I can't quite remember. We find a coffee stand, share a latte, eat a biscotti, so that Mom must go to the bathroom again to fix her lipstick. By the time the audience begins to arrive, she will have made four trips to the bathroom, not that I can blame her.

It feels like we are waiting forever. My feet hurt in those damn shoes. Whoever decided that high heels were a good idea for women should have had to wear them every day of his life, which would be punishment enough. Everyone smiles at my mother, and my own face hurts from so much smiling. I keep looking around for Ian, but know that with all the people there it will be unlikely that I will see him and have the chance to talk to him about getting into Curtis. The ushers arrive, and Mom decides to go backstage and check on Dino one more time before the show begins. I go back to the bathroom for lack of anything else to do, and to avoid the stares of the Dino posters. His hair is swept back from his face in them, silver and black, and he looks handsome and intense. It occurs to me that he is someone I know, someone I live with. But do I really know him? Anything about him, except the way he wants me to walk down stairs, turn a faucet off, close a door? This strikes me as sad—what a stranger he and his life are to me. In the bathroom, I wish for a vice—smoking, drinking. My best vice, Hostess Indulgence, sounds stomach turning and hugely lacking in vice-ly power at the moment. The bathroom has the paper towels stacked in a basket, and I wonder how long they will last before the dispensers with the twirly narrow handles will have to be used.

The bathroom begins to pack with perfumed women in sequins and big coats. I leave to find that the lobby is filling fast, with rushing people and lingering people, people in heavy jackets and others fanning themselves with their programs. It's amazing how loud it is in there, after the several hours where the only noises were footsteps on carpet. In spite of Dino's complaints about his venue, I know that the hall is one of the best for sound, a building built within a building to keep the life of the street out. Now in the lobby, we are standing in the middle layer, the protective atmosphere.

Mom comes out again, finds me looking out of the glass wall into what is now night. It's dark and has been raining, and the street is glossy. Cars are jammed up all along the road, and a light turns red and someone honks. In every one of those cars there is a story, or a hundred stories. For every light on in all of those huge city buildings, there is a story. No one knows what I am about to face, no one knows my story, and neither do I right then. I think about Ian and I scan the crowd for his face, and kick myself for not making a plan to meet him somewhere here. This place, a night like this, will be his place, too, his night. I wonder if his hands will shake as he takes a sip of water before his performance.

Mom grabs my arm. It's the second time she's done that. She tells me we have to hurry, that we should be seated by now. We walk past the ushers and down the sloped, carpeted ramp. Some of the family of the other performers stay backstage, but Dino has always preferred his support in the audience. I know from Mom's own performances that when you look out from a lit stage, all you can see is a blackness, the sky without stars. You wouldn't even know there were any living beings out there. I guess it's nice to know that there is something familiar and loving in that sea of darkness.

We travel down the rows of seats and I am lucky I don't fall on my ass in those shoes. All of those people in their suits and fancy clothes, holding hands or whispering to each other or reading their programs and scanning the names of all of the contributors to see which of their friends gave money, all of them are here to see Dino, to say that they saw him, to be able to tell the story tomorrow and in the days to come. You can feel the excitement in the air, in that reserved way of people in an elegant place—all good manners and shifting sideways to maneuver past each other and whispered *excuse me*'s.

We sit next to that weasel Andrew Wilkowski, and some other woman who is from the recording company, I think. I can smell her perfume from where I sit, one of those sorts that are not sexy so much as stalking. The strong odor jars me out of the nervousness that I feel, this psychic-hypercommunication that Mom and I have going between us, anxious electricity. The perfume is helpful because now I am just plain annoyed, and the annoyance puts me in full fault-finding gear. The woman has a little run in her stockings right at the point of her ankle. With any luck, we'll see it zip up her leg like a spider crawling up a wall.

I look behind me. Every seat that I can see is full. Every one. No one is even in the bathroom. I know that somewhere behind me, Siang Chibo sits with her parents. I know that Ian is there with his mother, tickets given to them compliments of Dino. I wonder if they can see me, if their eyes are on me. People in the front row turn to us and say things to Mom, shake her hands. They are probably the people whose names you see in the program under CONTRIBUTORS, the ones who have been in our house on Thanksgiving. We are in the second row by choice—my mom hates sitting in the front row. She says that all you get is a view up Dino's pant leg, but I don't understand how this is any better. If I had my choice, since I had to be there, I would rather sit in one of the overhanging pods, those special boxes that remind you of ladies with piled-up hair and opera glasses, or maybe of President Lincoln being shot, but Dino doesn't like us in the balconies. Better yet, I'd sit in the farthest back corner. I'd put my coat around me, close my eyes, and pretend I'm listening to him on a CD. The idea of him on the stage in front of us is too intense. It'd be more comfortable watching the surgery channel on a big-screen TV. This is not some stranger giving us a show—we will bring home his success or failure. We will live with the largeness of this event for days, the monumental fact of this one man with these people in his hands.

The lights dim, and Mom grabs my arm. We look at each other in the dimness, and I'm surprised at how fearful her face looks. We know Dino won't be performing right away, so there is no reason for this stomach lurching just yet. But when the curtain opens and there is such silence, only a few rustles and a throat being cleared, and the symphony is revealed, dressed in black, with instruments held in readiness, you know it has begun and whatever happens is inevitable.

The conductor enters, and we like him already. His hair is loose, and it is as swinging as his walk. He bows to the audience, and his wide smile says he is enjoying every moment of this, that we should relax and come with him where he is about to take us. The crowd breaks into applause—Peter Boglovich is well loved, known for his passion for coffee and pastries and other men. He steps up onto the conductor's stand, and raises his baton to a pinpoint in the air. And then they begin.

There is a frenzy of bowing, the slightly forward tilt of the musicians' bodies, their slight sway. I can feel my mother relax through the piece. I look over at her and see her smiling slightly.

The symphony plays two more pieces. After the third there is silence, and my mother takes my hand and holds it. Hers is sweaty, and I wonder if she has stopped breathing. Peter Boglovich is speaking, although his words are underwater. He turns to face offstage, applauds to Dino, who emerges from the wings. There is thunderous applause, which goes on for a long time, as Dino looks out into the black sea. In spite of all of the people around him, he looks alone, this one man who was once this one young boy. He takes off his tuxedo jacket, hands it to the conductor. Dino takes his place slightly left of center.

The first piece is titled *Giardino Dei Sogno*, Garden of Dreams. It is surprisingly upbeat, almost cheerful. He smiles as if he is remembering something sweet. His white shirt billows softly. The symphony joins him after a while, an easy, lovely mix of a walk in good weather. My mother's eyes never leave him; it's as if she is breathing for him. The piece ends. The crowd's applause is warm and full, but not overwhelming and astonished. Dino bows and his hair falls down over his face. He stands upright, gives the crowd a nod, and then raises up a hand in acknowledgment. This man, whom I share a house with and who uses the same silverware as I do, seems so removed from me that I could forget that I know him at all.

Dino walks offstage, and the curtain closes. The lights come up, and it is intermission. He will play again afterward. I hear my mother sigh a breath of relief, and then she puts on her smile to receive congratulations of the people who turn to take her hands again. They are being polite, I can tell. Underwhelmed. I stand and stretch, look around. Look up into the crowd and try to meet Ian's eyes, wherever they are.

My mother is leaning forward and talking to Andrew Wilkowski, who I notice for the first time is wearing a rose in his lapel. His wife is talking to the record company woman, who can't seem to take her eyes off of my mother. I check out the crowd and have a weird surge of panic at the sight of one man in our row across the aisle. For a minute, I think I am looking at William Tiero. I think the man looks just like him. In fact, I become sure in a moment that it is indeed William Tiero. This is what living with a paranoid can do; it makes you fear the worst things. My heart actually thumps around in anticipation of trouble. When Mom leans back in her seat again, I point out the man. *Isn't that William Tiero?* I ask.

Don't even think such a thing, she says. And then she tells me who she thinks he looks like, names someone I've never heard of, a movie actor probably. She tells me this man's nose and chin are too round, and that his hair is wrong. It is not William Tiero.

A woman comes to the front and asks if she can take my mother's picture. Andrew Wilkowski intervenes and says no, but my mother says she doesn't mind. The woman has a hard time figuring out her own damn camera, then realizes it hasn't been wound forward. Andrew Wilkowski reminds her to keep the camera in her purse during the performance, and the woman snaps something back to him about knowing full well the protocol. She gives us something to talk about until the lights dim again.

The symphony performs one endless piece and then there is Dino again. There is a long silence before he begins, and when he lifts his violin to his chin, he closes his eyes. It is a solo piece, parts of which I have heard again and again, but have never known the title of until I had picked up the program earlier that night. *Amore Dolce Della Gioventù*, Sweet Love of Youth. He begins to play, and for the first time I hear the piece unbroken. I see the entire picture. I know its name. It is strange to me that I have before this moment only known fragments and not the whole. I wonder what made him write it. I wonder if it was memories of his days in Paris as a young man, or if it was something more recent. I hear the notes, this most beautiful, tender arrangement of feeling, and I see him drawing back the curtain of the upstairs bedroom window of our house, see him watching Ian and me on the grass that night. Could he have seen something more than just his anger that night? Or is every person in this room feeling as if he was there the moment they fell in love? When the piece is over there is silence in the hall, and then frenzied applause. Shouts of *Bravo!* The record company woman wipes a tear from her face. He has triumphed.

He barely pauses to accept the applause before he moves to his next piece, the dreaded third composition that has given him so much agony. It is titled simply *Lunetta*. It is a piece that begins with just Dino's single, mournful violin, until the orchestra floats in, it seems, section by section until all the performers are playing so furiously that it is as if their instruments might alight at any moment. He has composed the music for each instrument, written every agonizing note, and it is true—he is a genius. The emotions pour forth, the definitions of love and life and struggle. Dino himself has his eyes closed—he is lost to this frenzied place. He grimaces, as if it is causing him pain; his shirt billows, comes untucked. His sleeves are swaying a rhythm of white, and this close you can see the sweat forming on his forehead. I hold my own breath—it is that kind of music, where you are almost afraid for what might happen next, afraid of where this group cry to the universe might bring us. I look over at my mother, and see her hands clasped in her lap. Her own eyes are closed, and she is smiling. She is gone to wherever music and passion can take her, and I see on her face why she loves this man and what it means to her to simply be part of this moment. I understand that that is what all this has been about—her ability to be here in a way that is more intimate than anyone else in the room. To have a piece of it that no one else has. This is why she has stayed.

I think of my father right then. I think how my mother has needs that he cannot fulfill. In some part of him, held secretly in his palm, maybe, I know he holds out hope that she will return to him. There is a part of me that right then opens up my own palm, unfurls the clutched fingers, and lets the hope out.

The audience is transported, and Dino is the one leading the trip. I am afraid for him—he seems so overcome, so lost and found at the same time that I wonder how he'll manage it. He leans over the violin, and the energy and fire he pours into that instrument is the brightest flash of light, a gamma ray burst, the death of a star and the creation of a black hole. The piece has ended, this piece that has caused Dino so much agony, and the audience explodes with applause, shouts, and rises to its feet. This surpasses triumph, but Dino looks depleted, exhausted to the point of collapse. He just stands there for a while, looking into the blackness of the audience as if wondering where he was and how he got there. *Lunetta*, I learn later means "Little Moon" in Italian. His mother's name.

Someone has the bright idea to turn up the lights a bit so that he can see the people on their feet, their hands in the air. His eyes settle on us, the record company woman, my mother and I, then move across the performance hall.

There are lucky and unlucky things about that night. The unlucky things are obvious. The lucky thing is that someone closed the curtain a bit too early. As the heavy velvet drapes shut, the applause finally quieted, and the rush out began immediately. That was the lucky part, that there were many people who had already made it through the doors before Peter Boglovich and a French horn player lost their grasp on a Dino who was trying to make his way out to the audience through the side curtain. He had thrown his violin down—that's how they knew that he was suddenly outraged and out of control. Thrown it hard enough to cause a thin crack down the back.

No one hears anything, although Andrew Wilkowski's envelope

wife would later claim she heard the splintering of the wood, which was an impossibility and a lie, given the noise in the auditorium and the chatter of the record company woman. We gather our coats. There is supposed to be a brief reception now for a few important people. This is fine for the record company woman, as her perfume is still going strong. I do not know that in less than a minute, Ian will know my secret. That everyone will.

The front rows are still making their way up the ramp when we hear it. This animal cry of rage. *You son of a bitch!* We turn to look, and in spite of everything that has happened up to that point, in spite of all that we have lived with over the past few months, the cry is a surprise, and I have no idea whose voice it is or what is happening. There is that sudden disorientation of trying to make sense of something unexpected.

And then I see him. Billowing white shirt, black tuxedo pants, and he leaps from the stage and stumbles. Andrew Wilkowski is the first one to understand that it is Dino, and that this is a disaster. He rushes down the ramp with a surprising degree of athleticism, but misses Dino coming up the side aisle. Dino is pushing past startled people, reaches the man who bears an unfortunate resemblance to Dino Tiero Cavalli's brother. He grabs a chunk of the back of the jacket the man wears and spins him around. He raises his fist, and with the force of the agony and pain of his lifetime, punches the man in his face, sending him reeling and crashing to the floor.

There are screams—my mother screams beside me. Dino is kneeling beside the man. He is putting his hands to the man's throat. Blood is coming from the man's nose. Andrew Wilkowski reaches them.

Dino looks into the face of the man, and realizes what we already know. He realizes that this is just a man, an aeronautics engineer who played the bass in his high school orchestra and who lucked into good seats through an online auction. This is not William Tiero, who he is certain tried to ruin him financially by getting him the psychiatric help he needed. Who shared the ugly history that Dino tried to escape from but feared he never could. As my mother said, his nose and chin are too round.

This is when Dino rises. The part of him that is sane and rational, if still a perfectionist asshole, looks shocked at what he has done.

Two ushers and a security officer are trying to move down the crowd of people to get to the injured man. Andrew Wilkowski has his arm around Dino's shoulder. But he doesn't know Dino's strength if he thinks he can hold him there. Dino wrenches himself free. He flees out the side door, the fire exit.

He runs out into the night.

Chapter Sixteen

Later, after the police had gone, the one thing I kept thinking about was Siang Chibo. I wondered if she had seen what had happened, or if she would only read about it in the morning. I thought about her reaction to this night even more than Ian's. I had such a profound feeling of having disappointed her. I kept seeing her finger, straightening that painting of *Wild Roses*.

Andrew Wilkowski was snoring on the couch, and my mother was sitting up in bed with the lights on. She'd told me to go to sleep, and I told her that sleep would be impossible. *Now,* she had said, and I guess she just needed some time alone to think. She had a lot to think about.

I'd been able to sleep, but it was a deep, dark sleep of restless dreams, full of Dino's music, full of the knowledge that he was gone, and that Ian was going away too. Finally I slept hard, woke up late, and emerged from haziness to the awful memory of what the night before had brought. It seemed so unreal that I had to convince myself that it was true. Dino was still gone. I called Ian quickly, and we spoke only long enough to arrange a meeting. There were things he needed to tell me. There were things I needed to tell him, too.

I stayed with Mom all day, on the Dino vigil. Andrew Wilkowski hid the newspaper and made sure the television and radio weren't played. There was no news of Dino from the police or anywhere else. After we tried to eat grilled cheese sandwiches and soup, I left Mom in the capable hands of Andrew Wilkowski, still in his suit, looking wrinkled and exhausted, his music-note tie discarded sometime the night before. Dog William snoozed on the living room rug, looking inappropriately content.

I walked down to the ferry docks. The day had been freezing but bright, too cheerful for what Mom was going through. White wisps of a foggy evening were beginning to form in the dusk, looking as if they could be cleared with a puff of my breath. Ian was there already when I arrived. I saw his dark coat all the way from the ticket window, where Evan Malloney's dad was working late.

Ian faced me, watched me walk toward him. He held out his arms and I got in. I let myself sink there and disappear.

"You saw," I said.

"Yes," Ian said into my hair.

"I heard about you, too, and Curtis."

"Bunny told me he saw you. There's so much to say that I don't know where to start."

"I don't either," I said.

"I knew Dino was . . . difficult. But Cassie, did he just snap?"

"No, not really. I knew something like this was coming. My Mom and I both did. There's been so much happening. . . . I was embarrassed to tell you. There was so much . . ." I still couldn't say the words. *Crazy. Mentally ill.*

"You should have told me. Look at us. We didn't tell each other the most important things."

"I was afraid of what you'd think."

"I was afraid of what *you* would think. God, we can't be so afraid of losing each other. I won't judge you. I love you."

I squeezed him under his coat. "But I *am* going to lose you."

"You're not going to lose me."

"But you're going away."

"Yes."

We stood there, just holding each other.

"It's what you have to do," I said.

"Yes."

"I don't want to talk about this anymore," I said. "I don't even want to talk."

"Okay."

"No sound. No music, no talking."

"Quiet as space," he said. "Is space quiet?" I held my finger up to his lips to tell him to shush. We walked down the dock. We didn't talk about where we were walking; we just kept going forward, in step with each other. We walked back toward town, went to the planetarium. Dave was just leaving, let us in and told me to lock the door behind me when I left. We walked into the dark auditorium, and I kept the lights off, turned on the projector and lit the ceiling with stars. We sat in the plush chairs, side by side and holding hands. Ian leaned over and kissed me, and we stayed there for a while like that. It got uncomfortable, and we lay down on the floor together for a while. What happened after that is nobody's business. It's my sweet, good memory. But I will say that I got my wish for quiet. Quiet except for the sweet, tender notes of *Amore Dolce Della Gioventù* playing in my head, and Ian's breath in my ear.

Alice came over and stayed with Mom when Andrew Wilkowski went home for a little bit. There was still no news of Dino. Alice seemed to know a lot about our life. Mom told more about what went on in our house than I ever did, it seemed. I wonder if my parents' divorce made me get too good at keeping secrets.

Alice brought tea and scones in a white bag. I guess she didn't have time to make them herself. A white bakery bag is one of the reasons life is good, if you ask me, and Alice's calm presence and kind voice did appear to work magic on Mom. Alice had her laughing, telling a story about someone else they knew, and I was glad to see that Mom had good people around her.

So it was Alice, anyway, not Andrew Wilkowski, who was there with Mom when she got the phone call. The call was from William Tiero. Mom was so happy and relieved to hear from him. Dino may have been right in his paranoid feeling that Mom and William kept in contact. They were two people who loved Dino, and they were looking after him. Mom's voice was warm, grateful.

"They found him. Thank God," she said, after she hung up. Dino had boarded a plane, flew to Milan. He had checked into the Principe De Savoia Hotel, was there now. He was alone, in bad shape. She needed to go immediately.

Mom phoned Dino's doctor and Andrew Wilkowski, who insisted on coming with her. The kind Alice called for plane reservations as Mom packed.

I sat on the edge of the bed. "How can I help?" I asked.

"Can you look in the top dresser drawer for my passport?"

I hunted around until I found the small blue book. I opened it up, looked at her picture. It was taken a few years ago, just before they were married. They had gone to Paris for a week for their honeymoon. She looked so young in the picture. I couldn't believe how much she'd changed. "Found it."

"I've never been to Italy," she said. "This wasn't exactly the way I intended going. This is not something I could have ever imagined. I cannot even believe what I am doing right now."

"Is he okay?" I thought about the *Wild Roses* painting. I thought about what Siang Chibo had told me. About what had happened with Vincent van Gogh after he'd painted it.

"You know what Dr. Milton said? Have I ever told you how much I can't stand Dr. Milton? Born with a reptile heart, I swear."

"What did he say?"

"He said I should commit Dino when I get to Milan. If he's alive by the time I get there. That's actually what he said. 'If he's alive by the time you get there.'"

"I still think he's a liar," my father said.

"He had reason. It's not that simple," I said.

"Crazy, then. I don't think anyone will dispute that anymore.

That poor man. His nose is broken. I can't believe he isn't going to sue. And that violin. Imagine how much that cost."

I hadn't seen a newspaper in a few days, but Dad had them all. He even had a few from other cities, for God's sake. Nannie was sitting in the chair with the pop-up footstool. She was doing the crossword puzzle in the *Chicago Tribune*. I saw it sitting open on the coffee table later. For "Elvis hit, 1956" she had written *artichoke dip* and had left two squares blank, and for "Hockey legend" she had written *puck*, leaving three squares blank. It just goes to show that if it works for you, great.

"Dino's suicidal in some hotel, Dad. I don't think they're thinking about that aspect of things right now."

"Look at what she chose. And our life together was so bad?"

I kept my mouth shut. Watched Dog William out the window, checking out Dad's backyard with a confused excitement. The gray whales had begun their migration in the sound that stretched out before us. But no one was thinking about whales, and that seemed sad and wrong.

"Flower parts, six letters," Nannie shouted. "What's a flower part, six letters?"

"Petals," my dad said.

She ignored him. "Flower!" Nannie said. She counted the letters. "Yep, that's six."

"I guess if your mother puts up with this, she'll never leave him," my father said.

I didn't tell him that I'd had the same thought. Instead, I took his hands across the table where we sat. The Dutch girls were still paired with the chefs—Dad had at last given up on Nannie's rearranging, at least with the salt and pepper shakers.

"I love you, Dad," I said. "I just . . . I wish you would let go, you know? Move on."

"I have moved on," he said.

"Dad." I gestured to the newspapers, spread out all over the living room.

He sighed. "Cassie?" he said. "There's one thing I know. You can't tell a heart what to do."

"All right," I said.

"Oh give me a home, where these roam. Seven letters," Nannie said. She was quiet a moment. Dad and I just sat there, our hands clasped together.

"Monkeys," Nannie said finally.

Mom's voice was there, coming across the ocean by phone. She sounded so close, she might have been phoning from the grocery store.

"I've got to get that doctor's home phone number," she said. "You've got to help me. It's an emergency."

"I can ask Dad to help me. He's a master sleuth. What's going on?"

"Just hurry. Call me back as soon as you can. He's gone, Cassie. We got here, and he's gone."

"Are you okay?"

"Something's happened to him. I can feel it. It's like I feel this . . . *separation*. I feel him gone in my gut."

* * *

After writing his *Principia*, Sir Isaac Newton collapsed in a nervous breakdown. Abraham Lincoln had several breakdowns, and was obsessed with thoughts of premature death and of going mad. F. Scott Fitzgerald and his wife, Zelda, were the dysfunctional couple of the century. He was wracked by alcoholism, and she died in a fire at a mental hospital. So much painful living, even for the seemingly most chirpy—Dolly Parton (depression), Charles Schultz (anxiety), Dick Clark (depression), Donny and Marie Osmond, for God's sake (anxiety and depression, respectively).

"What if he's dead, Ian?" I said into the phone. "What does dead even mean?" I couldn't get my mind wrapped around the thought. I couldn't picture him really gone. Forever gone, gone where? "I wanted him out of my life, Mom's life. But I never wanted this."

"I know."

"Tell me what dead means," I said.

"I don't know, Cassie. I just don't know."

Here is what happened, according to my mother. Dino took a cab, all the way down to the center of the country. A cab, if you can believe it, some 130 miles. Through Milan and Bologna. On to Florence, and a short while farther to San Gimignano, Tuscany. From there, just a few miles south to the hilltop town of Sabbotino Grappa.

My mother and Andrew Wilkowski took the train. They paid a man in an old Renault to drive them from the station to

Sabbotino Grappa. The man drove with one hand, and held a cigarette in the other, dangling it out the open window. They told him they were in a hurry, and he accommodated, although it seemed that all the cars on the roads drove with the same fury and absentminded recklessness, Mom said. Lots of veering and honking and driving up the curb until they were out of the city and the driver calmed down a bit. It was hot, Mom said, and they had to drive with all of the windows rolled down. You could see Sabbotino Grappa before you arrived there—from the highway it was a tiny town that looked balanced on a pinnacle. The town was built on the lofty hilltop location in the medieval days, so the townspeople could see who might be arriving to destroy them. Dino had done a good job in choosing Sabbotino Grappa, Mom realized. It was too far and too small to be of interest to tourists, and the trip up the winding road to the top too arduous. The village shared one phone, and traveling to that place in an attempt to check facts with the handful of people who lived there and who spoke only Italian would give anyone incentive to believe first Dino's and then Edward Reynolds's version of events. One look at this place, though, Mom said, and you knew that Edward Reynolds, the author of *An Oral History* made a decision about which story he would give to the world. Because there would be no canals up here. No canals in which to throw a bicycle.

The man in the Renault told them about all of the Americans he knew, asked if they lived in New York City. He'd been there once, and from what he saw of America, he hated it. They wound their way up the hill, arrived at a town so ancient and quiet, my mother was sure it was deserted. The man in the Renault let them out, and Andrew paid him. My mother took a big drink of warm air, looked out over the Tuscan valley, which stretched beneath them. The man in the Renault waved good-bye, the cigarette still smoking in his hand, and beeped his horn. As he headed back down the winding road, my mother worried about letting him go—the town, all yellow stone and small alleyways, seemed completely empty. It looked like an abandoned film-scene set, with its narrow passages and stone walls and buildings so old it was hard to believe anyone that lived there knew what year it was.

In the center of the town was a square, cobbled, with a church and three small stores, just as Dino had described. Just as Edward Reynolds had said. It just seemed so deserted, Mom thought; until she caught the movement of a curtain, saw the bulk of an old woman moving away who'd been watching them. Then she saw the window shade of a store pulled closed, a pair of shutters yanked shut, an old man hurrying off down an alleyway. They walked to the church and went inside. The church was freezing. There were three long rows of lit red candles, and a huge image of Jesus painted right on to the wall, chipped in an unfortunate place. Andrew Wilkowski called out, and an ancient priest shuffled into the church. He stank so strongly of wine, my mother thought she could get drunk just smelling his breath.

The old priest spoke only Italian, and Andrew Wilkowski made his best attempt to speak to him. The old man just shook his head *No, no, no,* until Andrew Wilkowski said Dino's name. When he heard this, he took Andrew's arms in his hands and nodded, gestured to the open doorway. My mother said she felt the most profound relief, until the old priest started shaking his head and mumbling softly, as if it was so sad, so sad.

They followed the priest out of the church and into the warm air of the piazza, followed him across the cobblestones and down a narrow alley. Up a flight of steps to a large wooden door. The old priest knocked with his fist. *Honoria!* He shouted. *Honoria! Apra il portello!*

The old priest kept banging, but no one answered. A cat appeared and curled around his legs, and he swatted it aside with his foot in a very unpriestly fashion. *Honoria!*

Finally he tried the doorknob. My mother and Andrew exchanged a look. Dread filled my mother. She thought she might throw up. The priest pushed the door open, and not knowing what else to do, they followed him into the house, through a dark hall with crooked hanging pictures, and into a kitchen. By that time my mother said she was expecting anything. An empty room, another crazy ride to another strange place, the news of Dino's suicide.

But she did not expect what she saw. He was lying on a couch, an old blanket tucked around him, his mouth hanging open. The nearly deaf Honoria Maretta was setting down a tray of tea and cookies beside him. Dino woke up, propped himself against some pillows, and smiled before he saw the trio come down the hall. He was smiling because he saw what was on the tray. Honoria had made him pizzelles.

Chapter Seventeen

As I said, the desire to be near fame and greatness can do odd and amazing things to people. That night, all the good people of Sabbotino Grappa came out to feast the returning son that was never theirs. Mom and Andrew were greeted warmly, now that the villagers knew they were strangers to be welcomed rather than feared. It wasn't too often, after all, that they got visitors. Antonia Gillette, the baker's wife, set up a table in the piazza and everyone brought food. The forever squabbling Mrs. Salducci and Mrs. Latore, both old as time, brought *pinzimonio* and risotto, and broke into an argument about where to place their dishes. Peter, the baker, made focaccia, though his daughter had to carry the plate as she held her father's arm to help him walk. Francesca and Lutitia Bissola arrived, clutching each other for steadiness, chatting and arguing and kissing everyone in sight after they had a few glasses of the wine that Father Abrulla brought from the church. Even Karl Lager came, bringing pomegranates from his store, and bruised apricots and olives. Father Minelli was dead and gone, as was the reclusive Frank Piccola. Almost everyone else, Mom said, was over eighty. She wondered what would happen to the town when everyone was dead, wondered who would live there anymore. The youngest people there were Maria and Eli Manzoni, and they were older than Dino, though Pia and her brothers arrived by car, bringing grandchildren that hid under the table and feasted on Honoria's cookies.

My mother got to see the sunset of Sabbotino Grappa, watched the sun as it dropped down into the Tuscan valley. She breathed in the smell of lemons, of plumbagos. Sat on the stone steps of the church with a plate of *budino di mele* balanced on her knees. Listened to the joyful language she couldn't understand.

And Dino, who had only previously seen this place in a book when he was sixteen and crafting a past for himself for his first interview, lavished in the affection of his "home" and "family." The children put almonds in his pockets, and the old ladies and old men kissed his cheeks. He feasted and laughed. Told stories in Italian. Finally, he picked up the old violin that Mrs. Salducci brought, hopelessly out of tune, and tried to play *Lunetta* for the townspeople. The sound was too awful, and so he gave up *Lunetta*. He played "Ballo di Mattina" (Morning Dance), a Tuscan folk song, instead, and Karl Lager danced with Mrs. Latore, and the Bissola sisters waltzed in tiny, careful steps with each other, and the children spun themselves in circles, the colors of their clothing bright against that yellow stone.

No wonder, my mother thought then, that Edward Reynolds

had decided to respect the version of Dino's life that he had chosen. It was a good story, with wonderful characters, in a beautiful setting. It made everyone so happy. And if you could make a choice, then why not pick happiness?

Late that night, over wine in glass jars and a short, dripping candle in Honoria's kitchen, Dino told my mother that he would be staying in Sabbotino Grappa. We would have to join him if they were to stay together—he had too long been in that second-rate musical city, and he would be near enough to Rome to play there.

My mother told him then what she said she'd wanted to say for a long time. That she loved him and cared about him, but that they could not live together anymore. She would file for divorce when she returned home. He could live with a family that wasn't real, made up of lies and things unsaid, but she had already been doing that for too long. She had a choice, and she wanted to pick happiness too.

Dino, Honoria's boy, slept on her couch that night, and my mother and Andrew slept on the floor. In the morning, Eli Manzoni drove them to Rome. They stayed in the Grand Palace Hotel, ordered expensive room service. My mother had a bath. They flew out the next day from the Rome airport.

Here was the funny thing. Her baggage never made it home, and she didn't seem to mind.

"You didn't even bring anything back," I said to her. "Not even MY MOTHER WENT TO ITALY AND ALL I GOT WAS THIS LOUSY T-SHIRT."

"Shopping wasn't a priority."

"Did you think for a minute you might want to stay?"

"Not for a second. Not even a split second. Or a split of a split."

"Are you okay?"

"Exhausted, depleted, war weary. Shell-shocked. It's been a long four years."

"It all feels so strange. It's so quiet."

"I know," Mom said. "It's hard to realize that it's done. I've been trying so hard to get everything to fit for so long, but it never did. You keep trying and trying, but you're just killing yourself."

"You've been through a lot."

"We've been through a lot. I've known this was necessary for a long time. But it's not easy to do what you know you should, especially when he's *ill*. God, he was so sick."

I didn't say anything. Just let her talk. I was so glad he was gone. There was air in the house again. Like someone had died, and the body and the illness and the sickroom were now carted away.

"I mean, where should your empathy stop? Your own compassion does you in. Gets in the way of self-protection. You've got an in-love feeling, but the relationship is damaging. When do you stop calling it love?"

"Meanness is still meanness," I said. "It's not a disease."

"It's true. And I've also got you to look after, thank God. I know how this has been affecting you, and I'm sorry."

"Are you going to miss him?"

She thought about this. "I'm sure there will be things I'll miss. I mean, when it was good, it was great. Especially in the early days. I know it's hard for you to understand, but I loved him. I really did. And it was exciting, it really was, being part of his world." She rubbed her forehead as if trying to get the thoughts to order themselves. "Right now, everything just hurts. But I'm also just so *relieved*. Mostly what I can see is that relief."

"Me too."

"You know how just now you asked if I was okay? That's why we're not doing this anymore. A daughter shouldn't have to worry about her mother. That's backward and wrong. And we should both be okay. Yes, it hurts. To get divorced again . . . God. But that's exactly it. A home is where you're okay."

"I'm proud of you," I said.

"I'm proud of us." She held up the coffeepot she was holding. "Here's to lessons learned. Lightness. Peace. Tranquillity. Knowing mostly what the day will hold when you get up in the morning."

I grabbed the nearest thing, a flower vase. We clinked them together. We toasted to a new life.

Siang Chibo still followed me home.

"You know he's not here," I told her. We were at the beginning of my street. I watched Courtney's brothers let themselves in their house, saw the blue glow of the television a moment later. "Even his study is getting packed up."

"You're my friend," she said. "That's why I'm here."

"Okay."

"It doesn't matter to me, you know. What happened that night," she said. "You act as if that changes something."

I stopped before we went in. Slipped my backpack from my shoulder and set it on the walkway. "He let you down."

"Let me down? You've got to be kidding." Her *Indiana Jones Temple of Doom* boy voice grew even higher pitched. "Were you not there? Did you not hear *Lunetta*? Did you not hear *Amore Dolce Della Gioventù*? My father was sobbing."

Dog William was out on the front lawn. We watched him chew someone's tennis shoe. I don't know whose it was. I was hoping he didn't snitch it from Mr. Frederici's front porch.

"I would have thought the rest of the night might've thrown a little cold water on the evening."

"Look what he gave us. Remember his painting? *Wild Roses*. That music. Beauty that could not be tamed. It was magnificent. Unforgettable."

I thought about this. "Yeah. Unforgettable, all right. And roses have thorns."

"Oh, Cassie," Siang said. "I want to be your friend even if you don't seem to get things sometimes."

I watched Dog William. I wondered if we should change his name. I tried a few out.

"Marley," I called. "Hey, Marley!" Dog William didn't look up. "José. Here, José. Archie!"

He ignored me. Kept chewing that shoe.

"William!" I said, and Dog William popped his ugly little chin right in the air, looked at me as if slightly exasperated at being interrupted.

"He is who he is," Siang said.

Ian and I spent the rest of the year together. It was a peaceful time—Janet apologized to me, even made me some cookies, and, of course, Dino was gone. A happy, happy time. Ian left for Philadelphia in August. Janet could not bear to take him to the airport, so Chuck and Bunny drove, and Ian and I rode in the backseat. I couldn't keep the tears from rolling down my cheeks.

"I don't want any blubbering," Bunny said. But he kept blowing his nose and sniffing a lot. Trying to keep the tears back.

It was five o'clock in the morning, already warm and smelling good, the air feeling promising and full of new beginnings. It broke my heart. Ian kept squeezing my hand and looking at me as if trying to get my features deep into his memory.

"Cassie, I . . ." He choked.

"Okay, all of you," Chuck said. "We're never going to get through this." But his voice was wavery, too. "On the count of three, think happy thoughts. One, two, three. Clowns."

"Clowns are creepy," I said.

"Gumballs. Cartoons. The beach. A vacation," Chuck said.

"Real good, Chuck," Bunny said, and honked into his Kleenex again. "Vacation? Travel? Planes?"

"There's so much to say," Ian whispered.

"We're going to be seeing you," Bunny said. Now his voice was hoarse. It was hard to keep back emotion. It always kept pressing, pressing at the edges of you, even if you didn't want it to. "It's not like we're not going to be seeing you."

We took the exit for the airport. The sight of the big planes there, parked and waiting, made my stomach feel sick. The airport was such a wonderful and awful place. For every arrival there was someone on the other side, left behind.

Deb Caletti

The plan was to pull up to the curb, unload Ian's bags. We'd say good-bye there. We wouldn't prolong it.

Bunny fought the cars and the shuttle buses and taxis, eased into a spot at the airport curb. "Kid," he said. His eyes were full of tears now. He leaned over and hugged Ian hard. "I love you. You be good."

Ian hugged Chuck, too, who was having a hard time holding it together. "Puppies," Chuck squeaked. "Sno-Cones. Heineken."

"Good-bye, Chuck."

I stepped out onto the curb with Ian. He was not wearing his long coat, as it was August and it was packed for a Philadelphia winter, but he was carrying his violin case. He took his suitcase from the trunk and set it down by his feet.

"I love you," he said.

"I love you." I hugged him. We kissed for a while. And then we separated, and I watched his back disappear into the sliding doors. I just watched him go. And like that, he was gone.

"Thank you for showing me how," I whispered.

And then I got back into the car, and let Bunny hold me as I sobbed.

Maybe love, too, is beautiful because it has a wildness that cannot be tamed. I don't know. All I know is that passion can take you up like a house of cards in a tornado, leaving destruction in its wake. Or it can let you alone because you have built a stone wall against it, set out the armed guards to keep it from touching you. The real trick is to let it in, but to hold on. To understand that the heart is as vast and wide as the universe, but that we come to know it best from here, this place of gravity and stability, where our feet can still touch ground.

My mother's divorce from Dino was finalized by the end of the summer. For a while, Andrew Wilkowski phoned her to let her know how Dino was doing. His health was improving, his health was worsening, his health was improving. His music was going well, going badly, going well. So it went. Andrew Wilkowski finally stopped calling with his reports after the record company woman flew to Sabbotino Grappa to discuss Dino's contract and ended up staying.

My mother is calm and happy. She plays her cello with love, not loss. She struggles like hell financially, but she looks more like herself. Her eyes are soft and relaxed. She's been out on a few dates with a poet-slash-advertising executive, a member of the creatively sane. She took in Alice as a roommate, and that worked great until Alice decided to move in with the French horn player in the orchestra. Mom is looking for a new roommate, and in a Bunny brainstorm, is having coffee with Janet to talk over the possibility. I wonder what it would be like to live in the same house as Ian's mom. It would be nice to be close to him in this way, I think, and Dog William would be thrilled to have Rocket on a regular basis.

A few times when Alice was around, Dad came over for a bowl of jambalaya. They all sat around the table and ate and drank wine and played marathon games of Monopoly and made up the rules as they went along. And yes, it felt like family. It was just as you hoped it could be, where everyone decides they can still love and care for each other, married or not. Where everyone just *gets it together.* That's all you really want or need—the ability to love both of your parents, and for them to see that a changed family need not be a destroyed one. I hope that is enough for Dad, to have Mom as family, and I hope he comes over still if Janet moves in. I like the idea of the three of them at that table together.

And Ian. I saw him once, over Christmas, and it was perfect but brief. It is too expensive for him to fly home very much, and long-distance phone calls, too, are few. We write each other, e-mailing as often as we can. Soon he will be winning awards, performing, traveling. He will make the circuit, following the path to certain success, maybe even fame. When I look at my bear, floating in the globe, I try to see him as free rather than unanchored. I try to think good thoughts about his freedom. More than anything, I try to keep him from spinning out of control.

I don't know what will happen with Ian and me. What I do know is that when I close my eyes, it is him that I see. When I think of love, it is his name etched always in my mind. And it is his music that I hear. When the notes fill my head, I do not imagine anymore the lemon trees and curved streets of Sabbotino Grappa. I do not imagine old ladies smelling of salami and olive oil, or a child running on yellow cobblestones. No, now Ian's music is his own, and what I see is a winter forest of fir and cedar and evergreens. I see diamond flakes beginning to fall, landing on a joyful, upturned face, drifting to settle in my beloved's hair. I see poplar and spruce, solid and sure, covered in the softest, quietest white. The snow glitters like a sky filled with stars, like a galaxy on a planetarium ceiling.

The Nature of Jade

To Mom and Dad—my biggest fans,
as I am yours.

ACKNOWLEDGMENTS

Gratitude first to Ben Camardi and Jen Klonsky, as ever. My work is better because of you, but so is life in general.

Thanks as well to the superb folks and my happy family at Simon & Schuster, particularly Jennifer Zatorski, Jodie Cohen (woman of a thousand shoes), and Kimberly Lauber. Appreciation, too, to U.K. Scholastic and Amanda Punter. Love and admiration also go to my favorite local and not-so-local independent bookstores. Thank you for your continued and priceless support. Special thanks, as well, to the Washington Center for the Book and Eulalie and Carlo Scandiuzzi for their acknowledgment of my work.

I owe a debt of gratitude to the work of Frans de Waal, Jeffrey Moussaieff Masson, Cynthia Moss, and Jane Goodall, which helped me better understand evolutionary processes and the emotional lives of animals. Appreciation, too, to Dr. Jerry Kear, who provided essential information on therapeutic methods, along with just plain fascinating conversation.

Finally, love and gratefulness to my family, who are there through every bump and joy and storm of chaos. You are very patient people. And to Sam and Nick—as always—it is a privilege to be your mom.

Part One:

Sea Boy and Desert Girl

Chapter One

Humans may watch animals, but animals also watch humans. The Australian Lyrebird not only observes humans, but from its forest perch, imitates them, as well. It's been known to make the sound of trains, horns, motors, alarms, and even chainsaws . . .
—Dr. Jerome R. Clade, *The Fundamentals of Animal Behavior*

When you live one and a half blocks away from a zoo like I do, you can hear the baboons screeching after it gets dark. It can scare the crap out of you when you're not used to it, as I found out one night right after we moved in. I thought a woman was being strangled. I actually screamed, and my mom came running in my room and so did my dad, wearing these hideous boxers with Santas on them, which meant he'd gotten to the bottom of his underwear drawer. Even Oliver stumbled in, half asleep in his football pajamas, with his eyes squinched from the light my parents flicked on.

The conversation went something like this:

Dad: God, Jade. Zoo animals! *Baboons*, for Christ's sake.

Mom: I knew we should never have moved to the city.

Oliver (peering at Dad with a dazed expression): Isn't it August?

I was told once, though, that we really would have something to fear if there ever were a big earthquake, like they're always saying is going to happen at any moment here in Seattle. Then we'd be living in the most dangerous part of the city. See, all the electrical fences are, well, *electrical*, and so if the power went out for any length of time there'd be lions and tigers (and bears, oh my) running loose, panicked and hungry. You hear a lot of false facts around the zoo—you've got the husbands incorrectly correcting wives ("No, ha-ha. Only the *males* have tusks, honey"), and you've got those annoying eight-year-olds you can find at nearly any exhibit, who know entirely too much about mole rats, for example, and who can't wait for the chance to insert their superior knowledge into any overheard conversation ("Actually, those teeth are his incisors, and they're used for protection against his greatest enemy, the rufous-beaked snake"). But this bit of frightening trivia came from one of the Woodland Park zookeepers, so I knew it was true.

That's one of the reasons I have the live zoo webcam on in my room to begin with, and why I see the boy that day. I don't mean I keep it on to be on alert for disaster or anything like that, but because I find it calming to watch the elephants. I also take this medicine that sometimes revs me up a little at night, and they're good company when no one else is awake. Besides, elephants are just cool. They've got all the range of human emotion, from jealousy and love to rage and depression and playfulness. They have one-night stands and then kick the guy out. They get pissed off at their friends and relatives or the people who care for them, and hold a grudge until they get a sincere apology. They are there for each other during all the phases of their lives. A baby is born, and they help it into the world, trumpeting and stamping their feet in celebration. A family member dies, and they bury the body with sticks and then mourn with terrible cries, sometimes returning years later to revisit the bones and touch them lovingly with their trunks. They're just this group of normally abnormal creatures going through the ups and downs of life with big hearts, mood swings, and huge, swingy-assed togetherness.

When we moved into our brick townhouse in Hawthorne Square by the zoo during my first year of high school, I had this plan that I'd go there every day to watch the gorillas and take notes about their behavior. I'd notice things no one else had, make some amazing discovery. I had this romantic idea of being Diane Fossey/Jane Goodall/Joy Adamson. I liked the idea of bouncy, open-air Jeeps and I liked the outfits with all the pockets, only I didn't really want to live in Africa and be shot by poachers/ get malaria/get stabbed to death. Bars between gorillas and me sounded reasonable.

I went over to the zoo and brought this little foldout chair Dad used for all of Oliver's soccer and baseball and basketball games, and I sat and watched the gorillas a few times. The only problem was, it felt more like they were watching me. They gave me the creeps. The male was the worst. His name is Vip, which sounds like some breezy nickname a bunch of Ivy Leaguers might give their jock buddy, but Vip was more like those freaky men you see at the downtown bus stops. The ones who silently watch you walk past and whose eyes you can still feel on you a block later. Vip would hold this stalk of bark in his Naugahyde hand, chewing slowly, keeping his gaze firmly on me. I'd move, and just his eyes would follow me, same as those paintings in haunted-house movies. If that wasn't bad enough, Vip was also involved in a tempestuous love triangle. A while back, Vip got gorilla Amanda pregnant, and when she lost the baby, he ditched her for Jumoke. He got her pregnant too, and after Jumoke had the baby, Amanda went nuts and stole it and the authorities had to intervene. It was like a bad episode of *All My Primates*.

So I moved on to the elephants, and as soon as I saw Chai and baby Hansa and Bamboo and Tombi and Flora, I couldn't get enough of them. Baby Hansa's goofy fluff of hair is enough to hook you all by itself. They are all just so peaceful and funny that they get into your heart. When you look in their eyes, you see sweet thoughts. And then there's Onyx, too, of course. One notched ear, somber face. Always off by herself in a way that makes you feel sad for her.

I didn't even need the little soccer chair, because there's a nice bench right by the elephants. I went once a week for a few months, but after a while I got busy with school and it was winter, and so I decided to just watch them from home most of the time.

There are two live webcams for the elephants, one inside the elephant house and one in their outdoor environment, so even when the elephants were brought in at night, I could see them. Twenty-four hours a day, the cam is on, for the pachyderm obsessed. I got in the habit of just leaving the screen up when I wasn't using my computer to write a paper or to IM my friends. Now I switch back and forth between the cams so I can always see what's going on, even if the gang is just standing around sleeping.

I never did really write anything in my "research notebook" (how embarrassing—I even wrote that on the front); making some great discovery about elephant behavior kind of went in the big-ideas-that-fizzled-out department of my brain. But the elephants got to be a regular part of my life. Watching them isn't always thrilling and action packed, but I don't care. See, what I really like is that no matter what high-stress thing is going on in my world or in the world as a whole (Christmas, SATs, natural disasters, plane crashes, having to give a speech and being worried to death I might puke), there are the elephants, doing their thing. Just being themselves. Eating, walking around. They aren't having Christmas, or giving a speech, or stressing over horrible things in the news. They're just having another regular elephant day. Not worrying, only *being*.

That's why the elephant site is up on my computer right then, when I see the boy. I am stretched out on my bed and the elephants are cruising around on the screen, but I'm not even really watching them. My room's on the second floor of our townhouse, and if you lie there and look out the window, all you sce is sky—this square of glass filled with moving sky, like a cloud lava lamp. Sometimes it's pink and orange and purples, unreal colors, and other times it's backlit white cotton candy, and other times it's just a sea of slow-moving monochrome. I'm just lying there thinking lazy, hazy cloudlike thoughts when I sit up and the computer catches my eye. The outdoor cam is on, which includes a view of the elephants' sprawling natural habitat. Chai is there with baby Hansa, and they are both rooting around in a pile of hay. But what I see is a flash of color, red, and I stop, same as a fish stops at the flash of a lure underwater.

The red—it's a jacket. A boy's jacket. When the outdoor cam is on, you can see part of the viewing area, too, and the people walking through it. At first it's this great big voyeuristic thrill to realize you can see people who are right there, right then, people who are unaware that you're watching them from your bedroom. There's probably even some law that the zoo is breaking that they don't know about. But trust me, the people get boring soon enough. It's like when you read blogs and you get this snooping-in-diaries kind of rush, until you realize that all they talk about is how they should write more often. People's patterns of behavior are so predictable. At the zoo, they stay in front of the elephants for about twelve seconds, point to different things, take a photo, move on. The most excitement you get is some kid trying to climb over the fence or couples who are obviously arguing.

But this time, the red jacket compels me to watch. And I see this guy, and he has a baby in a backpack. The thing is, he's young. He can't be more than a year or two older than I am, although I'm pathetic at guessing age, height, and distance, and still can't grasp the how-many-quarts-in-a-liter type question, in spite of the fact that I'm usually a neurotic overachiever. So maybe he's not so young, but I'm sure he is. And that brings up a bunch of questions: Is he babysitting this kid? Is it his huge-age-difference brother? It can't be *his*, can it?

The boy turns sideways so that the baby can see the elephants better. Baby? Or would you call him a toddler? I can't tell— somewhere in between, maybe. The boy is talking to the baby, I can see. The baby looks happy. Here is what I notice. There is an ease between them, a calm, same as with zebras grazing in a herd, or swallows flying in a neat triangle. Nature has given them a rightness with each other.

My friend Hannah, who I've known since I first moved to Seattle, would say I am interested in the boy on the screen only because he's cute. Hannah, though, seemed to wake up one day late in junior year with a guy obsession so intense that it transformed her from this reasonable, sane person into a male-seeking missile. God, sorry if this is crude, but she had begun to remind me of those baboons that flaunt their red butts around when they're in heat. Talking to her lately, it goes like this:

Me: How did you do on the test? I couldn't think of anything to write on that second essay question.

Hannah: God, Jason Espanero is hot.

Me: I don't think it's fair to give an essay question based on a *footnote* no one even read.

Hannah: He must work out.

Me: I heard on the news that a fiery comet is about to crash into the earth and kill us all sometime this afternoon.

Hannah: He's just got the sweetest ass.

It *is* true that the guy on the screen's cute—tousled, curly brown hair, tall and thin, shy-looking—but that's not what keeps me watching. What keeps me there are the questions, his *story*. It's The Airport Game: Who are those people in those seats over there? Why are they going to San Francisco? Are they married? She's reading a poetry book, he's writing in a journal. Married literature professors? Writers? Weekend fling?

The boy doesn't take a photo and move on. Already, he is not following a predictable path. He stands there for a long time. The baby wears this blue cloth hat with a brim over his little blond head. The boy leans down over the rail, crosses his arms in front of himself. The baby likes this, pats the boy's head, though the boy is probably leaning only to relieve the weight of the backpack. The boy watches Hansa and Chai, and then Hansa wanders off. Still, he stands with his arms crossed, staring and thinking. What is on his mind? His too-youthful marriage? His nephew/brother on his back? The college courses he is taking in between the nanny job?

Finally, the boy stands straight again. Arches his back to stretch. I realize I have just done the same, as if I can feel the weight of that backpack. You pass a bunch of people in a day— people in their cars, in the grocery store, waiting for their coffee at an espresso stand. You look at apartment buildings and streets, the comings and goings, elevators crawling up and down, and each person has their own story going on right then, with its cast of characters; they've got their own frustrations and their happiness and the things they're looking forward to and dreading. And sometimes you wonder if you've crossed paths with any of them before without knowing it, or will one day cross their path again. But sometimes, too, you have this little feeling of knowing, this fuzzy, gnawing sense that someone will become a major something in your life. You just know that theirs will be a life you will enter and become part of. I feel that sense, that knowing, when I look at this boy and this baby. It is a sense of the significant.

He stands and the baby does something that makes me laugh. He grabs a chunk of the boy's hair in each of his hands, yanks the boy's head back. Man, that has to hurt. Oh, ouch. But the baby thinks it is a real crack-up, and starts to laugh. He puts his open mouth down to the boy's head in some baby version of a kiss.

The boy's head is tilted to the sky. He reaches his arms back and unclenches the baby's fingers from his hair. But once he is free, he keeps his chin pointed up, just keeps staring up above. He watches the backlit cotton candy clouds in a lava-lamp sky, and it is then I am sure this is a story I'll be part of.

Chapter Two

In the animal world, sisters are frequently caretakers. Wolf sisters become babysitters when their parents leave to find food. Sister acorn woodpeckers take care of their siblings from birth, even giving up their first year of adult freedom to stay behind in the nest and look after them . . .
—Dr. Jerome R. Clade, *The Fundamentals of Animal Behavior*

You are wondering about the medicine I take, so let's just get that part out of the way so you don't think I'm dying or something. I'm going to describe it logically, but there's really nothing logical about it. My illness is like instinct gone awry, and there's not too much sense you can make of that.

So, number one: When I was fourteen, my grandmother died. If you want to know the truth, she wasn't even a particularly nice person, which you can tell by the fact that we called her Grandmother Barbara and not the more cozy things you call the relatives you like, such as Granny, Nana, Grams, et cetera. Grandmother Barbara would give you horrible clothes for presents and then ask why you weren't wearing them the next time you saw her. She was impatient with Oliver when he was little, wore a nuclear cloud of perfume, and hugged like she wished she could do it without touching. Once I caught her snooping in my room during a visit, looking for evidence of my rampant sex life or my hidden stash of drugs and alcohol, I guess. God, I still wore Hello Kitty underwear at the time.

She was also the kind of relative that had a bizarre, inexplicable obsession about your romantic success. Starting somewhere around the age of five, up until the last visit I had with her, our conversations went like this:

Me: So, lately, school's been great and I've been getting straight A's and I'm the vice president of Key Club and a member of the Honor Society and do ten hours of community service a week and have discovered a cure for cancer and successfully surgically implanted the kidney of a guppy into a human and . . .

Grandmother Barbara: Do you have a boyfriend?

Still, she was my grandmother, and she was dead. She'd had a heart attack. She had been overcome with this shooting pain down her chest and arm—she told my father on the phone before he called the ambulance—and that was that. Alive; not alive. There was a funeral and this box she was supposedly in, this ground. Her body was there in the dirt, the same body that walked around and snooped in my stuff and stunk of Chanel.

See, it suddenly struck me that there was such a thing as dead, and all of the ways one could get dead. I'd wake up in the night and think about it and become so frightened at the idea that I wasn't going to be here one day that I could barely breathe.

Then, number two: A few months later, my parents went away on a trip. Hawaii. Second honeymoon, because they were fighting too much after it had been decided that we were moving from Sering Island, which Mom loved, to the city, which she already hated. She was pissed and he was trying to buy her good mood with a swim-up bar and a couple cans of macadamia nuts and "memories to last a lifetime." Or so the hotel brochure said.

My mom was nervous about leaving—she wrote pages of instructions for my aunt who was staying with us, and just before they left for the airport I caught Mom in the kitchen. She was holding a paper lunch bag up to her mouth.

"Mom?"

I startled her. The bag came down. "Jade," she said, as if I'd caught her at something.

"What are you doing?"

"Planes. I'm just. Having jitters. About. Flying. It's supposed to help. Breathing in a bag." She had gotten an electric starter-tan, but her face was pale. My dad walked in then.

"Nancy. We're going to be late."

"I'm coming."

"What are you *doing*?" Dad looked crisp, competent. He had a golf shirt on, tucked into khakis, a travel bag over his shoulder.

"Nothing," she said. She put the bag on the counter.

"Thousands of people fly every day," he said. "I, for one, don't want to miss the plane."

Hugs good-bye, off they went. My aunt looked slightly lost at first, clapped her hands together and said, "Well! Here we are!" with too much cheer and a dose of desperation. She's got that nervous thing around kids that childless people have. Like if they turn their backs, you're going to blow something up. And they're not sure quite what to say to you—either they ask what you're learning in school, or they talk about the economy.

The evening was going along fine. Aunt Beth made macaroni and cheese, with very little butter because she was on a diet, so it wasn't so great, but oh, well. We watched a video she brought over, some National Geographic thing about pyramids, which Oliver loved but I was about snoozing through. I decided to go to bed but I wanted to get a snack first, so I walked into the kitchen. I don't know what had been going on in my subconscious for the last few hours, but here's what happened:

I see the bag on the counter. It has my mother's lipstick around the edges. Something about that blown-up bag makes me think of those oxygen masks that pop down from the ceiling of airplanes. I think about those airplanes that crashed into the World Trade Center, the hijackers, and my parents on an airplane. I think of those people on that burning plane, and the ones jumping out of the buildings, and suddenly I get this sharpness in my chest, like my grandmother had, and I can't breathe. I literally can't catch my breath, and I feel like I'm in some really small box I've got to get out of or I'm gonna die, and there's no way out of the box.

I clutch the counter. I almost feel like I could throw up, because suddenly I'm hot and clammy and lightheaded. I can't really be dying, right? Fourteen-year-olds don't have heart attacks, but even though I'm telling myself this, my body isn't listening, because I need out of this box and there is no out and I'm *gonna die*.

I'm gasping and I don't even have enough air to cry out, same as the time in second grade when I landed hard on my back after falling off the jungle gym. I am aware, too aware, of my heartbeat, and then Oliver comes in. I'm panicking, shit, because I can't breathe, and Oliver must see this in my eyes and he goes and runs and gets Aunt Beth. I hear him call her name, but it's really far off, and I'm in this other world where there's only this fear and this pain in my chest and no air and this feeling of Need Out!

"Jade? Jade, are you choking?" Aunt Beth is there, and she takes hold of my shoulders and I don't want her to touch me, but on the other hand I want her to put her arms around me and make me breathe again. "Water," she says, and lets me go. "Get a glass of water, Oliver."

I am so cold and hot and clammy all at the same time, that pass-out feeling. But instead of passing out, I throw up. Right on the kitchen floor, and I'm sorry for the gory details. I hate throwing up. No one likes it, I know, but I detest it, and that feeling of choking is the worst. My heart is beating a million miles an hour, and I'm shaking and Aunt Beth gets me to the couch to sit down. The pyramid show is still going on, I remember that.

Oliver stands there looking worried and holding a glass of water.

"It was that macaroni and cheese," Aunt Beth says.

Only it wasn't.

Because it kept happening. Three years later, it still happens sometimes. The medicine helps it happen less. That week, though, I succeeded in doing two things—I convinced everyone that I was nuts, and I convinced Aunt Beth never to have children.

My parents came home early from their trip. My father seemed pissed, my mother, sort of relieved. They took me to a doctor, who found nothing wrong. They took me again and again, because I *knew* something was wrong. They kept saying I was fine, but, excuse me, I know when my own body isn't acting like it should. I *felt* the symptoms in my heart, my chest, this shortness of breath. Maybe it was a cardiac problem. I could have a hole in my heart or a murmur, whatever that was, or *something*. I know what I felt. And what I felt was a real, physical happening.

I only threw up that one time, but the other feelings kept coming, at night in bed, and in school—God, once right during PE. I held on to the gym wall feeling like I was going to pass out, sweat running down my face and the jocks staring at me and then going right on playing basketball. The male teacher (twit) thought I had cramps and sent me to the nurse's room. Ms. Sandstrom, she's the one who called my mom and told her I had what she thought was a panic attack. She said we should see a psychologist. Actually, she said this after about my sixth or seventh visit to the nurse's room. See, I kept avoiding the gym, in particular, because I thought it would keep happening there since it happened there once, so Ms. Sandstrom was seeing a lot of me. This same thing had happened to Ms. Sandstrom, she told me, when she first moved away from home and went to college. Panic disorder. Anxiety. She had her first attack in the campus dining hall and didn't go back there for five months.

I saw a psychologist, and then also a psychiatrist, who I only visit now if my medication seems messed up. I see the psychologist every two to four weeks, depending on how things are going. I really like the guy I have now, Abe, which is what I'm supposed to call him. His last name is Breakhart, so you can understand the first-name-basis insistence. For a guy that's supposed to be fixing people, it seems like a bad omen. The psychiatrist finally put me on medicine because these episodes were making my life hell. I was sure I was dying, only no one knew it yet except me. Nothing made sense. I tried to logic myself out of it, not to have the thoughts, but it wasn't like it was always thoughts = attack anyway. Sometimes it was more like attack = thoughts. Once I had attacks, I started worrying about getting more. After I had the first episode, I started listening hyper-carefully to see if it was going to happen again. Was my chest tight? Did I feel short of breath? Could I feel my heart beating? Was I about to lose all control in public? Was I going to die after all, and were all those people who said I wasn't going to feel horrible that they were wrong? Your body does all kinds of things that are disturbing when you start really paying attention, believe me.

And I had no idea when it might kick into gear. It wasn't like I panicked every time I was somewhere high up, or in an enclosed space, or during a storm. It could be none of those things, or all of them. I could (*can*) panic in a car, a new situation, any time a person feels a twinge of nerves. It's a twisted version of *Green*

Eggs and Ham: I could panic in a train! I could panic on a plane! I could panic on the stairs—I could panic anywhere!

I didn't even want to go to school, because what if it happened there again? In class or something, when we were taking a test? How many cramps can you have? What if I threw up during an assembly, with the whole school there? People who have these panic attacks sometimes have "social anxiety," which means, basically, you don't want to go out in the world. But I think sometimes they've got their cause and effect screwed up. Would you want to get on a bus if you thought your body might do this? Would you want to be in a crowd of people? Sitting in math? That kind of fear, that kind of physical out-of-control is . . . well, private.

Anyway, I am not my illness. "Girl with Anxiety," "Trauma of the Week"—no. I hate stuff like that. Everyone, *everyone*, has their issue. But the one thing my illness did make me realize is how necessary it is to ignore the dangers of living in order to live. And how much trouble you can get into if you can't. We all have to get up every morning and go outside and pretend we aren't going to die. We've got to get totally involved with what we're going to wear that day, and how pissed we are that another car cut us off, and how we wish we were in better shape, so we don't have to think about how little any of that really matters. Or so we don't think about how we're just vulnerable specks trying to survive on a violent, tumultuous planet, at the mercy of hurricanes and volcanoes and asteroids and terrorists and disease and a million other things. We concentrate on having little thoughts so we don't have BIG THOUGHTS. It's like those days when you've got a really bad pimple but you still have to go to school. You've got to convince yourself it's not so bad just so you can leave the house and actually talk to people face-to-face. You've got to ignore the one big truth—life is fatal.

I hurry home after school the day after I see the red-jacket boy. I want to see if he and the baby will reappear. I drop my backpack at the foot of the stairs as I come in, head up to my room.

"Jade?" Mom calls from upstairs. She's in her bathroom, I'm guessing, judging by the muffled sound of her voice.

"Yeah, it's me."

"How was school?"

"Fine."

"The day went all right?"

"Uh-huh."

"I got my dress for homecoming," she says.

Yeah, you read that right.

My mom has gone to more homecomings than I have—four for four. I went once, with one of my best friends, Michael Jacobs, during a time we thought we liked each other more than friends but didn't really. As vice president of the PTSA, my mother chaperones the dances, which means she goes when I don't. I swear, she's got more pictures taken in front of phony sunsets and palm trees and fake porches than I do (with Mr. Robinson, my math teacher; Mitch Greenbaum, Booster Club president; Mr. Swenson, PE, etc.), more corsages pressed between pages of our *Webster's* dictionary, more shoes dyed to odd colors. She's involved in every other committee and program my school has too, from fund-raising to tree planting to graduation ceremonies to teacher appreciation days. Most irritating is The Walkabout Program, where "concerned parents" walk the school hallways in between classes to promote safety and good behavior, i.e., to spy. They even wear badges around their necks that read SAS—Safety for All Students. One time, some kid got into the badge drawer with a Magic Marker and swapped all the first and second letters, giving you an idea of how appreciated the program is.

Don't get me wrong. I love my mother, and I feel bad having these mean thoughts. Because Mom, she's one of the few people I can really talk to, who understands me. Sometimes she knows what I'm feeling before I even realize it. And we have a great time together. We make fun of the really bad clothes in the discount stores, and put ugly and embarrassing things into each other's carts when the other person's not looking. We tell each other about good books and talk each other into ordering a milk shake with our cheeseburger. But sometimes it just feels like she's this barnacle we learned about in biology. It discards its own body to live inside of a crab (read: *me*), growing and spreading until it finally takes over the crab's body, stealing its life, reaching its tentacles everywhere, even around its eyes. Well, you get the idea.

"Wanna see?" Mom calls.

"In a sec," I say.

I want to get to my computer. I want to be there if the red-jacket boy happens to come back. I knock on my doorframe three times, which is just this thing I like to do for good luck, then I go in. I log on, and sit down. Then there's a knock at my door.

"What do you think of the color?" Mom asks. Rose-colored

taffeta, no sleeves, sash around the middle. The dress actually swishes as she walks. "With the right bra . . ."

"It's real nice, Mom." It screams homecoming. Or bridesmaid.

"You don't like it."

"Not for myself, but it's great on you."

She checks herself out in the mirror on the back of my door. She lifts her blond hair up in the back, even though there's not much to lift. She tilts her chin, sucks in her stomach. Something about this makes me sad, the way women with eighties-style permed hair make me sad. The way old ladies in short-shorts make me sad.

"I think it makes me look slimmer," she says. She's always worrying about this—pretty needlessly, because she's average weight. Still, we've got low-fat and "lite" everything, and tons of those magazines with articles like "Swimsuits That Flatter Every Figure" and "Five Minutes a Day to a Tight Tummy." It makes you realize how basically everything we do comes down to a) mating or b) competing for resources. It's just like *Animal Planet*, only we've got Cover Girl and Victoria's Secret instead of colored feathers and fancy markings, and the violence occurs at the Nordstrom's Half-Yearly Sale.

"You don't have to look slimmer. You're fine."

"God, I'm just glad for fabric with spandex. Just shove in the jiggly parts and zip. Are these considered unhealthy weight issues that'll make your daughter turn anorexic?"

"Nah," I said. "I think they're completely normally abnormal. Besides, you know how I hate throwing up."

"Okay, whew. I can chalk that off my list of concerns."

"Yeah, stick to worrying about me robbing banks."

"Or your drug dealing. I've been thinking that it's something you should quit. I know you like the money, honey, but it's just not right."

I laugh. "You're not going to make me give *that* up." I faux-groan. This is my favorite version of Mom. The relaxed, watch-romantic-movies-together Mom. The let's-stay-in-our-p.j.'s-all-day Mom.

But suddenly she takes a sharp left turn into the version I'm not so thrilled with. The I-want-more-for-you Mom. I hear it in her voice, which goes up a few octaves. "So? How was school today?" she asks.

"Fine. I told you." I'm trying to keep the edge off of my words, but it's creeping in anyway. "And, no, no one asked me to home-coming."

"Jade. Jeez. I didn't say anything."

But I know it's what she's really asking. It's in the way she says "So?" As if it can unlock a secret.

"Are you getting your period?" She narrows her eyes.

"No! God. I hate that. I hate when every negative act is blamed on your period." Sometimes bitchiness is just bitchiness, happily unattached to anything hormonal. It should get full credit.

"I'm sorry. I hate that too. It's just . . . You. I want you to have a great year," Mom says.

"I don't even *want* to go to homecoming. And no, it's not because of anxiety." We'd been mother and daughter long enough that I hear *that* in her voice too. When you've got a situation like mine, people are always looking at you sideways, trying to figure out what's you and what's the illness, as if there's some distinct line down the center of my body they should see but don't. "It's because of people dancing like they're having sex while you're trying not to feel weird about it and everyone all made up and phoniness and because somewhere inside you're always wishing you were home, eating popcorn and watching TV." In my opinion, dances like that are one of those painful things we all pretend are fun but really aren't.

Mom sighs. Her dress rustles. "I hear you. I do. Wait, what am I saying? I never even *went* to a dance when I was your age. But your *senior year*. It should be fun. It should be one of the happiest in your life."

"You always tell me how much you hated your senior year," I say.

"I hated *all* of high school," she admits. "I was so glad to get to college, I cannot tell you. Let's just say, I was a late bloomer. College, now, that was a good time. College, I was good at. I had friends, went to parties, got good grades—the whole thing. But high school. Oh, my God."

"Ha-ha. You ate lunch in the *library*."

"Don't remind me. Not that there's anything wrong with the library."

"*I* don't eat lunch in the library. I'm happy," I say. "Look." I put on a huge, toothy smile. Wiggle my index fingers in the air. "See? Yay, happiness is flowing throughout me."

Mom smiles. "You goof."

"Happy happy, joy joy. Three cheers for late bloomers."

"What do you keep looking at? It feels like you, me, and your computer are having this conversation."

"Nothing." I focus on her. "Just elephants."

"All right. Okay. I'm going to go change." She says this reluctantly, as if getting back into her jeans will change everything back, coach to pumpkin, glass slippers to the big yellow Donald Duck ones we gave her for her birthday and I think she actually hated.

I'm glad when Mom leaves, because I don't want to miss that red jacket. I was so sure he'd be back that I'm bummed when I finally realize I must be wrong. No boy. No anyone, except for the Indian man in charge of the elephants.

I try to do homework—Advanced Placement American Government, Advanced Placement English, calculus, Spanish, and biology, which shows why I barely have a life. It's hard to concentrate, though. I keep peeking up, still holding out impossible hope for the nonexistent red jacket.

Another knock—Oliver, this time. You wouldn't believe how many years it took to train that kid to knock. He's ten years old, so minus one before he could walk—nine years. See, I'm not in calculus for nothing.

"What?" I say, and he comes in. I bust up when he comes through the door. I could never quite get over the sight of Oliver in a football uniform. Oliver's kind of small for his age, and he has this narrow face and thoughtful, pointy chin. His hair is a soft blond like Mom's, where mine is black like Dad's. He looks too sweet for football. He *is* too sweet for football. That's why he's coming to see me.

"Don't laugh," he says. "I hate it. Help me." He holds his helmet under one beefed-up arm, just like you see the real football guys do. He waddles over, sits on my bed.

"Talk to him. Tell him how much you can't stand it." Him, meaning Dad. My father, Bruce DeLuna, is a financial officer for Eddie Bauer, and a bit sports obsessed. To him, there's nothing that can't be cured by a brisk jog or vigorous game of touch football, even anxiety. He had this whole "cure" mapped out for me once, which actually included calisthenics. Dad's the kind of person who thinks he knows "what is what" and how exactly things should be, which means he misses the point about most everything. I've gotten him off my back, though, mainly by using his narrow-minded female stereotyping to my benefit. Shameless, but it's a survival tactic. See, I'm a *girl* (the "just" hovers somewhere nearby in his mind, you can tell), and even though he constantly reminds me that I should be doing my "cardio," he lets me off the hook on the team-sports thing. He tried me in softball for a while, but I'm one of those wusses that flinch when a baseball flies at my face. A ball hit me in the leg once, and after that, all I could do was crouch and hover and wonder when it was going to happen again. I'm sorry, it's not my idea of a good time to stand alone while someone pelts a hard object my way, with basically only a stick and my bad hand-eye coordination for protection.

I know I'm making Dad sound like a dad stereotype, but it's how he is. He loves sports and understands sports, and I see him as viewing the world in this sports-themed way—win/lose, right/wrong, yes/no. The garage needs cleaning: yes. I should buy you your own car: no. You can slack off on your grades every now and then: wrong. Sports are a good idea for girls and mandatory for boys: right.

So I can get off the athletic hook, but Oliver, who is a *guy*, can't. Even if he hates sports and just wants to play his viola and read his Narnia books, he's constantly signed up for soccer, basketball, Little League, and even the Lil' Dragons karate course in town. I swear, the kid has so many uniforms, I don't remember the last time I saw him in regular clothes.

"You know talking to him doesn't do any good."

"'Being accountable to a team builds character.'" One of Dad's expressions.

"I hate it."

"'There's no "I" in *team*.'"

"These other guys—they're *machines*."

"'Sports are good practice for life. You've got to be able to hang tough.'"

"Please, Jade." He's almost crying. I can see fat tears gathering in the corners of his eyes. "He's going to be home any minute to take me to practice. It's so stupid. Guys smashing into each other, shoving each other down. What's the *point*? The coach calls us men. 'Okay, men, in formation.' We know we're not men. And why? Why are we doing it? I've got *homework*."

"'A good athlete makes time for work and sport.'"

"Please. I can't do this. I can't." A tear releases itself, slides down his nose. "What can I do?"

My brother was born when I was seven. I was old enough that I can still remember him as a baby, with his tiny toes like corn kernels and chubby wrists with lines around them, as if a rubber band had been placed there too tightly. Ever since he first grasped my finger and held on (a reflex, I was told, but who cares), I felt a responsibility toward him. He was my brother, which meant I both loved him and wanted to kill him often, but that there was no way I'd ever let anyone else lay a finger on him. "Okay, Oliver. Let me think."

"Hurry."

"Okay, okay." Broken arm, broken leg—too drastic. Run away? Nah, he'd have to come home sometime.

"Help me, Jade."

Sick. Yeah. Really sick. Undeniably sick. "Meet me in the bathroom."

"He's gonna be here in five minutes."

"Just meet me there."

I hop off my bed, tromp downstairs to the kitchen. Root around in the fridge. Even if we don't have any, I can whip up a batch with some catsup and mayo. But, no, the phony-illness gods are with me. There, behind the milk and the jam and the single dill pickle floating in a huge jar of green juice, is the Thousand Island dressing.

I head up the stairs, and halfway up, I hear the garage door rising. Dad is never late when it comes to taking Oliver to sports practice. Once, I had to drive Oliver to soccer, was ten minutes late, and learned that there had apparently been a misprint in the Bible on the Ten Commandments thing: Thou shalt not murder, thou shalt not commit adultery, thou shalt not be late to soccer. My father was so pissed, I practically had to get the lightning bolt surgically removed from my back.

I shut the bathroom door behind us. Oliver rises from where he was perched on the edge of the tub, the shower curtain a plastic ocean behind him. "You're going to have to do some groaning, look bad," I say as I unscrew the cap.

"Okay."

I squirt a blob of the dressing down the front of the football uniform. Smear it around. Perfect.

"Oh, gross, it looks like I threw up."

"That's the idea, Tiger."

"It looks so real," Oliver says.

"Smush your bangs up with some hot water. But get a move on. He's coming. Call out for Mom. You're so sick, remember? *Bleh.*" I hurry. Screw the cap back on. Hide the dressing bottle in a towel.

"You're a genius, Jade," he says.

I smile. Feel a rush of sisterly competence and good will. It makes me happy to help him. He's my brother, after all, and I love the little guy. It's important I stick by him. Your sibling, after all, is the only other person in the world who understands how fucked up your parents made you.

Dad is ticked off that night, you can tell, probably because he got off work early for football practice for nothing. His dark eyes look as flat and hard as asphalt, his jaw line stone. Even his black hair looks angry, if that's possible. It's like he knows he can't get mad at a sick child, so the anger just simmers around in there and presses from the inside out, making his face tight and his footsteps heavy on the stairs after dinner. He stays in the basement all evening, working on his train set, something he's been building for a couple of years now, since we moved to Seattle. He's got a mountain with a tunnel and the start of a town, and a place for a river sketched out on the big board that's the base. His own world. He can move mountains, and no one complains. If he goes downstairs, you don't bother him, or rather, it's just pointless to try. The conversation goes something like this:

Me: Hi, Dad.

Dad: Hi.

Me: How's it going?

Dad: Good.

Me: I got a ninety-six on my calculus test.

Dad: Oh, mmhmm. Great. Can you hand me that glue bottle over there?

Me: I also built a bomb in a Coke can and set it off in the cafeteria during lunch.

Dad: Oh, super.

So we leave him alone there, and it's my personal opinion that he's immersed in the project just to get away from us anyway. I love my dad. And he's not always a father stereotype—sports fanatic, go-to-work-then-come-home-and-disappear. Sometimes he just cracks me up when he's really relaxed and he is laughing so hard at his own jokes. He's a lot of fun when he goes off his healthy eating regimen and buys a big bag of Doritos that we munch happily, our fingers orange and salty. He's an incredible basketball player, even if he's just average height, and makes the best fried chicken I've ever eaten, even if it's the only thing he cooks. And I really like it when he watches dog shows on TV and talks to our dog, Milo. Milo's a beagle and is a bit on the insecure side. He always walks around with his blankie in his mouth. It's like he's perpetually lovelorn, without the love part. Cover boy for Dogs Who Love Too Much. But Dad tries to boost his self-esteem. He'll watch the parading boxers and terriers combed to perfection and he'll scruff Milo under his chin and around his floppy ears and tell him what a good-looking dog he is, even if he's a bit overweight. How he is the best dog, and if there were ever a dog show around here, there wouldn't even be a contest. All the other dogs would just have to go home.

And Dad wasn't always . . . missing in action. He used to come home when we were little and we'd all ride bikes together or he'd play board games or we'd roughhouse. Lately, though, I have the feeling he's been taking single pieces of himself out of the house, one at a time. One, and then another, and another, until all of a sudden, you notice he's not there anymore. Sure, he's busy—he gets up in the morning, goes to the gym or for a run before he heads off to work, and then after work, he plays basketball a few evenings or stays late at his office or goes downstairs to do some more building on the train. But he's most missing when he's right there having dinner with us, or when we're all driving in the car together, or watching TV. When you have a conversation with him, it's less like he's listening than he's being quiet while you talk. His eyes are looking your way, but he's not really with you. It makes me wonder if his absence is really just concealed disappointment. I get this feeling that he's lived by all these rules all his life and tried to get us to live by them too, just like he was supposed to, but now it's turned out to be something of a letdown. As if he'd followed step-by-step instructions on how to build an entertainment center and ended up with a nightstand instead.

The bad part about my Oliver-saving plan is that Oliver doesn't get dinner—his stomach needs to settle, according to Mom, so all he has is ginger ale and a couple of saltines. After we eat, I bring him up some confiscated slices of that thin, rubbery orange cheese wrapped in cellophane, a couple of peanut-butter granola bars, and a banana. He is sitting up in bed, looking as happy as a released prisoner. He's reading *The Narnia Fact Book* by the light of the clip-on lamp attached to his headboard. A shelf of trophies (for participation, not skill) is directly opposite him, the frozen figures packed tight and looking on the verge of a golden war, with their upraised arms and kicking feet and swinging bats.

Oliver thanks me for the food, folds a piece of shiny cheese into his mouth. "What was Lucy's gift from Father Christmas?" he asks.

"Days-of-the-week underwear."

"Come on, Sis."

"Okay. Magic potion."

"Close."

"Magic dust."

"No. Flask of Healing."

"Sounds handy. Okay. I've got to go finish my homework."

"Who was the 'sea girl'?"

"Oliver, I've got a ton of math."

"'Sea girl,'" he reads. "'An undersea girl in *Voyage of the Dawn Treader* that Lucy sees as the ship passes. They become friends, just by meeting eyes, though their worlds cannot meet.'"

I shut the door behind me. I pass Mom and Dad's room, see Mom sitting on her bed in her sweats, watching a travel show on television, small squares of construction paper around her. Everything in the room matches—floral duvet, matching floral bed skirt and valance above the window. It's take-no-chances decorating.

"Jade! Come here for a sec."

I pop my head into the room.

"Invitations for the principal's tea next week. What do you think?" Blue on yellow, green on blue, yellow on green, green on yellow. *Come meet Mr. Hunter, your principle pal at Ballard High!* It's funny how we've developed tool-making skills over billions of years only to use them for invitations for teas and wrapping Christmas presents and folding napkins into swans.

"I like the green on blue," I say. I'm used to these decisions. Valentine faculty parties and mother-daughter teas and graduation cruises. I've seen more invitations than the White House mailman.

"Really? It seems a little dark. I was thinking maybe yellow on blue."

"Sure."

"That'd be zingier. Is that a word? More zingy."

"Uh-huh." I remind myself a little of Dad right then. The travel show is visiting some amazing beach with beautiful, clear water and women in tiny bathing suits walking on the sand. "Where's this?" I ask.

"I've lost track. Australia?"

It doesn't look like Australia, but oh, well. I watch for a minute.

"You should have seen the pool they just showed. Wow. Water slides, swim-up bars, a lagoon."

"You should go. You and Dad."

"Australia's got *sharks*. You can't even swim in the ocean. No, thanks."

"Then don't go in the ocean. Just tan by the pool and sip drinks with umbrellas in them. Or go to London." We'd heard the story a thousand times about how she'd planned to live in London for a year with a bunch of her girlfriends after they all got their business degrees, but how she'd married Dad straight out of college instead.

"Jade, all *right*. If I want to go, I'll go, okay?" Her voice prickles. And I guess I understand. It's a role reversal from her wanting me to go to the dance. Mom sighs, looks down at the paper in her hands. It's the way I sometimes catch her looking out of the window. As if she's staring somewhere way beyond, to a place I can't see. "I'm sorry I snapped," she says. "I guess . . . It just makes me feel you expect more of me, and I already expect more of me enough for the both of us."

"Man, we're hard on ourselves," I say.

"You're so right," she says. "Let's make it a way-after-New-Year's resolution not to be."

"Deal," I say.

She sets the invitations on the bed. Looks at them a long while. "Yeah, yellow on blue," she says finally.

I tap my doorframe three times, same as always, and go into my room. I let myself be swallowed up in the comfort of my deep blue walls, the warm light of my paper lanterns, and my patron saint candles (long glass cylinders decorated with pictures of saints, lit when you feel in need of a little protection and good luck) on top of my dresser. It occurs to me, then: four people, four different rooms. We are in our own cages, unlike the elephants, who stay all together in their adopted family.

I do a mind-blowing two hours on calculus and another brain-frying hour on research notes on Faulkner. I spend forty minutes on essays for my college applications. I spend ten minutes online talking to Michael Jacobs about how much work we have to do. I spend five minutes thinking of things I could do if I weren't such a freaking overachiever. I could read something without a theme. I could paint my fingernails. I could make an igloo out of sugar cubes.

All the while I keep checking out the computer screen, hoping the guy in the red jacket will appear but knowing it is too late, past the hours the zoo is even open, for God's sake. I'm just so disappointed at how he hadn't come when I'd been so sure he'd be back. It was one of those times you feel a sense of loss, even though you didn't have something in the first place. I guess that's what disappointment is—a sense of loss for something you never had.

Dad is still in the basement, Oliver is asleep, Milo is cuddled with his blankie, and Mom's light is off when I go to bed.

I shut off my own light, prop up on one arm. The moon is almost full, bright and round in my window, illuminating the blue-black clouds hanging around while deciding on a direction. The computer screen glows an eerie greenish gray. The image on my desk is of an empty viewing area, a still, dark night. Only the trees sway a bit; that is the only movement, until I see the bulk of a figure enter the bottom corner of the screen.

I sit up in bed, get up, and bend down over the computer. Yes. It's true. A figure is there. I can only see shoulders—the night zookeeper, maybe? A watchman of some kind? At night I usually switch to the elephant house, where they sleep, so it's possible this is routine. That's what my front-stage mind is saying. My backstage mind is thinking something else. Accelerating just a small bit with crazy-but-maybe possibility.

I send the figure a mental request: *Turn around! Let me see you!* If he turns around, I will know if it is the boy. Maybe if he looks toward the camera our eyes will meet, him a sea boy, same as Oliver's sea girl. Our eyes will meet from different worlds and still we'll connect. Two points in need of a line.

The figure goes to the rail, leans over, and rests on his elbows. This is not what a watchman would do. Not what anyone who worked there would do. It is a visitor's pose, so whoever it is had snuck in. The man does not have a baby in a backpack, and it is too dark to see a jacket color. But he just leans there for a long time, gazing into the darkness of the elephant pen.

It is when he leans back, tilts his head up to the moonlit clouds, that I know it is him. It is that same profile, full of questions, full of thought. My heart *ba-bamps* in my chest. I feel this surge of happy. My inside voice too often screams unreliable things at me, misinformation—that I am in danger, that someone I love is in danger, that now is the time to panic, to flee. I am happy, because it is just so good to know that it can give a whispered message, a simple, quiet knowing, and that it can be right.

Chapter Three

Animals have anxiety. Primates will pluck their hairs or injure themselves in times of stress. Dogs are also very vulnerable. They are pack animals, and rely on the others in their pack for a feeling of safety. Separation and death are innately intertwined. When they are left alone, without their human "pack" some dogs become anxious that their owner may never return. They bark, chew, urinate, or try to escape by scratching. If left alone frequently or for long periods, some become ill, in a form of depression . . .

—Dr. Jerome R. Clade, *The Fundamentals of Animal Behavior*

Jenna's the only one of my friends with her own car, so she's the designated driver to take us to Starbucks for lunch. As seniors, we can go off campus to eat, and so we all leave, because no one wants to sit in the cafeteria that smells like gravy and tuna fish and cut apples turning brown when you don't have to. Plus, that's when Mom and the other "concerned parents" (read: *bored PTA mothers*) roam around and see which kids were raised badly so they have something to talk to each other about. I know how mean this makes me sound, and I'll probably be either unable to have children of my own or end up roaming the cafeteria myself one day for saying so, but you'll notice that none of the parents of the kids who really need spying on are ever part of these things.

The first time I drove with one of my friends, my chest got so tight and my palms so sweaty that I thought for sure I was going to have an attack. I had to crack the window and ride like one of those dogs with his nose stuck out, even though it was January and freezing. It was nuts at first, because I kept thinking of all those teen driving accidents you see on the news, where there's this really handsome guy in his football uniform and crying girls interviewed by news reporters saying how he was the nicest person. I had to increase my exposure to the whole situation bit by bit, like Abe, my psychologist, has said, and that worked for the most part. I had to remember to breathe from my diaphragm and not my chest (hyperventilation causes a lot of the symptoms of anxiety), and I had to tell myself (a zillion times) that what I was feeling was not dangerous, just a nuisance. A problem I was making, not a real one. Restructure my thoughts. I still bring my cough drops along on the ride, because I find that if I've got a really strong flavor in my mouth, it helps me keep both my front-stage and my backstage mind off of plotting any ambush. I don't know why it works, but it does. Plus, it keeps my breath fresh.

Anyway, I don't mind driving with Jenna too much because she's a careful driver, and she's also got this cross hanging from her rearview mirror. I'm not a hugely religious person—the members of my family are Christmas Eve Catholics—but the cross does make you think that maybe this gives you a few safety points. Probably like if you saw a sweet old lady reading a Bible on an airplane you're on, you'd feel a tiny bit better about flying—that kind of thing. God couldn't kill her off, right? They say religion is about love, but you wonder how much of it really is about fear.

"Do you realize how many calories are in those butterscotch bars?" Hannah asks me. I've got a small brown bag in one hand, a cup of chai tea in the other. We settle into a table surrounded by coffee mugs and espresso machines for sale. Today it's me, Michael, Jenna, Hannah, and Akello, this friend of Michael's from Uganda who hangs out with us sometimes.

"Frappuccinos have more calories than a Big Mac," I say as Hannah sips hers. I don't particularly care how many calories it has, anyway. I love those butterscotch things, and besides, I'm too skinny. My mom says it's nervous energy, and I'm thinking she's right. I've probably burnt the calories I've set down on the table just by worrying about the grade I'm going to get on the Faulkner paper I've just turned in.

We pull a couple of chairs over so everyone can sit. Michael's been reading my mind. "That Faulkner paper killed me. I was up till two in the morning doing the citations."

"Like you won't get an A," Hannah says.

"What's that supposed to mean?" Michael says.

"Michael, have you ever *not* gotten an A?"

"Yes," he says, a guilty yes that really means no. He probably hasn't, but so what. "Some of us want to get into a good college. Some of us want to go to med school and become doctors and not just meet some guy and have sex." He's noticed about Hannah too.

"Some of us actually want to have a social life. You've been more intimate with your laptop than an actual female."

"I don't own a laptop," Michael says.

"For God's sake, you'll still be a successful adult one day if you get an A minus," Hannah says.

"Please," Jenna says. "Don't."

"What?" Hannah says. "He's getting obsessed. He started his American Government project practically before the teacher finished handing out the worksheets. We had two weeks to do it. He's like the teacher's pet in the Kiss-Ass School of Life."

Michael looks murderous.

"Not that," Jenna says.

"What?"

"For blank's sake. I wish you wouldn't say that."

"What?" Hannah says. She squinches up her face.

"Who's blank?" Akello says, twisting open the cap from his juice bottle.

"You know. What you just said. 'For blank's sake.' Taking the Lord's name in vain."

"Oh, fuck," Hannah laughs. "You're kidding me."

"It's offensive."

"You're kidding me," Hannah says again.

"Maybe we should change the subject," I offer.

"Yeah. Back off, Hannah," Michael says.

"Me? God," she says.

"Hannah!" Jenna says.

"What? Jeez. I'm sorry! I can't help it! I say 'God' all the time. You never had a problem with me saying 'God' before. I don't think it makes me a bad person."

"It's sacrilegious. You just shouldn't do it," Jenna says.

"Like, 'Thou shalt not fight in Starbucks,'" Akello says. I'm beginning to like him.

"Oh, for Christ's sake."

"That's enough," Jenna says. "That's it." She shoves back her chair. Gets up, slams her balled-up napkin into the garbage can, and walks out.

"Great," Michael says. "That's our ride. If I'm late to physics, Mr. Geurnley's gonna kill me."

"She's gotten psycho lately with the whole Christian thing," Hannah says. "Shit, it's annoying." She's right, really. Jenna had gone from this really cool, fun person to someone who wouldn't listen to rock music. We went together to my first concert, an alternative band that played at the Sit 'n Spin, the Laundromat–concert place downtown. Two years ago, she'd had the side of her nose pierced, and that's gone too, ever since she started going to this Bible study group at the end of last year.

Then again, my group of best friends, these people sitting around this tiny round table who are now realizing we'll have to walk back to school, these people I'd done every memorable thing with over the last three years, have all gotten a bit extreme. It is true, Michael is grade obsessed—he even has one of those shower curtains at home decorated with the vocab words and definitions that most often appear on the SATs. And Hannah is so guy magnetized that I even saw her flirt with Jake Gillette the other day, who's this seventh-grader who comes over from the middle school to be part of my calculus class. He's about four-foot-seven and sixty-eight pounds, and rides over on his skateboard that has a parachute attached to the back. The other day, Jake raised his hand to answer a problem, and then gave an answer to which Ms. Arnold responded, "Uh, these guys don't know about that yet. Let's hear from someone who doesn't know as much."

Akello starts reading a newspaper. He is bored with us. I can't blame him. I'm bored with us too.

"I don't think it was very Christian to leave us stranded here," Hannah says.

"It's your fault. If I get marked down, I'm blaming you," Michael says.

"I thought she was Buddhist," Hannah says.

"Just because she's Asian, doesn't mean she's Buddhist," Michael says.

"Yeah, just because I'm Italian, doesn't mean I'm in the mob," I say.

"I'm not in a tribe, but at the moment, it sounds kinda nice," Akello says.

Michael tilts his head back, drinks the last of his coffee. "We'd better get walking. Next time you piss off my ride, you can pay for a cab," he says to Hannah. He crushes the paper cup in a manly fashion, causing the plastic lid to pop off and go flying onto the floor. After he retrieves it under the table of two businesswomen, we walk outside.

"Did you get their shoe size?" Akello says.

"Shut up," Michael says.

I realize it's cool, suddenly, almost seriously chilly, and I'm in a T-shirt. Fall is like that. It's the only season that sneaks up on you. Every other season gives you advance notice, builds up, but fall—even if you're determined to see it coming, it's not there and then it is. The leaves are orange, bam, the air is cool, the furnace goes on, and there's that sad, something-finished feeling. I rub my arms for warmth. Great, and I'm feeling like I'm getting a sore throat. I'll probably get strep and miss a ton of school right at the start.

We walk about a block, and there's Jenna, waiting for us with the car idling.

"Get in," she says. "But no more garbage."

Everyone keeps quiet on the ride. Jenna turns on the Christian rock station and we listen to some frenzied, pounding song about loving Him being easy, and no one even says a word.

"So, how're you feeling," Abe says.

"Like shit," I say. I put my hand to my throat. "Ach."

"Lovely," he says.

"I was out in the cold. I'm probably going to catch pneumonia," I say.

Abe works with teens mostly. Or, as he says, "The Jung and the Restless." He's pretty young himself, for a psychologist, at least compared to the others I've seen there. He doesn't wear doctorish clothes, just his jeans and a khaki shirt with the sleeves rolled up, with some T-shirt on underneath. It looks like he gets dressed in five minutes. He barely shaves, either, so he's always got a face half-full of bristles. "Do you think you're going to catch pneumonia?" he asks. He peers at me with his eyes, set a little too close together on his face. But they're twinkling. He's testing to see if I'm bullshitting him.

"My great-grandmother's sister died from pneumonia," I say. This is true. Whenever we look at the old pictures, that's what they say about her. She was only twenty-two. I look in her face, wonder what she was like when she was twenty-one and only had a year to live but didn't know it.

"Yeah, that was a billion years ago, before they invented good drugs," Abe says. "And speaking of, how are yours? Any more insomnia?"

"No. A little zingy at night, but it's okay. Things have been good." Here, he writes a few things down in my chart. He shares some of this information with my psychiatrist, Dr. Kaninski, who works down the hall and who I can skip visiting if my medication is okay.

"School?"

"Yeah, I go to school."

"Great, terrible, mildly crappy?"

"Somewhere in between." I tell him about school. How my friends have all been going their own directions lately.

Abe listens. He leans back in his chair, folds his hands and rests them on his chest. Behind him are pictures he took from a trip to Tibet. Prayer flags flapping, the brown, eager faces of a group of children, tents at a mountain base. "Why do you think you're feeling this separation now?" Abe asks.

"Distancing?" I guess. "Kind of distancing beforehand?"

"I think you got that exactly right."

"When I was in the fourth grade, I had this best friend—April Barker," I tell him. "We did everything together. Made forts, baked our own recipes." Blue cupcakes, I especially remember. "Then, in the fifth grade, she moved. We got in a big fight the day she left. I guess it's like that. Same as you've said before about Mom and me—trying to get to our own territory."

"Senior year," Abe says. "Everyone gets thinking about going their own way. . . . Everyone starts bugging you, huh? Best friends, parents. Everyone is themselves in the extreme, which is annoying as hell, right?"

I laugh. "Really right."

"What's the latest on your college applications?"

"I've been working on them."

"Which 'them'?"

"Same as I told you last time. University of Washington, Seattle University, SPU. You know. The ones around here."

"The applications your mom sent away for." Abe rips open a tea-bag package on his desk, plunks the bag into his cup of hot water, and dips it up and down, up and down. His cup says WORLD'S GREATEST GOLFER on it, which is a crack-up. Abe's just not the golfing kind. Golf sweaters? Abe? Ha-ha. I can't see him in any sport that involves matched clothing. I'm guessing he's snitched it from Dr. Kaninski, who I know for a fact is big on golf.

I once saw him get out of his Lexus in the parking lot. His license plate read BO-GEE, and the plate holder, "I'd rather be driving my club," which probably has Freudian undertones.

"Yeah," I say. "But I'm filling them out."

Abe takes a sip of his tea. "Last time, we talked about the upsides and the downsides of going to school so close to home. You were going to consider applying to other schools. How did that go?"

"I thought about it . . ."

"Mmhmm."

"It just seems like such a hassle."

"You have a common application, right? What's the hassle of applying to other schools? Maybe you'll have to write an extra essay question?"

"It's not just that. Mom'll freak if I go out of state. And it's expensive."

"With your grades? Read my lips. *Scholarship*. All those AP courses? You just breaking your butt for your good health?"

"No . . ."

"You'll be applying for scholarships anyway?"

"Yeah."

"Is Mom getting a degree, or are you?"

"Shut up, Abe." I appreciate the fact that I can tell my psychologist to shut up and he won't scribble notes in my chart.

"Whose job is it to make this decision?" Abe thinks I try too hard to please people. He's trying to get me to do it less, but he doesn't understand that sometimes fighting is just not worth the hassle. It's too much pain and effort. Maybe Abe doesn't mind climbing a mountain to see the view on top, but I'm happy with a postcard.

"Mine." I bite an annoying bit of skin at the edge of my fingernail. "I was thinking I'd just live at home and go to school."

"And if that's your decision, I applaud you one hundred percent. Just, *your decision*, right? There's no magic here. If you don't change direction, you'll go where you're heading."

"Okay." I know he's right, but I still feel the battle inside—Oliver's White Witch and Aslan going at it.

"I'm going to give you a little homework. For us to discuss next time."

"You want me to get a scholarship *and* you're giving me more homework? I already have no life."

"Do a little research. Bop on the Web and look around. Find three schools that look cool. Away from home. And then let's try applying to one."

"Oh, God, Abe." I groan.

"What's the worst that can happen?"

"Mom refuses to write the check and starts crying hysterically. No, wait. I actually *get in*."

"Dad can write the check?" Abe suggests. I nod. "If you get in, do you have to go?" he asks.

"No," I say.

"We've tried things in the past and it's worked out all right, yes? You've trusted me."

"Of course I trust you. Even if you have no fashion sense."

"Hey . . ." He mock-scowls. "This is about you. You pretending you can go anywhere you want. Palm trees? Homework on a beach? No problem. Bring me pictures. Tell me what you like about them."

"Fine," I say.

"All right," he says. Abe always finishes up by looking at his watch, which he does now. Then he says, "Anything else I should know?"

"No," I answer. I'm not going to tell him about the guy with the baby. I'm not telling him that I've seen the boy appear at the elephant exhibit for eight days in a row now, enough to know there's a pattern. He comes with the baby at three thirty most weekdays, and if not, he comes at night, alone. Then, he just stares, lost in thought, like he's trying to work something out. It doesn't even matter if it's raining or not, he still comes. I don't tell Abe how much I look forward to seeing the boy appear, how much I think about why he's there and who that baby is, because that's all mine. It's like a little present I can count on—a happy something to look forward to.

"You know how to handle anything," Abe says. "You can take any step you want and be okay. I'm proud of you."

He always gives me that rah-rah right before I leave, no matter what kind of bad shape I'm in, but that's all right. I kind of like it, even if I can see through it.

"And you," I say. "Work on your klepto tendencies." I point to the cup. Abe looks down. Smiles.

"Fore!" he says.

When I get home, I start my Abe homework. I'm not going to see him for another week, but he'd made college hunting sound like a quest for a vacation spot, and it sounds better to dream a while with an excuse than to do my AP English. Also, it requires me to be at my computer. Flicking back and forth between websites and the elephants. On the screen, I can see Chai rubbing her side against a tree, and baby Hansa nearby. They're never far from each other. A nine-year-old elephant still spends half of its time only five yards from its mother. If they were in the wild, Chai and Hansa as mother and daughter would have a bond that would last fifty years or more, just like a lot of humans. They are the most fun to watch, because Chai just loves that Hansa so much. She puts her trunk under Hansa's butt to help boost her up the hillside, and she tucks Hansa underneath her on a hot day to keep her cool. She'll steer Hansa around by holding her tail, or Hansa will follow behind, holding Chai's.

The Abe homework is harder than it seems. I narrow it down to the west coast (no way I want to go farther), choose only sunny climates (I like Abe's palm tree idea, and besides, I'm one of those people who are cold all the time). I narrow it further to colleges with animal studies programs. It's all getting complicated and overwhelming. *University of California Davis*, I write down, though it looks huge and busy and crowded. *University of Arizona*, smaller, thank God, and because I love the desert. *University of New Mexico*. Same reasons, smaller yet. Animal studies and cool adobe architecture. And I write down *University of Hawaii*, just because it sounds warm and daring, though it's a bit like those posters in hair salons—hip, unusual styles that look possible in the hair spray scented, pop music fortified moment of why-not, but that you know have nothing to do with your real life.

By the time I'm done, my head hurts and my nose has gotten

so clogged my sinuses feel like the human body equivalent of a sofa cushion. I think I might have a fever. I go downstairs to find Mom, who has ingredients for tacos spread across the counter. She's grating cheese on to a paper towel, the shredded orange growing into a pyramid.

"Am I hot?" I ask.

"Not you, too. Just when Oliver's feeling okay . . . Boy, I thought he'd never get better."

Oliver had used the alibi as long as he could, but now he was back at practice. Maybe that's what you get for faking someone's illness—a real one. Mom sets down the grater, wipes her hand on a kitchen towel. She sets her hand to my head. "Nope. You feel fine."

I have the small, backstage thought, *If I'm sick, it might be the flu, and if it's the flu, am I nauseous?* Just this small thought, which begins as a spiral somewhere inside, a wide circle, which will grow ever smaller. Smaller and tighter. Tighter and faster.

"Are you sure I'm not hot?" See, my chest. Got tight. Like I was running. Out of air. Like I'd just. Run up. This huge hill. In the cold.

"You're fine, Jade. You've got a cold," Mom says. "An annoying but harmless cold."

"I've got to . . ."

"Are you all right?"

"Lie down."

I head back up to my room, knock three times, sit on my bed. See, you come to understand this thing, come to notice it when the circle of thought is still wide. You catch it, before it starts spiraling so fast, so fast upward to where it clutches your heart and grabs your throat so you can't breathe and you're sweating and about to pass out. I find the quiet place in my mind that Abe taught me about. For me it is the desert, empty and calm. No sea, no tidal waves that sometimes visit my dreams. Just the desert, and cacti, and other plants and animals that have adapted to a harsh environment, hardy and long living, from the time of the dinosaurs. I breathe in, and out. Picture red and rolling forever desert. I knock out of my thoughts the huge cement campuses and pictures of shiny glass buildings and enormous libraries. Enrollment forms, campus tours—out. I knock out the secret thoughts that still visit, even if I know they're illogical. That I really am about to die. That I've been right all along, only no one's discovered what's wrong yet. Desert. Just the dry desert, sprawling and timeless. Creatures evolving and surviving throughout thousands and thousands of years.

Breathe in and out, and the shakiness subsides, and the sense that I can feel and hear my own heartbeat diminishes. In and out, now is all that matters, and now, this minute, everything is okay.

I decide not to have dinner, and then decide to eat a little. If I don't eat, I will certainly feel more nauseous. So, dinner and then my homework while I watch for the boy. I'm guessing this will be a night-visit day, as it was last week.

"You know, you need to be more aggressive out there, Oliver," Dad says at the table. His head is tilted sideways as he bites his taco. Oliver still has his football shoulders on. "You've got to hustle if you want to stay open."

"Bruce," my mom says.

"What? I don't see the point in us going out there to practice and play if he's going to hang back and not give it everything he's got," Dad says. He eats his taco in twenty seconds flat, which is the way you've got to do it. Still, he ends up with a plate littered with bits of meat and lettuce. Milo's under the table, wearing his wishing-and-hoping eyes.

"Maybe football's not his thing," Mom says.

"Football's not my thing," Oliver says.

"I don't think basketball's his thing either. Or soccer," I say.

"I'm not going to have my son be one of those kids who sits in front of the TV or computer all day," Dad says. "You guys really have no idea of the importance of athletics." He holds up a finger. "Social skills." A second finger. "Mental well-being." A third. "Physical health."

I take my Kleenex out of my sweatshirt pocket and blow my nose loudly.

"God," Dad says. "You guys don't have a clue."

"Uh-oh. You said 'God,'" I say.

Dad looks at me like I'm nuts.

"I certainly must need some basketball myself, since right now my mental well-being is suffering," Mom says. Her mouth is cinched upward in a sarcastic smile, but her eyes look hurt at the way he included her in the clueless camp. I feel a pang of sadness for her. Sports Dad can be such an asshole. I pet Milo with my foot. Drop him a bit of meat, though I know I shouldn't. I blow my nose again, meanly wishing the germs toward Dad's perfect, athletic, physically and mentally healthy self.

"Sis, you need the Flask of Healing," Oliver says.

* * *

I help Oliver with the dishes and listen to him explain how Aslan means lion in Turkish, and how Lucy spends more time in Narnia than any of the other human characters, four hours longer than Edmund. I hear the *shi-shu, shi-shu* of Dad sawing something downstairs. Mom leaves for a PTA meeting, leaving dueling puffs of perfume and mint in the air. Milo is turning in circles, waiting for the right view before he plops down.

I do my homework, then lie on my bed with the light out, watching the computer. I think about the day, about Jenna and Michael and Hannah, about Mom and Dad and Oliver and anxiety and palm trees and deserts. It seems right then that my world is very small. Small enough to fit inside a cage, small enough that it's as if it has a lock that I cannot see.

The boy finally comes into view on the screen, that known/unknown figure, wrestling with his own questions. I close my eyes, so it feels like we are just two people in a room, thinking quietly together. The sea boy and the desert girl. We both have decisions to make, it seems.

And so I decide something. I decide that I don't want to live in a cage. I decide my world should be bigger than that. That's when I know that after school tomorrow I am going to the elephant house. I am going to go and see what happens if we meet, because I can handle it. I can take any step I want and be okay.

Chapter Four

In captivity, an animal will sometimes create unnecessary problems or challenges for himself to solve. A lion will pretend to
"chase" its food by throwing it in the air. A raccoon will search for
food in a stream, even if he lacks a stream. He'll drop his food in
his water bowl, hunt for it as if it is not right there in front of him.
Then he'll pummel it, "kill" it, and finally fish it out . . .
   —Dr. Jerome R. Clade, *The Fundamentals of Animal Behavior*

When I get home from school, I whip my shirt off and change.
It's a cold, rainy day, and they'd had the heat turned up too high
in the building and I feel sweaty and damp. I'm thinking maybe
I should just wait and go to the zoo another day. One, it's rain-
ing, and by the time I walk over there my hair will look like shit.
Two, I still have my cold, and my eyes are hot and tired and I

have to blow my nose every two seconds. Three, I have a lot of homework, which isn't unusual, but still. Four, the shirt I just put on looks bad and is wrinkled, and figuring out what else to wear suddenly seems as monumental as a death in the family.

So, I plunk on my bed and take my shoes off, and this little feeling of self-disgust starts to creep up my insides. I try to ignore it by popping a few of those miniature Halloween chocolate bars that my mom has bought early. I'd seen them on the counter and wouldn't have had any without asking, except I'd noticed that she'd already poked a hole through the bag herself.

I'm opening up my third baby Snickers and the self-disgust is not drowning out as it's supposed to, but getting worse. It makes me more restless, and damn it, I get my shoes back on. Oh, man, I get up and look in my closet again and try to find something that I don't hate myself in, because I guess I'm going to the zoo after all. Me and myself try to talk I into not going, but uh-uh. Black sweater. Armpits smell fresh. No wrinkles. I look pretty good in it. To the bathroom, brush the chocolate out of my teeth reluctantly. It's tough to go from all of that gooey, chewy comfort to the business-like sharpness of toothpaste. Comb out my long hair. Pull it back? Keep it down. Ponytail? I look at myself as if I've never seen me before, or else I try to. Black hair, dark eyes, narrow face. I keep my hair down, as I look older that way. He's got a baby. He might have a wife. *Wife* is a word that means that all of this dress-up is just teenage playacting. I feel the difference between teen and adult, a difference that usually just seems like an annoying technicality. But now it feels real enough that I get this jolt of stupid-and-ashamed at the fact that I'm putting on lip gloss.

Actually, this *is* stupid, I'm sure. He's got a baby. What does this mean for his life that he has a baby at his age? And what if he's not as young as he looks? What kind of fool would I be then? What if he asks me to babysit, like the old Brady Bunch episode where Marsha gets a crush on the dentist?

Mom's downstairs, looking for something in the coat closet. She's got that pissy, can't-find-it distraction.

"Where're you going?" she asks.

"Just the zoo. Fresh air."

"Drive carefully," she says.

"I'm walking. The *zoo*." It's two blocks away. I don't know if she wasn't really listening, or if she's doing the suburban thing again. Where we used to live, Sering Island (a suburb of Seattle), people drive their cars everywhere they go. If they have to mail a letter a block away, they drive. In the city, you walk. In the time it takes to find a parking space, you can go on foot, do whatever you're planning to do, and get home.

I'm not sure my mother has ever forgiven my father for the move from Sering Island, and I'm not sure he's ever forgiven her for not forgiving him. We moved to the city when my father got a new job with Eddie Bauer. It's not like Sering Island is far enough from Seattle to make commuting an issue (it's only a twenty-minute drive in good traffic), but my dad had always wanted to live in the city. He had this idea of us broadening our cultural scope (being buddies with people who have henna tattoos), seeing *films* (instead of just going to the movies), eating fine food (not fast food). This was a way to build a healthy intellect along with our healthy bodies. He wanted it so badly that he pushed the issue hard, and so we moved.

My mother had a full-blown passive-aggressive episode about us going—Sering Island has the best schools in the area, and the only serious crime occurred in 1983, when the ex–Mrs. Drummond brought home a young drifter she'd met in a bar and ended up getting murdered. Several decades later, people still talked about it. The only other crime news to gossip about was the two hundred dollars that got stolen from Janey Edwards's BMW, and everyone knew her son Zenith did it anyway. Sering Island was *safe*. Besides that, Mom had channeled the energy and organizational skills from her left-behind business degree and had become PTA vice president at my middle school. A move meant she'd have to build up her reputation from the bottom, the CEO going back to the mailroom, as she put it. She'd have to attend every poster-making meeting and chaperone every field trip, even the inevitable one to the Puyallup Fair, which she hated. Her friends at school didn't like going in to the city. Besides that, she'd have to find a new post office and craft store. Figure out which grocery store had the best produce. Leave the comfort and reassurance of the suburbs.

Funny thing is, three years after our move, Mom is busier with school projects than ever, and Dad only comes out of the basement for his own or Oliver's sporting events. I don't think he really likes the city. We went to one foreign film, got there late, and had to sit in the back. Dad forgot his glasses, so he couldn't read the subtitles. We went to one Ethiopian restaurant, and Dad seemed vaguely uncomfortable eating with his hands, using up more napkins than the rest of us combined. The food was actually good, even the pile of brown stuff that looked like what Milo used to leave on the carpet when he was a puppy. I think city life just turned out not to be Dad's thing after all, but now he can't admit he was wrong about moving, and Mom can't admit she was wrong about moving either.

"Take the car," Mom says to the inside of the closet. "It's raining. You don't want to catch pneumonia."

Milo trots to the door, gives me a pleading look. "I'm sorry," I say. Milo's the kind of dog you are always apologizing to. I close the front door behind me, ignore Mom about the car. We live in a brick townhouse built in the 1920s, one of ten joined together in an open oval, which surrounds a center rose garden and fountain. It's smaller than my old house—less modern, but more charming, with its intricate molding around the ceilings and windows, and its elaborate fireplace and stairwell. Everyone knows one another. There are the Chens next door, with little Natalie and the new baby, Sarah; old Mrs. Simpson, with her bird feeders and favorite Energizer Bunny sweatshirt her kids gave her for her eightieth birthday; and Ken Nicholsen, with the perfect house, inside and out. Hank and Sally Berger, who treat their parrot like a kid. It's a comfortable, safe place.

I walk down the porch steps and through the garden. When you leave our enclave, it's city houses and the Union 76 station and Total Vid, the video store where Titus, one of the guys who works there, always tries to rent you his favorite movie, even if you've seen it before. *Riding Giants* is this surfing movie, and Dad's brought it home three times now because Titus is so convincing, even with his bleach-blond hair and favorite/only attire of jeans and a T-shirt with a large pineapple on it that cryptically reads JUICY PINEAPPLE. Total Vid has, I swear, a hundred copies of *Riding Giants*, since Titus tells everyone how gnarly and bitchin' it is. Anyone in Total Vid's radius knows more about surfing history than the average person.

One more block over, and you hit the zoo parking lot. That's how close we are. I walk, counting my steps in groups of eight. I show our family pass to the older lady with the big button that reads ASK ME ABOUT BECOMING A ZOO PAL, then push through the revolving metal gates. Someone who had snuck in would have had to climb the stone border around the zoo's perimeter.

My cell phone rings—Jenna—but I ignore it. I'm feeling too nervous to talk. I look at the face of my phone, though, to see the time. Three fifteen. He usually appears about three thirty.

I take the path past the giraffes and zebras, around the African savannah. I hear weird bird calls, exotic messages. Hippos, the meanest and most dangerous animals on earth, are off on their own, like we put away prisoners. Down the path a bit farther is the elephant house, and the outdoor enclosure, a large, mostly flat area of bamboo fields with its own "watering hole" and a few trees. As far as the rain Mom warned me about, it is more of a drizzle, a sprinkle, a mist. We've got a thousand words for rain here, same as Eskimos have for snow.

I duck my chin down and walk fast. The rain means the zoo is nearly empty of visitors, except for this one mother, who looks slightly dazed and is pulling on the hand of her sticky toddler. God, I'm nervous. I have this wound-up, hyper feeling, energized fear, and I'm thinking this is about the nuttiest thing I've ever done. And stupid. And maybe dangerous. He's a stranger. He has a baby, which makes him seem unlikely as a rapist, but come on. I don't know him and here I am going to meet him, and I barely feel good about talking to guys I don't know at my own school. This could be one of those horrible stories you hear about, where some dumb girl meets some guy she's talked to on the Internet. It's either the bravest thing I have ever done or the most idiotic, and I suddenly realize how hard it is to tell the difference.

There is an overhang by the outdoor viewing area where I can stay dry, and that's where I head. I sit on the bench for a few minutes; I look out at Onyx, an Asian elephant and the only animal I see out there, except for a few pigeons pecking at the ground in a bored, halfhearted manner. My stomach is flopping around in anticipation. I watch Onyx for calm, her swaying body, her trunk that rises to explore the upper leaves of a tree. Onyx isn't the best choice for calm. Onyx is pretty old, I think—at least she looks old and acts old. She moves more slowly than the others, her movements dull and cranky. Her eyes look sad and sweet, dark and down-turned, as if she's asking for something but would refuse it if you offered. She makes me think of those days you have sometimes, when you're pissed off and driving everyone away with your mood, but what you most need is for someone to love you in spite of yourself. I've seen Onyx be aggressive with the others— shoving and nudging with her trunk, refusing to move when it would be the friendly thing to do. I know it sounds silly, like those people who have their dogs analyzed, but she seems depressed.

I'm getting cold just sitting, so I stand and lean against the railing. Just because it's three thirty, I shouldn't panic. He could be late. I'm sure he's still coming. I hope my hair still looks okay.

I search off in the distance, hoping to see a red jacket. My heart thumps around at the thought of actually seeing and maybe talking to the real him. No one is around at all, and it's just me and all of the sounds around me. Rain falling, a strange twittering of some bird, the eerie warbling of another. I can hear water rushing somewhere, maybe from the brown bears' river, I'm not sure. I look back at the camera where it is perched at the corner of the elephant house, and I give a small wave to the me's out there who are watching.

Red jacket! I mentally call. Where are you? Only five minutes, but forever passes. I take out a Kleenex, blow my nose again, which is when he'll probably come.

But no.

I blow it again, just to give him a second chance to meet me at a bad time. I hear an elephant trumpet, not Onyx, who is just standing under that tree, sniffing its bark. More twittering. The trees *shh-shush* with a bit of wind. One of the pigeons hops around by my feet and pecks at pieces of dropped, soggy popcorn. God damn it, red jacket!

I sit back down. Go through the list in my head again. He's babysitting. It's his sister's baby. It's his baby, and he's married. Too young, unhappily. Happily married. Divorced, raising a baby alone. What I am doing here today is a stupid thing. It's a brave and bold thing. I say the phrase over again, It's a brave and bold thing, count off the words using the fingers of one hand. *It's* is my thumb, *a* my forefinger, et cetera. I start again from the next finger and count until the sentence ends on my pinkie.

My butt is cold sitting on the bench, and so are my hands,

shoved in my pockets. My Kleenex supply is dwindling. It's three forty-five, which doesn't necessarily mean anything, but probably does mean something.

I stand up again, hold the railing and lean back, face to the sky like he does, rain falling on my cheeks and eyes and chin. Maybe he's done with elephants, moved on to a different animal. Maybe he's just moved on, period. Maybe I'd missed my chance by waiting too long. By just watching and not doing.

Four o'clock. He'd never been this late before, unless he came at night. I see the green pants and green shirt of the zookeeper who seems to be in charge of the elephants, an Indian man with a curving mustache and beard. He catches me watching him and waves and I smile. He disappears into the elephant house. I walk over to the house, peer inside at the glass windows of the huge stalls where Hansa and Chai and Tombi are snuggled, eating. The zookeeper isn't there, but a young woman feeds them something out of a metal bucket.

Outside again, the rain has turned from drizzly to insistent, consistent, drenching. I think maybe my chest feels heavy, a bit heavy—does it? From standing outside in the cold that long? That kind of heavy means a chest-heaving cough is coming on. Bronchitis, maybe. *Pneumonia*, my backstage mind says. There is not a red jacket anywhere, and my Kleenex is now a small, basically unusable wet ball, a soggy clump.

I walk away from the elephant house. My stupidity and I head home. We are both dripping wet, my hair becoming plastered to my face. In the zoo parking lot, I see Jake Gillette, the idiot genius, riding around on his skateboard in the rain, doing tricks, the parachute still attached to the back. That parachute looks optimistic in the gray wetness—trying hard even as it becomes heavy with rain—and something about this pitiful sight annoys me. I pass Total Vid, see Titus in his pineapple shirt behind the counter.

My shoes are sopping, my hair is too; even my pant legs are drenched when I get home. I don't want to see Mom, or for her to see me, so I close the front door very quietly, avoid the squeaky parts of the stairs. I knock on my doorframe softly three times. I take off my clothes, which an hour ago were confident and daring but are now soaked and humiliated. I drop them on the floor in a heap, leave them there where they belong. I have a bad headache. So bad that my headache has a headache.

I put on my robe. The only item of clothing that gives you unconditional love. I have dinner with my family, do my homework. The rumble in my chest is getting worse, I am sure. It feels dark, deep. I eat about ten cough drops to keep any anxiety under control, and because they have medicinal purposes.

And, yes, I watch the screen, in case he appears that night. But he doesn't. He's gone.

I turn the light off in my cage. Watch the screen. There are no flickering images. Just the muddy black of darkness lying on bamboo fields.

The next day, there's excitement in the air. It is a cliché to say so, I know, but it's true. And the reason there's excitement in the air is because the homecoming dance has finally arrived. Oh, yay. My mom is up early making breakfast for us on a school day,

French toast, when we usually just have cereal. She's got the kind of looking-forward-to-it excitement that gives you culinary energy. Mom, though, doesn't eat any of it herself, she says, because she has to fit into her dress—like one piece of French toast is going to suddenly split her zipper. I know I'm just pissed off and am acting horrible and will probably get struck by lightning for all the awful thoughts I'm having. And I know none of the homecoming stuff is meant to hurt me—Mom's explained that she has to go as one of the dance coordinators. Still, she's obviously revved up, and her cheery anticipation makes me want to fling French-toast triangles like boomerangs.

"I'm just glad I finally found my beaded purse," Mom says, as she flips a couple more pieces of toast onto Oliver's plate. They're perfect, too. Browned, yet still fluffy. Buttery, but not heavy with grease. "In the coat closet! With Oliver's dirty cleats and soccer socks and your old school backpack piled on top. It's a metaphor for my life. Buried under everyone else's."

"I wish there was a dance every day," Oliver says, and pours more syrup on his breakfast.

I glare at him. "Don't even joke," I say.

"What?" he says.

Mom doesn't hear us. "I've got a hair appointment at one, so you'd better pick up your brother after school in case I'm late," she says.

"Cretin," I say.

"It's not my fault," Oliver says, which is true, but who cares.

Ordinarily, I might have been sick enough to stay home, but there's no way I can deal with this all day. Calculus even sounds like more fun. Dad must have felt the same way, because he'd left for work early.

"Dad took the bus so we'd have the car. In fact, if you can take Oliver this morning too, that'd be great. I've got so much to do yet to get ready."

"Fine."

"Jade? Is there a problem?" Her spatula stops midair.

"No, Mom. I said fine."

"It's just your *tone*."

Ah, yes—the tone. The nasty traitor. My tone has gotten me into more trouble over the years than any actual behavior. And as much as I knew she'd hassle me about it, I couldn't help but let it slip. My tone is like one of those guys who commit crimes right under a surveillance camera.

"I'm sorry," I say, not in the least sorry, or maybe just a small bit sorry. I give Milo the rest of my French toast, even though he's too fat already. "Hurry up, Oliver. If you make me late, I'm going to hurt you."

"God, I didn't *do* anything."

I change all the radio stations in Mom's car. We drive along to rap music, which I actually hate. I hate it all the way to Oliver's school.

"Sis, do you ever get the feeling our parents are wacko?" Oliver asks.

"All the time, Tiger." I pull up in front of Oliver's school, past the flag whipping on the flag pole and the little kids with drooping backpacks waiting obediently at the crosswalk. I am feeling a little bad about how I treated him, though, because I really do like him. He's my brother, and we go through things together that no one else will ever understand. I have the thought that he's sure to get hit by a school bus or be killed in a school shooting now that I'd been mean to him. He'd be dead and I'd have guilt forever and never have the chance to make it up to him. "Have a good day, okay?" I say.

"It'll be a good day since it's the last one I'll have with all my limbs. The first football game is tomorrow." He scoots across the seat, opens the door.

"Oh, man. I'm sorry, Oliver."

"Not as sorry as I am."

He shuts the car door. I watch him walk toward the building. From behind, Oliver, too, is mostly all backpack. He seems too small for a big world. Which is funny, because I'm feeling too big for my small one.

"Why don't you come hang with Akello and me tonight," Michael says. "Forget all this homecoming crap."

It sounds good, but I don't like how Michael drives. And I'd never driven with Akello before, so he might be reckless. He's nice, but that doesn't necessarily tell you everything you need to know. I could always meet them wherever they were going, though. "Sure," I say. "What are you guys doing?"

"Movies?"

"Okay."

"Should we ask Jenna?" Michael asks. Hannah's going to homecoming, with this guy named Jordan from another school, so she won't be there.

"Nah. If we ask Jenna, we'll have to watch *Mary Poppins*," I say. It isn't nice, but I'm not feeling nice. I have this bone-deep ticked-offness, like those days when no clothes look right and your jeans are too tight, and you feel so negative you know you're going to end up working in a 7-Eleven the rest of your life, with only an occasional robbery to look forward to for excitement. I get a 96 percent on my Faulkner paper (big deal), am asked by Ms. Deninslaw to run for an Honor Society office (so what). No way in hell I'd do it anyway, as it would mean giving a speech in front of the club, and I'd rather walk around naked in Costco during free-sample hour than give a speech. I smiled and thanked her, though, and told her I'd think it over. Just another moment brought to you by the Politeness Equals Bullshit network.

After school, I pick up Oliver, who isn't dead, and we head home. Now that he is still alive, he's annoying me again, telling me that Narnia is the name of an Italian town, that J. R. R. Tolkien criticized *The Lion, the Witch and the Wardrobe* so much that C. S. Lewis almost didn't finish it, something Oliver's told me at least three times. The house smells all perfumey when I get in, and it isn't even time for Mom to leave yet. This can only mean she is back from the hairdresser's. Hairspray fumes. If aerosol could destroy ozone, God knows what it could do to our insides, so I hold my breath. Mom's dress hangs on the back of her door, and the sight of it, plus my extreme, bordering-on-homicidal mood, makes me go into my room and hunt around in my box of patron saint candles.

We're not devout Catholic or anything, but I like the patron saint idea. There's a saint for everything. There are patron saints for rain (Gratus of Aosta), rats (Servatus), respiratory problems (Bernadine of Sienna), riots (Andrew Corsini), and ruptures (Florentius of Strasburg), and that's only the Rs. They've got these cool candles for each different one, a column of tall glass with a picture of the saint on the front, and a matching prayer on the back, one in English and one in Spanish. They are pretty in-depth prayers and do a way better job of kissing up to God than you could ever think up on your own. For example, a prayer to Anthony of Padua, a full-service saint who protects against ship-wrecks and starvation, helps you find lost things, and protects old people, pregnant women, and fishermen, reads like this: *Glorious Saint Anthony, my friend and special protector, I come to you with full confidence in my present necessity. In your overflowing generosity you hear all those who turn to you. Your influence before the throne of God is so effective that the Lord readily grants favors at your request, in spite of my unworthiness.*

Or, for the Spanish among you, *Santo Glorioso Anthony, mi amigo y protector especial, Vengo a usted con confianza completa en mi actual necesidad. En su generosidad . . .* You get the idea. The grammar isn't always the best, but who cares. It's like Cliffs Notes for praying. You light one up, and if anyone is listening and in need of a lot of flattery, voilà.

It's tricky to choose, because I don't really have any candles for Intrusive Mothers Who Can't Live Their Own Lives. So I pick Saint Philomena, Patron Saint of Lost and Desperate Causes. Anyway, her picture is one of my favorites. She seems like a really nice person.

I move a few other saints over on my dresser (saints wouldn't mind) and put Philomena front and center and light her up. Hopefully, the match won't set off the fire alarm, causing Mom to come running in with her hair just done from the hairdresser's, and her nails all long and glossy. That, I do not want.

I wave my hand around to dissipate the small poof of smoke. And then I have this realization, and that is, I just don't want to be here at all as Mom is getting ready to go. I know she has to leave early to help set up, but I still have a good hour and a half or more where she is bound to come out and want me to take her picture and admire her and be excited for the fun she's going to have at my senior-year homecoming. I know I should be a bigger person about this, but that knowing and what I feel are in enemy camps. Maybe I'm just an awful person, but I'm not in the mood to be one of the mice that helps Cinderella before the ball. Abe says I have to stop trying to please everyone, so fine.

I watch Philomena burn for a while as I figure out what I want to do. I know there's a little piece of me already working on the possibility of going back to the zoo in the hope that the red-jacket guy just missed one day and isn't really gone after all. It isn't like stalking or something if I go back again, is it? My brain starts negotiations. If I go, I can't torture myself with humiliation and embarrassment if he isn't there. If I go, I can't get all invested in the idea of seeing him. Besides, I do want to go to the zoo, just because I admire and appreciate the zoo.

Something about this still seems obsessed-fan like, so I cut-and-paste the plan. I won't exactly go to the zoo again, I decide. I'll just take Milo for a walk. Past the zoo entrance. Past the zoo entrance he'd have to go through, right around the time he'd have to go through it. I check the clock. I'll have to hurry if there's going to be a coincidence.

Milo is so thrilled when he sees his leash that he leaps around and starts barking, tripping over himself with excitement. It makes me feel a little guilty because, honestly, he's just being used. His little black lips are smiling. His pudgy rear end is waddling back and forth, back and forth with joy.

I clip Milo to his leash and escape out the door. I don't even check to see how I look before I leave, so I'm really not even expecting to cross paths with the boy in the red jacket, and that way I'll hardly be disappointed when we don't. I've discovered this about things you look forward to or dread. Fate likes the surprising detour, the trick ending. When you're really excited and looking forward to something is when it turns out ho-hum or completely and devastatingly horrible. And when you think you are about to have the worst day of your life, things generally turn out okay. So I play this trick, and when I'm excited about something, I tell myself it's going to be lousy, and I think of all that might go wrong. Which is what I didn't do last time when I was going to meet the boy in the red jacket. Stupid me, I let myself get all excited, and look what happened.

Milo is walking me, instead of me walking him. For a small dog, he's really strong. Since he's a beagle, he's basically a nose on legs. Supposedly, he can pick up a jillion more scents than we can. He puts his nose to the ground and just goes. It's like he's reading a bunch of stories, following timelines in history. If you are in a car and reading a map, tracing a path with your finger, you are doing exactly what Milo does with his nose—he even takes these little sudden turns and then veers back again. He stops for a while when the story gets a little longer or more interesting. Or else it's just where another dog peed.

I have to really yank on Milo's leash to get him to break focus and go where I want him to go, and then he gets settled on a new trail and I have to yank him again. Walking him is a whole lot of work, a constant battle of forcing someone to stop doing what they're really into. Like those poor mothers trying to get their kid out of the McDonald's play tubes.

We arrive at the zoo, and the same round woman with the ASK ME ABOUT BECOMING A ZOO PAL button is at the window, and she smiles at me this time. I feel kind of funny hanging around there with her watching, as if I've done something wrong already. Even though she's smiling, it's the same feeling you get in some stores when the saleswoman follows you around as if you are about to shoplift at any moment. So I decide on another plan, which is to walk Milo around the zoo's rose garden, where dogs are allowed and where there's a clear view of the zoo entrance.

I haul Milo into the garden, which turns out to be a huge mistake because there are a couple of squirrels jetting around, which drives Milo into a frenzy of pulling and barking and straining at the leash and straining at my patience. I can barely hang on to him, he is yanking so hard, and I get worried he might win the tug-of-war and break the metal clip that connects him to his leash. Let me just tell you in case you don't know— letting a beagle off his leash can have disastrous consequences. They are at the mercy of their nose and this screaming drive to follow the scent to wherever some animal might be. They will follow it into eternity or into a busy intersection or into the wilds or into the path of a truck or a ferocious dog simply because they can't help themselves. Beagles have to be protected from their own instinct. One time Milo got off his leash and flew his fat self like a speeding train through the Chens' yard, across the street, past the center fountain. Mom was chasing him in her robe. Luckily, he got pinned in the corner of the front gate, his face bent down in captured shame. He could easily have been Squashed Milo in morning traffic.

Anyway, he is behaving atrociously. He really needs more practice getting out. It has to be right around three thirty now. It'd be just great if the boy in the red jacket came now. Milo is straining and barking and bulgy eyed and practically frothing at the mouth. He starts making that horrible *heck-heck* sound, that dying cough he gets when he practically strangles himself. He's so loud, Mom can probably hear him from home. I lean down and pick him up, cart his heavy, squirming self out of the garden, away from the squirrels who make that creepy semisqueak at him as they cling vertically to the tree trunks.

Now I am sweaty and covered in dog hair and drool. Milo is not generally a drooler, but get him near an animal and he's a Saint Bernard. I set him down back near the zoo entrance. I decide to handle the whole ticket-saleslady-worry with authority. I give my face that look of determined searching, check my cell phone clock with annoyance as if I'm waiting for someone who hasn't shown, which I guess I am. Milo sits politely and stares off in the distance as if waiting for his bus, as if that crazed, frenzied fiend back there was someone he didn't know and wouldn't care to.

I look around and fold my arms, pissed at the faux friend who hasn't shown, but actually searching for the red-jacket boy. I'm half-hoping he really won't show, because I'm sure I smell of sour underarms and a situation out of control. Me looking like shit, and smelling bad—I am giving him his best shot to appear. Milo and I stare toward the parking lot, at an assortment of minivans with baby seats, Fords and Subarus and who knows what; I'm not so good at car identification. A big RV with a license plate that reads CAPTAIN ED and a bumper sticker HOME OF THE BIG REDWOODS takes up two spots.

Three forty-five. Three fifty. Jake Gillette shows up with his skateboard under his arm, sets it down carefully on a large, empty patch of parking spaces. He whips around with exaggerated style, showing off. I see our neighbor, Ken Nicholsen, go into Total Vid and come out a few moments later carrying a copy of *Riding Giants*, the big white wave on the cover obvious even from across the street. Milo starts to pant, which isn't too surprising after all the barking he'd done back at the squirrels.

Four ten.

He isn't coming.

In spite of my resolve, I feel an avalanche of disappointment. God, it's been a shitty day. And Mom is still home, no doubt, putting on her nylons and more mascara.

I decide to leave, but before I do, I notice the elephant keeper in his green shirt and pants, coming out toward the parking lot, carrying what looks to be a file box out to a truck parked in a front space. He sets the box on the hood, fishes for his keys in his pocket and unlocks the door. He puts the box inside, then looks up suddenly and catches me staring at him for the second time in two days.

"Elephant girl," he says. His voice is deep, almost musical from his accent. I smile. "He's a fat one," the keeper says, and nods his chin toward Milo. It might have been not nice, except he then pats his own stomach and smiles. "Like me. Like my wife at home. Too many treats."

Ordinarily, I'd have felt a little more wary—adult man, unknown. But I don't get any creepy vibes, and I'd seen him so many times with the elephants. He's all right, I can tell. He has smiley crinkles by his eyes, a kindly brown face, black beard and mustache turning gray. "Have to watch those treats," I say.

"Ah, such a shame," he says with a sigh. "So, you like the elephants? I've seen you come and stay."

I'm embarrassed. The kind of embarrassed you feel when you've been watched and didn't know it. "Chai, Hansa, Bamboo, Flora, Tombi . . ." I count on my fingers. "Who'd I forget?"

"Onyx," he fills in.

"Oops."

"Onyx hates to be forgotten."

Milo's manners are impeccable. Or maybe he's just exhausted. He doesn't strain toward the man with his usual desire to sniff pant legs. He just sits nicely and smiles. "Next time you come," the man says, "you work instead of sit. We always need the volunteers."

"Okay," I say. I'm not sure if I mean it. As nice as he seems, I don't know this man, and as much as I love the elephants, being right near their actual selves with their huge, stomping legs and powerful bodies is another matter. I'd have to think that over. For a long time. Maybe such a long time that I'd never come back. Or maybe just long enough that if I did come back, he'd have forgotten he'd mentioned it.

"There's plenty of elephant dung to always shovel," he says, grinning.

"I'm sure."

The elephant keeper locks his car door again, waves a good-bye. I wave back.

I walk Milo out of the zoo parking lot and around the nearby neighborhood. I let him lead, because wherever he goes, there are no red jackets, and no mothers in prom dresses. Finally, it is time to go home. The house is empty, and I reward Milo for that fact with a huge glass mixing bowl of the coldest water. He gulps and slurps happily, making a mess all over the floor. Then he looks up at me with water droplets glistening on his beard. He smiles gratefully, which I guess means that one of us, at least, is satisfied.

Chapter Five

Male elephants live in a warm, loving family of females until they are ten to fifteen years old. When the male is of age, he is slowly but strongly forced out of the herd. He continues to follow the herd at increasing distances, until he is finally living alone. He lives alone for the rest of his life, except for siring children. When he is with the herd, his interactions with family are gentle and courteous, but little else. Male elephants are viewed by the females as dangerous to their children, and are not welcome after the baby is born. Their lives are solitary ones . . .

—Dr. Jerome R. Clade, *The Fundamentals of Animal Behavior*

I go to the movies with Michael and Akello and have a pretty good time, and then we head over to Smooth Juice and buy a fruit drink and a pretzel. B-plus fun, but better than pretending the school gym is some tropical paradise with basketball hoops.

When I get home, Oliver is back from football practice and is asleep in front of the television, and an exhausted Milo is curled up with his blankie and doing his dog-dream flinching. The basement is quiet, but Dad's car is parked on the street, so he's probably down there. It seems only polite to say hello, since we haven't seen each other all day, so I tromp down the stairs and open the door.

"Dad?"

The train set is built on a platform that Dad has put on top of our old dining room table to make it easier for him to reach. Each week, it grows more elaborate. There is a little town with brick streets and tiny plastic people. A general store, a church with a steeple, a train station. A perfect little place. Now, the train is pointing out of town, which is the area of the platform Dad is working on lately. He is building the road out. It aims toward a tunnel that goes up and over a mountain to another place altogether. You can't tell what that place is yet. So far, it's just an empty area that only Dad sees in his imagination.

I don't see Dad at first. He isn't standing by the platform as he usually is, bent over it, painting or gluing or sanding or sawing. But then I realize he's just sitting in the corner in this chair from our old house that we put down here because it didn't go with any of our new furniture. That's what's mostly in the basement—all the stuff that doesn't fit us anymore, from the dining room table and the recliner to a shelf of Dad's college textbooks, and my and Oliver's old clothes that Mom's packed in boxes and labeled with our ages in black marker. There's no decorating, really, except for a framed picture of a castle Dad got on a trip to France he took after he graduated, and a tacky advertisement for Rainier Beer painted on a mirror.

Dad is wearing the gray sweatpants he wore to Oliver's practice, his Mariners sweatshirt. His hands are folded across his chest, his eyes open and just staring. The footstool is up, and his sock-clad feet are resting on it. I surprise him and he jumps when he sees me, sits up suddenly, causing the chair to pop back into upright position, footrest gone as if it had been doing something it shouldn't have.

"Jade," he says.

"What are you doing?"

"Just sitting here. Thinking."

"Are you okay?"

"Sure," he says. "Of course I'm okay. Is your mom home yet?"

"Not yet."

Silence.

"Jade?"

"Yeah?"

"I'm sorry. You know—about that."

"What?"

"You know. Mom. The dance."

"It's all right. It's not your fault."

"Maybe. Maybe not."

We both don't say anything for a while. It's awkward, him saying stuff like that to me. His voice is low and quiet. This isn't the kind of conversation I have with Dad. Mom, maybe, but not

Dad. Dad asks how school is. How I did on tests. Dad talks exteriors, Mom talks interiors. He doesn't share the corridors of their relationship like this, or of any relationship. I don't really want to be standing there anymore. It makes me kind of nervous. He's my dad, but I feel some sense of responsibility to keep the conversation going, and have no idea how. *Maybe, maybe not.* I count the syllables on my fingers, May-be-may-be not, but end up on my pinkie the first time, so it's no good. I want to be back in my room, with the elephants and Philomena, but it's one of those times you can't just turn around and leave, yet you don't want to stay, either. I pick up this package on the table, a new, tiny house in a bubble of plastic just bought at the train store. I pretend to study it.

"Where's this going to go?" I say finally.

"I don't know yet," he says. He is still just sitting there, looking at his hands. Then he says, "Why don't you put it where you think it should be."

This is a little weird too. See, Dad's train isn't this father-child bonding project, where we get to move the little people around and paint the moss on the rocks. Nope, this is hands-off-Dad's-big-toy-if-you-touch-it-he's-gonna-be-pissed. The whole thing is making me uneasy, and I don't know why. He's not acting like the dad stereotype I know and understand. He's somehow gone from Mr. Black-and-White to something hazier and gray, and right then I prefer the him I'm familiar with to this guy.

"Anywhere you want," Dad says, and I realize then that this is an attempt to reach out to me, to set a tiny bridge across where there are now two separate pieces of land. And I don't want to say no. So I just say, "Okay." I open up the package. I walk around the

platform slowly, the little house in my palm. "This is a very serious decision," I say, hoping to lighten the mood. I put it on top of
another house. Pretend to contemplate. "No, the neighbors would
complain." I put it on top of the train station. "Too noisy," I say.

And then I stop messing around, because I know where it
should go. That new blank area outside of town, through the
tunnel, where nothing is yet. I set it down there, appraise the situation. It looks funny, this house on this bare piece of undeveloped
plywood. Kind of empty, but the start of something new.

"There," I say.

I'm expecting a protest, or a grunt of disapproval, or even a
laugh. But he does none of those things.

"That's what I was thinking too," Dad says.

The next morning, our house has this disheveled, morning-after
glow. Mom's wrap is draped over the banister, and her hair clip
is on the coffee table, next to a photo of her and Mr. Dutton, our
librarian, in a homecoming folder with the date on it embossed in
silver. Their hands are clasped and they are standing under a faux
sunset. Mr. Dutton looks happier than he ever has in the library.
It pisses me off. Actually, it makes me feel kind of sick. A wilted,
browning orchid is in the fridge, next to the milk carton.

Mom is bouncing all over the place, yelling cheerfully at
everyone to hurry up or we'll be late for Oliver's game. She'd slept
in her hairdo, which had barely moved, which meant either she'd
gotten in pretty late and barely slept on it, or that the hairdresser
had used a shitload of hairspray. I sort of wish she'd walk by an
open flame right then, actually. Mom is doing this casual ignor-

ing of me, not mentioning last night, and making the nonverbal point that she isn't bothered in the least about my bad attitude, meaning, of course, that she is bothered enough to be on the edge of really mad.

Oliver is dawdling, which is making Dad tense. At least, that's why I'm guessing he's tense. Oliver can't find his cleats, then his shoulder pads, and then, when we're finally all in the car, he says he's left his water bottle in the house. Passive-aggressive behavior must come down the family line on your mother's side.

I don't always go to Oliver's games, or that's all I'd be doing every weekend. I usually have too much homework, plus it's cold and boring standing out there with all those parents and their big golf umbrellas bought at Costco. But it's his first football game, and I figure he could use the moral support. Jenna's brother is also on the team, so Jenna and I decide to meet to keep each other company.

Oliver rides with his chin down and his water bottle in his lap, just picking at the threads of his pants. I jostle him with my elbow, but he doesn't respond. He forgets his gym bag in the car when we get there, and I have to run back and get it. I plunk it down with the other bags. Before he runs off to join the others on his team, I tell him not to worry, because I've brought the Flask of Healing.

"Football is so brutal," Jenna says.

"And too cold," I say. "Baseball's sunny at least." I stick my hands in my jacket, jump up and down a bit. It's early-November gray, the sky filled with flat, stubborn clouds. My legs are already getting cold through my jeans. If standing out on a muddy field way too early in the morning isn't enough fun for you, make it cold enough to stop feeling your fingers.

"Baseball games go on forever, though," Jenna says. Her brother plays every sport too. He even *wrestles*. "What's with your mom's hair?" Jenna says.

"Homecoming. Chaperone."

"Oh, that's right. Did you tell her it's *over*?" This is the Jenna I like. We both chuckle at ourselves.

"You're lucky your mom *works*," I say.

We watch our brothers. I don't know anything about football, but, basically, they line up, run two feet, crash into each other, and line up again. The dads on the sidelines are this tribe of jumping, screaming, pacing men, mostly wearing some form of athletic attire and shouting orders to their sons as they parade up and down the chalk marks at the edge of the field. The women talk and pretend to watch the players, except for this hard-core mom that's screaming, "Get in the game! Get in the game!" as she stands there all comfy in her down coat, holding her steaming coffee cup. Every sport of Oliver's is the same—parents who look like they themselves would have a coronary jogging halfway across the grass, yelling at their kid to do it faster, better, harder.

The whistle blows, and no one quite understands why. There's more lining up. Occasionally, our quarterback, the coach's son (the coach's kid *always* gets the best position), breaks out and runs from the pack, throwing the ball in a wide pass, where it lands on the ground and bounces on its nose. The coach shoves his hands in his pockets, looks down, and kicks the ground with the toe of his shoe. You can see the puff of air his sigh makes when it escapes into the cold.

"They're killing us," Jenna says.

"How can you tell?"

"Just look."

She nods her head at our sidelines, toward three scared-looking kids, another who is crying, and one who has just gotten hurt and is holding his arm tight against his chest. The dads crouch over the players, hands on their fatherly knees, giving "pep" talks. I've heard plenty of these, and they are all a version of the same theme: If you really *wanted* to win, you would. It doesn't matter if the other kids are twice your size and look like they're already shaving, it doesn't matter if they are just plain better, or have more players, or have a team that's been playing together since they all were in the womb—it's about *attitude*. Shout the team name, boys, loud enough so the other team hears and is scared out of their already-shaving wits. It all reminds me of animals that eat their young.

My own dad seems to have lost all of his introspection from the night before. He is wearing his nylon training pants with his Seahawks sweatshirt; his hair is combed in rigid perfection. When the game begins again, his jaw is strong and tight as he walks up and down the sidelines, yelling at Oliver, pausing only to turn his head and spit. It's a miracle, I decide then, if team sports don't make a kid hate his father.

"So far, at least, Jason and Oliver are okay," I say.

The words are barely out of my mouth when the whistle screams a fierce *breeeep*! The players stop, look around. One kid is still running forward until the news from his visual cortex catches up to him. Kids huddle around a fallen body, but you can't tell who it is. The assistant coach runs out and clears the kids aside, who all gather to stare like motorists at an accident. That's when I see it is Oliver.

"Oh, shit. It's Oliver," I say.

Dad has stopped pacing and just stands there, then folds his arms as if it's nothing to be concerned about. The mother Mom is talking to points, and Mom stops chatting and sees that Oliver is down. She watches with her hand to her mouth.

Oh, my God, Oliver. He doesn't seem to be moving. Thoughts crash—a broken neck. Oliver in a wheelchair. People's necks got broken playing this stupid sport, didn't they? What if he never walks again? Is he breathing now? I picture an ambulance with lights whizzing, blaring onto the field. He isn't moving at all. The other coach runs out too, and at this, tears start welling up, and my throat shuts. Goddamn it. Oliver didn't want to play. Maybe he knew this would happen. Maybe that's why he didn't want to play—a premonition. Now he is broken.

"He's okay," Jenna says. And it's true. Or else, he's okay enough. He stands with a coach on either side, limps off the field with their help. The parents clap. Injury always gets applause. His face is streaked with dirt and tears. Some other kid jogs reluctantly out to take his place; they tell him to hurry, and the game goes on.

"I'm going to see if he's all right," I say to Jenna. I head over to Oliver, who's trying hard to stop crying. He isn't having much luck. His chest is heaving up and down. Sobs catch in his throat. "What happened?" I ask. My heart hurts.

"That big guy," he says. His voice is high and tight. "Number forty-six. Jeez, he just bashed his shoulder right into my chest, and when I was on the ground, he steps on my leg with his cleat." He sniffs hard, rubs his nose on his sleeve, doesn't meet my eyes.

"That bastard," I say. "The minute he gets off the field I'm going to kick him in the balls." Oliver laughs a little, his eyes filling up at the same time. "He'll never know what hit him. His balls are gonna go flying, I promise you that. People will wish they brought their catcher's mitts." Oliver half laughs. Dad is there now.

"He's all right. He's fine," Dad says, his usual line whenever Oliver gets hurt. It means: Go away. Don't baby him. Don't show too much compassion. The other dads do this too. It's some kind of group hysteria, based on some fatherly fear that says compassion equals homosexuality. Parents and sports—I've come to the conclusion that it's all about fear—fear that your kid won't come out on top, be a success. Forcing him into these brutal encounters will a) make damn sure he is a success, and b) allow you to see evidence of that success with the added bonus of a cheering crowd. This means that sports are supported with an almost desperate enthusiasm. The football team gets catered dinners before a game. Honor Society is lucky if it gets a cupcake. Academic success—forget it. That requires too much imagination. There's no scoreboard.

Dad moves in close, hunches over Oliver. I know he's going to say what they all do in this situation. *You're okay, you're okay! Come on, get up! Be a winner! Shake it off!* The kid is bloody and bruised and can't move, but, hey, what's your problem? You've got another leg!

I walk back to Jenna. Mom is sending glances their way, weighing, as she always does, whether or not to interfere. She catches my eye. Gives her head a little shake and rolls her eyes upward to communicate her disgust with the whole masculine display. I nod back in agreement. It makes me miss her a little. Makes me remember that we were usually on the same side. I feel a pinprick in the oversize inflatable beach ball that is my anger. Dad bends down to talk to Oliver. Oliver is looking at the ground.

"Is he okay?" Jenna asks.

"I guess."

"Wow." She sighs.

"I don't see any redeeming value to this stupid game. None."

"Really. The best part for the players is when they get the snack after the game," Jenna says.

"Not even," I say. "Look."

"Oh, man. Granola bars." She points to the box of snacks on someone's foldout chair. Everyone knows there is an aftergame snack hierarchy. It moves from cupcakes and doughnuts at the top, to granola bars and raisin boxes at the very bottom.

My chest is recovering from the feeling that it had been me who'd been hit. Poor Oliver. Poor guy. The "men" line up again. Then their helmets clack together, same as those big-horned sheep doing battle over a mate. The players fall on the ground. Jenna has her eyes closed. I wonder if she is praying or something. Maybe that her brother, Jason, won't get hurt next. Maybe that these fathers would soon find a more evolved way to usher their sons into manhood than this mini battle reenactment.

Praying seems like a good idea. I stand in respectful silence. But then Jenna pops her eyes open again.

"Man, I got something on my contact," she says.

Everyone is quiet on the way home. It is the edgy silence of unmet expectations. I can see everyone's reflections in the car windows. Mom, with her hair that has gone from inappropriately frivolous to somehow ashamed; Dad, with his disappointed profile; Oliver, with his faraway face, lost in another place where children fought beasts way bigger than themselves and where potions fixed the worst evils.

It's turning out to be a lousy weekend. Hannah has already left two messages on my phone about homecoming the night before, and my family feels like jigsaw pieces, each from a different puzzle. I have so much homework I'm thinking AP stands for Addicted to Pain. And the red-jacket guy had gone back to his own world, back out to sea, maybe. Gone forever.

That's when I decide that shoveling elephant shit would be better than this.

Part Two:
Elephants Are Just Like People, Only More So

Chapter Six

Animals will sometimes offer help to others of a different species. In Kenya, an elephant was witnessed attempting to lift and free a baby rhino that was stuck in the mud. Its own mother charged when she saw the elephant, but then went back to eating when the elephant retreated, oblivious to her baby's danger. The elephant waited, then returned and attempted once more to save the stuck baby . . .

—Dr. Jerome R. Clade, *The Fundamentals of Animal Behavior*

I do sometimes shovel elephant shit (which has its own, sunny name: zoo doo), heaving it onto shovels and into wheelbarrows used just for this purpose. After all, each elephant contributes eighty pounds of it a day. Consider yourself informed if the question ever appears on *Jeopardy!* But when I'm at the zoo, I do many different jobs. I spread new hay and slice fruit and fetch Flora's tire whenever she has to be moved, and I set up the microphone for Rick Lindstrom's Saturday elephant talks, featuring the happy-to-oblige Bamboo. I help feed, water, and look after the physical and mental health of the elephants, check their trunks (adequate saliva on the tips means they're drinking enough water), mouths (rosy-pink means no anemia), skin (should be elastic, not dry), pulse (taken below the chin), and prepare their enrichment exercises, which include such things as hiding watermelon in various parts of the habitat so they can hunt for it, and hanging traffic cones from rope.

A little over two months ago, that day after Oliver's football game, my determination to volunteer at the zoo ran out right about the time I got to the elephant keeper's office. I'd followed the directions of Sheila Miller, the zoo's volunteer coordinator, and then, when I got there, I just stood in the hall. I didn't knock. I had nearly convinced myself to go home, when the door opened and startled me.

The keeper let out a little shriek. I guess I'd startled him, too. "Can I help . . ." Then he smiled. "Hey! Elephant girl!"

"Jade DeLuna." I held out my hand. "I'm here to work."

"Damian Rama," he said.

I waited in his office while he gave some direction to Rick Lindstrom, his assistant, a lanky postgrad zoology/animal behavior student with long bangs and a soft voice. I studied Damian Rama's office while he was gone—the window that looked out on to bamboo fields; the sill filled with elephant figures in ceramic, glass, wood, even straw; the messy desk with paper stacks and ring binders. And photos—a picture of him and his wife (he was right—they *were* both chubby), both with wide grins against a background of trees with curving, reaching branches; a family group by a riverbank; a black-and-white image of a barefooted boy riding an elephant across a band of water; and a large photo of Damian Rama embracing an elephant. He looked so happy, and so did the elephant. I liked him already.

When Damian Rama returned, we discussed the hours I could work and the jobs I would do. It was nuts with all the classes I was taking, but I was committed to coming after school every day if I could. My homework would kill me, but my inner overachiever reminded me it was community service, and my inner psychologist (who had Abe's voice) told me it was good to get out of my house and that I could handle whatever I chose to.

"I like your photos," I said.

Sometimes a person on first meeting will do something that tells you all you need to know about them. Or at least the most important thing. Damian Rama did not pick up the photo of his wife, or his family. Instead, he lifted the black-and-white image of the barefooted boy on the elephant.

"This one is my elephant, Jum."

"Wow," I said.

"Here, too," he said, and handed me the recent photo of the two of them.

"She's beautiful."

"Indeed. And a good soul." He looked at the picture and smiled. It may as well have been Jum's school pictures, with him the proud parent. "You like her?"

"Very much."

"Oh, we'll get along fine, then, won't we?" He chuckled.

That day, I met the elephants for the first time, in person. This is what the house smells like, I learned—wet concrete, hay, apples, the sweet/sour of crap. There would come a day, Damian warned, when we wouldn't even be able to be with the elephants one-on-one anymore because of the liability risks. Someone might get hurt, someone might sue. Some zoos already had elaborate systems of leading the elephants where they needed to go, caring for them with a barrier between human and animal, between human and lawsuit. But not at his house, Damian said. They need the touch, as we, too, need the touch, he said. As the saying goes, elephants are just like people, only more so.

An elephant is much, much larger when you are standing beside her than when you are watching her from a distance as you sit on a bench, especially with words like "danger" and "liability risks" in your head, and with your hands full of forms both you and your parents must sign relieving the zoo of responsibility in the event of your injury or death.

Damian brought me to each of them so we could be introduced. First, he buzzed me through the locked gates of the elephants' private quarters, where I met Flora, the smallest of the Asians (only six thousand pounds), with the pink around her ears and trunk, who is never parted from her tire; and Bamboo, the matriarch, with her high arched back and long straight tail. Outside (and for the first time *inside* the enclosure), I said hello to Tombi, the only African elephant, easy to spot with her large ears; sad, old, Onyx; Chai, young mother with the notches in her ears, and baby Hansa.

"Go ahead, touch her," Damian said as I stood before Hansa.

I put my hand out, flinched when she moved her trunk to smell me.

"Oh, my God." I wanted to scream. I almost did.

Damian laughed. "They are not tigers," he said. "Here. Blow in her trunk. It is like saying hello, or shaking hands. Once you do, she will never forget you."

He holds Hansa's trunk out to me, and I blow gently inside. "Oh, my God." My heart was beating so fast, I cannot tell you.

"You must approach them with confidence," he said. "It's essential. Do not show your fear."

I held out my hand, and did as he said. That day, I learned that an elephant feels tough and soft at the same time. Wrinkled, warm. And I learned that you can be brave, if you must.

In the two months that followed, Hannah had four more boyfriends, and Mom had the principal's tea, the holiday bake sale, and the Winter Art Walk. We had Thanksgiving and Christmas, and celebrated my eighteenth birthday. Oliver's football games wrapped up and Dad signed him up for basketball. Michael and I both got letters telling us of our automatic acceptance to Seattle University. I was glad; I knew at least one place wanted me. Seattle University—just a few minutes from home, on a quiet, small campus.

In those two months, I had also gone through two new patron saints when my reoccurring nightmares appeared again—dreams about tsunamis and wings ripping off of airplanes. I hauled out

Raphael, my other favorite multipurpose do-gooder, who guards against nightmares, and who also protects young people and joyful lovers and travelers and anyone meeting anyone else. Also, Gratus of Aosta, who is my usual natural-disaster guy (lightning, rains, fire, storms), but who I also discovered protected against animal attacks, which I hoped would give me a little extra protection when I worked with the elephants. In the two months I had also dated Justin Fellowes, this guy in my Spanish class, though after three weeks we decided we should "see other people," which in my case was a joke, but it beat hearing him remark on everything I ate. *I don't know why girls are always on a diet*, he'd say when I ordered a Diet Coke, and *You should watch your starch intake* when I had a muffin. I scarfed a Snicker's bar behind my locker door when I saw him coming once, and that's when I knew his time was up. If I decide to have food issues, they're going to be *my own* food issues, thanks.

You don't think much happens in a couple of months, but, looking back, I guess a lot had. I had many new people in my life now, in addition to Damian Rama. There were lots of volunteers at the zoo—ours were Elaine, a grad student with long black curls tied back in the functional fashion of her cargo pants and boots, who spent almost every day with the elephants; Lee, an older woman with deep wrinkles and a cigarette-husky voice; Evan, an accountant who was apparently recently divorced and expanding his new life. There were others, too, who worked days and whose names I knew only from the work charts or from the few times we gathered as a group. The zoo itself had many volunteers, from gift-shop workers to fund-raisers.

And I had Delores from the ticket booth, my favorite of all the volunteers. I should never have worried she'd be suspicious of me that day at the rose garden. Suspicious wasn't a Delores word. Her words were good ones, like "funny," and "kind," and "cozy." The people in the photo at her station were her daughter, son-in-law, and granddaughter who live in San Francisco. Delores drives a Mini Cooper and actually has a wicked sense of humor. She once said she saw Sheila, our volunteer coordinator, by the hippo pen and thought one had escaped—a comment more about Sheila's personality than her body type. Delores used to be a nurse in a cancer ward, and it just got to her one day and she couldn't handle it anymore. She and her husband "cut back," as she put it, and now she just gives her time to the zoo, where there's more living than dying. I've tried to get her to come out of the ticket box and interact with the elephants, but she just wants to stay there, selling tickets and examining passes and doing her seek-and-find puzzle books.

And I know so much more. I now know that it's disrespectful in India to ride an elephant with your shoes on, and that you should not approach one unless you have a peaceful mind. I know how to hose down an elephant, which is not something I'd have ever thought I could do two months ago. They roll on their side real nicely for you, like Milo wishing for a tummy scratch. I've learned there are mean-spirited people who shouldn't be let into zoos, who throw their paper cups and old gum into the enclosure or yell insults *Hey, stupid! Fat Ass!* to them. And that there are others, gentle men, grown mothers and daughters, who come to see the connections, rather than to reassure themselves of superiority. You get to thinking that maybe the dividing line shouldn't be *animals* and *people* but *good* and *bad*.

As far as peace of mind goes—I've gone through a lot of cough drops. But I'm proud of myself. I had this idea, and I did it, even though it was new and I didn't know what might happen. Especially at first, because I was thinking how elephants are wild animals, which means they are unpredictable. But I've learned that animal behavior makes sense. Much more than human behavior. Also, you look in their eyes and they look in yours and you see each other. It's not like you see *animal* and they see *human*, just that you both see your bond. Living being to living being. No words necessary. It's simple and uncomplicated and honest to the point of purity. And besides, I've learned that Hansa likes the smell of cough drops. She puts her trunk right up by my cheek, which could really freak you out, but I love it. Her good intentions make me forget to be freaked.

In those two months too, I had almost forgotten about the boy in the red jacket with the baby. Well, maybe I didn't forget about him, exactly. I just revised him, cut-and-pasted the feelings I had when I first saw him on the computer screen. Momentary sugar high, temporary happy-feeling buzz, boredom looking for a target. Just another good-idea thrill that wasn't so good, like my original intent to study gorillas. File it under Oh, Well.

But there were these moments, I confess, when I lay on my bed, a candle flickering on my dresser, just staring at my framed piece of sky, and thoughts of him would visit, uninvited. When the clouds picked up speed and raced from one place to another as if in a hurry to get somewhere, or when they lazed in one spot, the way you do in your robe on a Sunday morning, that boy would appear with his head tilted back and the first, encompassing feeling I had on seeing him would fill me again, as the elephants (now well known to me) walked and swayed on my computer screen. I would unwrap the thought of the boy, like you would a treasure kept in folded tissue paper and hidden in your underwear drawer. I would open it carefully, examine it from all angles. It was the kind of memory that had the bittersweet taste of unfinished business.

"You'll never guess what happened this morning," Damian Rama says when I find him in the elephant house. I take my overalls off the hook, step into them.

"I saw," I say. "That tree stump in the center of the field. Who did it?"

"Of course it was Onyx. She dug it up, threw it in the air. Ah, she must have been quite angry."

"Why?" I ask.

"Baby Hansa? Life?"

Damian Rama sighs over Onyx and the tree stump. Onyx had been a growing problem lately; she was becoming less solitary, more aggressive. She had gotten a parasite, and Dr. Brodie, one of the zoo vets, said she had to be separated from the others for a while. This only made her crankier.

"Onyx is angry," Damian says. "Onyx has a right to be angry. You've got to remember, for many elephants, their life is that of a human in a war-torn country. Ravaged homes, killed relatives, separation," Damian says. Here's another thing I've learned over two months—every elephant here has a sad story. Every captive elephant's story is one of loss and separation. Something to remember every time you see happy people getting elephant rides.

Onyx was a cull orphan, which meant, Damian taught me, that she had been taken from her family as a baby. She'd been weaned too soon, stolen from her mother and all of the other, older female caretakers. Even elephants that witness another one being culled, Damian says, can suffer problems like depression and can react to stress with aggression.

"Poor Onyx," I say.

"Well, if you don't feel secure, safe, you'll never feel free. If you're not free, you can't be secure," Damian says. He strokes his beard as he says it, as he always does when he is thinking. I love Damian; we all do. He's easy to love, with his warm eyes, the smile wrinkles embedded into his skin the color of toast. His goodness comes through in the way he handles both the elephants and the people who care for them.

I set two metal buckets of apples on the floor, in preparation to file Tombi's nails. Inspecting the elephants' feet (its cuticles, nails, and pads) and removing any stones from the feet is part of their daily care, but often their nails need to be filed, too. Tombi is already in the house. The pen has a separate door near the floor where the elephants can stick their feet out. My job is to distract Tombi with apples as Damian uses the long, grooved knife to scrape and file her nails. It's important when you do things like this to be aware of just where their trunk is, to avoid being injured. Most of the elephants know to put their trunks against the palm of your hand, for example, when they are being examined. The end of their trunk feels firm but kind of pliable, like the cartilage in the end of your own nose.

Damian lifts the small, square metal gate and latches it. Tombi is so well trained, she just sticks her foot right out. Man, if only Milo were that maturely behaved. I stand by the bars, feed Tombi a piece of apple. Tombi is an African elephant, which means she has two fingerish points on her trunk (Asians have only one), which is how she grabs the apple and brings it to her mouth. An elephant's trunk is pretty awesome—it smells, grabs, breathes, strokes. They suck water up through it and shoot it into their mouth, the same way you get a drink from the garden hose on a hot day. Hansa will shoot you with it, same as Oliver when he's asked to water the front yard.

"I've only known one other elephant to suffer so much. More," Damian says. He sits down on a stool in front of Tombi, puts her huge foot on his lap.

"Who?" Tombi crunches her apple.

"Jumo."

"Your Jum?" I'm surprised. I imagine the pictures on Damian's desk, the happy pair, remember the stories Damian tells me sometimes when we work together. How Jumo would blow in his face to greet him. How sometimes when they traveled, he would sleep with Jumo beside him, Jumo's trunk wrapped around his waist. How Jum would give Damian a push and then run away so he'd chase her.

"Yes."

"You never told me she was unhappy."

"It is a sad thing. Upsetting. She suffered as a baby. She is still suffering."

Damian is quiet. I'm sure his thoughts are there, in India. Damian had been a *phandi mahout* in India, he's told me. *Mahout* means "knower of all knowledge." A mahout is an elephant trainer, or keeper, or sometimes a driver. Damian is from Assam, where being a mahout is looked upon with awe and wonder. In other parts of India, mahouts are lower class, but in Assam, it's a privileged profession, and often passed on from generation to generation. Damian's father wasn't a mahout, but Damian had his own elephant when he was a child, Ol Bala, and he fell in love with elephants because of Ol Bala (and also probably because mahouts got the hot girls). Mahouts actually have their own kind of "university," he's said, where you have to pass certain tests about elephant care and training. You can become a *phandi* after passing these tests, and then a *baro phandi*, which is like a master's degree in elephant behavior. They are held in highest esteem of the other mahouts and the elephant owners, and even the government. That's how Damian knows so much about elephants.

Damian became unhappy in Assam, because elephant management was deteriorating. Younger mahouts, Damian has said, didn't have the traditional initiation into the "art," didn't have the proper knowledge to do the work, or the proper respect for it. They used violence to control the elephants, and Bhim, the elephant owner Damian worked for, was doing nothing about it. Damian argued with Bhim and almost lost his job, and when Damian was granted a U.S. visa just shortly afterward, he and his wife, Devi, left their home and family and even Jum to set up life here, where Damian got a job first as a keeper, and then as the elephant manager.

"Is Jum okay?"

"The first time I met her, twenty years ago, she was a baby. Still crying. She and her twin were dragged from their mother, kicking and screaming. She'd been crying for days, because just before I came, her twin died during the breaking process."

"What do you mean?"

"The breaking process? It's the first step in training an elephant. They are restrained and beaten."

"Why?"

"So they will listen to the new owner. What they are trying to break . . . It's the elephant's love for his mother."

Damian raises the long file to Tombi's foot, scrapes it rhythmically across her nails as she reaches out to me with her trunk for more apple. I look at Tombi, happy now, and think of poor Jum. Elephants don't just wail their pain—people think their eyes get watery with tears, too, just like us. "That's horrible. I don't get why that's even allowed," I say.

"Thousands of years of tradition. People don't see the humanity that lies in the animals, same as people don't see the animal that is within humans. The first time I saw Jum, she was trying to lift her dead brother up with her trunk. She was trying to get him to stand again. She'd even stuffed grass in his mouth to try to get him to eat."

I don't say anything. I imagine Chai being taken from Hansa. I imagine Oliver being taken from me.

"And when I left, many years later, she was broken again."

"Because you left? She was brokenhearted?"

"Yes, she was brokenhearted. But she also had to be broken again. *Ketti-azhikkal.* The process where a new mahout takes control over an elephant. They do not easily accept someone new. You see, an elephant is a very cautious animal. She needs to take time to see if something is safe. If you are trying to get her to cross a bridge she's never been across before, she must sniff it and test it, and will only cross if she is convinced of its safety. She will not allow her baby to cross until she has done so. Then she will go back and help her calf over. They are very curious, but very cautious. A new mahout, well . . ." The file *zsh-zshishes* over Tombi's nails.

"It should be a slow process, and he should work with the old mahout to understand the elephant. He should assist with chores so that the elephant will come to trust the new mahout. But in recent years, *ketti-azhikkal* has become violent, and mahouts will use physical force to control a new elephant quickly. One of the elephant's front feet will be chained, one back foot. Then, two or more mahouts agitate the animal, try to get it to chase while it is still chained. The new mahout gives the elephant commands, and the elephant resists. They beat the elephant with the *valiya kol*, the long stick, and *cherukol*, the short stick, until the elephant is exhausted and gives in to the commands."

The vision of this makes my stomach drop. Elephants get angry and show joy and are sad and playful. They are vulnerable, full of tenderness and feelings. Hansa put her trunk around my waist once, just as Jum did to Damian, in a huglike greeting. And then there is Flora, with her tire. Captured in India, she grew up alone in a zoo. She had a tire in that zoo. When she moved here, Damian says, she claimed an old ignored tire in the yard as her own. Like Milo and his blankie, or Oliver and the stuffed Easter chick he's had since he was a baby. When he was little, Oliver wouldn't go anywhere without it, and Mom had to sew the head back on twice. It's so dirty and looks like stuffed-animal roadkill, but he still keeps it on a shelf in his room.

These animals feel. They think. They love. People, one another, beloved old black tires. Chai was moved here because she was chained at her former zoo. She learned to undo the chain, and to fasten it back up when the trainers came. When she figured out how to undo the bolts in her holding area, she was transferred to our more open environment. I know people who aren't that smart. I know people who aren't as sweetly affectionate and loving. I know that feelings should be dealt with gently. Elephants don't have a voice, the power to defend themselves with words, and that only makes them that much more fragile. Four tons of fragility, a funny joke from Mother Nature.

Damian shifts Tombi to her other foot, which she does happily. I give her more apples, and she takes them, twists her trunk to her mouth. "Damian, it makes me sick," I say.

His eyes are sad, and he strokes Tombi's leg. He is very gentle. "My brother. He goes and sees Jum," Damian says. His voice is small. "She stands, rocking herself. For comfort."

"I'm so sorry. I know how much you loved Jum."

"Loved? *Love*. She's my child. I'm her mahout."

I don't know what to say. I can see his pain in the slump of his shoulders. I just keep handing Tombi apples.

"I left her. I fled. And now she is twice broken."

My two hours after school at the elephant house always speeds by, and when I have to leave, I do it reluctantly. Passing Delores in her ticket booth, walking out through the metal gates, always feels like a tough transition, an abrupt transfer between two worlds, like Oliver's Narnia books, where Lucy must pass through the wardrobe, leaving a snowy, magical land to return to the everyday coldness of the empty room in the huge country house where the wardrobe stands. I would walk through the parking lot, where I would often see Jake Gillette riding around on his skateboard with the parachute on the back, flying off homemade ramps and clocking leaps and jumps with a stop watch. Then I would pass Total Vid, where Titus in his pineapple shirt would be sliding *Riding Giants* across the counter to another customer. Sometimes he would look out at me, and I would look down, feeling too embarrassed to acknowledge him. I would count my footsteps on the way home, groups of eight.

I would open my front door and there would be the cooking smells of dinner, the sounds—the *siss* of something frying or the hum of the oven, a wooden spoon scraping against a pan. Milo would rush over from wherever he was and start barking maniacally (he is very sensitive to all door sounds—sometimes he'll bark when a doorbell rings on television, and other times he'll listen for when a door is not completely shut so that he can nose his way in). He'd turn to and fro and looking for his blankie, a toy, a sock, *something* to bring me; he's generous that way. Dad would be just arriving home, or he and Oliver would be returning from practice, Oliver's skinny legs sticking out from his satiny basketball shorts, his eyes tired and miserable. New invitations for some school function would be spread over the dining room table, and my phone would be flashing its mailbox icon, with the lid opening and closing, opening and closing, with messages from Michael asking for help with proper footnote form, and Hannah asking if she should break up with guy of the moment, and Jenna saying she couldn't do anything on the weekend because she had Bible camp. My mind would be pulled from the animal world into the human one, my hands still smelling like hay. This transition between two worlds—I felt a little like the rocket that burns up on reentry through the atmosphere.

That day, after Damian and I finish with Tombi, I help Elaine hang some hay sheets for enrichment, then change out of my overalls. I head up the path to the viewing area, in my regular clothes now, my backpack stuffed with homework and slung over my shoulder, and that's when I see him. Them. Just like that. Two and a half months later, at five o'clock in the evening—an unexpected time, an unexpected meeting, an unexpected veering in my day, week, life, and oh, my God, oh, my God, there he is, right there, and the little boy in the backpack, too, with his sweet baby cheeks rosy red from the cold.

A rush of adrenaline zaps through me, an all-hands-on-deck, Code Red, physical emergency that basically fixes it so I can't move. I'm stopped in my tracks, like an animal suddenly face-to-face with his predator, only my body is messing me over again, as my mind is saying how happy I am. I am a deer, who can die of a heart attack if it is touched.

The red-jacket boy points. "Look, Bo," he says, and there is his voice, too. Gentle, deep. Soft.

There he is, in front of me, not the object of my imagination but a real person, with a real voice. He stands, a hand around each of his son's legs. Of course it is his son. The baby's hair is bright blond and the boy's is brown, but his touch on that patch of the baby's bare leg, just there between the cuff of the baby's pants and the top of his sock, is too tender to be anything other than a parent's touch.

My legs decide that they can walk again. What I decide to do next, or decide not to do, is to just walk past them, that's all. Just walk past, smiling briefly.

Because I am a cautious animal. And this, too, is a bridge I have never before gone over.

Chapter Seven

The marmoset father carries his babies wherever he goes for the first two years of their lives . . .

—Dr. Jerome R. Clade, *The Fundamentals of Animal Behavior*

Casual, regular day. No big deal. Casual, regular day. Calculus. Spanish test. Starbucks with friends. Elephants, as usual. Nothing special, I am telling myself the next day after school, before I head to the zoo. Hair pulled back. Nothing sexy, nothing different. I'm going to work with elephants, shoveling crap, among other things. No new sweaters allowed there. Anyway, if I'm going to offer anything to anyone, I'm offering just me, and if he doesn't like it, too bad. But I probably am not going to offer anything, because this is a casual, regular day, so stop thinking anything else! Okay, no new sweater, but a little lip gloss. I'd worn lip gloss to work before, because your lips get dry. Okay, fine. My favorite older sweater. Goddamn, I'm going to ruin this, I just know it, with my own thinking.

There is no time for the perfect patron saint, so I light Raphael, the nightmare guy, so that this doesn't turn out to be one. I light him, blow him out, head downstairs. Mom has made a bowl of peanut butter cookie dough and is eating it off the tip of her finger. Cookie making is never simply cookie making. It is a direct result of an elevated mood, good or bad. It is either joy inspired (see the related French Toast Incident, previously described), or depression inspired—PMS, broken heart, listless boredom, agitation that can only be cured by the near inhalation of fat and sugar. The clues—no baking sheets out yet, the oven still cold—means this is *not* about joy.

"I suppose you'll be home for dinner," she says. Her tone sags. Bingo: depression.

"Five thirty. Or so."

"Don't be late without calling." Finger dip, consume. "Want some?"

"No, thanks."

"Jeez, it seems like I barely see you anymore." Her voice is a ball rolling downhill.

"Busy time," I say.

"You're not going to be around your family forever, you know," she says.

"Well, I could get married and have six kids and we can all live in my room," I say.

"At least we'd still do stuff together. Watch a movie every now and then. Eat cookie dough out of the bowl like we used to. Make valentines."

"Valentine's Day was two weeks ago."

"We used to make valentines together, remember? I'd buy all those paper doilies and the glitter . . ."

"When I was *six*."

"I loved that," she says.

"I've got to go," I say.

She doesn't answer. I leave the kitchen, close the front door behind me. I have this creepy, gnarled feeling inside. Guilt. God, what'd she want me to do, eat paste and have her tie my shoes for me forever?

The task of the day is to finish the elephant cleaning started by the morning interns. This means Bamboo and Flora, and Flora's tire. I work with Elaine and Evan, who is embroiled in some kind of divorce depression that day and barely talks, except to the animals. I know how it is—sometimes you're sure only they'll understand and/or put up with you. We clean the dirt out from the bottoms of Bamboo's and Flora's feet and give them baths, and when I am done, the legs of my overalls are soaked. Picture washing a four-ton car, only the car is moving.

The task is involving enough that the time goes fast, and I check my cell phone clock only a couple of times, because I am holding one of the hoses. I change out of my overalls about ten to five. My pants are also wet too from the mid-thigh down, so walking around, out toward the viewing area, just before five, after combing my hair and putting on new lip gloss, is also probably a good idea. Not because of anyone, but just so that the air can dry my pants a little. And then back to the elephant house because he isn't there yet, and then out again, and then, oh, shit.

Oh, shit, he's there. He's there, and now I have to breathe, only it's impossible because my lungs are collapsing, folding in on themselves.

I watch him from a bit up the path (stalker!) so that I can catch my breath and until he becomes just the same old him. We practically know each other. Okay, he doesn't have a clue who I am, but I can tell a lot about him already. He is familiar to me now, I remind myself.

Every big happening has a moment of *plunge*, that moment of decision, usually instantaneous even if you've been thinking about it forever. That *now*! Toes at the edge of the pool, looking at the water, one toe in, looking some more, and then, suddenly, you're in, and it's so cold, but nice, too, and you don't even remember where in there you decided to jump.

"Look, Bo, look who's coming. Remember that one? With the tire?" Flora. She's ambling out of the house into the yard with her new manicure. "She sure likes that tire. See, Bo?" The boy points, I can hear the nylon of his jacket swish as he moves his arm, but the baby just squirms in the backpack.

"Dow," the baby says.

"And that one. Remember him, with the really big ears?" Actually, *her* with the really big ears. Tombi. Stomping out with newly bathed cheer.

"Dow," the baby says. "Dow!" The word turns into a half screech.

"Okay, fine." The boy says. He sounds tired. "But no running off."

The boy swings the backpack off his shoulders and around, giving the baby a mini amusement park ride. He holds the baby under the armpits and lifts him out. I still can't tell how old the baby is. A year? A little older? I'm not too experienced with babies—my only real exposure was with our neighbors', the Chens', little girl. They wanted me to babysit when I was about fourteen, but Mom got nervous that something would happen that I couldn't handle, so they had Natalie come over to our house. She was only a couple of months old, and her head was as floppy as my old doll Mrs. Jugs.

The minute the baby's little tennis shoes hit pavement, he takes off running, in this rigid-limbed, forward-leaning way. It seems so unsafe. Like a windup toy headed for the edge of a tabletop. My own feet start moving then, heading to the viewing area where they are. I have this insta-vision—the baby running to me, grabbing my legs. Looking up at me, then smiling. I am going forward, because this is the moment, right now, when the boy and I are going to meet. Two points in need of a line, and now the line is being drawn.

The baby is running in my direction, just like I envisioned. And, yes, when I am in front of him, he stops and looks up. His face freezes in this look of half pleasure/half alarm. I smile. "Hi," I say in a small-children voice. Here is where he is supposed to smile back, big and beaming, the red-jacket boy seeing the connection we already have.

But instead, the baby's mouth twists, contorts. He looks up at me, and his face turns red. And then he begins to cry. Scream, actually. A wail so loud and terrified, even Onyx looks up with concern, and a couple making out by the savannah enclosure stop to watch who might be being kidnapped in case they're interviewed on the news.

"Oh, no," I say. "Oh, I'm sorry." Oh, my God. Horrible. Way to go, Jade! Perfect first impression—his baby screams in fear at you! You make the kid cry, for God's sake! Thanks bunches, Raphael—good job on the nightmare thing!

The boy comes over, lifts his son up in his arms. The baby sobs into his shoulder as if he's been traumatized so terribly he's sure to need therapy far into adulthood. "He's not good with strangers," the boy says over the cries. "Bo, hey. It's okay. Hey, kiddo." He bounces him up and down, pats his back. "She works with the elephants. Right?" he asks.

The baby is still crying, but my shame backs up a step. He'd seen me. He'd been here, when I was here. When I didn't even know it. Sea boy, desert girl.

"Yes," I say. "I help out whenever I can. Almost every day."

"We watched you before," the boy says. "You were hiding pieces of watermelon all over."

"Enrichment. It keeps them interested, working things out."

The baby, Bo, is quieter now. His chin is tucked into his dad's shoulder.

"The little elephant likes you. He sniffed your hair."

I laugh. "Hansa," I say. "She likes smells. You know, my shampoo . . . Hansa's a real handful."

"I know all about that." Bo peeks from the safety of the red jacket.

"I bet. Is this little guy yours?" I ask. I'm bold. I can be. He'd seen me. He'd noticed things about me, as I had noticed things about him.

"Oh, yeah." He smooches Bo on the neck, and Bo wriggles himself further into his dad, into that red jacket, which is right there in front of me. The real red jacket, the real boy, talking. To me. Having a regular old conversation. I am listening to his voice, this real person, this person who is not just an image in my thoughts. "All mine. This is Bo. Say hi, Bo."

Nothing doing.

"Hi, Bo. I'm Jade." I peer back at him.

"Jade?" the boy says. "Wow, that's really pretty."

Heat rises in my cheeks. God, don't blush. Please don't blush. Okay, I'm blushing. I think I'm flaming red. Blushing is so unfair. Might as well wear a sign: WHAT YOU THINK MATTERS TO ME.

He doesn't offer his own name. The conversation stops. Awkward silence. Well, that's it.

"And you?" I have to at least know this. Just this—his name.

"Oh," he says. He seems startled. "Sebastian. Sebastian Wilder."

Awkward silence again.

"Well, I'd better be going," I say.

"Yeah, I better get this guy fed. He's got maybe twenty minutes before he goes ballistic."

"Good luck," I say.

"Maybe we'll see you again," he says.

"That'd be great," I say. "I could show you around."

"Sure," he says, but he doesn't seem sure. Maybe I'd gone too far. Shit, I'd gone too far.

"See you," he says. "Maybe tomorrow." I hadn't gone too far. Okay, I hadn't. I'd done fine.

"Bye," I say. "Bye, Bo."

No response, not that I'm expecting one. I walk away, am almost down the path, when behind me I hear a small voice: "Ba-ba." Bye-bye.

I smile. I refrain from doing what I really feel like doing—leaping and hugging things. Hugging and shouting and doing good deeds for people for the rest of my life. Joy spirals through every part of me, spins and sparkles, lifts up my heart and makes everything look right. Jake Gillette is in the parking lot with his skateboard again, racing over a new ramp, and even his parachute looks bold and majestic.

"Cool skateboard!" I shout, and Jake smiles and does another leap for me. I pass Total Vid. Titus looks out, and this time I wave. He raises his pinkie and thumb in the Hawaiian "hang loose" greeting. The world—it sits in the palm of my hand. It's all mine, if I want it.

Mr. Chen is getting out of his car, coming home from work. "Hi, Mr. Chen," I say. I hear the singing in my voice.

"Hi, Jade," Mr. Chen says. He sounds surprised. He holds his briefcase and a clump of mail.

"Have a good evening!" I say. The day is one of the most monumental and spectacular in the history of days. I have met the red-jacket boy. And he did not have a wedding ring.

* * *

I see the letter on the kitchen counter when I come home, an acceptance to the University of Washington, just a ten-minute drive from home. Mom has already opened it.

"Did you see that, honey?" she shouts from the living room.

"I see it."

"You don't sound too excited. This is wonderful. God, I'm so proud of you."

"I am excited." I am. Everything is working out beautifully. The best school in the state, a red-jacket boy. I'm not sure why I feel this small, grating annoyance. The sense of something being scraped against something else. Maybe I'm just pissed she'd opened my mail. I tell my backstage mind to shut the hell up. I don't want anything to intrude on the happiness I'm feeling. Soaring, red-jacket happiness.

"Well, it's no surprise, though, with your grades. Bring it here so we can read it together."

She has her feet up on the couch, a book open on her knees. She sits up to make room for me and I sit beside her.

"You've got your whole life ahead of you. Wow. God, I'm a greeting card," she says.

"At least not, 'Sorry for your loss.'"

"Really. It's corny, but it's *true*. Can you believe we're looking at this? A letter from college?"

"I know. Freaks me out."

"I'm sure. This is *huge*. Dad hasn't seen it yet," she says. "He's getting changed for dinner. He'll be so pleased."

I hand her the letter, check out the book she is reading. "*The Life and Times of Alexander Hamilton?*"

"It's interesting. Quit with the look. It really is."

"Since when do you read history?"

"I read history," she says. "Mr. Dutton recommended it. It's fascinating. I couldn't put it down. Did you know he was illegitimate?"

"Mr. Dutton?" I say.

"Alexander Hamilton! Not Roger."

Roger?

"Oh. Wow," I say.

"Pretty shocking for those days . . ." she says.

She's missed my sarcasm. I turn it up a notch. "Now I understand why you're reading a"—I check the back of the book—"682-page book about the guy."

Mom does this thing with her mouth that reminds me of the time Dad took Oliver and me to a trout farm, just after we'd caught the poor targets, pulled them out of the water, and laid them on the dock.

I don't have time to follow this up, because Dad's voice booms from the direction of the kitchen. "Should I be taking this out?" he yells.

"Oh, shit," Mom says. "Dinner. I forgot." She tosses aside my acceptance letter and leaps up. I follow her into the kitchen. Dad is wearing an oven mitt with smiling vegetables on it, and he's holding a pan. The vegetables are the only things smiling. There's a small dark item the size of my fist in the center of the pan.

I crack up. "Was that a roast? Toasted roast. Toasted *mini*roast."

"I didn't even smell it burning," Mom says. "It's supposed

to cook slowly, but probably not for . . ." Mom checks her watch. "Oh, my God. Three and a half hours. " She chuckles and so do I.

Dad sets the pan down on the stove with a clatter. He seems pissed. Big deal, so she forgot. You know, give her a break, for God's sake. In the last ten minutes, I've been annoyed at her for opening my mail, and at him for being mean. When Oliver comes downstairs to help me set the table, I'm so glad to see him, I sock his arm. It's one of those times where you look for someone to like just so you don't hate everyone.

At dinner, Oliver chews his roast dramatically. It's pretty impossible—a piece of tire that had self-destructed on the freeway would have been easier. "Okay, all right," Mom says. She is half grinning, too, because, really, it's pretty funny. But Dad actually spits an attempted chunk of beef into his napkin and then shoves his plate away. He's being a real ass, if you ask me.

"I guess reading comes before dinner," he says.

Mom ignores him. She scoots her rice around with the edge of her fork. She doesn't apologize (good), acts as if no one has spoken. She puts a mouthful of rice in, then looks up and meets his eyes. She's daring him to say more—her eyebrows are raised in a silent statement of *Anything else you care to say?* They stare at each other for a moment, saying a thousand unsaids. Oliver has gotten very still. I'm not sure he's even breathing. The silence crawls around into the corners of the room, scary-movie-music style, something-bad-about-to-happen. I count the syllables in *Reading comes before dinner* and end up on my pinkie on the second try. Finally, the silence is more than I can take.

"Oh, my God, I forgot," I say. My voice seems loud. It's better than the silence, though, better than them staring like animals about to fight. "Coach Bardon called yesterday. He canceled practice tomorrow. Good thing I remembered! Work or something." Mom's head pops up. She looks at me. Her eyes ask the question, and my eyes answer. She rubs the bridge of her nose, hides her smirk behind her hand. She's pissed enough at Dad to go along.

"I don't understand why he took the position if he's never going to show," Dad says.

"Well, don't say anything to him about it," Mom says quickly. "He's a *volunteer*. They're never appreciated as it is. Boy, don't I know."

"I never said I was going to say anything to him. I'm not *going* to say anything to him. I just don't think he should volunteer if he's never going to show. It's a lousy lesson to teach the team. That's his third cancellation."

Oliver kicks me under the table.

"He's obviously a busy man," Mom says. "Who also has a *life* besides *sports practice*."

"We're all busy people," Dad says. "If this continues, I'm talking to the league, volunteer or not."

Oliver kicks me again. After dinner, Mom mouths *You're good!* as we get up from the table. I snag a piece of Oliver's sweatshirt. "Let's get out of here."

"Okay," he whispers.

"I'm starving. Dairy Queen? Something with butterscotch."

"Ice cream like Mrs. Cartarett's hair," he says. Mrs. Cartarett was his kindergarten teacher. She did have that hair—tall, with a curl on top.

We take Milo, too. He hates the feel of the leather seats of Mom's car, so he gathers himself up and perches on the carpeted mound of the side armrest, tail up, butt against the window and mooning every car we pass. Every time we turn a corner, he balances against the curve like some surfer in *Riding Giants*. Gnarly hot doggin', Milo. Bitchin'.

A few moments later, Oliver and I are happily clutching our pink plastic spoons.

"Don't ever say I don't take care of you," I say.

That night, I lie on my bed and look out my window, into the darkness. It's supposed to be sunny and clear tomorrow, one of those rare February tastes of spring, and so the stars are out, getting ready. I replay my conversation with Sebastian—*Sebastian!*—a thousand times. I watch the white and red lights of an airplane move across the sky. I am soaring, too, like that plane, so full of hope that for once I don't think of the weight of its metal, hanging improbably in midair, the impossibility of that. No, instead I wonder about the people up there. I wonder who is reading a magazine, who is fishing around in their purse for a stick of cinnamon gum, who is quieting a baby. I wonder where they are all heading. I think not of wings falling from the sky, but of wheels touching down, just as they should. The airplane landing. One piece, whole. I think of the doors opening, revealing a new place—a place so bright and welcoming it would make you blink.

Chapter Eight

Animals who are bored in captivity will think of ingenious ways to amuse themselves. A chimpanzee will pretend to get his arm stuck in the bars of his cage, or will hang by his teeth from a piece of string he's found and spin around. One lion realized that if he urinated at a certain angle, he could spray his visitors and make them shriek . . .

—Dr. Jerome R. Clade, *The Fundamentals of Animal Behavior*

American Government is group anesthesia. It's so mind numb-ingly dull that I stoop to counting the ceiling panels and the floor tiles. After that, I watch Jason Olsen flick pieces of pencil lead, trying to hit the bottom of Alicia Watanabe's shoe. He actually succeeds once, and I have to refrain from clapping. Of course, Mr. Arron isn't teaching us the fascinating, page-turning, and dinner-burning excitement of Alexander Hamilton's illegitimacy, so who can blame me.

I bolt out of there, but so does everyone else, and we jam up the doorway like cattle moving toward the slaughterhouse. Or calculus, rather—same thing. After that, Jenna drives me and Hannah and this other new friend of Hannah's, Kayla Swenson, to McDonald's for lunch, and even that model of fast-food frenzy seems slower than a stationary bike on a freeway. I am so looking forward to getting to the zoo later that time has turned slow and oozing.

"I really liked the rest of the campus, and then the tour's almost over and I have to go to the bathroom," Jenna tells us. "I go in there, and I'm washing my hands, and I see this sticker on the tampon dispenser. It says something like, 'The apostle Paul says to let the love of Jesus Christ guide your every action.'"

"*Every* action?" Hannah says.

"That's just it," Jenna says.

"On the tampon display?" Kayla says. "That's just twisted." The weatherman was right about the day's weather—it is crisp and blue but still February cold, which doesn't stop Kayla from wearing this tiny skirt that barely covers her ass, thanks for sharing. Kayla is a cheerleader, so ass showing is part of her regular daily routine, same as some people brush their teeth.

"I'm just thinking that maybe the student population there isn't as serious as they should be," Jenna says. She crumples up her fries bag, wipes the table with napkins even though we haven't spilled anything.

"Isn't that a good thing?" Hannah says.

"Yeah, you know, I don't see how you're going to have any fun at a Christian school," Kayla says.

"Depends on what kind of fun. There are lots of different kinds of fun," Jenna says.

"*Fun* fun," Kayla says. Her Coke straw has lipstick on it. "Guy fun. Party fun. Drinking fun."

I'm staying out of this. It's the whole culture of all-consuming nowness I try to avoid. Ever present and screaming its message in the halls, on television, on everyone's personal web pages. Do me, I'm yours. I'm part of the counterculture who actually thinks about the future. Subversive activities are always best kept a secret, so I keep my mouth shut. I take the lid off my milk shake, watch the blob of ice cream come sliding down the cup, heading for a collision with my face.

"You guys just don't get it," Jenna says.

"Isn't it time to go?" Kayla says. "I don't have a watch."

I open wide, slide in the ice cream, aim the lid back on the cup, and get up. "Yeah, we better get back."

Jenna is silent on the ride back, but it doesn't matter, because Hannah and Kayla don't shut up the whole way.

It goes something like this:

Kayla: I'm just about to go into the dressing room, and I turn and there's Chad, and I just about have a heart attack because I haven't seen him since all that, and I just freeze, and of course he still looks so hot, and then I say to Melanie, 'Let's get the fuck out of here,' and I just get in line with what I've got because it looked great on the hanger and if I put it back and come back later I know it's gonna be gone, so I buy it and now

I've got this pink shirt and it's got this elastic right here . . .

Hannah: Ugh.

Kayla: I know it. But, shit—*Chad.*

Hannah: I'm a sucker for guys with sexy eyes. And Chad . . .

Kayla and Hannah: Has sexy eyes! (laughter)

The whole time, Jenna is breathing out her nose like a cartoon bull about to charge. I'm biting my tongue, because I'm trying not to remind Hannah that she's not a sucker for guys with sexy eyes, she's a sucker for guys with any eyes at all.

I am starting to get that vaguely irritated feeling again, that sense of fingernails scraping down my internal chalkboard. We are friends, it seems, simply because we've always *been* friends. Like Milo and his blankie, Flora and her tire. My friends are a habit, same as the way I always put my socks on before I put on my pants.

"Great, Abe. Everything's terrific." I'm hoping to make this quick. My weekly appointment and I can't cancel without my parents finding out and it being a big deal. If I hurry out of there, I'll still have an hour or so with the elephants, and a chance to see Sebastian.

Abe taps his pencil, just waits. I know he does it so I'll fill in the blank space between us with words. I know it, but, shit, it always works.

"Terrific, really. You know, except for my parents' having a long-distance relationship even though they live in the same house."

"You think they might be growing through some changes?"

Another Abe-ism. "Are you a vegetarian, Abe?"

"No. I've tried. But I can only go about three days before I'm craving some huge juicy cheeseburger." He lets out a little groan of carnivorous pleasure.

"When you say things like 'growing through some changes' you sound like a vegetarian. I don't think they're growing so much as about to kill each other."

"I didn't say growth doesn't hurt." Another thing he says often. So often, in fact, he has a poster on one wall: ALL NEUROTIC PAIN IS CAUSED BY THE AVOIDANCE OF REAL PAIN—JUNG.

"Can you kill with silence?"

"Oh, yeah. Absolutely," Abe says. "How do you feel about that silence?"

"Makes me nuts. All the unsaids are like a heavy-metal band playing at some higher vibration only me and dogs can hear."

"And you manage the stress how?"

"I get out of the house. The volunteering's been great." No way am I going to tell him more right then. I look up at the clock in his office.

"Attacks?" he asks.

"Just an almost-once, but I'd had a cup of coffee, which was stupid." Coffee is not my friend. It gets me feeling agitated and looking around for a reason why.

"Are you late for your plane?"

"What?"

"You keep looking at the clock."

"Oh. No. It's just . . . I'm going to meet a friend."

Abe smiles. Taps the damn pencil.

"I'm kind of . . . looking forward to it."

"Jade?" Abe says.

"Yeah?"

"Go. Get out of here."

I have my mom's car, which is great, because I basically have this traveling freshening-up station. Don't get me wrong—I'd never put on makeup while I'm driving or anything like that, because I could just see me running over some bicyclist and killing him because I had a mascara wand stuck in my eye. No way in hell. Just the idea of it makes me want to unwrap a cough drop, quick. But as soon as I park, I swipe on the travel-size deodorant I keep in my backpack and put on a little makeup. I want him to accept me as I am, but I want to look good too.

I change into my overalls, and notice that Onyx isn't in the elephant house. I go around out front, look for her saggy old self in the enclosure. No Onyx. Maybe she's just out of range, but I get this little seed of worry. I find Damian in his office.

"Good afternoon," he says.

"Hi," I say. "Where's Onyx?"

"You didn't hear."

"Oh, no." I have a sick feeling. My stomach rolls up, sinks in sadness preparation.

"Chai charged her. She's being treated. She's all right."

Relief. *All right.* All right meant *not dead.* It hit me then with tidal-wave, lightning, hurricane force—how much I cared for them. The devastation I'd feel if something happened to one of them. What we risk when we invest in one another.

"What happened?"

"Baby Hansa. Onyx was being aggressive with her. Butting her, shoving. Mama Chai was furious. It was a dangerous situation for Elaine, who was there. And Hansa. I was just on the phone with Point Defiance. She'll have to be moved if this continues." Point Defiance—the zoo in Tacoma. "They'll take her, but Onyx is suffering. More rejection—is that the answer? I think not. But I have to think of Hansa and our humans, too."

"I feel so bad for her," I say.

"Every elephant you see in captivity who was not born there, each is a witness to violence, abused, abandoned. Broken animals. Sometimes I do not feel like an elephant keeper. I feel like a social service worker."

"At least they have you, Damian."

"They have me. And I'm glad for that. But I can't help thinking of my Jum. Jum has no one."

My task of the day is to take over Lee's place in watching Hansa after Lee goes home. Hansa had been eating sand over the past few days, and there is worry that she might fatally clog up her stomach. Victor Iverly, the zoo director, thought that maybe Hansa's diet was deficient, but Dr. Brodie disagreed. Damian personally oversees all diets, and he had another answer. Every time anyone turned their head, Hansa would dart across the yard to a patch of dirt and start shoveling it in her mouth, causing whoever was nearby to hurry over to her in a panic, yelling, "Hansa, no!" This was what she was after, Damian said. She just loves the attention she gets, all the shouting and running. So now we have to watch her, and if she does it, just very calmly and with no fuss redirect her trunk from the dirt with the bullhook.

I love Onyx, but I am kind of glad she is out of the yard when I get there. I think about Elaine and the morning's incident—Elaine with her functional cargo pants and firm demeanor would have handled it, no problem—but a charging Chai would have freaked me out. It makes me remember that release I had to sign, about my death or injury. My mother started trying to talk me out of the whole thing when she saw it, until my dad told her to hand it over, bearing down hard on the pen as he signed. If I didn't take risks, he'd said, I'd end up being one of those people who live limited lives, too afraid to take airplanes and swim in the sea and ride on boats. People whose fear of death becomes fear of life. Still, there are risks, and then there are RISKS, and Onyx, beloved as she is, is a bit like this kid in my fourth-grade class—usually quiet and sweet, but once frustrated enough that he picked up his desk and threw it across the room. I think they sent that kid to Point Defiance too, and I'm only half kidding about that.

Anyway, the dirt-eating Hansa doesn't make me nervous. She's just a really large toddler. So I babysit her for a long while, and I don't mind just standing there, because even though it is February, the sun is toasty enough and everything looks bright and the tang of elephant shit warmed by the sun smells kind of good. It's a positive smell, somehow, like when you drive past a farm with your windows rolled down and it's the kind of day where your tank top makes your arms feel free and brown and healthy and the backs of your legs stick a little to the vinyl car seat. That grassy, cow-crap-and-livestock smell that means it's been a day of open windows. Life is good babysitting this elephant, and Hansa is behaving too, except that I can tell she is watching me out of the corners of her eyes. Finally, sure enough, I turn my head, and off she jets to the patch of dirt.

I'm probably not the best person to be safeguarding Hansa's digestive health, because the reason I turn my head is that I see Sebastian coming down the path, his jacket over one arm. Once I see him, I really don't want to turn away. I'm sorry, Hansa, if you ate extra dirt because of me. But I see Sebastian and my heart lifts and I just want to watch him, same as I used to when he was on the computer screen. I want to see him walk toward me and know that there will not be a world between us this time. Someone walking toward you is such a simple, happy-to-be-alive thing.

Bo is with him, asleep in the backpack. Bo's cheek rests against Sebastian's back. Sebastian waves when he sees me and I wave back, then go to retrieve Hansa from her dirt feast.

"Is she digging holes?" Sebastian asks.

"Worse. Eating sand."

"Oh, man, Bo used to do that. Out on the beach. Once, he was rolling something around in his mouth and I stuck my finger in and fished around, and he was sucking on a rock." Sebastian laughs.

"Yum," I say.

"You'd think I never fed him, the way he was going at it."

"Maybe they're tastier than we think. Do you live near the water? You said 'the beach.'"

Our back-and-forth stops. He pauses. "Well, I did . . . I . . . Not now."

I've said something wrong, hit a tender place. Awkwardness butts in; it's a rude person shoving to the front of a line. Maybe he'd had an upsetting divorce. Maybe his wife left him. Maybe a thousand things. Maybe I am too eager to get information. Maybe I am pushy.

A couple appears with a small child and a baby in a stroller. The man, in a baseball cap, says the usual. *See the elephant, Jakey? See? Say Hi. Say hi, elephant.* Jakey ignores Dad, picks a leaf off of a tree. Mom rattles the ice in a drink she's carrying. *Let's go see the monkeys,* she says. *They're not so boring.*

"That's what their neighbors say about them," I say to Sebastian.

"This one guy threw an empty Fritos bag in there once. I wanted to kick his ass."

"Or dump garbage on his lawn."

"Really." The uneasiness is gone again.

"Bo's just sleeping away today," I say.

"He's been a monster. He's just resting up for more, I'm sure."

"This one too," I say, nodding my chin in the direction of Hansa. "See her looking at me?" I ask. "She's watching me."

"She sure is," he says.

"The minute I turn my head, she'll go cruising over there." I keep my head straight, watching Hansa. It's easier that way. Sebastian is so close to me that my heart is going nuts—not in the usual, full-anxiety mode, but in this new, soaring, zipping, full way, same as those planes at air shows. The fence is between us (always something between us), but I am near enough to smell his breath, and I think he's just eaten a mint. Little poofs of freshness bounce in my direction.

"Bo does the same thing with the telephone. And the remote control. Or my grandma's record albums. Or just about anything."

"It must be exhausting."

"Oh, man."

"Your grandma helps you?"

"Yeah. She lives with us. She watches Bo while I'm at work. She saved us, she really did." He looks away, rubs his jaw line with his hand.

The question sits between us, large and unspoken, just like, well, an *elephant* in the room. The question about her, the mother, the one who had given Bo that white-blond hair so unlike Sebastian's brown curls. I want to ask. I want to *know*. I'd lived with the mystery of him for months now. But I don't want to go to the tender places when we barely know each other. Maybe he needs to cross bridges carefully too. He is here, I am here, both of us in front of the camera, and that's all that matters for now.

Hansa has lost interest in the sand. She wanders away. Damian was right—our calm reactions take away all the fun. "She's going off to think up more trouble," I say. Sebastian smiles. He has the perfect smile, meaning slightly imperfect, just a little off. There's something about exact, white, ordered teeth that seems insincere.

"I should let you get going," he says. "You're busy."

"I'm about done," I say. "I'm heading home." I can't tell him what I am heading home to—AP American Government, calculus, AP English. Schoolwork. Maybe a phone call from Hannah so she can tell me about some shoes she bought, or an IM from

Michael asking about what pages we're supposed to read. Dinner with Mom and Dad. My life seems so far from what his must be. My life seems so *young*.

"Have you worked here long?" Sebastian asks.

"Just a few months," I say. "Do you come here a lot?" *As if you don't know, Jade.*

"I used to come every day, or, you know, when I could. I'd bring Bo after work. Or just myself." *At night sometimes. You'd climb the fence. You'd watch the stars. You'd tilt back your head and look at the sky. You'd think it over, whatever it was.*

"Just to see these guys?" I say. "Or all the animals?"

"These guys," he says. "I read a book that hooked me. This man studied elephant troupes and then ended up raising an abandoned calf. So good, it made me want to see them in person."

"Sounds great."

"I could lend it to you," he says.

"I'd love that."

"I'll bring it next time," he says.

"Thanks," I say. We hit the sudden conversational roadblock, that place where you're talking along just fine with plenty of road and ideas before you, when, all at once, bam. The silence of the end of the line. Your brain races away like mad, trying to think of what to say next, but all the possibilities are fading fast, same as trying to remember a dream after you've woken up. No, too late.

"I'll leave you to your visit," I say.

"Okay. Well, bye."

"Bye."

"Jade?" he says. "Good to see you again."

"You too," I say. Casually, though my insides feel anything but. I wave, walk to the elephant house. I hang up my overalls and dissect the conversation, and I remember how I asked too many personal questions and how he had seemed uncomfortable, and then there was that awkward silence when no one said anything about Bo's mother.

I go to the bathroom to wash my hands, and then I see that I have a very noticeable set of brown mascara spider tracks under each eye, and I just about die. Shit, I'd sneezed when I was in the dusty pen, and should have checked then. I convinced myself I've completely screwed up because a) I'm a conversational imbecile, and b) I looked awful and had been acting like I looked great. He probably won't even come back. God, I'm an idiot. I unwrap a cough drop partly out of habit and partly because I'm suddenly feeling this steel ball in my chest.

And then I remember all the good things. He'd been glad to see me again. He was going to lend me his book. And that mint. A breath mint. A breath mint means you care.

I say good-bye to Damian, to Delores in her little ticket box. The sun is just in those beginning stages of going down, when it spreads magic light on everything. An orangey glow warms the trees and sidewalks and even makes the garbage-can lids look beautiful. Jake Gillette's parachute, too, is golden and glowy, and gives me that bittersweet sense that time is passing. The "76" ball at the gas station glints in its slow twirl. I don't see Titus in his pineapple shirt, but I do see Mr. Chen coming home from work. The fountain is on in the center of our building complex, and the grass is yellowed with twilight.

"Beautiful day," I say to him.

"Ah, yes," he says, as he hauls his laptop from the backseat. "In spite of being rag-dolled at the office." Rag-dolled—to be drilled, rolled, and tumbled by a wave. He'd seen *Riding Giants*, too.

I hurry through an average, nonburnt dinner. Dad goes downstairs to work on his train, Mom leaves to call volunteers for the Winter Art Walk, and Oliver heads to his room to read *The Ultimate Narnia Fan Handbook*. I'm anxious to get through my homework, and I ignore the message from Jenna, who wants to talk about Kayla and what a bitch she is. I think she actually said "witch" in the voicemail, but if that's what she means, I don't see what difference the vocabulary makes.

I finish my homework by about ten fifteen, and it could have taken me longer, but I want to have some time to think, so I rush. After I pack everything away in my backpack, I clear my dresser of all the patron saints except for St. Raphael. I give him front-and-center billing.

Raphael flickers, and I sprawl on my bed and look through my lava-lamp frame, at the stars glittering, at the wisp of a cloud drawing across the sky like the tip of a paintbrush. I hold up the moments with Sebastian, gaze at them again with a gentle eye, with careful hope. I do the necessary work of falling in love, that time spent alone with your imagination. I close my eyes, remember the smell of mint, the baby's cheek against his back, his smile, not quite perfect.

The scent of a blown-out match, melting wax, fills my room. St. Raphael, patron saint of meetings, of young lovers. Patron saint of joy.

Chapter Nine

During a sparring match between chimpanzees, female chimpanzees will stand on the sidelines, wave their arms, jump up and down,
and screech their encouragement. In other words, chimps have
cheerleaders . . .

—Dr. Jerome R. Clade, *The Fundamentals of Animal Behavior*

"Didn't you have a friend with a car?" Kayla asks. She's going
home with Hannah, and we are climbing the stairs of the bus. I
see Michael and Akello, and I walk down the aisle and sit down
in the seat behind them.

"She got a job after school," Hannah says. They take the seat
across the aisle from me. The three of us never would have fit in
one, because Kayla has brought her pom-poms, which she holds
on her lap and clutches like an old lady with her purse.

"I haven't ridden a school bus since we had a field trip to Pioneer Village in the eighth grade," Kayla says. She bounces on the seat a little, making her pom-poms *chsh-chsh*. "I never get why these things don't have seat belts."

"I never got that either," I say.

"Where'd Jenna get a job?" Akello asks. "I need a job."

"Her church," I say.

"That's out," Akello says.

"If I had a job, I'd never keep up my grades," Michael says. The bus rumbles to a start, lurches forward in takeoff.

"I always thought it'd be funny, you know, when we have to job-shadow? To do a priest or something," Kayla says. Actually, it's mildly funny for once.

"The pope," Hannah says. They both crack up.

"Pope for a day," Hannah says. She's on a roll.

"It could be the prize on some radio station. Be the seventy-seventh caller and you could win," Kayla says.

"Call in when you hear . . ." Hannah says.

"'Jive Talkin'" by the Bee Gees," Akello says. Michael and I laugh. Hannah and Kayla stare.

"Do you guys want to go to the movies with us tomorrow night?" Akello says.

"Saturday?" Kayla asks.

"Yeah, that'd be right, since today is Friday," Akello says. Michael whacks him on the arm. "What?" he says. I like that about Akello. He doesn't get the social rules—*Don't insult the intelligence of a cheerleader, no matter how tempting*—or else he just doesn't care.

"Par-tee," Kayla says. "We're busy." Kayla is in "the popular group," obviously, since she is a cheerleader. "Popular group" is a phrase that's slightly embarrassing to use. If you use it, you aren't in it. I always think it's kind of weird how everyone knows who this group is and who it isn't. How does it form, anyway? It's not like there's some sign-up sheet. But you know and they know. I never can figure out what the separating factor is. It isn't just pom-poms or looks. Take Hailey Nelson, for example, with her orange hair and plain face, who is as popular as they come; and Renee Desiradi, who is gorgeous and shy and who no one pays attention to. Someday she's going to be famous and they'll show her year-book picture on television and none of us will even remember her. No, what I think it comes down to is who asserts a sense of dominance, just like baboons. It isn't necessarily the strongest and biggest and best-looking baboon that'll be the leader, but the cockiest and most self-assured, the one who assumes he'll win any fight. I guess we tend to believe people's high opinion of themselves, whether it is earned or not. And don't go buying into that psychology BS that says overly confident people only act that way because they don't feel good about themselves inside. They feel *great* about themselves. They can be stupid, irresponsible, a smart-ass, with failing grades or a sex-will-save-me pout, and will still walk around with the self-esteem a Nobel Prize winner should have but probably doesn't.

I'm thinking we ought to rethink the whole self-esteem thing. It should almost be a dirty word. I mean, look at Kayla. She has the intelligence of a tree stump, and its sense of humor. She's less about real attractiveness than she is about advertising, like those cereals with zingy boxes and toys inside and that make the milk turn chocolate but taste disgusting. The weather had turned rainy again, and she's still wearing this tiny T-shirt and this tiny skirt with rhinestones on the back pocket, like she's Western Barbie. Humiliating, only she'll never realize it. She's the kind of girl who shows how hot she is because she has nothing else to offer, who doesn't realize that hotness has an expiration date. Yet, I'm still a little nervous talking to her, like she's holding a lottery ticket she just might or might not decide to hand over to me. It is nuts, if you stop to think about it. I give her this power, and it's kind of like voting some idiot into office. But, hey, we're good at that too.

"Sorry we can't go to the movies," Hannah says. Now that they'd become friends, Hannah is hooked to Kayla like life support.

"I mean, you guys can *come*," Kayla says. "To the party. If you."

"Sure," Michael says.

"It's at Alex Orlando's," Kayla says. "You know where he lives."

"Oh, yeah," Michael says. He has no idea, I am positive. He'll have to MapQuest it. This seems particularly humiliating, Michael sitting at his computer, typing in Alex Orlando's address that he'd found in the phone book. "You'll come, Jade."

"I don't know. Probably," I say. This I know: It's easier to say yes and cancel later then to say no when people are right there. Lying on the spot is an acquired skill. Already, I am feeling the heavy ball forming in my chest, this weighted hand pressing down. It's new-situation anxiety, this time, rather than about-to-die anxiety. Mom would love it, me going, but, hey, my skirt with the rhinestones is at the cleaners.

My inner turmoil isn't noticed. In fact, everyone has already moved on. Akello has pulled out his Twain reading for English, and Michael is writing something down on his calendar that I can only imagine—ALEX'S PARTY—in stubby pencil. Hannah and Kayla are talking without saying anything. Their conversation goes like this:

Hannah: Uh-huh.

Kayla: It was like, ugh!

Hannah: I know.

Kayla: *Shit.* Come on!

Hannah: Well, you know, whatever.

Kayla: I guess, but still.

Hannah: Yeah.

Kayla: You know?

Hannah: Yeah.

The bus arrives at Hannah's stop and they both get up. Kayla adjusts her clothing, tugs on her hem, then twists her skirt so the zipper is centered.

"Aren't you freezing?" Akello asks her. Michael whacks him again. "Whaat?" he says.

"You would have loved it, Sis," Oliver says. "They had this camera, hidden in a pile of crap. Or this stuff that looked like a pile of crap."

"Cool," I say.

"It was. They followed the herd that way. They even showed a baby elephant being born. All the elephants gathered around to help it stand up. And then the male came, and they all circled around the baby to protect it."

Oliver is telling me about the video they'd seen in science that day. I pour myself a glass of cranberry juice, which is supposed to be full of antioxidants to keep you healthier. It is going to compensate for the brownie I am going to eat before I go over to the zoo. I have to be careful. The way I eat, my arteries are going to clog and I'm going to have a heart attack at thirty-five, like those type-A businessmen.

"Imagine the camera guy who has to hide it there." I take a swig of my drink.

"No, seriously," he says. "It was great." I can tell I am frustrating him a little, which makes the sicko part of me want to do it more. "It was awesome."

"I still want to know if it was real crap or manufactured crap. That'd make a difference."

"Sis," he says.

"You know, smell versus no smell," I say.

"Quit it," he says. His voice is so full of disappointment that I feel bad.

"Okay, I'm sorry. Tell me about it quickly, 'cause I've got to get out of here or I'll be late."

"Never mind."

"Come on," I say.

"I'll tell you later."

"O-kay."

"You would have really liked it," he says sadly.

My conscience would be guiltier if I weren't in such a hurry, and if I weren't so looking forward to getting to the zoo. I finish my snack, brush my teeth, zip through the dining room. I don't know where Mom is, but there's a stack of books on the dining room table. *The Jefferson Connection; The Forefathers at Home. Washington and Delaware.* Okay, it seems strange. But I figure I don't have to worry until she starts wearing a three-cornered hat and hanging old pistols above the fireplace. Then again, just because I worry about everything, doesn't mean I worry about the right things.

"Elaine and I can do it," I say to Damian. Bamboo and Flora need to be washed.

"Elaine is babysitting Hansa. And besides, washing them is one of my favorite things," Damian says. "It's so satisfying. Damn the administrative work."

"It's my favorite too," I say.

"Prepare to be drenched, then."

"All right," I say. I'm glad I won't be in the same place as yesterday if Sebastian comes, sitting there like I'm waiting for him. Okay, I *am* waiting for him, but I don't want to seem like it. Plus, Damian is right—washing the elephants is satisfying. It is like washing your car, as I've said before, but it makes the car happy too.

The elephants have a bathing area outside in their enclosure, but it's so important to keep them clean that we try to give them a daily bath as well. Baths are a big part of their lifestyle in the wild, and baths protect them from disease and insect bites and from getting too dried out. It also relaxes them, just like us with our bath beads and scented candles. The best time to bathe them is in the morning, but sometimes there isn't enough time for everyone. The one thing you've got to watch out for is that the elephant hasn't just done a bunch of exercise, or the sudden change in temperature can make them sick—like if you jumped into a cold shower after running a marathon.

We bring Flora and her tire in first. Flora lies down so I can squirt her with the hose. I have to be careful not to aim at any of her tender areas—inside her ears, near her eyes, her genitals, the tip of her trunk. Damian does the actual washing, because he can do it safely and quickly. In India, they bathe the elephants in the river, he's told me. He washes Flora's face and tusk, her stomach, and hind legs, scrubbing with a pumice stone. We wash her tire, too. All the while, Flora is making these little squeaks of happiness. The elephants love the water, but maybe it's just baths of any kind they love, because they take mud baths, too.

We work hard with Flora and then Bamboo, and then we let them out into the enclosure. Bamboo strides off (probably to cover herself in dust, same as Milo rolls in the grass after a bath), and Damian and I watch her, like a couple of proud parents. Damian chuckles.

"What?" I say.

"I was thinking about how scared you were when you first came," Damian says.

"Real funny," I say.

"It was funny, all right," he says, chuckling away.

"Well, you know, they're kind of *large*."

"You are progressing," Damian says. I look over at him and he grins at me. He nods. "Yes, indeed."

We admire Flora next, as she ambles over to the others. I know it is about time for Sebastian to come, and I keep checking and watching until I finally see him. Suddenly, he's there, and my heart just rises up again. Part of it is happiness, and part relief. I guess I halfway expected him to just not show, to disappear, taking this new joy with him. But no. He's there and he sees me and waves, and I wave back.

"Ah," Damian says.

"What?"

"Hmmm," he raises his eyebrows up and down.

"Quit," I say.

"You are progressing more than I even realized."

"You're embarrassing me."

"He has a baby on his back."

"I know. He's not married, but . . . Is it a bad thing? He's got . . . a different life."

"He's a responsible young man. Look, do you see? He has given the child a graham cracker even if it means the crumbs are sure to be in his hair. And you are a young woman. You are not an animal in an enclosure. And he has waved at you and you are still standing here."

"Damian? Thanks."

"I'll see you tomorrow."

I run back to the elephant house, take off my wet overalls, wash my hands. I hurry out to the viewing area—*Don't leave, don't leave, don't leave*—and hope I don't look as awful as I probably do.

Sebastian smiles when he sees me approaching. Bo ignores me, intent on his graham cracker, and Damian was right about the soggy pieces of brown that have dropped from Bo's hands and landed on the side of Sebastian's head. It's the third time we've seen each other, and something about this is significant. I can feel the change between us. The third time means the start of familiarity.

"Hi, guys," I say. "I'm a mess, and I'm embarrassed to see you." It's that trick prosecuting attorneys use, right? Where they bring up all of the flaws in their case first, before the other guy does?

"No, you look great," he says. Which I'm sure I hear wrong. What he says is, *You're muddy and wet and smelly.* What he says is, *You've got mascara there, under your eye.*

"I was washing Bamboo and Flora. Flora—there, the small one with the pink around her ears? And Bamboo—the big one. She's the matriarch."

"You think they all look the same at first. But then you realize," Sebastian says.

"I know. And their personalities are so different."

"I brought you that book," Sebastian says. "But I left it in the car. I can't believe I forgot it. I can go get it. . . ."

"I'm heading out," I say. "I can walk with you when you guys are ready."

"We're ready. We only came by for a minute. I like to take Bo out for a while when I come home. It gives him and Tess a break from each other."

"Tess? Your grandmother?"

"Yeah."

"Do you guys live around here?" We start walking. It's nice walking beside Sebastian. There's a coziness to it. The easy normality of heading in the same direction.

"You know where the houseboats are? By the Fremont Bridge? We live in one of those."

"Wow. That must be great." Seattle has a couple of houseboat "neighborhoods." Floating houses moored in rows along docks. They range from narrow and grand to quirky shingled shacks, a mixed-up combination of bobbing lives all packed close.

"Not the easiest with a little guy who just wants to *go*. Not much room to run around. And he's in this fearless stage, where he bolts and doesn't think. And all I do is see danger everywhere—him falling in the water, him escaping and us not realizing. Every other word out of my mouth is 'no.'"

I understand that, seeing danger everywhere. We leave through the entry gate, pass Delores in her little box. She pops her head up, raises one eyebrow at me. Man, I can't get away with anything in this place.

"That water all around would make you a wreck," I say.

"Exactly. I want to put him in a life jacket every time we walk to the car. Maybe I can just keep him in a life jacket the rest of his life. Here we are."

He has a really old Volvo, one of the square, boxy ones, with a car seat in the back, along with assorted children's books and toys and bottles and crumbs. It's the same way Mrs. Chen's car looks, while Mr. Chen's is vacuumed and ordered and spotless.

Sebastian swings the backpack off his shoulders, sets it down, and then lifts Bo out. "God, Bo, look at you." Bo has made a smeary mess with the graham cracker. He has it around his face, his hands, and down the front of his shirt. "How much of that got in your mouth?" Sebastian says.

"You had fun with that, didn't you," I say to him.

"I've got to warn you, he hates the car seat." Sebastian holds the crackery Bo away from himself, aims Bo's rear end toward the seat, and backs him in. Sure enough, as soon as Bo is ducked into the car, he straightens himself and stiffens. He starts to shriek. "Come on, Bo," Sebastian pleads. They wrestle a bit, until finally Sebastian is able to get the strap over Bo's head and buckle him in. He clicks the belt shut, closes the car door. Bo's face is red and devastated, still screaming behind the glass.

"Whew," Sebastian says.

"Whew," I say.

"All right," Sebastian says.

"I hate to even mention it, but the book?"

"Oh, God, I forgot." Sebastian opens the driver's side door, letting a few of Bo's protests escape. "Come on, Bo," he says. "Relax, man." Sebastian takes off his coat. He roots around in the front seat, plucks the book from the passenger seat, and shuts the door again. His face is flushed, and he stands there in his curls and a navy blue cotton shirt, and, God, he looks good. His shoulders are broad and strong.

"Here," he says. I laugh. He's just gone through a lot of effort to say that word.

"Thank you," I say. I pretend to read the back, but the text just floats meaninglessly past. "You look so good," I say, and shit! Oh, God, that's not what I meant. Shit! "*It* looks good. The book." I feel the blush coming, stampeding in. I curse my backstage mind. I can't believe it. Oh, my God.

"Jade, I . . ." Shit, what? Am I right? He's hesitating, struggling with something. I am such an idiot! But, wait a sec. I'm not sure he's flushed from wrestling Bo. It's not really a flush. It's more . . . Is *he* blushing? "I've got this child," he says.

I wait.

"And I know we don't even know each other, but it's been great, you know, just talking a little to someone who's not either under two or over sixty." He laughs.

"I'm glad," I say.

"Since we moved here . . . I mean, I don't have a lot of time to go out, you know, with Bo. But I work at this bookstore, and there's a coffee place there, and I was wondering if maybe you might want to come by tomorrow night, because I'm working. I mean, I'll be working, but I could take some time . . ."

"I'd really like that." I would love that. I would so love that.

"I know this isn't the usual thing, guy with kid, not the kind of *date* you're used to . . ."

I shoot past humiliation, roller coaster to relief again. I'm feeling so light, there's the possibility I might take off right there, lift up, like those dreams you have where you suddenly realize you can fly.

"That would be great."

"The store—you know Armchair Books?"

"No."

"Greenlake?"

"I can find it."

"Right by the place where they rent bikes."

"I can find that," I say.

"Eight-ish?"

"That's great."

"All right." He claps his hands together.

I look at him, and do something I would have never done if I'd had time to think. I raise my hand, take a chunk of graham cracker from his hair. He reaches for my fingers, turns them to see what I had retrieved. "Oh, no," he says, and brushes my hand clean. Then he holds my fingers for a moment, just a moment, and looks at them as if he'd just discovered something.

I, too, discover something right then, as he holds my fingers. I look up, and realize that I had stepped onto the bridge, that now I am on the other side. I am on the other side, and there is Sebastian next to me, looking at my hand, both of us, it seems, wondering how we'd gotten there.

Chapter Ten

Beavers make specific mate choices. They may completely ignore members of the opposite sex until they see "the one." Then the pair will go off, play, mate, build a home. They stay bonded though life, though if a partner dies, the beaver may eventually "remarry" . . .

—Dr. Jerome R. Clade, *The Fundamentals of Animal Behavior*

"He's pretty cute," Delores says on Saturday when I come for work.

"You noticed," I say.

"I noticed he had a baby, too. Is it his?" Delores circles a word in her seek-and-find book.

"Yes."

"Where's the mother?"

"I'm not sure yet," I say.

"I'd make that a priority to find out," she says.

"Okay."

"It could be complicated."

"I know," I say. I did know.

"You're young, and a child . . . whew."

"Okay."

"He's young. And a child . . . You know?"

"I know."

"But he sure is cute," Delores says.

The early morning jobs at the elephant house are cleaning stalls, laying new hay, washing elephants, and feeding them. On weekends we try to do this before the zoo opens, since we get the most visitors then, and it's best to have the animals out where people can see them. Enrichment tasks, like hiding fruit and adding new toys, are best done in the afternoon, so zoo goers can watch. That morning, I find Damian (who only takes Sundays off and is on call even then) scrubbing Onyx.

"Damian, I think you must spend half your life soaking wet," I say.

"Oh, I don't mind. I could give this job to one of you, but then I'd be miserable."

"Hey, Onyx," I say. "You big old girl. You old softie." Onyx is smiling, her lips curled up.

"Washing these beasts, it relaxes me. You, too, right, Onyx?" He pats her side. "Thinking time. I remember my home, the river, and my Jum and family."

"Your poor hands. Permanently wrinkled."

He stops, looks at his hands. Onyx lifts her big head and nudges him, same as Milo when you're done petting him. "Maybe so. And what of you? I'm surprised you are here today. I thought you would be on a date with that responsible boy."

"Tonight."

"Ah. Falling in love is such a magical time."

"We just met, Damian. I'm not in love."

Damian laughs. "I am going to have you clean the stables today, since you are already so full of shit."

"Great," I say. "Thanks a lot."

"Every job will be a pleasure today," Damian promises.

When I get home, I tell Mom I am going to a party at Alex Orlando's house. She knows who Alex Orlando is, of course. She looks so excited, I worry for a minute she'll want to come along. Suddenly, she's overly interested in my clothes, and she's suggesting this really short skirt I bought when I was in one of those stores with the loud, pumping music—the kind of store that makes you think you're brave enough to wear anything, until the music is no longer and reality hits. It's weird she's acting this way, because this is the woman who's been telling me for years that a guy should appreciate who you are, not what you look like; that you demean yourself if you advertise that you're just someone for them to have sex with. She's never really been one of those mothers who'll let you wear anything if it helps your popularity. But then again, I've never been invited to Alex Orlando's house. She hands me the too-tight sweater bought with the above-mentioned skirt. If she knew I would wear what she suggested to meet a guy of an undefined age who I had just met, who has a *baby*, she would have strangled me with her new leather belt she's just also offered to lend me. But to Alex Orlando's house, no problem. Alex Orlando, who ran for ASB president with posters showing him with his shirt off. Who won on the campaign slogan, "Vote for Alex. He'll make you feel gooood." Mom has lost all sanity with such riches at our fingertips—she's suddenly turned into a popularity pimp.

I decide on a pair of jeans and a nice sweater instead, and Mom gives up with a sigh. I'm not Barbie, and Sebastian's not Ken. Mom has a talk with me as I hunt around for the car keys, which I'm sure I've lost, meaning Mom will have to drive me in Dad's car to Alex's, or something else that will result in me missing this night. Her lecture goes something like this:

Mom: If there is any drinking at this party, I want you to come home immediately. If the environment gets destructive or out of hand, it's okay to leave. You know that, right? We have to look out for ourselves in situations like that, no matter what people may think. And if you do anything stupid like actually drink if there is alcohol there, I'll be very disappointed, but I'll still love you, and the important thing is to *call* and I'll come get you no matter what time it is. I don't care what time it is, because I'd rather get up and be inconvenienced than have to sit by your hospital bed. And speaking of the hour, I want you to come home by midnight, because all of the drunks are out on the roads after midnight, and remember that you need to say no to boys in a way that they understand you mean *no*.

Me: Have you seen the keys?

Anyway, by the time I get out the door, I almost forget where I'm actually going. I've been so convincing about going to Alex's party that I have to stop for a minute and realize I'm not really going there.

I wait until I'm out of the driveway and around the corner before I start shifting gears and thinking about seeing Sebastian. I have this ever-so-slight backstage-mind thought that Mom will pick up on my guilt somehow, my lying vibes. As I head for the bookstore, though, I have a huge natural-disaster wave of nerves. Are my jeans too casual after all? I don't want to seem like that's all I wear. Or too schoolgirl. He'd maybe been married, and I had barely kissed anyone on a date to the movies. In terms of our life experience, we really were from two different worlds. I start to get that foolish feeling, where you're embarrassed at yourself and haven't even done anything too stupid yet. Anticipatory humiliation. And I was going saintless—I'd left without even lighting Raphael or anyone else.

Seattle has two lakes right inside the city—one, Lake Union, where Sebastian lives, and the other, Greenlake, where Armchair Books is. Greenlake is small, about three miles around, and people go there to jog, walk, swim, lounge on the grass, and walk their dogs. Cozy businesses dot one end of the lake; peaked-roof houses in various shapes surround it. If you keep driving south, you'll eventually hit the zoo. Armchair Books is tucked between a bakery and a place that rents bikes. It's small and narrow, and an armchair is painted on the front window. I can see a fireplace inside, a couch and two plump chairs in front of it, and a large braided rug on the floor.

The store hours are listed on the door, and I have a plunge of disappointment when I see them. The store closes at nine, and it's eight already. It's going to be a short date. But what did I expect, anyway? He probably needs to get home to Bo. He has just a few more demands on his time than an upcoming history test.

I push open the door, and the bells on the handle jangle. It's quiet in there, only the voice of some old jazz singer softly playing in the background. There's just one customer that I can see, a man with a backpack who doesn't look up from the book he's perusing when I come in. The fire is lit, and there is the nice, warm smell of coffee and cinnamon and bread, probably from next door. The ceiling is high, and books rise up along the walls, reached by rolling library ladders, and where there aren't books there are posters, pictures of authors, I guess—I recognize Hemingway in his big beard and wooly sweater—and scenes of Paris bookstalls and quotes about the pleasures of reading. The building is long and thin, with a winding staircase that leads to a second level. A set of doors to one side opens to the bakery, dark now, but which I can see has a few tables and chairs, and a large glass cabinet.

I pretend to look at books in that slow, meandering way that bookstores require, all the while looking casually around for Sebastian. I consider going in and out the front door again to make the bells jangle some more, and would have if the man with the backpack hadn't been there.

I wander; I tuck myself between two rows not far from the register. I am staring with Academy Award–winning interest at a shelf of books when I hear my name.

"Jade?"

And there he is, Sebastian, with his dark curls and dark eyes, in a nubby brown sweater and jeans. Comfy, happily worn student clothes. "Hi," I say. "This is a really nice place."

"We've got many fine gardening books," Sebastian says.

I look at him, puzzled, and he gestures toward the books I'm staring at: *Tips for Northwest Gardeners. Terrace Gardening. How to Garden at Night*—okay, that one wasn't there, but you get the idea.

"I may be a little nervous," I say.

"Okay, I'm really glad you said that, because I just went to the back room to put on more deodorant," Sebastian says. He flaps his arms a bit. "I probably shouldn't even have told you that. Those aren't the things you're supposed to admit."

"No, I'm glad," I say. I *am* glad too. I thought of my own car-freshening, and this makes me happy. If nothing else, we have sneak deodorant swiping in common. His nervousness calms me.

The bells on the door ring again, and Sebastian takes my elbow. "I'm sorry—do you mind? I've got another hour, and then it's just us. I've got to do some restocking, but we won't have customers." I get a shot of happy, a direct injection to my veins.

"It's all good. I don't mind at all. Do what you need to," I say. I try not to grin like an idiot. "I've got all these gardening books to get through."

I like the way Sebastian looks behind the counter, the way the big lady with the canvas book bag who just walked in asks him questions that he seems to have the answers to. I like the way he rings up the man-with-the-backpack's purchase, and talks to him about the weather. I like that when an old man with a shiny bald head comes in, he knows Sebastian's name, and Sebastian knows his. More than anything, I like just being there while he works, doing what he knows to do, in his own place. A place that I now know is his own place. I like the way he looks my way and rolls his eyes or twirls a pen between his fingers to make me smile. I could have gone home right then, and it would have been the best date I ever had.

A little after nine, Sebastian takes a ring of keys to the door and locks it. The jazz singer is still singing over the speakers, but it feels suddenly quiet. Sebastian turns the sign to CLOSED, looks out on to the empty street.

"I like this time of night," he says. I can see his reflection in the glass. It is the red-jacket boy that I remember, the one who has big thoughts to think, decisions to make. It is the same red-jacket boy who comes to the zoo at night, who I now know works in a bookstore with posters of Paris on the walls and too many gardening books, with customers who call him by name.

"Okay, now for the fun part of the date," he says. "This is pathetic, because now I have to restock." Sebastian runs his hand over his forehead and through his hair.

"Let me help," I say.

"You want to?"

"Sure."

"All right," he says. "I'll be back in a sec." He disappears through a doorway in the rear of the store. Suddenly, the music changes. It's cranked up. The kind of rock that's all guitars and energy and lyrics with a message. "God, that jazz puts me to sleep," he says. We work together. Sebastian shows me how to check the computer for sales, how to fill the empty spots where the books are leaning lazily against each other. The music keeps us moving fast. When we are done, Sebastian looks around.

"Man, we did that in record time," he says. "Thanks to you."

"It was fun," I say.

"You're kidding, right? You, who gets to work with amazing, fantastic creatures?"

"No, I really liked it."

Sebastian looks at his watch. "It's early, still," he says. "I'm not expected back until eleven thirty or so. It's my late night. Can you stay? This is the time I was hoping for."

"Sure," I say.

"Okay. Great. All right. Come here," he says. He takes my arm, leads me to the reading area by the fireplace. "Have a seat. I'm going to get us something."

I sit down on the couch, all old soft leather, and it's like sinking into an oversize baseball mitt. The fire is in front of me, still blazing, and I notice for the first time that it's electric, which explains the lack of firewood and the ever-glowing flame. Sebastian trots to the back room again, changes the music. A woman singing, quieter, the voice of creamy liquid poured over ice. Then he heads through the doors to the dark bakery. He disappears from sight, and I look out the window. The street is quiet and it is beginning to rain. Drops patter against the glass, making me feel warm and tucked inside. I can hear dishes clattering from the bakery, and then the crashing sound of metal falling.

"Shit," Sebastian says.

"Are you all right?" I call.

"Aside from the broken foot," he yells back, but his voice is cheerful.

He appears a moment later, carrying a tray. He sets it down on the table in front of the couch. Two mugs, filled high with whipped cream, a plate with a pastry—a strawberry tart of some kind—and two forks.

"Wow," I say. "What's this?"

"Something for hanging out with me at work on a Saturday night when you could be at a party, or something," he says. I remember, suddenly, that I actually am supposed to be at a party. I feel sorry for the people there. That life seems far away, and the memory of it annoys me. It intrudes, same as the phone ringing during a really good movie.

"I don't really like parties," I say. "Actually."

Sebastian hands me a cup. Hot chocolate with whipped cream, or, rather, whipped cream with a little hot chocolate. It seems another good reason to be falling in love with Sebastian. He knows how to get the balance right.

"I don't really like them either," he says. "All that phoniness. Pretending you're not uncomfortable. I can *do* it, I just don't *like* it. And drunks never look good to anyone except other drunks. You've got to have a bite of this. It's my favorite thing over there." He taps the plate with his fork.

He's right, it's incredible. Buttery, and the bright sweet-sour of strawberry, and thick vanilla custard. "Oh, yum," I say.

"Isn't it?"

"The best." I put my fork down. Maybe it's the faux fire and the rain and the sinking couch, I don't know. Or maybe it's his soft clothes and warm eyes, but I'm just comfortable there with Sebastian. Some guys give you the edgy feeling of dogs behind chain-link fences, and some give you the nervousness of high heels you're not used to. But Sebastian—he makes me feel like I just buried my nose in warm laundry. It gives me a casual bravery—not how I'd be with anyone at school. With Sebastian, I am new.

"Okay," I say. "Here's what I know about you. Your name. That you work in a nice place and know a lot about books. That you have a son; that you appreciate elephants and live in a house-boat with your grandmother that you call by her first name."

"Tess isn't the type you call 'grandmother.'" He laughs.

"She sounds unusual."

"That's one way to put it. She raised my mother and my aunt by herself, used to have a community theater . . . But she's always been an activist. Give her a cause, she's happy. Old-growth forest—great. Picketing the NRA—no problem."

"Wow," I say.

"Tess is one to get carried away. She once led this secret uprising to switch the voice boxes of Barbies and G.I. Joes. When they hit the shelves, G.I. Joe said, 'Let's go shopping!' and Barbie said, 'The enemy must be overtaken.'"

I laugh. "No way."

"Yes way. Sex-role stereotyping in children's toys, all that. She calmed down for a while when she hooked up with Max. Weaver. You ever heard of him by chance?" I shook my head. "He used to run the Iditarod. He was an early climber of Everest too. Great

man. She was peaceful with him. But he died last year. Lung cancer. He didn't even smoke."

"I'm sorry."

"Me too. I think Bo gives her a distraction from her grief."

"I'm sure." We sit quiet for a moment. "So, what else is there
to know about you?" I ask.

He sips his chocolate. He has cream on his upper lip. "That's
a big question," he says. "Although maybe not so big. I wish I had
more to say. Mostly, I'm all about Bo right now. I'm Bo's father.
It freaks me out to say it sometimes. I'm someone's father. God.
It shouldn't be allowed. But you have a baby and they take over
your world. One little person and . . ." He put his palms down,
gestured a spreading, a widening. "Your whole life."

"Was he planned?"

"Oh, shit, no," Sebastian says. He half laughs, runs his hand
through his curls again. "When I found out . . . I thought my life
was ruined. I was pissed, scared . . . Man, so scared, I cannot tell
you. I was ready to start college . . ."

"Did you ever consider other . . ." I looked around for the
right word. "Options?"

"I would have, absolutely, only I didn't know she was pregnant until too late. She hid it from me. Everyone. Herself." *She*.
Bo's *mother*. I wonder where she is. Who she is. "Now that Bo's
here, I can't imagine him not here. The first time I saw him,
man, that was it. Something happens to you I can't explain. But
then, I was ready to start college . . ."

"You were just out of high school?"

"Just finishing. I wasn't even eighteen."

Quick math calculations. Sebastian is somewhere around twenty. We have a two-year difference, no big deal. Not to me. But with me still being in high school and him with a child, we are a lifetime apart.

I decide to let him know, get it over with. "That's where I am," I say. "It's hard to imagine dealing with that now."

"Oh, yeah?" Sebastian says. "I thought you were older." So that's that, I think. I consider taking a last swig of chocolate and heading out. What was I thinking? He had a baby. I had a locker.

But Sebastian seems to have moved on from our age difference just fine. "You seem older," he says. "Maybe it's the way you care for the elephants."

"I graduate in June," I say. Might as well hammer a few nails into the coffin lid.

Sebastian holds his mug between his hands. His elbows rest on his knees. "Are you going away to college?"

"Probably not. Probably here. Is college out for you now?"

"I hope not. I wanted to study architecture. *Want.* When Bo gets a little older . . . I can't burden Tess too much. It wouldn't be right."

I sip my chocolate. The mother question is there again—I can almost feel it. It is the rain on the windows, though, the music, the feeling of being in a cocoon, that makes me slip off my shoes and tuck my feet under me and ask. There is nothing like safety to make you feel bold, I was learning. "What about Bo's mom? Can she help you?"

"She's . . ." It almost seems as if he has to think about this. "Dead. Died."

He gets up from the couch. Walks to the window. Folds his arms around himself.

"Oh, my God," I whisper. Oh, my God, oh, my God. He hadn't wanted to talk about it, and now I know why. Shit, that explains things. And I had to go and open my big mouth. I could be so stupid. I could be so bad at reading signs. My instinct spoke in a foreign language.

"Yeah," he says.

"What happened?" I whisper. This—it requires soft voices. I feel sick with horror. He doesn't speak for a while.

"She died. . . . Childbirth," he says finally.

"Oh, my God," I say.

"Yeah."

Childbirth. Oh, God, how awful. How traumatic. How rare was that? And what guilt he must have. I can't take it in. I can't picture his life. It's like seeing some disaster on TV. The words go in, even the pictures, but there's no way to grasp it and make it real. Real tragedy, not the kind of my imagination.

"I'm so sorry," I say.

"Can we . . . talk about something else?" Sebastian says to the window. "You know . . ."

"I am so sorry," I say.

"It's . . . what happened." He stares into the street. "I just want to say one more thing," he says at last. A gust of wind blows the trees outside, and splats of rain hit the window. I picture people under umbrellas on the grounds of a cemetery. "This thing that happened between Tiffany and me . . ."

Tiffany. A real girl. With white-blond hair . . .

"Getting pregnant and all . . ." Sebastian crosses his arms, looks up at the ceiling for a moment. "I didn't go around doing that, you know, having sex with people. Tiffany . . . She was someone I loved since I was like, eleven. Her parents were really overbearing. They put all this pressure on her. She would cry and tell me about it and I would just break in half. This sad, beautiful little person I wanted to watch over. She said when she was with me was the only time her life was *true*. When we finally got together, I mean really got more serious . . ."

"It's all right," I say. I don't know what is all right. Nothing, really.

"We don't know each other, but I don't want you to get the wrong idea about me because of Bo. Me having Bo. 'Getting a girl pregnant'—I mean, it sounds like someone who's this . . . I didn't even go on *dates*."

"I appreciate your telling me. I didn't think that, anyway. . . ."

"You—you're like the only other one I've even *noticed*."

I don't say anything, mostly because my insides are tangled. Sad, happy, heavy, dancing. I want to cry. I want to smile.

"When that baby elephant put his trunk up to your hair, and you kind of pulled back, surprised . . . And then you rubbed his trunk. *Her* trunk. It was really . . ."

"I *was* surprised. . . ."

"Caring," he says.

"You can't *not* love them," I say.

"Oh, I'm sure some people could manage," he says. "Most people, it seems like they've only got one part of the equation down. Caring for themselves, or caring for someone else. And I've learned how important it is to have both. I don't know. . . . Look, I'm sorry about all the deep talk for one night. I feel like a fuck-up. First date, and I make you work in the store and then we discuss these things, and I don't even take you to the movies or something. And I don't even know your last name. . . ."

"DeLuna," I say.

"Jade DeLuna. God, that's pretty," he says. "It fits you. I'm so glad to know, because it's been bugging me. One of those things you're embarrassed to ask after too much time passes. Something I should have found out a while back."

"Like how old Bo is," I say.

"Fifteen months," he says. "Tess tells me we stop counting his age in months after a year and a half. If not, he'll be five and we'll still be saying he's sixty months."

"Yeah, that might embarrass him."

"That's supposed to be part of the job, right? I'm looking forward to that."

"My mother was great at it," I say. "She brought me my lunch once, when I forgot. I was a sophomore. She came to my math class."

"Ouch." Sebastian laughs, and then we are off, talking and laughing, and things are easy and there are no sudden road-blocks. We are in front of a blazing faux fire, surrounded by books, the reflection of the streetlights showing on the wet pavement outside. Later, he reaches for my stockinged feet, puts them in his lap.

And that hand on my foot—just that, is one of those uncommon moments, those times when you don't wish for something else, for even one thing to be different; when you have no other needs and no worries, where your insides are calm, and everything you were ever restless about, anything that had ever given you angst, is quieted to stillness. No steel ball in your chest, no breathless fear. No blue numbness of nearly passing out, no nagging doubts of the backstage mind. All of that, forgotten. It is just rightness, so rare.

We say good night outside the store, hug briefly. He'll be coming by the zoo soon, he says. I head to my car. The fir tree I parked under is decorated with raindrops. They glisten white and magical under the streetlight, cling to the needles of the tree, and then slide off. I tilt my chin to the sky, to that treetop. I take in the night, Sebastian-style. I let the drops dot my face. I feel that hand on my stockinged foot again. I breathe the night air. I drink in its cold, wet happiness.

Chapter Eleven

A rhesus monkey mother will sometimes do a "double-hold." She will grab her own baby, along with the baby of a high-status monkey, when its mother is not looking. She will hold them both together in her arms, thereby encouraging a bond between her child and the high-status offspring . . .

—Dr. Jerome R. Clade, *The Fundamentals of Animal Behavior*

When I get home that night, I see that Mom's been waiting up, reading. I tell her I'm too tired to talk, that the party had been great. She's obviously pleased. She tightens the tie around her robe, puts her arm around my shoulders, and kisses my cheek.

The next morning before breakfast, I switch on the elephant cam and watch for a while. I won't be going in to work—I've got so much homework, I'll need a shovel and one of those hats with the lights that miners wear just to get out from under it—so I want to see how everyone is. Watching the elephants also makes me feel closer to Sebastian. I replay our night in my head—restocking the books, drinking hot chocolate, hearing about Tess and Bo's mother.

It was such a perfect night, but when I play it back, my brain keeps snagging on something. Maybe it's a sabotaging snag. Maybe it's an important listen-to-me-now snag. How can you tell the difference? My body sometimes told me I was in mortal danger when I was taking a calculus test, so, you know, how can you trust your instinct? I want to tell my thoughts to shut the hell up, but I still keep going over what Sebastian had said about Tiffany. Dying in childbirth. The way he'd told me she was dead. The way it had almost sounded like it was a surprise to him, too.

It's stupid, I know, to think like I'm thinking, because what did I know about any of this? I couldn't have any idea how someone might feel or act if something so awful had happened. Maybe you'd feel distanced from it. And he did seem a little distanced. He had sounded sad about his grandmother's friend, Max Weaver, dying. When I'd said I was sorry, he'd said that he was sorry too. But not so with Tiffany. Had he said "I'm sorry too" about her? I didn't think so, but maybe I was remembering wrong. Maybe this was more of the psycho revisionist editing my brain was so fond of. Maybe he just couldn't bear to think about it because the pain was too much. Maybe he didn't want to overwhelm me. Maybe my backstage mind just likes to screw things up whenever something feels okay. Whenever something feels great.

I am watching Chai and Bamboo hanging out near the water when an instant message pops up.

YOU MISSED OUT, Michael types in these huge letters.

So sad, I write back.

More booze than a liquor store convention

I smile. Tap the keys. **You drink?**

Had half a beer and I could barely talk

Moron

No answer yet. I wait. **Felt like one of those foreign films where the soundtrack doesn't match the moving lips**

Lost all respect for you. Not that I ever had any

Stupid party. Should've done homework. Alex's dad came home early and . . .

My door opens. Shit, my door opens, and Mom stands there in her robe.

"Hi, honey," she says.

No knock, nothing. My heart pummels my insides, fueled by this panicked surge of guilt, and I reach around for the mouse to click off Michael's messages. Getting that little arrow into that little X is tough to do with shaking hands, suddenly as tricky as those pathetic vending machines where you have to pick up a stuffed toy with a mechanical claw.

"What was that?" she asks.

"What was what?" God, I'm guilty. I sound so guilty. I'm so guilty, my hands are trembling with double-shot espresso shakes. Man, I'd make the worst criminal.

"Up on the screen."

"Just Michael, messing around." She saw. I knew it. She saw, Goddamn it.

"It says, 'You missed out.'"

"Oh, yeah. He went with Akello to a party for Akello's dad."

"I thought you said he was going to Alex Orlando's last night."

"I did say that. But he changed his mind at the last minute. Akello's dad had this thing and his parents made him go and he was just begging Michael to go, so, you know, he wouldn't be the only one under forty, and so, you know, Michael went, because that's the kind of guy he is. . . ."

"So how was the party?"

"Michael said it was boring. His dad had a lot of alcohol there and the adults got embarrassing."

"No, your party. Alex's."

"Oh, it was great. Yeah. I had a really great time."

"What'd you do?" She sits on my bed. Crosses her feet at the ankles. Folds the flap of her robe closed so I don't see unshaven legs. She's all comfy. I feel an ungenerous, inward groan. Sometimes living with Mom is like trying to walk in those new shoes you buy at the drugstore, the ones connected by plastic string.

"Oh, you know—talked, listened to music, ate. Some people danced."

"What did you eat?"

If you want any further evidence that my brain is a vicious and cruel traitor, then here you go. Eat? My thoughts zip crazily. What did we eat? I rack my mind, try to come up with some food, and for some reason, the question feels like something off of *Jeopardy!* Food, food! All that's coming to me is this vision of Titus from Total Vid. Why Titus? Why right then? I have no idea, but that's what's there. Titus, giving me the "hang loose" sign.

"Pineapple," I say.

"Pineapple?"

Oh, my God. Oh, for God's sake! Who had pineapple at a party? Pineapple? Jesus!

"It was Hawaiian themed," I say. "Pineapple. And pork."

"Pork."

"Yeah. You know, that barbequed kind they have in Hawaii."

She thinks about this. "Oh."

"Tiki lamps outside." Shit!

"Wow. Were there costumes? Were you supposed to wear a costume? If we would have known . . ."

"Yeah, I could've worn my coconut bra if I hadn't grown out of it. No! There weren't any costumes . . ."

"I'm sorry. How am I supposed to know?"

"Alex in a hula skirt. Whoa."

"So, do you think it went well? I mean, do you think you'll get asked again?"

I want her off my bed, then. With that question, I just want her *away*. This anger boils up inside, spills over in sarcasm. "Well, you could slip him a couple of twenties to invite me next time."

"Jade! Come on."

"Or maybe you can try out for cheerleader. Then you could be invited to the parties yourself."

Mom's face falls. "That is so mean. Jeez, Jade. I was only

wondering if you had a good time. If you'd be going again." Her mouth turns down. She looks like she might cry.

"Okay. I'm sorry." Mom stares down at her hands. Studies her fingernails. Shit. I shouldn't have said what I did. "Yeah, I'll be going again. Maybe next weekend."

"God, Jade. After everything I do for you. You didn't have to say those things."

Guilt creeps around, plucks at my insides. I feel like I have stolen something. Maybe her dignity.

"I'm sorry. I'm just . . . tired. It was a late night and I didn't sleep well, and now I've got all this homework . . ."

Mom smoothes her robe against her knees.

"I didn't mean to be mean," I say, even though I did.

She is quiet, and then finally she says, "Okay." And then: "I'm still glad you had a good time. I think it's important to try new things, mix with new people."

I think of all the beaches she won't go to and boats she won't ride and trips she won't take, and I keep my mouth shut. Blue ribbon in self-control.

"I'm going to get dressed," she says.

I remember, then, something Damian had told me. About an elephant that had been part of a circus for fifteen years, who had suddenly broken loose and gored one of the trainers. I don't know why I think about it right then. All I know is that I do. This thought, it makes me sad. I feel like a traitor, but more than that, I just feel the weighty, fullness of loss. For the times we used to talk. For that time we were in the bathroom at the mall, and she was being silly, thinking we were the only ones there. *Shouldn't have had that Slurpee. Get it? Slur-PEE? Ah! Ah! Ah!* She fake-laughed, real loud. It was only after we'd washed our hands that we saw a pair of clogs underneath the far stall, causing us to laugh our heads off for a good ten minutes as soon as the door closed behind us.

I go downstairs to have some breakfast. Milo appears, sits at my feet, and looks up with pleading hope. "You, with the fur. Quit staring," I say. I pour the last bit of Cheerios in my bowl.

"Eyuw," I say to Oliver, who has come downstairs wearing the pajamas that make him look like a husband in a fifties TV show.

"What?"

I show him the bowl.

"Cereal dust," he says.

"I'm not eating it. Don't tell." I empty my bowl into the garbage.

Oliver checks the freezer. "Waffles," he suggests.

"Okay."

Oliver reaches into the waffle box and pulls out a couple that had seen better days. If we had an ice pick and a few hours, we could probably chip away and eventually find them.

"'Always winter and never Christmas,'" Oliver says.

"Think if Aslan comes, he'll bring some Eggos?"

"Sis, if you're wishing, you can wish for anything. Not just waffles. How about a whole breakfast? Bacon and pancakes with strawberries and whipped cream."

"I'm always too practical in my wishing," I say. I use my inhuman strength to break off a waffle. I put it in the toaster and push the lever down, and that's when we hear this shout.

Dad. Yelling. Man, is he angry.

"Tell me!" he says.

Then Mom's voice. Too quiet to hear.

"Why hide it? Huh? What are you trying to hide?"

His voice shoots down the stairs, bounces and crashes against all the regular parts of our kitchen—the coffeepot and the fridge, the pot holder hanging by its loop on the stove. Oliver looks at me with wide eyes. See, our parents never fight. Well, they fight, but *disagreement* is the word that comes more to mind. Someone would say something a bit sharply and the other would stare off or leave the room. And then the issue would just fade away, like invisible ink after the lemon juice has dried. No one ever *yelled*.

Oliver and I just stand really still, looking at each other. Milo is still too, but he's just waiting for a waffle.

I gesture for Oliver to follow me. We tiptoe over to the stairwell, like a couple of burglars. Listen.

"Since when are you so interested in this stuff? That's what I'd really like to know."

"You're making a big deal out of nothing," Mom says. "Roger just thought I'd like these. He's trying to be helpful. I *am* interested. . . ."

Roger. Mr. Dutton? Dad was jealous of my *librarian*? Giving Mom *books*?

"And they're under the bed—why?"

Nothing.

"Goddamn it, Nancy, answer me."

Silence.

Answer, I plead. Books, for God's sake. Big deal! Answer!

"Well, that tells me what I need to know. Fuck, this is great." Oliver practically gasps. *Fuck* is not part of Dad's usual vocabulary, at least that we know. It was the kind of thing he'd say when he was fixing the kitchen sink, or as part of a joke to the car mechanic when they both looked under the hood of Dad's car— *Carburetor is French for* Don't fuck with me, *is what I believe.* But it was nothing he would say to Mom. Nothing he'd yell at her in anger.

"No!" Mom says. "Stop it! I don't know why I hid them . . . There's no real reason to hide them . . ."

"And what about our household, huh? It's a mess. There's no food in the house. The laundry—"

"I never get to the laundry. Okay? I'm a criminal."

"It's overflowing. There's no coffee. The kitchen's a mess. . . ."

He might have been a little right.

"I noticed that too," Oliver whispers.

"You don't even care about this house anymore!" Dad shouts. "Us. Me."

"That's all I do. Care about everyone else. Do everything for everyone else! You are all capable people who can clean the kitchen and do your own laundry. Who does my laundry? Who cares for me?"

"I don't even know you anymore," Dad says.

Mom starts to cry. Shit, she starts to cry. I hear her voice break down. A lump starts in my own throat.

Oliver whispers, "Are they going to get a divorce?"

The word is huge, catastrophic. A word like *earthquake*, or *tidal wave*, or *plane crash*.

"Of course not," I tell him. "Not in a million years."

We listen to Mom cry. Then I feel Oliver's hand slip into mine. We sit like that for a while. Oliver seems small in his husband pajamas. I can't take it anymore. My heart hurts. First, Mom in my room; now this. I feel all hollow with grief.

* "Come on," I say.

"What?"

"Get dressed as fast as you can and meet me downstairs."

I step to my room quietly, knock three times softly. I throw on some clothes and pull a few bills from the wad of money I have in my sock drawer. Every time Mom or Dad gives me any, or I get a birthday card with money tucked inside from one of my relatives, I stash it. I'm not much of a spender. I prefer the comfort of those bills in a fat lump to anything I might think I want for a moment.

I feed Milo some of his food, which looks like a brown version of Capn' Crunch with Crunch Berries. Oliver hunts in the closet for his shoes. The waffle has popped up, and I know how it will taste anyway, that stale, frozen taste of things in one place too long. I leave it there. It will be a waffle statement. I grab Mom's keys from the kitchen counter and we leave out the front door.

"Where we going, Sis? Are we coming back?"

"Of course we're coming back." I swat his leg. "Okay—clue. 'If you're wishing, you can wish for anything.'"

He still hasn't guessed by the time we turn into Yvonne's House of Pancakes parking lot (or YHOP, for the acronym minded). Yvonne's had been there forever, or at least from the seventies. Big, ugly brass flower sculptures decorate one wall. The menus have thirty years' worth of stickiness, and the waitress still has a crush on Tony Danza, but the pancakes are big and buttery. Strawberry pancakes, bacon. Large orange juice with pulp clinging to the empty glass. We go from starving to stuffed in twenty minutes.

Then I suggest we go to Total Vid. "I don't want to see the surfing movie again," Oliver says, but that's not what I have in mind. Titus in his pineapple shirt apparently has the day off, but this other girl wearing pigtails and a leopard-print shirt helps us find the nature videos. They don't have the spycam-in-crap one that Oliver wanted me to see, but we get another one about elephants. Back at home, there are only the usual sounds. Dad is downstairs; I can hear him hammering. Mom has the television on in her room. I guess the fight is over, but it seems like Oliver and I are still recovering. Something feels bruised.

I have so much homework that I'm bound to be up all night for the next few days, but this is more important. Oliver puts in the movie and we sit on the couch together. We watch a herd, followed over several years. We watch babies being born, elder members dying. We watch as the family struggles through a drought, through a flood, through a long voyage in search for food. We watch as they stay together, through mourning, through celebration, through all things. Depending on each other for their very survival. Family, always.

I find Damian in his office the next time I go to the elephant house. He is leaning back in his chair, his hands folded across his stomach.

"You look sad," I say.

"Jade," he says. "Good afternoon. I've posted a new list of jobs this morning."

"Are you okay?"

"Oh, yes."

"But why do you look like that? No smile." Damian never looks this serious.

He sighs. "It's Onyx. They want to transfer her."

"They've said it before," I say. "They can't get rid of her." I love Onyx. Onyx is troubled and sometimes mean, but she looks like she knows things, the way people who've seen pain know things.

"No, this time Victor Iverly is preparing. I need a plan," Damian says.

"What?"

"I don't know. But I don't have much time. Victor has given her three weeks. He's making her travel arrangements. He's worried about 'public safety.'"

"I'm sorry, Damian."

"I'm not giving up yet. There's got to be something that will help. An idea that will work without banishing her. I don't think she can take another move, another break."

"You're like a father to them."

"Some fathers aren't driven from the herd, I guess. Some stay."

I work with Elaine on enrichment, hanging up the big chain wrapped in a fire hose, which gets put up after January so that tires and barrels and treats can be strung from it. We also help drag over a huge pine tree that had formerly been with the

Siberian tigers, and we dump it in the fields. The elephants love anything with a new, strong scent, and before we even get out of there, tails are up and ears, too, and the elephants start vocalizing and Tombi and Bamboo sway on over. It makes you happy to give them something new and interesting to check out, same as giving Milo a new rawhide.

. Sebastian comes alone that day, right as I am finishing up. I'd been trying not to obsess over the would/wouldn't, and I am rewarded, because there he is—an appearance that is expected and unexpected at the same time.

"They sure are excited over that tree," Sebastian says.

It's true. In the time it took for me to change and come out to see Sebastian, Tombi and Chai are already throwing it around. You should have heard the noise. Like thunder and happy elephants.

"And they're getting great exercise," I say. "But I wouldn't be surprised if that tree lights up like Christmas." It looks as if it's about to get tossed, in the direction of the electric fence.

"Will they get hurt?"

I'd asked Elaine the same thing. "Nah. They'll just pick it up and throw it again. In a day or two, they'll get bored and we'll have to haul it out."

"Like Bo with a new truck. He's so into trucks right now, I'm worried he's going to end up with a CB radio and a girlfriend named Wanda who works at a diner."

I smile. See, these are not the kind of conversations you'd have with an Alex Orlando. Sebastian thought about things, filtered them through his own sea-boy lens.

"I'm glad to see you," I say. And I am. My insides are all cheery again. He's erased all the ugly feelings about Dad being angry, about Mom and her sudden, nutty interest in history books. "Where *is* Bo?"

"At home. I've got a weird schedule this week, because Derek, the owner, is on vacation. So I probably won't be here in the next few days. I wanted to tell you that."

"Oh," I say.

In a second, my backstage mind has already opened up the door. Thoughts fill in the crack of his hesitation. He does think I'm too young. And maybe I was the only one who'd been having a good time the other night. I was stupid to ask about Bo's mother and all. I'd moved too fast. I should have lit Raphael, at least.

"So that's why I came by."

"Well, thanks."

Sebastian runs his hand through his curls. "Jade, I . . . I'd really like to see you again, you know? I just feel kind of bad to ask, with Bo and all. . . ."

"I had a great time, Sebastian. I really did. It was my kind of night."

"No way."

"Really."

"Tiffany's so into parties and all that . . . I'm just surprised. It was my kind of night too."

"It was cozy. I like cozy."

"Well, then, I'm going to go ahead and ask you for dinner. At the houseboat this week, if you can. I've got the night off,

Wednesday, and Tess has got a new group she meets with. But, it'd be the three of us. Bo . . ."

"Sebastian, it's fine. I'd really like that."

"This is new for me. Dating with a kid . . . It's really bizarre."

"I'd love to come."

"Sevenish? Macaroni and cheese?"

"I'll bring the hot dogs."

He laughs. "That's great. That's terrific."

I ignore the mind-snag, the realization that he used Tiffany's name in the present tense. I mean, she isn't going to parties anymore, is she? I banish the thought. Grief has got to play all kinds of tricks on you. Maybe it's hard for him to imagine she's really gone. I let it go; instead, I just let the Sebastian-happy fill me. The relief of not messing up after all. It practically lifts me from my shoes. I am flying when I go home. Sure as Jake Gillette's skateboard parachute.

Chapter Twelve

Animal kin sometimes appear to feel each other's pain. An entire pod of whales will beach itself so as not to abandon a beached clan member, and chimpanzees will touch, pat, and groom a family member who has been a victim of aggression. A grandmother lemur once attacked the mother of her grandchild, after the mother ignored and rejected the injured infant . . .

—Dr. Jerome R. Clade, *The Fundamentals of Animal Behavior*

"A barbeque? But it's raining."

Why'd I say barbeque? Why not just dinner? Why did lying make you so stupid? It's like there's some eerie morality department of your brain that just tries to trip you up and teach you a lesson.

"Well, you know, Alex's dad will probably just jet in and out with the food."

"Kind of strange to have it midweek," Mom says.

"It was a spur-of-the-moment thing. No big deal."

"I just wish you felt you could have your friends here some-times."

"I do. I will. I would. They just have this big house, I guess, so people go there."

"Oh."

"One of those places with a living room no one goes in. You know, like it should have a red velvet rope across the doorway and a plaque telling about the furniture."

Mom is quiet.

"I can never understand having a room no one uses. A whole room just to look at but that you still have to dust."

This seems to make her feel a little better. "I know it," she says.

"It's stupid. What a waste."

She's still quiet, though. Like she's tried to file away sad, but can't quite close the drawer. "Alex told me he thinks you're cool," I say. It's shameless, and my insides fold up with guilt, but I know this is the big parental prize, something that makes them inexplicably happy.

"Really?" she asks.

"Who knows why," I say.

She socks my arm. "Well, just make sure the meat's cooked all the way," she says.

It's raining really hard when I get outside, and I duck into Mom's car and then see we're out of gas. I stop by the 76 station. The old guy at the counter whose nametag reads ROGER greets me with a Yooit Wahine (Greetings, Female Surfer), as he rings up my gas and the package of hot dogs I've just remembered that I said I'd bring.

I wind my way toward the water of Lake Union, peer in between the banks of trees to find the right dock. I park in a strip of gravel, swing open a gate, walk through a gnat cloud and down the ramp. For anyone who's never seen a houseboat, they really aren't boats at all. They are houses built on floating logs or cement, and they don't move from their location like a boat would. They stay put, if you don't count the ups and downs of moving with the sways of the water. It's getting dark, and tiny Christmas-like lights in yellow and red are draped overhead, running the length of the dock. Most of the houses are snug cottages, shingled or painted bright colors and adorned with hanging flower baskets and pots. There are several two-story houses with modern angles, though, too, and all of the houseboats are separated by thin bits of water strewn with sailboats and kayaks. For a neighborhood with no ground, there are a lot of gardens—climbing vines and roses and hanging baskets of fuchsia.

I look for Sebastian's house, Number Three, as a cat winds its way around my ankles and another plunks himself in my path. A dog hears my footsteps and appears in a window to bark. Someone calls his name— "Sumatra!"—tells him to quiet down. I can see the end of the dock up ahead, and the sprinkle of white city lights on the other side of the water.

I find Number Three. It's a combination of styles, a narrow two-story house, but old looking. Painted red with blue trim, a

small, crow's-nest deck on top. Pots of plants decorate the platform the house floats on—there's a palm tree, some ferns and
marigolds. A cement Buddha sits in one leafy pot, a bullfrog in
another. An ancient, half-rusted watering can with a whirligig on
a rod sticking from it is propped in one corner.

I step onto the float, and feel it dip with my weight. There's a
set of rubber yellow gardening clogs by the front door, and a tiny
set of rubber rain boots painted with dragonflies and insects. A
grass welcome mat sports a sunflower. After I knock, I realize
something: I have tapped three times on the doorframe, just like
at home.

At the sound of the knock, I hear little running steps, and
Bo's shout, "Da!" Then bigger steps, and the door opens and
there is Sebastian in this new place, this homey and wonderful
new place. Bo grasps him around the knees again.

"You made it," he says. "It's okay, Bo. It's Jade." He picks
Bo up so that he can peek at me from the comfort of Sebastian's
T-shirt.

"Hi, Bo," I say. "He said 'dad,'"

"I know it. It blows me away. First, that lately he's got these
words for things. Second, that I'm his *dad*. Come on in." He steps
aside. "A dad is the guy that does the taxes, you know? Not me."

"This is such a cool house," I say. A denim couch and a
rocking chair are crowded in with a table and Bo's toy chest.
Big windows look out onto a wide canal of water that eventually
opens into the lake. Colorful, plump pillows are strewn on the
couch, and there's a tall bookshelf that follows the staircase to
the second level. Black-and-white photos in every shape and size

cover another wall. There's a woodstove, and a viney plant that's making its way up and around a side window.

"It's my great aunt's place. Tess's sister. Mattie and her partner came into some money and bought a bunch of little houses all over. They're living in Santa Fe now."

"I love Santa Fe," I say. "At least by the pictures. I've never been." I think of my college application, my Abe homework. University of New Mexico, the one I had chosen to apply to. A piece of me that is actually there, right at this moment.

"They love it too. Mattie's taking some time off. . . . They've got this amazing adobe house there. Anyway, let me show you around. The grand tour takes about thirty seconds."

The house is small. It makes you want to take careful steps and sideways moves, but it also feels sturdy from years of love and use. "Ta-da, the kitchen . . ." Painted in green and yellow, with cups of all colors hanging over the counter. There's also an Indian rug on the floor, and horseshoes along the tops of the walls. The lamp is made out of an old gas can—MOBIL is still painted on the side, along with a red, winged horse. The windows are steamy, and a pot with a lid boils on the stove.

"Mac 'n' cheese?" I ask.

"Well, no. I actually cooked. This is the one thing I know how to make. Maybe I shouldn't admit ability in case it's awful. Chili?"

"Yum. Oh, and I brought hot dogs."

"You'll be Bo's friend for life, now. Bo—gogos!"

"Gogos?" Bo seems worried he heard wrong.

I take them out of the bag and show him. He reaches out, and I hand them over.

"Maybe we can put those in the fridge. Okay, Bo? You do it." He sets Bo down, opens the rounded door of the old refrigerator. He pats one of the shelves. "Right here, bud. Then we'll have them for dinner." Bo places them on the shelf. "'Atta way, bud." Bo runs off to the living room, the plastic of his diaper *chsh-chshing* as he moves. "That's a victory lap," Sebastian says. "Did you notice how nothing is on the bottom shelves?" He opens the door again to show me. "He can open this. One day, Tess found his trucks in there and the apples all over the floor. We figure he's got about a minute and a half alone, max, before he gets into trouble. He's doing this climbing thing too. If you can hear him, it's okay, but if he's quiet . . ."

"Oh, man," I say.

"Exactly. I found him sitting in the middle of the kitchen table once."

Sebastian continues the tour. "Dining room." A wood kitchen table with three chairs and a high chair, all looking out on to the kayaks in the water outside, and a pair of fishing poles on the dock. "Bathroom." I poke my head in. A tiny wood-wrapped room with a small claw-foot tub and a porthole for a window. "Study." He gestures to the wall of books and I smile. "Now, upstairs."

We pass Bo, who is fishing through his toy box, taking out all the toys one by one. "I just picked up all those, of course," Sebastian says. We walk up the narrow stairs. Through one arched doorway is a tiny bedroom that is all quilt-wrapped bed and view, and another small bedroom, obviously Bo's, with a crib and toys and a bright, woven wall hanging. "He's almost getting too big for his crib," Sebastian says. "And here's my room." It's not a room, exactly, but a bunk. A doorway and three laddered stairs to reach a bed on a platform. A shelf above the surrounding windows holds photographs and train cars and metal sculptures of animals. "Mattie's decorating, but I don't mind," he says.

"What a view," I say.

"You get used to the motion. Sometimes it's a surprise to see that everything out there is rocking up and down."

"I bet."

"Up those steps?" He points to a wall ladder. "There's a deck. But if Bo hears them creak, he'll want up, and he'll have to be wrestled down."

"That's okay," I say. "Another time."

"Oh, shit—dinner," Sebastian says. He jogs down the stairs and I follow. He trots to the kitchen and lifts the lid and stirs. Yanks open the oven door and takes out a pan of cornbread with a towel, warm, sweet smells following.

"You made that? He cooks, too?"

"Tess's friend, Max? He taught me how, but I didn't pay attention. This is 'add water and stir.'"

"Can I help?" I love it here. The cups above the counter, the wicker chairs at the table, the old California license plate hanging over the stove. Sebastian cutting hotdogs into small, Bo-size pieces.

"Nah. I got it covered."

I wander back out to the living room, examine the wall of pictures. "Hey, Sebastian, is this you?" I call. Curly-haired little boy. Overalls. Standing in a sprinkler fully dressed. Mini-Sebastian eyes.

He pokes his head out of the kitchen. "Which one? I'm in a lot of them."

"Sprinkler."

"Oh, yeah."

He appears next to me. "And there. That's Tess and me and my sister, Hillary, fishing at Tess's old place where we used to live, Ruby Harbor. That's Tess on her motorcycle."

"Oh, my God." Tess, a gray-haired, strong-looking woman wearing jeans and a bright orange shirt, atop a Suzuki.

"Mom got it for Dad, but he thought he was too old for it, so Tess bought it off them." He points to a separate grouping of pictures, on the space next to the window. "That was my great-grandmother, Lettie. And Mattie and her partner, Lou. Tess and her daughters—Mom and Aunt Julia. Mom painting." Sebastian's mom has brown hair pulled into a ponytail. She is pretty, with a kind face and a paintbrush clenched playfully in her teeth. These pictures, mothers and daughters and sisters—they make me think of elephant clans.

"She's an artist?"

"Mostly for fun. She's sold a few." He points to the main wall again. "There's my dad." Standing next to a swimming pool and wearing a funny long bathing suit, hoisting a water wing like a barbell.

"They all look so nice."

"You know, they are nice. That's my Aunt Julia again, Mom's sister, and her husband, Tex Ivy, and their twins." A really beautiful, long-legged woman in cutoffs. Her husband, an outdoorsy guy who looks a little like Abe, with his long hair and bristled cheeks. One girl and one boy, about four or five, both beautiful like their mom but with their father's hair. "The twins are monsters. Good thing they're so cute."

"And look at you there," I say. It is one of the typical high school dance pictures, the kind Mom has plenty of, with Sebastian looking kind of goofy, actually, in a tux, his arm around a girl with straight blond hair.

"Don't look. God, I look stupid."

"Not your most relaxed. Is that Tiffany?"

"Yeah."

"Jeez, Sebastian, she's gorgeous." She is, too. Perfect nose, the kind of cheekbones you see in magazines. Tall but thin. This smile that's Tampax-ad happy, free. It's weird to see her. That was her, alive. Now she's dead. Bo's mother. Sebastian's lost love.

"She used to do a lot of competing—you know, beauty pageants. Her parents made her at first. She *hated* it. I felt so sorry for her. I was like, eleven, and I wanted to save her. Hide her in my room, or something. She was so . . . *fragile* to me. She seemed like glass." He cups his hands in front of him, holding something delicate. "Later, she just gave up and got into it. It was sad. She wasn't the same person who just wanted out, to live like a normal girl instead of on some perpetual stage. She got to liking all that stuff. From this really sweet uncertainty . . . She changed. It took me a long time to see it."

"Wow." It leaves me speechless. I mean, I've been told I'm pretty, but no one would put me in an evening gown and a tiara. "She really is gorgeous."

"Jade? You know what? I think you're the beautiful one."

It's not a beautiful-one, high-self-esteem thing to do, but I actually laugh.

"I mean it. Tiffany was so focused on her looks. It got . . . ugly. *She* got ugly, to me."

It seems kind of mean. To say all this about this girl, now dead. I try not to look at the picture too hard, but I want to. Same as I used to look at those pictures of my great-grandmother's sister, who died of pneumonia all those years ago. See, Tiffany didn't know when she was standing there that she wouldn't be for very much longer. That she'd get pregnant and die. I'm looking at her when I know the end of the story but she doesn't.

"Bo sure does look like her."

"I know." I watch Sebastian for signs of sadness, but he seems okay. He seems happy, really. "I think we're ready for dinner," he says. "Come on, Bo!" Bo has taken all of his trucks from his toy box and has lined them up on the carpet.

"No," Bo says.

"Dinner. Gogos."

"No."

"Power tripper," Sebastian says. "He knows about eight or ten words, but that's his favorite. Close your ears, Jade." He swoops Bo up and Bo screams. He zooms Bo to his high chair and plunks him in. Tosses the hot dog bits on his tray in a flash, and Bo suddenly stops screeching.

"You have that down," I say.

"Man's got to be quick."

I move around in the tiny kitchen, help carry out the bowls

he's laid out, and the silverware. I sit in one of the wicker chairs, and Sebastian brings in the rest of the dinner.

"Cheers to our first meal together," he says. We clink our soda cans.

Bo munches on his hot dogs, which he smashes up toward his face. Sebastian gives him pieces of cheese, some crackers. A sippy cup of something that smells sweet and sticky, apple juice maybe.

"You have this handled so well," I say. "You just think, *Young father* . . . You know, that you'd be tearing out your hair."

"Oh, I do that." He laughs. "I do a lot of that. This is a show of togetherness to impress you."

"But you know what to *do*. How do you know what to do?"

Sebastian sprinkles some cheese on his chili. I have a bite of mine. It is way too salty, but who cares. "I don't always. I mean, I have a lot of help. My family." He gestures at the wall. "Without them, forget it. Even then, when Sebastian was first born? They gave him to me, you know, at the hospital. When it was time to go home. I almost handed him back. It felt so wrong. Like they shouldn't give him to me to take anywhere because I might wreck him. Or break him or hurt him. Later, I was so tired. I'd never been so tired in my life. It's not like you have an all-nighter and can sleep the next day. It goes on and on. . . . I'd feed him in bed with a bottle and we'd fall asleep there, and I'd jump up in this panic that I'd rolled over him and suffocated him."

"Scary."

"I was so crazy about him. This love just . . . overtakes. But, shit. Suddenly your whole life is dominated by this one thing.

I can't even explain the adjustment. Like someone just hung a bowling ball around your neck and you've got to go on like you used to. That's not quite right, because the bowling ball's got to be kept alive. Needs to eat every few hours, cries and spits up and needs to eat again. Gets a cold and can't breathe . . . You've got to handle any need of his right then, not when you feel like it. There's this little demanding human and he is yours every day, every minute, and sometimes I'd have to step outside of the house and shut the door. Just, I was so fucking exhausted. I didn't think I could do it."

"What happened?"

"Well, we were with my mom and dad then, and they helped. Took over if things got too crazy. And just, day by day, I guess. You get to know what you're doing. I got used to the demands, and then the demands changed. Now it's demanding in a whole new way. Honestly? Sometimes I want to strangle him. But, look." We watch Bo munch his hot dog. His shiny hair. His rows of tiny, white teeth. He tries to scoop up some cut bananas with a spoon, with maybe 20 percent accuracy. "I go to work and I miss him. I go out without him and I feel like I've forgotten something. I think, *Wallet? Jacket?*" He laughs.

"It's strange, because here you are, just two years older than me, and every guy my age seems like he's still thinking about his video games or sex or football."

"Na-nas!" Bo says, holding his spoon in the air.

"Don't get the wrong idea. I used to love video games. I can't wait until Bo's old enough—man, that'll be a kick. I just don't have time. That all feels like a lifetime ago. Sometimes I feel like

I'm fifty. Sometimes I feel like I was just seventeen and had this experience where someone hypnotized the real me and took over my life and, shit, look what they've done."

"I'm impressed, though."

"Don't be. It's not heroic. Someday you'll see Tess tell me to pick up my socks like I'm seven. Or hear me yell at Bo, and then feel like he'd have been better off adopted. But, talk to me about you. I'm not kid obsessed, really. Maybe a little. But tell me more about you. Your family—start there."

So I do. I tell him about Mom and her prom dresses and her parents in Florida, and about my dad and his sports obsession and Oliver and Milo and my dad's family. I tell him how Dad once tried to teach us all to ski and how Mom had the television on all day every day after 9/11, and how she even bought masks for us in case of chemical warfare, and how I accidentally knocked out Oliver's first tooth and how my mother used to sometimes cry and stay in her room with the door closed before we had to go over to my dad's parents' house.

Bo has basically smooshed or examined everything on his tray, which now is all half swimming in what is definitely apple juice. Then he wants "Dow!" and off he runs, and Sebastian tries to clean his face with a wet paper towel, which Bo distinctly hates.

"Want to get your jams on?" Sebastian says, which cues Bo to fling off his socks and begin a frustrating attempt to take off his own clothes. Sebastian finishes the job, and Bo has a glorious minute of naked freedom, running around like a cupid.

"Hey, Turbo," Sebastian says. "I'm gonna getcha!" Sebastian catches him and they wrestle Bo's pajamas on. "He can take off most of his clothes, but no way can he get them on yet," Sebastian shouts over the noise, and I carry our plates to the kitchen.

The phone rings and a newly p.j.'d Bo dashes to it, beating Sebastian easily.

"'Lo?" Bo says, then drops the phone where it is. You can still hear a voice coming out from where it lies on the floor.

Sebastian retrieves it. "Hi. Yeah. My secretary. Hey, can I call you later?" He pauses. "No, like tomorrow." He rolls his eyes toward the ceiling for my benefit. "She's supposed to be back late. FFECR meeting." He pauses again, listens. "Say it fast and it sounds like a word we don't want Bo to learn. Mmhmm. Okay. Tomorrow. Promise—jeez! Bye.

"My mom," he says.

"Hey, I should let you get going. Get Bo to bed."

"Let me just get him his toothbrush. He thinks he's brushing, but basically he sucks on it. He loves it, though, so it'll give me a chance to say good-bye."

"Ba," Bo says, and blows me a kiss. "Mwah!" he says, movie-actress style.

"Not yet," Sebastian says. "Hey, man, she's still here."

He finds Bo's toothbrush, and he is right, of course. Bo sits right down on his diapered bottom and sucks that toothbrush like a Popsicle. Sebastian walks me to the door.

"I really enjoyed this," I say.

"Go home and take a couple Tylenol," Sebastian says.

"No. Come on, he was great. This place . . . I had a terrific time."

"Me too," he says. He gathers my hair behind my back, lets it fall. We are close enough that I can feel his warm breath on my face. He leans down, and sets his lips not quite on mine. Just to the edge of my mouth. A light brush, oh, God, and then I perfect his aim.

We kiss for a while, not long enough. His mouth is chili-warm. We pull apart. Sebastian, my red-jacket boy, looks at me for a while. He puts his hand behind my neck, pulls me to him and kisses my forehead.

"Good night," he says.

"Bye," I say.

"Bah," Bo says from the living room. "Mwah!"

Wow lifts me up, plunks me outside into the cold, misty-wet night air. The lights that are strung along the dock reflect in the water of the lake. Ripple, dance. I head past the flowerpots, am just about to step off the dock, when I almost bump into a figure coming on. I barely see her, in her dark coat with the hood up against the rain. The hood comes down and out pops a fluff of gray hair, eyes direct and blue as the color of the china some old ladies have.

"Well, you don't look like a burglar," she says.

"I'm Jade. DeLuna. A friend of Sebastian's."

"Uh-huh."

She just stands there, drilling me into the ground with her eyes. This is Tess, I know, the one with the smile and the fishing pole in the pictures, the one with her arm around the big, bearded man, the one sitting with her sister on a rock wall somewhere that looked over the sea. Somehow, though, it doesn't seem like a good idea that I know who she is. That knowledge makes me too close, and she is already shoving me back with her gaze. I decide to fake ignorance. For a small woman, she seems capable of lifting me up in her fist and throwing me into the water. She seems too fierce for yellow gardening clogs.

"And you are . . . ?" I say.

"Early, it appears."

My insides gather up in some kind of shame, huddle together against her bad feeling of me. "Excuse me," I say. "Good night." I walk past her, feel her eyes follow me down the dock. The wind picks up and the houses rock up and down, their moorings creaking. I have gone from happy to humiliated in less than a minute, and as I walk to the car, I start getting that creepy, alone in the dark/someone about to jump out/victim of violent crime/check your backseat feeling. My chest starts growing dark and heavy, my palms sweat a little. I have a flash of fear that I won't be able to catch my breath, and so I get in the car in a hurry, lock all the doors and sit for a minute with my hands cupped over my mouth and nose. Breathe. In. Out. It's okay. I can. Handle this. Nothing is wrong. Only my body. Giving me. The wrong signals. Breathe. In. Out. From the diaphragm. See? There is no danger. Only the sense that I suddenly have something important to lose.

Chapter Thirteen

Some animals are emotionally invested in the help they give others. Rescue dogs, for example, become depressed if instead of saving lives they only encounter corpse after corpse. After the Oklahoma City bombing, the search dogs became morose, wouldn't eat, had to be dragged to work. No amount of treats or rewards could alter their sense of hopelessness. Only after a live "victim" was placed where the dogs could find him alive did their joy in their work resume . . .
—Dr. Jerome R. Clade, *The Fundamentals of Animal Behavior*

"So, Abe, how do you know what to listen to inside?"

"What do you mean?" Abe sips his tea. He'd stolen another one of Dr. Kaninski's coffee cups. GET A GRIP! it reads, with a cartoon guy holding a club in a half-swing. Probably what Dr. Kaninski felt about his patients, too.

"Well, how do you know if something is a good thing for you or a bad thing?"

"For example."

"For example, you meet someone. And they're great. Really great. But there are these other parts of it that people would generally think of as not good. Maybe your insides think those things are okay, even nice, but you have some other worry you can't put your finger on. How do you know? When to trust your inner voice?" Sebastian—God, he's warm and funny and smart and caring. But something is still nagging me about Tiffany. His reaction to her, the loss of her. Then again, maybe everything is getting wrapped up in his grandmother's reaction to me. I felt like I had been caught stealing and wasn't sure if I could go in that store again.

"Why are these questions important to you now?" Abe says. "Tell me about the person you've met."

"Don't get all psychologist on me, please? I just want to know how you know what to listen to. Person to person. Your human being knowledge."

"Shit." Abe sighs. "That's a big question. You're looking at instinct like it's a foolproof system. Like it's a global positioning device."

"I thought that's why we have it. That's why animals have it. To protect."

"Sure, but it's a tool. Not THE tool, one tool. More like an old-fashioned map, not a GPS. You know, it's great to have a map, but there's the chance you can hold it upside down, read it wrong. Sometimes you just have to see where the road leads."

"But instinct should be *right*."

"It's mostly right. Think about it. You're descended from the very first person or creature that existed. Think what they had to do for you to be here in this time and place. All of your ancestors came from someone before, and you're the end product. You have Australopithecus ancestors."

"Who?"

"The guys with the big jaws, small brains."

"Are you insulting my father?"

"Ha. But think about it. Even before that. I love this stuff! You have ancestors that made fire and fought saber-toothed tigers and explored new territory and traveled oceans and went to war and survived the Great Depression." Abe gets up. His shirt is coming untucked. He refills his teacup with hot water, bobs a tea bag up and down.

"I never really thought about that."

"Well, look. They have. Your *ancestors*. You didn't just, poof, appear. You have the pieces of every person that came before you, from the dawn of time. You've *lasted*. That's what you're made up of. You've done pretty well, huh? Made of strong stuff."

"Me? Always afraid? They'd laugh."

"Think what a huge force fear must have been. Imagine being out in the dark, alone in the elements. Fear, great enough to change the formation of all living things—eyes on the side, eyes in the front, protective coverings, spikes, and venom. Other protections, too—shyness and anxiety and superstitions—all remnants of fear. Rituals and rain dances, gods and mythology. Living in groups . . . It goes on and on. Fear causes the greatest changes, when you think about it. Fear is a monumental force."

"Maybe my ancestors left behind too much of it. My instinct sucks."

"Sometimes it can get drowned out by other things. Maybe it gets tweaked by people in your life. Urged in one direction. Sometimes that's just the way you come."

"Or it gets broken . . ." I think about Onyx and the other elephants. How they will become afraid to the point of harming people after they've been hurt, even people who try to help them.

"Nothing about you is broken, Jade."

"I'm not talking about me. Just . . . in general."

"Sure, okay." He rocks a bit in his chair. "Instinct's an awesome thing, but we don't have to be a prisoner to it." He scratches his whiskers. "So. Anyway. What's happening now that's brought all this to mind?"

"I met someone. Not just someone, but *someone*."

"You're in love." He grins.

"Quit it." I glare at him. I look away, stare at his bookshelf and his photo of Tibetan prayer flags, waving yellow, red, blue, green in the wind.

"Your instinct is there and in fine working order, okay? You've just got your fear turned up a little loud. Like your stereo with too much bass. Makes it hard to hear the lyrics."

"I don't want to get hurt."

"How does a person stay safe, always? Lock yourself away? You're looking for a guarantee and there are no guarantees. If you love, you'll feel loss. You can't 'careful' yourself into avoiding loss. You're trying to get day without night."

"All the marshmallows without the cereal," I say.

"Summer vacation without the school."

"We can stop now," I say.

Abe sighs. "I was just getting going."

"I've got a new plan for Onyx," Damian says to me when I arrive at the elephant house. "It's brilliant, if I do say so myself." Damian is checking health charts when I find him. His warm, brown face is soft and pleased with himself, his eyes bright. "I could barely sleep last night, I was so excited. It's so simple."

"What?"

"What Onyx needs. A mother. Her own, full-time mother. Consistency. Unconditional love."

"Okay . . ." I wait for more.

Damian faces me, clasps his hands together. "Delores!" he says.

"Delores?"

"She's perfect. The solution has been right here all along."

"Delores? Are you sure?"

"Of course I am sure. She is a caregiver. She is a mother with a loving heart. Do you see those pictures of her children?"

"Yes, but have you asked her to do this?"

"Well, that is my one small problem. She says no."

"That seems like more than a small problem." I step into my overalls, zip them up.

But Damian's eyes are still all gleaming and dancing. "That's where you come in!"

"Me?"

"She likes you. You will coax her out of that little box she hides in."

"Damian! I barely know her."

"You are young and you make her smile, I've seen it. And she is missing her daughter. Get her to come out of her box and just *see*."

"If she doesn't want to, what can I do?"

"Try," Damian says. "And try quickly. Onyx is running out of time."

I work a little cleaning stalls, and then hang a traffic cone on the chain for enrichment. Hansa is the first one over. She saunters right over to it and sniffs to examine it. She sets her trunk to my head as if to get me to play too.

I pat her, rub her trunk. I love its roughness under my hand, and her funny little face. The fluff of hair. "Sweet one, you are," I say to her. "Funny girl."

As it gets closer to leaving time, I watch for Sebastian. After Tess and her reaction to me, I don't know if he'll even come.

And I am right. It's a nice day, and there are several visitors in the viewing area. *See the elephants! Say hi to the elephants!* But there is no Sebastian and no Bo.

I pass Delores as I leave the front gate. She is in her booth, doing word searches and drinking a can of Diet 7 Up.

"Wow, you look down," she says. Her voice is small and echoey from behind her window.

"I do?"

"Written all over your face. That boy?"

I nod.

"Complicated," she says. She picks up her purse from the shelf near her feet, fishes around inside. She pulls out a pack of cinnamon gum and offers me a stick through the half-circle hole in the glass. "Here. I just got to give you *something*," she says.

She's a person with a loving heart, just like Damian said. "I'm supposed to talk to you about Onyx," I start.

"I don't want to hear any more about it," she says. She unwraps a piece of gum for herself, folds it into her mouth.

"Delores, you'd love it."

"I'd get attached, I'd get all involved, I'd never leave. . . ."

"That's the idea."

"I had that in my old job, remember? That's why I left. No more. This is perfect for me."

"You're missing out," I say.

"So, I'm missing out." She chews her gum, smacks it all juicily.

"Hansa would love that gum. The smell," I say. "She'd put her trunk right up to your cheek."

"Go," Delores says.

"I'll be back," I say.

I walk the long way home, through the rose garden, hoping Sebastian will still show. The garden is mostly green sticks, an improvement over the brown sticks they were a month ago. Green stick bushes and hedges, a pavilion at one end. In the summer it will be beautiful there, but now it is harsh and prickly. Jake Gillete isn't in the parking lot, and Titus is too focused on his work to wave. Through the window of Total Vid, I can see Mrs. Porter, our mail lady, perusing the display of *Riding Giants* as Titus heads her way, determined as a salesman in the Nordstrom shoe department.

When I open the door of my house, I can hear my mother talking on the phone in the kitchen, laughing. I shut the door loudly, to let her know I am there. I don't know why this feels necessary, except that her voice has something different about it. A lightness that erases the mother parts of her. That makes her seem like a girl. Her voice—it's like ice cubes tinkling in a glass.

"I have to go," she says. I hear the phone clunk to its cradle. "Jade?" she calls.

"It's me."

"How was your day?"

"Fine."

"I've got to pick Oliver up from basketball. Oh, and can you start dinner? Hamburgers? 'Cause I've got a meeting at seven."

"Okay."

I take everything from my patron saint box, look at each candle carefully. Saint Dymphna is the best choice. I know it sounds like a growth that should be surgically removed, but really she's this young woman with a handkerchief over her head and an understanding look. In her picture she holds something that looks like a box of chocolates, but I don't have a clue what it really is. Maybe some kind of cure, some magic released when the lid is off, like in one of Oliver's Narnia books. She is the patron saint of family happiness, of possessed people, of therapists and nervous disorders and runaways. I figure she'll do the trick for Tess and Sebastian, close enough, and I feel qualified on the nervous disorders end. Even Abe will be watched over, and I figure it's the least I can do, considering all he does for me.

I have a ton of homework, but I don't care about reading twenty-five pages of biology right then. I'm too worried about Sebastian, about that angry white-haired lady with the blue eyes that he cares so much about. Instead, I lie on my bed and look out the lava-lamp window. I watch the white clouds make shapes against the sky, drifting, but with purpose. As if they know just where they are going.

After dinner, Mom leaves for her meeting, and instead of helping with the dishes, I am bouncing Oliver's basketball around in the kitchen.

"Jade, you better help," Oliver says.

"If you think we're doing your plate, just know you'll be seeing it at breakfast," Dad says.

"Go out for a pass," I say. I bounce the ball Dad's way. He ignores me and it crashes into the oven door.

"Something's going to get broken," he says.

"I'm giving you another chance," I say. I dribble around the kitchen table. Scoot beautifully around a blocking chair. It doesn't have a chance. If I were this good in PE, those people never would have laughed. I give the ball a single bounce toward Dad. He turns in a flash, drops his kitchen towel, and neatly catches the ball.

"Now you're in trouble," he says.

And I am. See, as I've said, Dad's a really good athlete. Even in his dress slacks and shirt, his tie slightly loosened, he moves around the kitchen as if he's on some gym floor with his tennis shoes going *sweek-sweek* and the crowds going wild. He stops, dodges, and advances. Already, he is over by the refrigerator. I approach, but he is gone again. Just dribbling, oh, so full of himself, back by the stove now.

"Help me, Oliver," I say.

We pounce, and Milo starts barking like crazy and Oliver lets out a tribal war whoop. Dad dances and jets around and we keep reaching out, grabbing at nothing.

"I-I'm whip-ping your bu-utts," Dad sings.

"Get him!" Oliver screams. I'm not sure whose team Milo is on, but he should be kicked off for unsportsmanlike behavior.

Oliver has his hip right against Dad's. Then he moves ever so slightly in front of him, neatly snatching the ball. Suddenly, Oliver is over by Milo's water bowl, dribbling with that same smug look Dad had.

"Yes!" I screech. I jump up and down. "Victory is ours!"

"Well, look at that," Dad says.

"I learned it from Coach Bronson," Oliver says.

"Game over. Let's have a beer," I say.

Dad shoots me a look.

"Kidding!" I say.

We finish up the dishes and then follow Dad downstairs to see the train. "Wow," I say.

The new part of his town has been filled out—there are patches of nubby green trees and serene rolling hills, a small lake, all surrounding the house I had set there. Off a bit from the house is a very small town, one store, with its own tiny gas pumps, and a truck beside them getting filled. There's only a small corner of board left.

"You're almost done," I say.

"What do you guys think?"

"I like it there," Oliver says, pointing to where the new house is. It's true—it's the prettiest part of the board, away from his old center of town with the streets and people and miniature trucks and stores and factories.

"Me too," I say. "What are you going to do with the corner that's left?"

"Don't laugh," he says.

"What?"

"An ocean."

"Cool," Oliver says.

"I've never seen a set with an ocean before," he says. "I'm still trying to figure out how I can craft it."

"Then you'll be done," I say. "And then what?"

"I don't know," he says. He takes his tie off, tosses it on the chair.

"The train goes on its first trip," Oliver says.

"I guess you're probably right," Dad says.

We leave Dad downstairs.

"Jade?" Oliver says. He's been thinking about something.

"What?"

"I still don't like basketball."

"That's okay," I say. "More than okay."

I knock on my doorframe. I settle in front of my computer for homework, try to concentrate on things I don't care about instead of obsessing about where Sebastian might be. I flip over to the elephants, hoping for even red-jacket cyber contact. Anything. I would have called him if I weren't scared to death of his white-haired grandmother. I watch Tombi swaying, moving her feet in that restless way. I know how she feels. I do more homework, pop on the web, and try to look up FFECR. Maybe it would help me understand something about Tess. I stop looking for it after three pages of French phrases and medical conditions, nothing I'm guessing Tess would be at a meeting for.

I clomp back downstairs to feed my misery. I have a couple of chocolate chip cookies left in the bag from about six months ago, which are lifeless and stale. Milo appears with his blankie, and I give him a big new rawhide to brighten his evening. It cheers me up to make him so happy. He takes it from me, gently, politely, and then trots to the living room with it sticking sideways out of his mouth. I watch him. He paces, hunts around for just the right spot to bury it.

"Chew on it, don't hide it," I advise.

He ignores me. Continues his quest with the focused, got-to-find-it obsession of someone in a long checkout line hunting for that last nickel. He tries out one place, under the couch, decides against it. No good. He walks to the potted fern and sniffs, but no. Under the armoire with the television in it? Maybe. He sets it down, looks, decides it is not quite right. He finally sets it next to the basket of magazines. He pushes his nose against the carpet over and over, burying it with imagined dirt. It sits there on the rug in plain sight, and Milo looks at it as if it weren't there. It's kind of embarrassing. But you can tell even he knows he's kidding himself.

Milo stares up at me with his deep brown eyes. He seems like he's at a loss at what to do, and this makes me sad for him. "You did a great job," I say. "Awesome. I don't see a thing."

I pat his soft head. Talk about broken instinct.

It's one of those life rules that when you don't care about guys noticing you, they most often do. The next day at school, with my thoughts on Sebastian, I catch Ben Nelson checking me out, and in Spanish, I have an unexpected encounter with Jacob Leeland, manic pothead. Another rule of life is that if you are a decent and hardworking student, you will pay for it by always getting placed by your teachers next to some hyperactive headline-of-the-future. Your reward for your responsible and respectful behavior is to be "a role model"—basically, babysitting junior borderline criminals. You will have the honor of putting up with them rolling pencils at you, cheating off your tests, throwing paper clips, borrowing your pens (which they never give back), and sitting in a reeking cloud of marijuana or cigarette smell, the haze of which drifts around their jackets like fog in a field on a cold morning.

Jacob Leeland is one of those. Señora Kingslet always pairs us up, primarily so Jacob can at least get a decent grade on the stuff we do in class, and we are supposed to be developing a dialogue that would take place in a restaurant. Our conversation goes something like this:

Me: So, you're the waiter, and you say: *¿Qué usted tiene gusto de ordenar, Señorita?* (What would you like to order, Miss?)

Jacob: Do you find me attractive?

Me: Huh?

Jacob: Do you? I think you're hot.

Me: (Pause) So, anyway, then I can say something like: *Quisiera los pescados, por favor.* (I'd like the fish, please.)

Jacob: You didn't answer my question. We'd be a cute couple (scoots closer).

Me: (Scoots away) Then you say: *¿Cualquier cosa?* (Anything else?)

Jacob: Does that mean, no, you don't find me attractive?

Me: You're a nice person, Jacob, but . . .

Jacob: Sure. (Sulks.) So where'd you get that shirt? My girl-friend would like it.

At lunch, we stay at school for once, sit on the benches outside since no one feels like going anywhere and Akello and Michael are broke. Jenna bows her head over her tuna sandwich. Hannah and Kayla squeal over their shared Cheetos bag, and Michael and Akello and I study for our AP Government test and eat Michael's Corn Nuts. I look up and watch the crowds, who remind me of cows—if one lies down, they all do. If one is standing, they all are standing. I have this ache inside. My insides pulling with a desire for too-salty chili in a bowl and a rocking houseboat and my feet in someone's lap. I belong there, and suddenly this bench in its plot of grass is the place I don't know, somewhere I've never been, and these people are the ones that seem like strangers.

"Come on, Delores."

"I told you, no."

"I'm not saying you have to do anything. Just come with me. Come out. I promise you, you're not making some kind of decision. You're just *looking*. See? Beverly is here to sell tickets. She can spare you for a sec."

Delores pretends to study her seek-and-find word book. Then she smacks her pencil down on the page. "Just to look."

"Okay, great! That's so great."

"Don't sound so excited. I'm only doing this to shut you up." Delores leans for her purse, then turns the handle inside her booth. I never realized there was a handle. It's the first time, actually, that I've ever seen her out of the booth. She steps out, shuts the door. She's a little shorter than I am, has those jeans with the huge back pockets that cover a wide, flat rear end. She wears tennis shoes and an orange sweatshirt and her big ASK ME zoo button. She carries her purse in her left hand, the one that sports one of those watches that have circles of various, removable colors. I notice gold hoop earrings peeking from her short, white-blond hair. She's a real person with a real life, and that seems like a surprise. I wonder what she does when she's not here. If she watches sports on TV or likes to cook. It reminds me of the time some little kid in the viewing area asked me if I lived at the zoo.

"Look at you," I say.

"What?" Delores says.

"You're out."

"Make it snappy," she says.

"I'm going to take you into the house first," I say. "But, warning—it smells kind of strong in there."

"I used to work in a hospital," she reminds me.

Delores's walk is efficient. I have to work to keep up with her. We go around the back, where Damian's office is, and the staff quarters. Then I bring her through to the stalls. Rick Lindstrom and Damian are washing Chai, who lolls on one side and rolls and sneezes like Milo on the lawn. Damian grins at Delores.

"I'm looking," she says to Damian. "That's all."

"Just look, then."

"Let's go out to the yard," I say.

I can see Tombi and Onyx out by the water, and Hansa near the viewing area. When she sees me, she ambles over. "Ambles" is not quite right for Hansa—she's actually quite fast. Hansa and I are special pals.

"They're rather . . . large," Delores says.

"Don't be nervous," I say. "The trick is to be the boss. Hey, I'm the most worried person in the world, and I handled it. It's a little intimidating at first, but trust me, if I can do it, you can. Come here, you," I say to Hansa.

Hansa stops near us and sniffs around to see if I've brought her any fruit or treats. "Sorry, girl," I say. I rub her side, and reach my palm for her to snuffle her trunk in. "Put your hand out," I tell Delores.

"Forget it."

"Honestly, it's okay."

"Oh, my God," Delores says.

"See?" I say. "I was so scared at first."

"Oh, shit," she says. She squeals a little when Hansa smells her palm.

"We should have brought some watermelon," I say.

"She's really cute, though," Delores says.

"Everybody loves her, except Onyx. There's Onyx. Over there. Not her best side." We're looking at Onyx's huge, saggy ass and her tiny tail, twitching from side to side. Funny thing is, I can almost picture Onyx in those same wide-pocket jeans Delores is wearing.

"She's really huge." Hansa is sniffing Delores's sweatshirt.

"But she's sad. Her anger is just too much sadness with nowhere to go."

Hansa's trunk is everywhere. In my hair, on Delores's shoulder. "You're a pest," I say.

Delores pats Hansa's side, like I do. "It's softer than I thought," she says.

"I know it. Like rough leather." I see that Damian has appeared in the enclosure to watch us. "Let's meet Onyx," I say.

"All right."

Delores follows me through the yard, looking over her shoulder as if she's in a rough neighborhood. We approach Onyx from the front. Onyx can still make me a little nervous, and I'm glad Damian is nearby. Still, it's so important not to let the elephants feel your uncertainty that I force myself to shake off any fear.

"Onyx, you big softie. Meet Delores."

"Hello," Delores says formally.

"Now you must blow in her trunk, like this." I show her.

"It's a handshake. An official greeting. Once you do, she'll never forget you."

I hold Onyx's trunk out to Delores, and she blows inside. Delores looks at Onyx and Onyx looks at Delores. "It's a pleasure," Delores says after a while. Here's what passes between them: the look of a couple of older women who have seen things in their day.

"Let me think about this," Delores says as we head back. "Don't go taking that as an encouraging response. I'm only thinking."

"You won't regret it," I say.

"You did a wonderful job," Damian says to me afterward. He is outside with Onyx and Flora. "It is like the car salesman trick, you see? Once you drive the car, you will want to buy it."

"You think?"

"I know. An elephant is impossible to resist. Look at that face," he says to Onyx. "What are they saying, those eyes?"

"They are saying, 'I want to be with Delores,' right, Onyx?"

Damian chuckles. "Those eyes know things."

I haven't even changed into my overalls yet, so I head back to the elephant house to do that. When I hang up my coat, I hear my phone ringing in the pocket. By the time I fumble around and get it out, I miss the call. But the words on the screen make my heart lift. ARMCHAIR BO the screen says. I press the call button, trying to wrestle my backstage mind, which is barreling in with thoughts and what-ifs. Tombi is making a happy racket in the house, so I go outside, lean my back against the building.

"Armchair Books."

"Sebastian? It's Jade. I just missed your call."

"Hi," he says.

"Hi."

"I'm so glad to hear you." The tension that had risen in me like one of the waves in *Riding Giants* crashes and breaks into relief.

"Me too."

"I was calling . . . I wanted to apologize for Tess. Can you hang on a minute?"

"Sure."

The phone clunks onto the counter and I hear Sebastian's voice far away, speaking to another man. Then he's back.

"That was so weird," he says softly. "This guy, he looked like an escaped con and wanted a book on puppetry."

"Do you have one of those buzzers on the floor, like they do at the bank in case of robbery?"

"I wish. Anyway, Tess . . . I know she saw you. I hadn't told her about you yet, and I know she overreacted. . . ."

"She just made it clear where she stood." A peanut shell is in the dirt on the ground, and I send it into a figure eight with the toe of my shoe.

"You always know where you stand with Tess. She's a good person, really, she's just worried about me. We got in an argument. She's repenting. Told me to ask you over here to dinner so she could meet you."

"Is that what you want?" I was wondering if it might be easier to roll around in some raw hamburger and visit the Bengal tiger, but, hey.

"I do. I mean, I'd really like you to know each other. I guess, actually, it's important to me. If it's okay with you. Is this . . . too much, too fast?"

"No. I don't think so."

"Well, great. Next Saturday? Are you free? Six? I'm not working."

"No, that's great. Great."

"Great," he says. "That was a lot of greats."

"It sure was."

"You should see who's standing in your gardening section now. Pierced lip, tattoo going up his arm. Some kind of dagger. Very Seattle. Oops, gotta go."

"Next Saturday."

"Bye."

"Bye."

We hang up, and I'm filled with excitement/loss. The happiness at his company, the sadness that his company is gone. But the sadness turns out to be unnecessary. A few hours later, after Armchair Books has closed, my phone rings again.

"I just thought you might want to know that I wasn't robbed after all," Sebastian says.

Glee is such an old-fashioned word. A corny one, but that's what my heart feels—the equivalent of every corny, ridiculous, gleeful scene. I'm the living embodiment of those musicals where people break into song at monumental moments, of square dancers twirling in bright, ruffled skirts, of glittery snow on Christmas cards.

"I'm so glad," I say.

"And the pierced guy bought *All About Bulbs.*"

We talk into the night. After that, he calls every night of the week before our Saturday date. When Mom asks, I tell her it's Michael with girl problems. Poor Michael's got a lot of girl problems lately, and poor me, I have to sit there and listen. When Sebastian calls, I get comfy, cross-legged on the floor, keep my voice low to keep from disturbing anyone—okay, to keep from anyone knowing how late we actually talk. Sebastian calls when he's stocking books. I picture him with the phone crooked between his shoulder and his ear, working in that cozy room with the faux flame in the fireplace. Occasionally, he drops me when he reaches a high shelf. There's a huge crashing clunk and then Sebastian's voice, far away—"Jade! God, just a sec! I'm here! Don't go anywhere!" And then he returns, his voice loud again. "Are you all right? Are you still in one piece?"

We talk about his customers and my school day, books we've read, some movie, a dog he used to have—small stuff. Then about God and the universe and why we're here—the biggest. One night, it becomes so late that we reach the hour where the rules and bindings drop away, where it's just the raw, feral pieces under all the rational ones. Sebastian confesses that he's always been afraid of things with wings—bats and birds and cicadas. I confess that I've been afraid of everything. I tell this to the darkness of my room, instead of to the boy on the other end of the phone. Abe says not to be ashamed, we all have anxiety to some degree, but sometimes I still am ashamed.

Sebastian asks questions—gentle, past-midnight questions. He has some knowledge of anxiety, from a friend of his. He tells mc it's okay, that everyone has something to struggle with. *Okay*—that's all that really matters.

It is a few nights after that, just before our scheduled dinner date with Tess, that I see Sebastian on the webcam in the elephant viewing area. We'd just hung up—he was heading home, he'd said. It is late, so he has snuck in again. It feels wrong to be watching him now that we know each other, but I do it anyway. I lie on my bed, my head propped on my hand, as he sits on the bench, his legs crossed in front of him. His own hands are folded under his chin, and he is still there after a long time. And then he bends his head down, forehead on his hands, and I realize what he is doing. He is praying.

This is not a place he has invited me to. I turn off the screen. I sit back down on my bed, watch the green light of the computer glow. In my mind, I take Sebastian's hand, hold his head against my chest and comfort him.

Chapter Fourteen

Animals can form kinship relationships with species not their own. In a Thailand zoo, a dog has raised three tiger cubs, and now resides with her "children"—three full-grown tigers and her own pup. Should the tigers be returned to their "own kind," however, their own kind would likely be viewed as some strange, alien, other. It is the dogs that are family . . .

—Dr. Jerome R. Clade, *The Fundamentals of Animal Behavior*

"I was hoping you'd be home tonight," Mom says. "I've hardly seen you lately."

"I thought you *wanted* me to get more involved in the social stuff," I say. Mom is unloading groceries. I get the happy what's-in-the-bag excitement that comes when someone's just gone shopping, especially since she hadn't been in so long. I peek in, hunt around for something worth the enthusiasm and only find plastic bags of broccoli and bananas and lettuce. Diet food—what a letdown.

"But what about us?" She turns to face me, a carton of yogurt in her hand.

"You got your hair cut," I say.

"Do you like it?"

"And highlights."

"Too much?"

"No, it looks nice." And it does. It's sort of flippy and fresh. The PTA women all look alike—hair that tries to look young but still seems like it has a list of things it needed to accomplish. Politician-wife hair. But this style is looser. Free. Oh, my God, that's not what it is. It's sexy.

"I just needed a change."

"Well, great. Anyway, I don't want to miss this thing at Alex's. I won't be late—you won't have to worry about me driving."

"All right." She sighs. But as I turn to leave, I catch her looking at her reflection in the dark glass of the microwave door. She angles her head to the side, raises her chin. Then she's back to the grocery bag, taking out a loaf of brown bread. I rush out of there. I get this weird feeling, like I'd seen parts of her that weren't my business. Like those times when you watch your parents at a party with their friends, or find some pills of theirs in the bathroom, or when you see too much as they're coming out of the bathroom—soft abdomens, an uncovered chest. That glance made me remember that there were pieces of her life that were only hers, that she had thoughts that had nothing to do with my report card.

I drive out of Hawthorne Square, wave to old Mrs. Simpson, one of the neighbors, who is clutching her sweater closed for warmth and walking toward Total Vid with a copy of *Riding Giants* to return. I can see her wrinkly fingers wrapped around the surfing guy on the front of the box. I am getting a tightness in my chest, the cinching. There is too little air outside, it seems, for everything that needs it. My heart sits right against the surface of my skin, and I try to breathe deeply. You can handle it, Abe would say. I count this on my fingers. *You-can-han-dle-it. You-can-han-dle-it.* I decide to count coffee shops to take my mind off of the fact that I am going to dinner at Sebastian's and am about to be devoured by a grandmother. One espresso stand near the 76 station, two coffee houses by the zoo, a Starbucks on the main drag, another across the street. Another espresso stand by the bank, count the one inside the Laundromat, two more on the street by Lake Union. Another Starbucks, then Seattle's Best, a Java Jive, and I am at the lake.

It is still light, and late-March cold and gray. The trees are uninspired, and the lake steely and determined. The city sprawls across the water, with the Space Needle dominating the sky with its white, spidery legs and alien-ship top. I shut my mouth tight against the gnat conference that is apparently ongoing there at the start of the dock, creak down the planks, step over another cat, and notice things I hadn't before—flags on sailboats whipping, their rings clanging against metal masts. The sound of wind chimes and seagulls. Ducks cruising around between the houses, stained-glass windows, door knockers in the shape of sailboats and whales.

I walk up the ramp of Number Three, and am struck again at how snug it feels there. The plants have just been watered—the earth in the pots is dark and wet and smells freshly upturned, and the dock wood is still drying. Spicy odors, something with tomatoes, drift from the house, and I can hear Bo inside making a racket. A pair of tennis shoes have joined the gardening clogs on the step.

Before I ring the doorbell, Sebastian opens the door. He is wearing jeans and a sweatshirt and looks tousled and relaxed; he's barefoot. He is the visual equivalent of a Sunday morning.

"I felt you step on," he says. And to my baffled expression: "The house tips when someone walks on the float."

"I just realized I never asked you what I should bring. I even forgot the book you lent me."

He took my arm, squeezes. "No worries. We've got everything. Come on in."

"I promised I'd behave," Tess shouts from the kitchen. Tomatoes, all right. Garlic. Bo driving trucks on the floor, some music in the background. Lit candles on the higher windowsills.

Sebastian guides me to the kitchen. "Proper meeting. Jade, Tess. Tess, Jade."

"Pleasure," Tess says. I think of Delores, saying the same thing to Onyx. Tess is wearing a sweatshirt too, but hers has the solar system on it and a little arrow and the words: YOU ARE HERE. She wears jeans, and a pair of wooly socks, and her eyes are as blue and direct as I remembered. You get the sense that with one look, she'd opened all your file drawers and read the contents.

"It smells great," I say.

"Shrimp Creole. Hope you're okay with shrimp." She clatters the lid back on the pot, wipes her hands on a kitchen towel. "So."

"Tess is restraining herself from asking you a ton of questions. She's probably going to ask for your résumé."

"I am not," she says.

Conversational roadblock, and oh, shit, so soon. Everyone's quiet. We all look at Bo, watch him drive his trucks around the floor. He is oblivious to the three pairs of eyes boring into him in social desperation.

"Hey, buddy," Sebastian says to him lamely.

Somewhere in my mind I must have something I can say to her. "Sebastian tells me you're an activist," I say finally.

"Well, I get *involved* in what I feel needs attention."

"That's great."

Silence. Just more silence and more staring at Bo.

Sebastian claps his hands. "Shall we get ready to eat?" he says.

"Oh, for God's sake, Sebastian, relax," Tess says. "She's too cute to bite."

"Not too tasty, either," I say.

"Well, Sebastian should probably be the judge of that," she says.

"Tess," Sebastian says.

"What? It's the truth. Do you fish?" she asks me. Those blue eyes again.

"Well," I say. I think. There was that one time at the trout farm. I remember dropping our lines in and pulling up a fish, easy as spearing a maraschino cherry with a toothpick in a glass of Coke. "Not much."

"Not much?"

"Once or twice."

"So, let's go," she says.

"Now?" Sebastian says.

"Why not?" She is already heading out of the room. "You need a jacket?" she calls.

"I'll be okay," I say.

"Now?" Sebastian says again. "We've got dinner, and Bo . . ." He looks at me, and I shrug my shoulders.

"Bo's fine," Tess says from the other room. "He loves the boat. Bring some crackers."

Tess appears again, wearing a zip-up jacket. She tosses me a blue wool coat. "You're skinny. You'll get cold."

"Ba?" Bo asks.

"Yep, I guess so," Sebastian says. He rolls his eyes at me, takes Bo's fleece jacket off a hook by the door, and then his own red one.

A few moments later, we are sitting across from each other, knees to knees in Tess's small motorboat. She is at the helm, manning the rudder, and Bo is on Sebastian's lap, his orange life jacket up around his neck same as those people who have to wear a white collar after a car accident. Fishing poles and a tackle box are in the back, and my own life jacket is snug around me. I'm having one of those moments where you don't feel like it's you in your own body. I'd gone from this warm house with garlic smells to a boat with a roaring motor, wearing Tess's wool coat, my hair flying around my face and catching in my mouth.

Tess kneels at the helm with her back to us, showing us the bottom of one rubber boot. Her nylon coat whips back and forth, and her white hair springs around with its own contentment. The sun slides out and the water twinkles, and we pass the rows of houseboats and head into the channel that connects Lake Union to Lake Washington. The water gets a bit choppy and we hit a wave with a big, jouncy thud, and I say a small prayer, *oh, shit,* that Tess knows what she is doing, and she must, because she pushes the boat's levered handle and slows the speed, until we are jostling gently forward.

I relax—we're obviously in good hands. Sebastian smiles at me, and I smile back. Cold air blows in my face and fills me with joyful wake-up. Bo could care less about the plastic bag of goldfish crackers Sebastian holds out to him. His blond hair is snapping around and he sits stone-still on his dad's legs, watching the waves, the houses, the big underneath side of a bridge we pass beneath. My heart is in-love happy, with this boy across from me, this boat, this ride, that baby, even that grandmother, who's shouting things in the wind she thinks we can hear but don't. Finally, she turns and we do hear.

"Marvelous, yes?"

I nod and smile. The wind, the ride, the bumping. The *outside,* so present, close enough to breathe in. The smell of gasoline on water, the sun-glints and the sky with drapey colors—it is binding. You take a boat ride like that with people and you're as close to them as if you've spent a hundred lunches together across tables in crowded restaurants.

She slows the boat to idling now. We are slopping around, and Tess has me hand her a pole, already hooked, and the tackle box, with its jars packed with bait—red eggs, yellow and pink marshmallows—and its shiny, odd lures and rolls of line, a container more varied and fascinating than any jewelry box.

"Sebastian watches Bo, I cast, and you hold the pole," Tess says. *Ssszink*, the line is in the water and she hands it to me. Tess tugs at the line. "Feel that? If you feel that, pull back hard to set the hook, then reel. Got it?"

"I think so," I say.

"Yes, you do. You're a fisherman from way back, I can tell," Tess says.

"Tess met Max fishing," Sebastian says. "Sort of."

"I found his old wedding ring, in a trout."

"You're kidding," I say.

"I am not. That's what happened. I saw his name engraved inside the ring, and I knew the man lived nearby. I returned it to him. And, basically, I never left."

"It was just his cooking," Sebastian says.

"It was just his everything," Tess says. Her voice wobbles a little. She clears her throat. "Yes, well," she says.

I feel my own eyes fill, and my throat tightens. Sebastian leans forward and takes my hand. I squeeze. I want to cry. See, she is a woman in love, and I suddenly feel the magnitude of that. I am one, too.

The sun is setting when Tess docks the boat by the house again, and we step up and out, handing each other the poles and the tackle box and life jackets, and Bo, who passes through the air with his legs dangling. Tess knows what she is doing, all right. By the time we all get out, we are working as a team, and Tess rests her hand briefly on the back of my coat. "Fine fishing," she says.

"I didn't catch you anything," I say.

"Fishing is about the expectation of good things," she says. "Not about the fish."

Inside, it feels warmer than ever after coming in from the cold. We shed our jackets. I'm starving. We set the table, put Bo in his seat, and I give him some spiral pasta and bits of ham and bananas. We eat hot, spicy Creole shrimp and bread, wash it down with sparkling lemonade. Tess sips a glass of wine, which makes her cheeks red. Sebastian has his hand on my knee under the table. Tess brings out a small album of Mattie's. She points to pictures of her and Mattie with locked arms (*My sis*, she says), of Sebastian's parents' wedding (*They were too young, but it worked out all right*), of Sebastian and his sister Hillary, standing in front of the tea-cup ride at Disneyland (*Puke fest*, Tess says. *This was the* before *picture*). We talk about my family and Tess tells stories about Sebastian when he was little, and we laugh and Tess pours another bit of wine.

"This has been so fun," I say. And it has. Further proof that when you are positive something's going to be great, it isn't always, but when you don't expect great, it just might be. We are all in that drowsyish contentment that fresh air plus good food brings. Bo has been snapped into his pajamas and is watching Elmo singing on a video.

"You can come back and we'll take the boat out," Tess says.

"Now that Jade knows you're a nice little old lady," Sebastian teases.

"Smartass. Ha. I'm younger than you in ways," she says. "I was *worried*, all right? No one could blame me. You getting involved. When you've got so much to handle. When your life is . . ."

"A mess?" he suggests.

"In flux. You know, after we left, after Tiffany's car accident and all, Sebastian was a wreck—"

"Childbirth," Sebastian says.

"Childbirth?" Tess says.

"Childbirth is what you meant." Everything is quiet. All you can hear is Elmo singing in the next room. What the hell is going on? Tess leans forward on her elbows. Sebastian runs his hand over his forehead. "Shit," he says.

"Childbirth?" Tess says. She shakes her head. "God, Sebastian. No one dies of childbirth anymore."

"What?" I say. The word is barely there. I don't understand what is happening here, but I know it's big, huge. I'm suddenly at the edge of a cliff, my toes hanging over. I feel the long drop down in my chest.

"She's got to know," Sebastian says.

"Car accident, Sebastian," Tess says. "For Christ's sake."

"I want her to know, Tess."

He has gone from the sweet, solid Sebastian I know to someone with pleading and desperate eyes. "What's going on," I say. "Please." I'm falling off that cliff, that's what it feels like. Freefalling, with nothing to grasp onto. I'm holding my breath. I'm waiting for the crash.

"This is the royal fuck-up I was afraid of," Tess says. She pushes her plate away from herself, as if she wants it all, everything, away.

"She needs to know. I hate this lie. Please, Jade. I want you to understand. Tiffany," Sebastian says to me. "She's not dead." His words are whispers too.

"What?" I don't understand. "What?" I say again. I picture Tiffany, her long, shiny hair, the beautiful face I'd made tragic. The face I'd seen in my mind a thousand times, imagining her unaware of her own fate, feeling real sorrow for her unrealized future. She's alive somewhere? Right now, she's somewhere, eating dinner, watching television, wearing sweats, or brushing her teeth? My mind attempts to make the mental shift, stalls in the bringing her back to life. I feel cheated somehow—the lie and my belief in it, all that misdirected compassion. I feel like a fool. I feel like I'm making the long drop down that cliff, with the ground rushing at me.

"Jade," Sebastian pleads. "See . . . I did something really stupid." He looks up at me, then down again, puts his head in his hands. "I'm sorry I lied. Bo . . . God, how do I say this? I've never said this out loud. I left with him."

"You took him?" Away from her? His mother?

"This is not simple . . ." Tess says.

"Tiffany—she didn't want Bo. Never wanted him. She wanted to give him away. We knew too late to change things, and she was so angry about that, like her refusal to face it was *my* fault." He is talking fast now. "She'd have these moments of guilt, you know? And she'd deal with it by shoving it all away. Calling the baby *It*. I guess I can understand that. I can. I just don't think I can *forgive* that."

"Bo is not an *it*," Tess says.

"She would cry. She cried *a lot*, but it was always about what was happening to *her*. Her body, her life. She was devastated by what happened, but it was never about the baby, or me, or my family, or anyone else. I thought she loved me. I thought we loved each other. But all she could see was how this would ruin her. Her parents . . . Everything they'd worked for with those stupid pageants . . ."

"God, those people . . ." Tess says.

"I saw Bo, and I couldn't give him up. None of us could. My mother, she just . . . no one could let him go."

"He's part of our family," Tess says. "We raise our own, Sebastian. This is not about a mistake. . . ."

"We had him for almost a year. Tiffany never saw him, Jade. Not once after she left the hospital. Not *once*. It, *he*, was done and gone for her. I didn't even know her then. She wasn't someone I ever even knew. Her parents came by once and gave him this cup, this silver cup with some prayer engraved on it. We all sat in the living room, my folks, them, me. Tiffany's mother held Bo and talked to him, and it just made me sick. Every minute she held him, I was just dying. She held him like this." He cradles his arms out, away from himself. "As if she couldn't even touch him."

I don't say anything. Part of me wants out of there. Part of me wants away from something way bigger than my normal life. Delores had been right. *Complicated*—she had no idea.

"I raised him, my family did. *Every day.* I didn't bail. I was the one who was there. Tiffany would ask how he was, but that was it. Little guilty questions, but all in all, more relief than guilt. She kept talking about what he'd done to her body. We met once, and I'll never forget this—she lifted her shirt and showed me the white lines on her stomach. Stretch marks. She said she felt branded by what happened. Talked about how depressed she was. How she was trying so hard to *move on.* She kept going on about school—college." His voice catches.

Tess puts her hand on his arm. Her hand, veiny and road-mapped. Highways and paths of her life in relief on her skin. My heart hurts for him.

"So then, a couple of months ago—four months, four and a half—she calls me. After I hadn't talked with her forever. She starts crying. Saying she fucked up. That her parents were putting all this pressure on her to have Bo in her life now. She was confused. . . . That they got a lawyer . . ."

Elmo stops singing in the other room. "Da!" Bo shouts.

"Come here, buddy," Sebastian yells back. His voice is full of tears.

"Da!"

"Here!"

Bo appears, the plastic feet of his pajamas *skush-skushing* along the floor. Sebastian lifts him, cradles him against his chest and rubs his back. Bo watches us, then gives up and sets his head against Sebastian's shoulder. Pops his thumb in his mouth.

"They got a lawyer. They were going to file for custody. And that's when I made the mistake. I took off. I told my parents I had to go, and I ran. Stayed with him in a motel for three days. I didn't know what to do. I didn't want to be around to get served any papers. And then, the fourth day, Tess shows up. She tells me that if I'm running, I'm not going to go through it alone. If I'm going to hide from those papers, I was going to do it right."

"I'm an idiot," Tess says.

"She saved my butt. Made a plan. We came here. The plan is, *was*, don't tell anyone who we are. Tess was pissed I told you my real name. Got involved . . ."

"No one can know where we are," Tess says.

"I understand." I don't know if I do. I think I do. Sebastian reaches for my hand. He looks at me, deep in my eyes, asking for my forgiveness. And then I'm not falling anymore. I've grabbed ahold of a branch, and I'm not going to hit the ground. See, it's still just Sebastian. I see him in his eyes as he looks at me, my sea boy.

"I'm not kidding myself," Sebastian says. "I can't run forever. I know that. I just believe that if she has to work at this too hard, she'll give up. I *know* her. I've known her since she was in elementary school."

"But it's her child," I say.

"It's not about him, for her. It's about herself. The looking, the waiting—she'll get bored. She'll lose interest. Too much *effort*. I *know* her."

"It's the parents I'm worried about," Tess says.

"Maybe it was a mistake to run. Though, I tell you, it doesn't feel like a mistake. The courts are going to think otherwise, but . . . Look at him. I'm all he's ever known. She's a stranger."

"I thought you were grieving," I say.

"I *am* grieving. If Bo . . . If I ever had to give him up, even part-time, to those people . . . I don't know. I just don't know." He kisses the back of Bo's neck, keeps his mouth there for a long time. Tess stands, begins to clear the dishes.

I want to cry for him. I guess now I am grieving too. "You could have told me," I say.

"I'm sorry. I wanted to. I'm a crappy liar, anyway. I hope you can understand. If anyone found out, someone who didn't get this, those papers would be on my doorstep within a couple of hours.

"I'm going to lay him down," Sebastian says. Bo is zonked. His thumb has fallen out, but his mouth is still sucking a little, as if the thumb were still there. His cheeks are rosy and his hair slick from the warmth of Sebastian's sweatshirt. Sebastian looks so young holding that baby.

I carry some dishes into the kitchen. Tess wipes the inside of a glass with a soapy sponge.

I just stand there. I don't know what to say, honestly.

"He trusts you," she says. "And I do too." She rinses the glass, sets it upside down in the rack, and dries her hands. "I'm sure this isn't quite what you were picturing."

"I care about him," I say.

"I can see that," she says.

Sebastian appears. "Can I walk you out?"

The wood planks creak under our weight. At the end of the dock, he takes my hands in his. "I can understand if this changes things," he says.

His eyes hold my own. I understand he's not guilty of anything except maybe loving too much. This boy, he is just . . . mine.

"No."

"I really want you in my life, Jade."

He kisses me then. And we are there outside, arms in each other's jackets, for a long time, and I stand with my ear against his chest, just listening to his heart.

Part Three:
Tsunamis, Hurricanes, and Doors Flying Off Airplanes

Chapter Fifteen

Chimpanzees will thrust their tongues in each other's mouths. In other words, chimpanzees French kiss . . .
— Dr. Jerome R. Clade, *The Fundamentals of Animal Behavior*

"This is Onyx," Damian says. "Onyx, this is Delores."

"We've met," Delores says. "It's nice to see you again."

"Give her an apple," Damian says.

Delores holds one in her palm and Onyx takes it, curls her trunk to her mouth. "She's crunching." Delores chuckles. "Hear that? She's crunching."

Damian smiles at Rick Lindstrom and me.

Delores pats Onyx's wide, crinkled side. "That's really cute. That's so funny. You're a funny old thing," she says to Onyx.

* * *

I was spending as much time as I could over at the houseboat. Sometimes with Sebastian and Bo, sometimes with Tess and Bo, and sometimes just Bo, if Sebastian was working and Tess was at an FFECR meeting—Fathers For Equal Custody Rights. I would bring my homework, and Bo would come and sit down in my lap and I'd put my nose under his neck and inhale his sticky-peaches scent. He would "work" while I did—scrawling big strokes of crayons on paper after sheet of paper, crazily waste-ful but quiet. I got to know what he loved—blowing bubbles, trying to haul big things around, saying no, words that rhymed, showing off by dancing, trucks, trucks, trucks. And what he didn't—getting his face washed, when a toy didn't work, when he had to leave somewhere before he was ready, the neighbor's dog, a black lab named Bruce. I learned his good points and bad ones—he threw things, got frustrated and would kick and grab everything he could, and he'd cry forever in a high-pitched half scream. But he was also cuddly, knew way more than he could say, tried to sing, and would bring his blankie over when he was ready to sleep. Plus, God, he was just so precious. His soft skin, and the way he'd sit in his overalls and study something, head bent down, so serious . . . well.

Tess left a key for me, hidden under the cement frog. I got to know Tess, too. The way she would swear and act tough but wasn't. How much she loved her sister, her daughters, her grandchildren, the way her eyes would brighten and her laugh would twinkle when she talked to them. How she disliked the dock cats crapping in her garden. How she'd sometimes write letters to Max that he wouldn't get anymore. How she made the best blueberry muffins you ever had in your life. How she loved her boat and missed her motorcycle she'd left back home, and how she worried she'd done the wrong thing by Sebastian. How she got fired up when she talked about injustice, causing her face to redden.

I learned about dock life. How on Tuesday summer nights the sailboats would race on the lake, the water packed tight with speeding triangles of white and spinnakers of starburst color. How any variety of boats might pass—tour boats with visitors waving; kayakers, who sometimes had dogs in life jackets as passengers; even flat, motored barges with dining tables atop and guests eating by candlelight with linen napkins on their laps. I now recognized the neighbors—Winston Grove, who was from Australia, and his wife, Trudy; and Gloria Montana, a woman who lived alone and made sculptures and was always having visitors. There were Annalee and Tony, who'd just gotten married. There was Bruce the dog and Jose the dog and Jazzy the cat and Sal and Brickhead, twin calicos. There was a beaver who was building a dam near the start of the dock.

And I learned more about Sebastian. Sometimes love is a surprise, an instant of recognition, a sudden gift at a sudden moment that makes everything different from then on. Some people will say that's not love, that you can't really love someone you don't know. But I'm not so sure. Love doesn't seem to follow a plan; it's not a series of steps. It can hit with the force of nature—an earthquake, a tidal wave, a storm of wild, relentless energy that is beyond your simple attempts at control. Thomas Jefferson fell in love at first sight, I learned from Mom at dinner one night, and so do butterflies and beavers and so did I. And so I had to go backward and come to know the person I loved. I learned he hated shirts with scratchy tags, that he knew everything about cars and read science fiction and spy novels. He could figure out what was wrong with a computer, drew sketches of buildings on napkins and phone books and spare pieces of paper, and often wore socks that didn't match. He hated to get angry, and instead just kept it inside until it came out in a rush that was near tears. His touch was gentle. He used the word "fuck" a little too often after he got to know you well, but rarely swore around people he didn't know. He liked anything barbequed—ribs, chips, hot wings. Sometimes he licked his fingers.

Our talks went something like this:

Me: If you could change anything in your life, what would it be?

Sebastian: I'd have met you sooner.

And this:

Sebastian: I wonder what animals think about.

Me: I do too.

Sebastian: Does an elephant think about heaven? And if he does, are there big, white fluffy clouds?

Me: Elephant angels with giant halos.

Sebastian: Do dolphins think about God, and if they do, does he sound like Flipper?

And this:

Tess: Fresh blueberries. That's one of the secrets. Not frozen— that'll add too much water and make them gummy. *Fresh*.

Sebastian: They're not cheap, either.

Tess: Sebastian, you ought to know more than anyone that some things are worth paying a high price for. Turn on the oven. Four hundred.

Sebastian: Bossy, bossy.

Me: And hand us that bowl.

Tess: You got it now, girl.

See, it wasn't just Sebastian I loved. It was all of them, that snug feeling of right. I craved their presence, their den, their lair, their nest. I loved Sebastian's tousled presence, his bare feet, his arms around me and him kissing me, my back up against a tree, his hand behind my neck, his hands, mine. I loved when he read to Bo, and I would lose the words, forget they had meaning, and would instead just ride with their rhythms, disappear in the music of his voice. I loved Bo's raw energy, the way he sucked in the world and used it to add to his knowledge. He was developing a sense of humor—calling an object by the wrong name to get a laugh. And Tess. Well, I loved the way she would overreact, loved the way she did everything with energy and heart. When she dug in the dirt, setting geraniums in the houseboat planters, she did it with her bare hands, and when she laughed, it was loud, and when she got into the boat, it was with a solid, sure step. She was *connected*. To her family, to her surroundings, to her life in general. She lived vividly.

And here's what happened. My anxiety—I sort of stopped noticing I had it. I'm not saying there's some simple solution here, because there isn't. I'm not saying if you do X, Y, Z, it will go away, because I don't believe that's even true. It wasn't gone— I don't mean that, and it'd be stupid to think so. Just, I stopped giving it so much attention. I felt more calm. I hadn't lit a patron saint candle for weeks, and they lay cold and still on my dresser, the top of the wax collecting dust. I even backed off some of my studying, which is probably normal for a senior in her last semester of school, but not normal for me. I got a couple of Cs on tests, something Dad would have killed me for, or at least given me the tight-jawed silence, had he known, which he didn't. He and Mom didn't know anything about Sebastian and Bo and Tess. They thought I had more hours at the zoo, and spent the rest of my time with Alex Orlando and gang. In truth, I would go to school, put in my time, head to the zoo. I'd clean cages and wash elephants and hide watermelon and watch Onyx follow Delores everywhere. Then I'd go to the houseboat and stay until the evening. During that time, I had stopped feeling the way I had for a long while—like a hamster on one of those wheels, running, running, running, his heart beating like mad, in his little wire cage. I had always felt like I was being chased, but I was on that wheel, and the only one chasing me was myself. Now, I wasn't looking over my shoulder, or trying to see the future, living for some other time. It was just *now*.

I finally felt a lack of fear, a sense that the most important things were safe. But instinct, as Abe says, is not a foolproof system. Sometimes it is a map we hold upside down. I was lulled into peace by a rocking boat, by the smell of muffins baking, by the love of a young father, and I forgot to imagine a beautiful young woman and her parents, driving in their BMW to an attorney's office, to the expensive building that housed the private detective they'd hired to find Sebastian.

I forgot to imagine all the ways the pieces of your life can be endangered. Just as the beaver by the dock was gathering and building his dam branch by branch, stick by stick, building a new life in a new place, there would be another dam elsewhere being taken apart—piece by piece or all at once, by a predator, by a storm, or just by the daily movements of the water.

We are sitting at a Starbucks table—two, actually, pushed together. It is decorated with swirls and contemporary hieroglyphics, cave drawings done by a factory, painted in black on tan, shiny wood. Michael raises his cup.

"I've got something to tell you guys," he says.

"You're gay," Hannah says.

"Shut up. This is serious," Akello says.

"Tell us," I say.

"I got accepted into Johns Hopkins."

I have a swell of feeling. My heart just fills—pride, excitement, that satisfaction of knowing that someone's hard work, at least, has paid off. I might have been wrong, but I could swear his eyes were teary. My throat closes. I grab his hands.

"You did it," I say.

"I know it. I can hardly believe it," he says. "I got the letter yesterday."

"That is so fantastic," I say.

"You earned it, Michael," Jenna says.

"Hey, if I get sick, there's no one I'd rather have figuring out what the deal is," Akello says. "You're going to be a kick-ass doctor."

"This is so great. This is just so great," I say.

"The thing I never got," Kayla says, "was why it's *Johns* Hopkins. Are there two of them? I mean, what's with that?"

"I know it. It's weird," Hannah says.

"See, this is what can happen when you work hard," Jenna says.

"To Dr. Jacobs," Akello says, and taps his cup against Michael's.

Michael smiles. Just shakes his head as if the news hasn't yet sunk in. "They've got something like forty libraries."

"Wow," I say.

"Speaking of *library* . . ." Kayla says.

Hannah laughs a little.

"Shut up, Kayla," Michael says.

"Shut up, Kayla"? From Michael? What is this? Kayla's mouth drops open, her straw halfway to her lips. Everyone is silent. Jenna traces a swirl on the table with her finger. A coffee grinder blasts on at the counter. Somewhere in my stomach, a sick feeling is starting. They all know something I don't. That's what's happening. I can see it now. Maybe there's a part of me that understands what's coming. Instinct buried. Buried no longer, because now is the time to look. Here it is.

"Really," Akello says. "You are such a bitch."

"Go back to where you came from," Kayla snaps.

"What's going on?" I say.

"Nothing. Ignore them," Jenna says. "Come on, you guys."

"Don't you think she should know?" Kayla says.

"Kayla, don't," Hannah says.

"Know what?" That sick feeling—it's moving. Working its way from my stomach to where it knows it belongs—my heart.

"Your mother and Mr. Dutton."

"What?"

"Shut up!" Michael says. "Don't even listen to her."

"Michael," Hannah says. "You know, maybe . . ."

"Someone had their tongue down someone's throat, is what I heard," Kayla says.

"What?"

"Brittany Hallenger caught them," Kayla says.

What I feel then is the ground, and it seems like it has been moved, taken away. My head feels strange too, like I could black out. Like there's no oxygen, suddenly, an important connection from lungs to heart to brain snipped.

"Let's go," Jenna says.

"Come on, Jade," Akello says.

"We're not finished," Kayla says. "Lunch isn't even half over."

Michael and Akello get up. Jenna, too. I go with them, and we get in the car and leave Kayla and Hannah sitting there. We go from the cool air conditioning to the sunny May air, the stifling heat of the car smelling of warmed vinyl.

"I don't want them in my car," Jenna says.

"I don't want them in my life," Michael says.

"I hope she chokes on her fucking Frappucino," Akello says.

No one speaks on the ride back. No one speaks, and Jenna squeezes my hand, and Akello offers to carry my backpack. Which means it was true. What Kayla had said back in the café, it was true.

* * *

I sit through biology and Government, and I get through by trying to focus on each and every word that is said. If I look out the window of the class, I'll see my mother's car in the parking lot, and I cannot, cannot, cannot (count the words on my fingers, starting with my thumb) think of that, or of the library or of Mr. Dutton, *do not, do not, do not*. I walk home. I don't take the bus. I count sidewalk tiles. I don't go to the zoo, can't face the elephants and their warmth and love and family life right then. I don't know what to do. I have no idea. I just open the door of my house, and it seems like a strange door. One of those bizarre moments when a familiar object seems completely foreign.

I have no plan. Maybe my backstage mind has a plan, because I drop my backpack to the floor with a thud when I hear her in the kitchen. *Her*, not Mom. Just *her*. In the kitchen—our kitchen, Dad's kitchen, this family's kitchen.

I am in the doorway. She's emptying the dishwasher, of all things. I don't know why this seems so extraordinary and why it pisses me off so much. The dishwasher—it seems so *innocent*. It's innocent to put away our glasses and forks after kissing another man.

"Good day at school?" I say. The sarcasm drips from my words like an icicle from a rooftop.

"Yes," she says. She turns, eyes me warily. She holds a plate in her hand.

"That's what I heard. I heard you had a *really* good day." The anger—it's there. Suddenly, it's there, in a boiling rush. So much anger, it scares me. I don't know how much is there, how much

I have inside. I didn't know that rage could sweep up like a wave, washing over everything else, drowning good things. It is bigger than I am. God, it's *huge*.

"Jade. What is the matter with you?"

"You *disgust* me."

She just stands there with her mouth open.

"Mr. Dutton and his *books*. The *librarian*, for God's sake. What a Goddamn *sex symbol*. You were *seen*, do you know that? Seen and talked about. You embarrassed me. You *humiliated* me."

"Jade." She is frozen there, shocked. Holding that plate. She has her jeans on, and the white blouse, opened too far at the neck. Silver jewelry. Is that what she wore? Was there more? Had she slept with him too?

"Who saw?" she says finally.

"Who saw? Who saw? That's what matters here?" There is guilt in those words. "Are you having an *affair* with him?"

"Jade, no! It's not that! It's not . . . what it seems."

"Oh, what—you were rehearsing for the school play? You're probably in my school play now too, right?" I want to cry, but I don't. Anger is taking all the space. It overtakes every piece of me.

Mom's face twists. "I'm sorry." She bends over, grasps the plate to her stomach. A sound escapes: grief. Just this cry of grief.

My heart wants to feel pity, it tries to, but I shove it away. Goddamn her. What was she thinking? How could she want to wreck our lives? "'I'm doing this for you, Jade,'" I mock. "'I'm doing all of this for you.' For me. Right." My voice rises. I'm yelling. My throat is raw with rage. "You were doing it all for *you*. It was never about me. You, you, you! If you wanted to do something for me, you would have left me alone. You would have let me have room to *breathe*."

I am screaming at her. This is not me. This is some cyclone inside, a furious evil person. I turn and run. Up the stairs to my room. I slam the door so hard I can hear one of the pictures that hang along the stairwell wall drop to the floor.

I sit at the edge of my bed. Clutch my pillow. My heart is pounding so hard. For a moment, I fear I won't catch my breath. She'd taken my air, yes, she had. I concentrate. Desert. Calm. In, out. Goddamn her. In, out.

"Jade, please." Her voice comes through the door. None of this is happening, which is a good thing. It's at a distance. It isn't my life falling apart.

"Get away from me."

"I want to explain." Muffled voice. Crying.

"Explain to Dad."

I count this phrase on my fingers. *Explain to Dad. Explain to Dad. Explain to Dad.* Breathe.

"Nothing happened. Nothing is going to happen. Jade! Jade, I was so lonely. I am so lonely." She is crying hard now. "He was . . . a friend to me. Okay? He took interest in me."

"Obviously," I say.

"Please," she cries. "Please . . . My life. It's always been so . . . decided."

I say nothing. I pick fuzz off of my bedspread. Build it into a pyramid.

"Your dad . . . I've been . . . alone. A long time. Roger was kind to me. I felt like . . . I remembered I was a human being. A woman."

I don't want her to say that. I hate that she says that. Right then, I hate that word, *woman*. It sounds dirty.

"I'm going to tell Dad," I say. "Of course I'm going to tell him. He should know." I don't know if that's true or not. That I will tell him. That he should know.

"Jade, no. I'll tell him. I'm going to tell him." She is crying. "Let me." Her words come in bursts. "What happened today—it was my fault. I'm sorry someone saw. I'm sorry I did it. That was all that happened. I swear to you. That was all. It won't happen again. I love you. I love all of you."

She is sobbing, hard. "God. Oh, God," she cries.

I rise from the bed. I open the door. Mascara drips down her face, which is red and puffy and small-eyed. Tears have dampened her blouse. Pain radiates from her body in waves. Maybe I should put my arms around her. Maybe I should, but I don't.

"I'm sorry for you," I say.

And then I shove past her. I take her car keys, swipe them off the counter. Hey, otherwise she might use them to see her lover, the librarian. I get in the car. I get the hell out of that place that's supposed to be my home.

I drive until I reach the water. I park the car, but by then it has already started. It's too late. I grip the steering wheel, fighting the feeling of no air. No air and the reality of what has happened are colliding forces, a shaking earth causing animals to flee and buildings to fall, and the sea to rise in one overpowering wall of water. I guess I manage to get the car door open, because an eternity later, Sebastian is standing there, the mail in his hand.

"Jade?"

"I . . ."

"Are you all right? What's going on?"

"I can't . . ."

"Come here. Come here. It's okay."

He helps me from the car. "Panic. I can't . . . Breathe."

"It's okay. It is."

He holds me to him. Strokes my hair. I think I might throw up. I can't throw up. It would be horrible if I threw up. But I might. His hand is firm, rhythmic. He strokes my hair. "Breathe with me," he says. "There, now. Like this. It's okay. See? You're okay. Everything is fine. I've got you."

The desert. His arms. The timeless, endless desert. Love, timeless and endless, too. Breathing, in and out. I start to cry. And he just keeps me tight in his arms and kisses my hair. "It's all right," he says.

Tess is home, but heading out. She changes her mind. She hangs her little knapsack-purse over the chair and pours me a glass of ice tea with a slice of lemon and listens with a care that is both efficient and gentle.

"Lost hearts." Tess sighs.

"Don't be sorry for her," I say. "After what she did."

Tess sighs again. Bo wakes from his nap in the other room, calls out "Da!" and Sebastian goes to him. "Jade," Tess says after a while. "You know how much I care about you. But you want everything to be either black or white. I've noticed this. You want to put things into separate compartments—right, wrong, good, bad. But not much works that way. Even black and white—mostly, it's just shades of gray."

"Are you saying what she did was okay? 'Cause if that's what you're saying, I don't agree."

"It was hurtful, yes, it was. But right or wrong? Was your dad wrong to spend so much time alone? Was your mom wrong to feel lonely? Were they wrong to grow apart?"

"They have Oliver and me."

"I don't know. The older I get, the more I just see how we've all got the same struggles, and then all I can feel is compassion."

"She chose to kiss that man, and that was wrong." I don't understand how Tess can't see this.

"And where is the beginning of that wrong? Where is the start of that thread? Good luck finding that. Go back eons. Did she do it because of him? Did he do it because of her? Because of their parents? Because of their parents' parents? Because of some deep, archaic need?" Tess is getting a bit worked up. Her eyes are blue and focused, and she leans into me so close I can smell her clean, laundry-soap scent.

"Maybe she did it because she made the choice to."

"Does the river make the choice to erode the rock?" Tess says, eyes blazing.

"I feel like I've walked in on open-mic poetry night down at the Flamingo," Sebastian says as he rejoins us. Bo is sweaty from sleep. Still groggy, his head rests on Sebastian's shoulder.

"I'm trying to tell her that everything is so interconnected that it is often impossible to sort out who impacts who, and how."

"'Every action has an equal and opposite reaction.' Or something like that, right? I got a C in physics," Sebastian says. He winks at me.

"More like we've got this big knotted ball of history and behavior and needs and drives."

"Sounds like a mess," I say.

"A real tangle. But, oh, what a lovely one."

"I'm angry at her," I say. "I don't want to try to understand her."

"Right," Tess says. "You're pissed and you want to lash out, but it's too hard to hurt something you understand."

"Yeah," I say.

"Well, when you're ready for compassion, that's where to look. The way we're all just creatures doing the best we can."

Tess leaves to do some errands and attend her FFECR meeting. Evening comes and Sebastian makes me scrambled eggs, and I read Bo's favorite story over and over to him before Sebastian calls halt and Bo disintegrates and finally winds down to sleep. I don't want to go home. Sebastian puts Bo to bed and I do the dishes. I am putting the milk carton away when Sebastian appears in the kitchen, takes my wrist, and brings me outside. We sit on the dock for a while, watching the ripples in the water, the city lights dancing on waves. It gets cold, so Sebastian goes inside and gets some blankets. We lie on the hard wood dock and wrap ourselves in the blankets and look up at the stars. I settle into the crook of his arm. I hear crickets, the drifting voices of someone's television, canned sit-com laughter. The water smells seaweedy, and a twinge of melting butter still clings in the air.

"Today . . ." I say. "In the car . . . My anxiety. I'm sorry." I feel the shame, inching around my insides.

"What are you sorry for? It's all right. I'm sorry you have to deal with it. It seems awful."

"It's like being held underwater," I say.

"God, that's got to be tough."

"I'm embarrassed."

"Embarrassed? Are you kidding me? I have a *kid*. You still accept me."

"Of course. He's part of you. He's great. Anxiety's not great."

"But it's part of you. Jade? I love you. All of you."

My heart soars. I find his hand in the dark. "I love you, too," I say. I want to cry. Happy cry, sadness, acceptance. The whole knotted ball that Tess was talking about. He loves me and I love him, and it is simple and immense, too.

We are quiet for a while. The dock creaks and groans with a passing wave. "You know, you handled it just right. In the car. It helped," I say.

"I'm glad." He turns toward me a little under the blanket, and his breath is warm in my ear. "Bo, sometimes he gets himself worked up, and he just struggles. . . . If I hold him, and just rub his back, or his head . . ."

Sebastian strokes my hair. We start to kiss. We kiss for a long while. His hands are gentle.

I guess that's the only thing that is necessary to know about Sebastian and me on that hard dock, the blanket around us. He is careful, so very careful with me. Then, I realize the importance of having another person who sleeps beside you, the survival-necessity of having a shoulder to shake awake during the middle-of-the-night terrors, those times when it is dark and you feel too alone.

I come home really late that night, and the house is quiet and dark. Milo doesn't even wake up to greet me, but when I go upstairs, the bathroom light is on and Oliver is coming out, his eyes all squinched up from the shocking blast of fluorescent brightness after dream darkness.

"Jeez, Sis, you scared me."

"Oliver, flush! God, don't be gross."

"I was sleeping!"

"If you're awake enough to pee, you're awake enough to flush."

He peers out of the slits of his eyes at me. "You're just getting home. You have your coat on."

"Congratulations, Sherlock," I say.

"You're going to be in trou-ble," he says.

"I'm eighteen, remember? I don't even have to live here."

"Don't say that," he says. "You wouldn't leave me."

I suddenly want to hug him, my little brother in his p.j.'s and with his sleeping hair. "How was tonight? Was everything okay?"

"Mom and Dad stayed in their room all night talking. I watched *Titanic Mysteries* on TV. I opened a new bag of Doritos and ate them for dinner and no one even said anything. Why is Mom crying?"

"I don't know, Oliver."

"He's being a butt."

"I don't know." I've had enough talk tonight about laying blame.

"If you ever don't live here, you can take me with you," he says.

I do hug him then. There had been so many changes, just in one day. I feel new and old at the same time. I feel like the first person ever to make love to someone else. I almost want to cry, from the loss of the old, from the moving forward. Part of me wants to hold on—it's going so fast.

"Jade, you're squishing me," Oliver says.

Chapter Sixteen

Animals lie, and they do so when the benefits of the lie outweigh the risks. Piping plovers fake broken wings and hobble around in acted-out injury to distract predators from a nest, and apes will hide food when other apes walk past. Monogamous European passerines, most notably the pied flycatcher, will hide their mated status, pretending to be "single" in order to possess several unknowing mates in several locations . . .
  —Dr. Jerome R. Clade, *The Fundamentals of Animal Behavior*

Everything in my house felt careful. Like we all understood that we were in a fragile place, and care was being taken not to break us. Door handles were twisted so that doors could shut quietly, steps were soft, voices low, and eye contact was avoided. Anger was too dangerous—anger would have shattered the hairline cracks snaking through our glass. Everything felt held in midair, just waiting, in temporary balance, in suspension. Like those surfers in *Riding Giants*, or Jake Gillette's parachute as he leaps off the skateboard ramp. We all moved carefully, slow moves, a Queen of Hearts in hand, gently placed on top of the card house. Will it hold? Will it fall? Nothing went forward or beyond, except for Dad and the building of his train set. He kept hammering and sawing, and the sounds coming from downstairs were both persistent and somehow mournful, a reminder that going forward always meant loss, too.

Even Milo was quieter lately. He would stretch, rump in the air and front legs reaching out, then he would lie back down again, his chin on his paws, paws on his blankie. His toenails clicked more quietly and slowly on the wood floors. He would sit patiently while his food was being scooped, his chin up, eyes watchful.

That night, after Milo eats, Oliver tosses Milo's old stuffed hedgehog in his direction. Milo wags, leaps after it, and then just slides flat on the rug, the hedgehog held between his paws.

"Give it here," Oliver says. He wears his white karate uniform, with its wide and swingy pant legs and cuffs, its thick, stitched belt. He claps his hands, but Milo just looks his way and stays put. Oliver makes a quick grab for the hedgehog, but speed is unnecessary. Milo lets him have it. Oliver dances the hedgehog toward Milo, gives the hedgehog an enticing growl, but Milo only sighs through his nose.

"What is wrong with you people," Oliver says.

"For your information, Milo isn't people. Milo is a dog."

"You're all acting dead or something. When are you going to start talking to Mom again?"

"I'm not *not* talking to Mom," I say.

"That is just . . . bullshit." He tries the word out. Says it as if he's just robbed a bank and is showing off the loot.

"Oliver."

He apparently likes the sound, and so he says it again, adds a flourish. "Bullshit. Mega-bullshit. I don't like what's going on here. It's like everyone's under a spell."

"The White Witch?" I suggest.

"Always winter and never Christmas," he says.

I think about this. He is right in a way. We are under a spell. Lies are delicate. You have to hold your breath around them.

"Hi-*yah*!" Oliver karate chops the hedgehog, but Milo merely rolls on his side, exposing his white stomach in a display of canine submission.

"So you haven't told anyone about Sebastian," Abe says. "Mom, Dad, Jenna—no one? Why is that?"

"You. I just told you."

"Besides me." He taps his pencil on his desk.

"No one else."

"Why?"

"I don't know. Maybe I don't want their interference."

"Does their knowledge necessarily equal interference?" Abe asks.

"Some things aren't their business."

"Agreed."

"Like sleeping with him." I test the waters. I look at Abe, but his face is still its usual calm self.

"That's a big step," he says. "How did you feel about taking it?"

"It was a positive experience," I say. "It felt right."

"And you protected yourself."

"Yes, Abe. God."

"Jade, these are big things, big changes in your life. Is there a place between letting people take over and shutting them out completely by keeping secrets?"

"She certainly has hers."

"Mom."

"Yes," I say.

"That may be true, but what about you? What do you get by lying to them? What are the upsides?"

"I keep them from charging in. They won't get it. There's no way they'll understand it—Bo and all."

"So, you manage the situation by trying to manage them."

"Right."

"And this can go on for how long?"

"I guess until someone finds out and freaks out completely."

"What are your other options? You're eighteen. You'll be graduating in a few weeks. Are Mom and Dad going to decide every relationship you have?"

"They'd like to."

"What happens if you give them a chance? Is there the possibility they might surprise you? They've surprised you lately."

"This is Mom and Dad we're talking about, here. They will *flip out.* Do you know what could happen if they found out? If they told someone?"

"So, it sounds like they find out either way. You tell them and they flip out, or they find out and they flip out worse, since you lied to them. Can you really control the outcome, how they're going to feel and how they're going to react, by lying?"

"It's working so far."

"So far? Jade, remember: Secrets have a shelf life."

A week passed. Maybe more. Mom and Dad seemed to be giving each other the small patching threads of kindness—she laughed at his jokes, he offered her coffee when he was pouring. I saw the politeness as forgiveness. I forgot that politeness is also the way we stay safe among strangers.

School was getting that end-of-the-year feeling, that loose, energized excitement that meant some things were ending and others starting. Yearbooks were splayed open on desks and cafeteria tables and steps, and there was that pressure to sum up relationships both deep and never really begun. Lies and promises (*I hope to see you again. Let's hang out this summer! Too bad we didn't get to know each other better*), definitions and secret memories (*You're so sweet! Don't forget about that time with the frog in Lab*). Four years of joint growth and incarceration. Everyone was talking about where they were going and what was going to happen next. We stopped having lunch with Hannah, though I saw she had tried to call me a few times without leaving a message. Michael was trying out his new confidence, and Akello was getting ready to go back home. Jenna still hadn't decided which

Christian college she wanted to go to, and my own decision to go to the University of Washington right near home seemed like an extension of the stuck-in-midairness of life at home.

But nothing stays in midair forever. What hangs there will fall, eventually. Sometimes caught. Sometimes shattered. Always irrevocably changed.

"Onyx and I had a falling-out yesterday," Delores says.

Onyx is on her side in the elephant house, being hosed. Delores is speaking loudly over the sound of the water. Rick Lindstrom is carefully spraying Onyx while Delores brushes her.

"I'd have never guessed by looking at her," I say. "She's smiling."

"Well, we had to have a chat. She smacked me with her trunk yesterday."

"Oh, my God, Delores. Are you okay?"

"I'm fine, but I was pissed at her." The sleeves of Delores's blouse that are sticking from her overalls are wet, rolled at the sleeve.

"What happened?"

"I've been getting to know the other elephants. I gave Hansa some apples. I guess Onyx got jealous."

"But you came back today."

Rick Lindstrom shuts off the hose, and my voice is suddenly too loud.

"I told you never to do it again, didn't I?" She pokes Onyx's big, old rough side. "You see, you must never be selfish with your love," she says to Onyx in the mother-of-a-misbehaving-preschooler voice. "I care about all the elephants, but you are my special one."

I don't know if Onyx understands Delores's words. Maybe, maybe not. But her tones and rhythms must be universal, because Onyx lifts up her head, pokes the air with her trunk.

"Be still," Delores says to her.

"Delores, I think you are a natural," I say.

"A natural."

"Yep."

"I think you may be right," she says.

I help clean the outdoor enclosure for most of the rest of the day, but the volunteer chart says I'm helping Damian weigh the elephants next. I look for him in the elephant house. Usually, he's there before I am, with his stack of charts and plastic tub of treats for good behavior. No Damian. I am surprised to find his office door closed, which it rarely is unless he is having a meeting with Victor Iverly. I tap softly.

"Yes?" he says.

"It's Jade. I was waiting for you at the scale."

"Oh, dear, dear, dear," he says. "Come in."

I open the door, and see Damian facing the window in his swivel chair. He doesn't get up. He keeps his face turned from me.

"I wondered where you were. Nothing's ready."

"I've had a distressing call," he says. He folds his hands together. They look like they're getting comfort from each other.

He swivels toward me. His eyes, usually brown and dancing, are sad and flat.

"Are you okay?"

"My brother called. It's Jum. My Jumo." Damian's voice wavers. "She . . . He went to visit. He is worried about malnutrition. She is not eating. He asked Bhim about her weight, her eating habits, and he just shrugged. He asked Bhim if he had examined Jumo's molars. You see, if there is a disease, a growth, it impairs chewing. Jumo is too young to show the ravages of age in her teeth, so it is likely something that can be helped. If he would take the time. He doesn't care, you see. And I have abandoned her."

"No, you haven't," I say. "You still love her."

"I am her mahout—she is like my child, Jum. My little one."

"What can you do?"

"From here, nothing." He shakes his head. "Nothing."

Tess can't contain her excitement. "Whoo-ee," she repeats. "Look at that. Look at him. What a specimen. What a beauty."

"Ish," Bo says.

"Indeed, it is!" she says.

"His eyes give me the creeps," I say.

Bo pokes his finger against the slick, cold scales, scrunches up his face.

"Really," I agree. "Blech."

"Copper River salmon!" Tess sings for the zillionth time. Tony, one of the houseboat neighbors, had caught several the day before and given Tess one. She is hopping around as if she had just unscrewed a Coke lid and found out she'd won a million dollars. The fish lies on some spread-out newspapers on the counter. His eyes are teeny glass paperweights, dull and unseeing, his tail thin and floppy, his middle thick.

"I'm becoming a vegetarian," I say.

"Wait until you taste this. You'll think you've died and gone to heaven."

"I'm happier when I don't think of my food as formerly living," I say. "I'm happy to think it all came from Safeway. Food shouldn't look at you."

"Circle of life," Tess says.

"If you sing, I'm leaving," I say.

"Ish, ish, ish," Bo says. Poke, poke, poke.

"Bo," I say.

"The fish doesn't mind," Tess says. She flaps his tail up and down in a fake swim and Bo squeals.

"Well, I hate to say it, but I can't join you. I've got this last big paper for humanities, and I need my computer."

"Coward," Tess says. "Chicken. Bawk, bawk."

"Awk awk," Bo says. "Ish."

"No, that's not what a fish says." Tess laughs. "A fish says . . . Hmm. Nothing, really."

"They just make those kissy-lips," I say. "Like this." I demonstrate for Bo. He tries to copy me, and purses his lips with this face so adorable, I could just eat it. I ruffle his hair. "Man, you're cute," I say. "You are so cute, you should be illegal."

"I can't believe you're going to miss this. Copper River salmon!"

"I really shouldn't have even stopped by. I just wanted to say a quick hello."

"I don't know what's keeping Sebastian," she says.

"Just tell him hi for me," I say. "And have fun with your fish."

"You don't know what you're missing," she says.

I walk down the dock and head up the steps to the street. My usual routine is to take the 212 bus that drops me off at home, or to have Sebastian drop me part way. I'm almost at the stop, down the narrow street, when I see Sebastian's car. He waves, pulls over to the side of the road. He rolls down his window.

"Don't tell me you're leaving," he says.

"Humanities paper," I say. I kiss him through the window. A stuffed Armchair Books book bag is on the passenger seat, along with a half-empty water bottle and a partial bag of barbeque potato chips.

"Damn. Now I'm really pissed I had to stay late."

"We'll have some time this weekend?"

"Yah. But I miss you now," he says.

"You're having Copper River salmon for dinner. He's lying in the kitchen. Fish corpse. Tess is beside herself."

"Thanks for the warning."

He takes a strand of my hair. He caresses my face with the back of his hand. "I love you," he says.

"I love you, too," I say.

For a few weeks, every time I saw Mom's car in the driveway, I got this sickening attack of messy, unsorted emotions. It was like looking at some automotive equivalent of shame. The car had been in the driveway a lot too, as she wasn't spending so much time at school. She was planning our graduation ceremony, of course, along with the other PTA ladies, like Mrs. Lenderholm, with her Porsche and brown hair roots showing through the blond; and Mrs. Thompkins, who, when she left a phone message, treated you like you were five and unable to spell a challenging phrase like "please call." But Mom usually worked from home. Maybe she had been embarrassed into hiding. Maybe she was avoiding Mr. Dutton and the dangers of his passionate temptations—overdue book fines, paper cuts, heartbreak.

Funny thing, on that day, her car just looks like a car. A regular, aging silver Audi, a vehicle that had done great things (like get me my driver's license) and bad things (like break down on the first day of school once), but that mostly was pretty reliable and had nice cup holders, too. I barely even notice it.

Mom's just sitting there when I open the door. Sitting on the stairwell with a white envelope on her knees. Her hair is pulled back into a small ponytail, and she is wearing Mom clothes. Jeans. A T-shirt with a zippered sweatshirt over top. She'd moved from being a woman-woman back to a mom-woman.

"Well, Jade," she says.

"Jeez, Mom. You scared me."

"I could say the same thing about you," she says. Her voice is uh-oh icy. Oh-shit icy.

I don't say anything. She just stays there and looks at me. I hold my backpack in one hand. I don't set it down.

"Something came in the mail for you," she says. She hands me the envelope. I drop my backpack finally. I can see that the top edge of the letter had been torn open, the contents read. I almost don't want to take it, but I do. I reach out, turn the envelope over.

University of Santa Fe, it says. I slip the paper out and unfold it. *We are pleased to inform you . . .*

I'd forgotten about it, that was the weird thing. I actually look at the words and have to urge them into meaning. I feel a surge of relief. *This* is what she's freaking out about? I can handle *this*. This was a betrayal that had an explanation, or at least one that I could blame on someone else.

"Oh!" I say.

"I guess there are things you aren't telling me, Jade."

"No." Yes. "I mean, this is just because Abe . . . Part of my homework was to apply to some other places. You know, not near home. I'm not planning on *going*."

"Jade, there's *a lot* you're not telling me."

My inner attorney tells me to keep quiet. Not that I can speak, anyway—a bolt of cold fear has shut my mouth. She knows. About Sebastian. My backstage mind realizes this. I want to run. I feel like throwing up. All I had to lose rushes forward, shows itself. My cheek burns where he had just touched me.

"I said I wasn't going. I had no intention of going. That wasn't even the point. I forgot about even sending it. . . ."

Her eyes look hollow. They have brown circles under them that I don't remember seeing there that morning. She still just sits on those steps. "You never told me. I was really hurt by that, Jade. I went to find you. I wanted to know why you'd kept this from me. I went to the zoo, but they said you'd left already. No one knew where you'd gone. I saw Jake Gillette in the parking lot. You know Jake?"

"Everyone knows Jake."

"I see him around school. I try to be friendly to him because he seems lonely."

Jake Gillette. *This* was who ruined my life?

"He was there, with his skateboard and this little ramp he'd made out of wood," she continues. "I asked him if he saw you this afternoon, or knew where you went. He said he saw you all the time. That maybe you went off with the guy that has the baby, like you usually do. What the hell is going on, Jade?"

My mother isn't the swearing type, same as Dad isn't. Maybe she'll swear at the aforementioned Audi, maybe at Dad under her breath every now and then. But not often.

"What is going on here?"

I don't know how to start. I don't know how to explain it so she'll understand. "I can't talk about this right now," I say. I need time to think.

"Do you think you have a choice? Is that what you honestly think?"

I leave my backpack where it is. I try to edge past her on the stairs. I want my own room. I want to light a candle, look out my window, watch the elephants wander on my computer screen. "Let me by," I say.

"No," she says.

"Let me by!" I shove past her.

"I want some answers!" She follows me up the stairs. The PTA ladies should see her now. Stomping up the stairs, shouting. This isn't in the parenting books, now, is it? This isn't part of the four-cassette pack of *Parenting with Love and Logic* they sold at the PTA meetings. *Now, Junior, this behavior makes me sad.*

"It's none of your business."

Oliver stands in his doorway, hands over his ears. I make it to my room, slam the door.

"As long as you live in my house, it's my business!"

She flings open my door. My heart is wild. Hers must be too—her chest is moving up and down as if she'd just climbed something steep. We stare at each other. It's amazing how much I hate this person that I love. Twice now, over a few weeks, our relationship had suffered deep gashes, the claws and teeth of a tiger tearing into solid, strong hide. I know her so well, yet she is a stranger standing there. I see things in her face I haven't seen before. More wrinkles around her eyes. A looseness in the skin of her neck. When was the last time I had really looked at her? Where had this time gone? It was a question I'd heard my mother ask often, a question I felt now, for the first time.

"You're wearing lipstick," she says. Her voice is quiet. "Not gloss. Lipstick."

I nod. I stare at her and she stares back at me.

"It looks really pretty." Her voice is almost a whisper. "Really pretty." Her eyes are filling with tears.

I swallow. I don't know if I can speak. "Thank you," I say, but the words are full of grief now, too. My throat gathers tight, tears roll down my nose. She puts her palms over her eyes, lets out a pained sound.

"I'm sorry," she cries.

"I'm sorry too." I sob. She comes to me. We put our arms around each other. I can feel her body wracking, and she likely feels mine.

"It's just . . ." she says into my shoulder, her voice high from escaping a throat closed with grief. "You're not . . . in your little bathing suit in the blow-up pool anymore."

I laugh, through tears.

"You know?" She sniffs.

I nod into her shoulder.

"You're not . . . making me plates of Play-Doh food. Wearing that pink ruffly apron, remember that? You have this *life* I don't know about. It went so fast, I never quite caught up." She sniffs again. "Jade, I really . . ." Her voice wobbles again. She speaks through new tears, a tiny, high voice. "I really . . . I've really loved being your mother."

"You're not going anywhere," I say. I have the high voice too. The back of her shirt is wet from my tears.

"I know," she says. I can hardly hear her, her voice is so small. "But you are."

We just hold each other. I hold her, the young mother who turned on the sprinkler for me to run through, the one who fished for the escaped magnet under the fridge with the broomstick handle so she could hang my crayoned art, who drove with one arm out the window on the way to the orthodontist's appointment, this woman who loved to organize and who liked kitchen stores and who made great lasagna and who was too afraid sometimes and who wished for things I didn't know about. And she held me, her baby, her toddler, her young woman who loved animals and deserts and watching the sky and who loved staying organized and who was too afraid sometimes and who wished for things *she* didn't know about.

"God." She sniffs. "Look at us."

"I know it," I say.

"I need a Kleenex," she says. *I deed a Kleedex.*

"We both do," I say.

She makes us some tea. We sit at the table in the kitchen, and she sips her tea and looks down into her cup, stares at the browned string of the bag, sips her tea some more. Her eyes are still red, her face puffy from emotion. My own tea is nearly untouched, except for the warm mug, which I wrap my hands around for the comfort of its heat.

"He sounds wonderful," she says.

"He is."

"His maturity, it's something you like."

"Yeah. It's so different. The guys at school . . . Well, you know the guys at school."

"Like Alex Orlando." She holds her cup by the handle, swirls the liquid inside, a mini-tornado.

"I'm sorry."

"The fact that you've been lying—that's the thing that really made me mad. It hurt. *Hurts.*"

"I can understand that."

"It'd be reasonable for your dad and me to freak out. He's got a *baby.* You know? This is not just you going to the prom. This is jumping into the deep end of adulthood. Sebastian's had . . . He's had deep relationships."

"Had sex, you mean. And you talk about the prom like it's this great big innocent punch-bowl-and-corsage life moment.

We don't even have punch bowls anymore. We've got *police*. The
prom's about sex, for most guys. Definitely for Alex Orlando. You
think Alex cares about love and dancing on prom night?"

"I don't just mean sex." She stops swirling her cup. "Not just.
Responsibility, too. Of having a child. You're not exactly going to
be having a carefree time."

"Can you honestly say that *any* relationship is carefree?" I ask.
I consider what I've just said. Mom and Dad, Onyx and Delores,
Sebastian and Tiffany, Me and Hannah, Jenna and God—Tess
and Sebastian, even. No relationship is carefree—more the tangle
that Tess talked about. Complicated, if beautiful.

"Mostly carefree, okay? Before it needs to be otherwise? And
why does Sebastian live with his grandmother? Where's his family? What's with Bo's mother? You never said where she was."

"Dead." The word slips out before I have a chance to think.
Quick as instinct. Like a python zipping under sand to hide, or
the tail of a gecko instantly dropping off to distract a predator.
Sometimes, they would be quick. Sometimes, not quick enough.

"Dead? She died?"

"Childbirth." Shit.

"Childbirth?" Shit, shit! "I know it happens," Mom says, "but,
Jade, that's really rare."

"I know," I say. My backstage mind has completely abandoned
me. I could see it off in the distance, waving its nasty little fingers at
me, *Whoo hoo! Jade! Over here!* Childbirth, for God's sake!

"I just . . . Jade, please. I want the truth."

I think for a moment. What comes to me then is Abe, his
words. His urging to give this truth a chance.

"Not childbirth," I say.

"No," my mother says.

"Mom, you've got to promise. This is important, and you've got to promise. . . ."

"Okay, Jade. *All right.*" Her voice pulls with impatience.

"You can't talk about this with anyone."

"What is going on, Jade?"

"The baby's mother, Tiffany. She didn't want anything to do with Bo after he was born. She never saw him. Sebastian raised Bo. And then Tiffany's parents, they talked her into getting him back."

"Sebastian?"

"No, Bo. The father, he's some hotshot plastic surgeon in Ruby Harbor, where Sebastian used to live. They've got a ton of money. They can afford all the attorneys they want. Sebastian is the one that took care of Bo. She didn't want anything to do with him."

"What are you saying? Are you saying he took off with the baby? Oh, Jade. Tell me that's not what you're saying."

"You don't understand. Bo doesn't even know her. She didn't care about him."

"Obviously, she does!" Mom pushes her chair away from the table as if it is something gruesome. "Does he realize how he's hurt himself now? What is this grandmother thinking?"

She doesn't know Tess. She doesn't know the first thing about her. It is shocking, really, how fast things can go from great to horrible. I think about my computer and its "system restore." How the whole thing can revert to an earlier time and place before the mistake happened. "He hasn't been served papers yet," I say. "He isn't in violation of any order. There is no order."

"Yet!"

She just doesn't get this. She doesn't understand Sebastian and Bo together. "He thinks Tiffany will get tired of this. Mom, she's a beauty queen! She doesn't want to be a mother."

"But she is, Jade. She *is* a mother."

"Knock, knock," Dad says.

My humanities paper is going along just great, as you can imagine. Who gives a shit about exploring history and author motivation in *After the Fall*? I am acting out my own play—*During the Fall*. I have lit one of my patron saints for support, the Infant Jesus of Prague. Patron saint of families and children, which is why he's been chosen. His picture looks a bit creepy, like those dolls well-meaning people buy for you when they visit a foreign country. Those beady, swinging eyes in hard plastic, elaborate dress. But he also wears a puffy velvet king hat with a cross on top. The picture may have been vaguely unpleasant, but the prayer on the back is user-friendly, and it has the essential elements:

1. Kiss-up: *Dearest Jesus, little infant of Prague. So many have come to you and had their prayers answered. I feel drawn to you by love because you are kind and merciful.*

2. Submission, aka I'm Counting on You!: *I lay open my heart to you in hope, as I am at your feet.*

3. Request: *I present to you especially* (and anyone else who's listening, if we're going to be honest) *this request, which I enclose in Your loving heart.* (Insert request here.)

Then, of course, you get the whole thing again in Spanish. The Infant, who isn't an infant at all (and I have no idea where the Prague part comes in), is also handy for colleges, freedom, travelers, peace, the Philippines, and foreign service.

"Come in," I say to Dad.

He is wearing his sweatpants and a Sonics T-shirt. There is something slightly embarrassing about Dad in sweatpants— something loose and childlike. Too *uncontained*.

"God, Dad, untuck your shirt."

"What?" He looks down, checks himself out.

"It's dweeby like that."

"I'm not here to talk about my fashion sense," he says, but untucks his shirt anyway.

"I'm guessing not," I say.

"Can you stop typing for a second?"

I look at him, and he sighs. "This thing, with this boy," he says. My backstage mind is hurriedly stacking stones to make a wall against the assault I know is coming. This is the man who told me I would have to buckle down and apply myself if I wanted to "get anywhere" after I got a B in science in the eighth grade. "Anywhere," I assumed, was someplace with a high credit limit and a BMW like his. "Anywhere" was where you listened to news radio and had a retirement plan and where you took a vacation once a year, which usually meant the falsely enthused idea of "Let's play tourists in our own city!" because your wife was too afraid to fly. This is the man who told me I would one day regret not "getting my cardio," who got pissed when I couldn't help him clean the garage that time they were having the Honor Society picnic. The anywhere Sebastian might bring me is certainly not the anywhere he had in mind.

Dad slings his first arrow at my stone wall. "We only want the best for you," he says. That all-purpose phrase, both barbed and soothing, which may be true but is too often used to cover a multitude of parenting sins, usually involving some sort of over-reaction on their part.

"When I was your age, all I had to think about was college and pretty girls . . ."

"And you had to walk to school in twelve feet of snow even though you lived in Arizona."

He sighs again. I wait for him to use Arrow Number Three in the parental arsenal: As Long As You Live Under My Roof. But he only stares at the flickering yellow from my patron saint candle.

"I sound like my father," he says. "I know I do."

I wait. He seems vulnerable, which makes me uncomfort-able. Dads shouldn't be vulnerable. Dads leave cave, kill meat, drag home. Dads protect and serve, bring home the bacon, fight fire with fire. Dads fix broken things and remove dead birds from the lawn on a shovel without getting squeamish. They don't hesi-tate, or look lost.

"Jade, I'm realizing as I get older that I know less and less, not more and more." He sounds a little like Tess, but noth-ing like Sports Dad. It occurs to me why people are so fond of stereotypes—their simplicity makes you feel the ground is safe and firm, more safe and firm, certainly, than the layers and com-plexities of the unknown. This man—I don't know him. I'm not even sure how, exactly, to start to know him. "I don't have any answers for you," he says. "Honestly, I don't. All you can do is make the best decision you can at the time after looking around from where you stand. That's all I can ask."

"That's all?"

"Yep."

"Okay." I'm relieved. Actually, I'm kind of shocked *and* relieved. He really doesn't have the answers, and he's not expecting me to have them either. There's something so, I don't know, *human*, about that. I feel a lightness that comes with a release of expectations. This vulnerability—maybe it's okay after all. Maybe we can just be human together.

"Is there anything I can do?"

"If Mom tells anyone about this . . . I asked her what she's planning to do, and all she'll say is, she needs to *think it over*. What does that mean? I've asked her not to tell anyone, but she just says she can't make that promise." God, oh, please, God, Infant Jesus of Prague, and everyone else.

"You want me to make sure she doesn't?" He gives his head the smallest shake, chuckles. It's the kind of laugh one gives when a friend asks for a favor—to spy on a boyfriend, to help them cheat on a test. The laugh of the stupid request, of the impossible. "I can try," he says.

He is right to give that laugh, I know, and that's what keeps me awake that night, long after the printer spits out the last pages of my paper, which is somewhere around one A.M. He has tried to get her to do lots of things—travel, ski, meet other couples. And she has tried to get him to do lots of things —understand her, hear her, accept her for who she is. The possibility that he would sway her is small, finished years and years ago, and this may mean I have ruined Sebastian's life, Bo's, Tess's, my own. Actions and their reactions, all right. I fall asleep finally, but have disturbing dreams. Tsunamis and hurricanes, the doors flying off of airplanes.

I wake about six in the morning. The sun is already out, the sky blazing blue. I watch the changing forms of the punctuation clouds—the casual wisp of a comma, an apostrophe, the curve of a question mark—turning now into seagulls flying.

Chapter Seventeen

A caged animal will come to fear his freedom. When first taken captive, put behind bars, he will fight and attempt escape. Finally, though, he will resign, and once resigned, the doors of the cage can be opened, but he will cower within . . .

—Dr. Jerome R. Clade, *The Fundamentals of Animal Behavior*

I go to school that next day, and then put in my time with the elephants, weighing them, cleaning the outdoor enclosure with Elaine. I hang out near Hansa, just because she makes me feel good, the way she sniffs my hair and hunts in my pockets for apples. I don't see Damian, and leave straight for home afterward. Jake Gillette, the traitor, isn't in the parking lot, but Titus gives me his usual "hang loose" wave.

I call Sebastian and tell him I won't be coming over. My

paper, I say, although I had turned it in that afternoon. It's the first time I've lied to him. I keep our conversation short—*That paper . . . crazy last days before graduation . . .* because I'm afraid I might tell him everything, panic him for no reason. Maybe I'm just delaying the fact that he will inevitably hate me for putting him in jeopardy as I have.

I also want to hurry home because I think if I stay near Mom, hover, watch, that maybe I can prevent her from doing anything crazy. She would have to look at me, remember who she would hurt. If I let her out of my sight, she might forget that. It might make it too easy for her to do what she feels is right.

Hawthorne Square is engaged in summer—Mrs. Chen is washing her car, her baby, Sarah, in a playpen on the grass. The fountain has been turned on, and little Natalie Chen is surfing her Barbie in the waves, *Riding Giants* style. Old Mrs. Simpson is filling the bird feeders hanging off her porch, and I am surprised to see my mother in the front garden of our house, her knees in the dirt, her hands around the roots of a geranium plant.

"Hey," I say.

"Hey," she says. She positions the geranium in the hole she's made, pushes the dirt in around it. "How was school?" She doesn't look at me. Natalie shrieks as her arm gets drenched in the fountain. *Don't get soaked now*, Mrs. Chen shouts, her own shorts wet from the leaking hose. I notice Milo standing in the window. Looking out with a face so devastated, you'd have thought we'd all gone away on vacation and left him behind.

"Good. You know."

"You get your paper done?"

"Had to stay up until one, but, yeah."

She stands, brushes the dirt from her knees. She rubs her nose with the back of one gardening glove. "Stupid allergies."

"Really."

"Jade, I think we better have a conversation."

"All right." Sunshine makes the lawn and the flowers and the bricks of the buildings look new and optimistic. I hear the music-box notes of the ice-cream man driving up the street, playing "The Entertainer." But it's black dread that edges up my insides.

"Can you run in and pour me a lemonade? It's getting hot out here."

"Sure."

Oliver isn't home yet, but Milo jumps around my legs and barks with nearly-abandoned-now-I'm-not joy.

"Relax," I say, but someone needs to say it to me. I feel a little light-headed. Am I light-headed? Am I going to faint? I think I'm nauseous. I stop with one hand on the refrigerator, trying to see if I'm nauseous enough to throw up. I can breathe, though. I am breathing, yes. In, out. In, Jade. Out. No, my heart isn't pounding, it just feels . . . It hurts. It feels like it might be broken.

I remove the cool pitcher from the fridge, clink ice into two tall glasses, and pour the liquid over the crackling cubes. This is what she used to do for me. Pour me a glass of lemonade in the summer, so that I could have it as I sat on a towel on the grass of our old house after running through the sprinkler. Lemonade, and those boxes of animal crackers with the circus train on the side, the elephants and giraffes and hippos inside. That red box with a string for a handle.

I carry the glasses out, pushing open the door with my foot, hedging sideways so Milo can't escape.

"Oh, thanks," Mom says. She's sitting on the porch step, her gloves tossed near her feet. She reaches for the glass and rests it against her forehead for a moment.

"It's warm," I say. It's what you do when you can't say what you need to—you talk about the weather.

She takes a drink of lemonade, and so do I. It's cool and sour-sweet.

"Jade—I just want to tell you that I love you." Those words— sometimes they aren't what they seem. Sometimes we say it to hear it said. Sometimes they're an excuse. Sometimes, an apology.

I'm quiet.

"You're not going to like what I have to say." She sets her drink on the brick step.

Dread, creeping blackness. Heart . . . yes, there it is. That heavy ache. Breaking. I can only think of one thing: I think of Bo, first with no mother, then taken from his father. I think of Bo, twice broken.

"No," I say.

"Jade, you can't keep this child from his mother. She has a right to be in his life. He has a right to have her in his life. It's wrong for you to take part in this."

"You don't understand. You don't know anything about this. About them."

"I called . . ."

"No!"

"I called directory assistance. For plastic surgeons in Ruby Harbor."

"No, no, no."

"There was only one. I left a message. An anonymous message, Jade. No one will know who called."

"How could you?"

"He can't go on like this."

"How could you do this!" I scream. I see Natalie Chen with her Barbie turn around suddenly. My hand is around the glass, wet with condensation. I throw it against our house, where it shatters.

I want out of there. I turn then. Oliver is just coming up the drive. He has his backpack on, and is carrying a large brown grocery bag, stuffed full. They've just done the end-of-school desk-cleaning ritual, I can tell, and he has likely walked home happily with his reclaimed treasures—glue sticks and half-dry markers, crayons with the paper rolled off, stubby pencils, bits of loose glitter and pieces of artwork taken down from the classroom walls, staple holes in the corners. That was always a good day in elementary school, bringing home your stuff, the ice-cream man playing as you walk. But now he just hugs his bag. He looks stricken.

I run past him. I head for the bus stop, the 212, but change my mind and go to the 76 station instead. I realize I've left my backpack and cell phone at home in the hall, but I dig in the pocket of my jeans for a dollar, get some change from the guy inside. I push open the folding door of the phone booth. That cramped sticky place where bad news is delivered, because only bad news has the urgency required to stop here. *I'll be late, honey. I'm lost, honey. I'm never coming home, honey.*

"Sebastian?"

He's at the houseboat. He's outside on the dock—I can hear the motor of Tess's boat in the background.

"Jade! If you finished your paper, come over. We're getting in the boat."

"I can't . . ."

"Your voice sounds funny."

"Sebastian," I cry. "I'm sorry."

He tells me to come over. He asks me to meet him. At the end of the dock. Where we would have some privacy. He needs to go now. He has to tell Tess quickly.

I am almost too ashamed to go. I wait for the 212, ride in silence in a seat by myself until a guy with an army jacket and body odor slides down beside me. I grit my teeth, feel deservedly punished. I get off the bus, walk to the dock. I wait at the end, near the street. No Sebastian.

It's like the old days, when I would wait for him, not knowing if he would ever appear. Sea boy and desert girl, the boy in the red jacket who was mourning something. Now I knew what. Now I would mourn too.

I wait and wait, and finally I hear the *thwat-thwat* of tennis shoes running on wood, see him, my Sebastian. "Jade!"

He's out of breath. "God, I thought you might not wait."

"I'm so sorry." I start to cry. He puts his arms around me. The hurt party is comforting the guilty one, and something is wrong in that. I can feel his heart thumping beneath the cotton of our T-shirts.

"It's not your fault."

"It is."

"No, it's not. It's mine. I'm the one who did this. I'm the one who's put us in this position. It's going to happen. Tess says it's the chance you take every time you get close to anyone in this situation."

"She's mad. She's furious, if I know her."

"At me. At herself."

"What are you going to do?"

I'm afraid I know the answer. I don't even want to ask.

"Mattie, Tess's sister, has another place. She's got a couple of rentals, where they like to vacation. There's a renter in their place in New Mexico now, so it looks like Montana. Besides, it's by a lake."

"You shouldn't even be telling me."

"Jade. Look at me." He holds me away from him, takes my chin in his hand. "I love you."

"I love you, too. Sebastian, I do."

"Jade, I want you to come. I want you to come with us."

The moment, it's as if it is suspended in midair. I look at him. Sea boy to my desert girl. He holds me with his eyes, and it is easy. So easy.

"Yes," I say.

"Yes? Are you kidding? Yes?" Sebastian grabs me to him. Kisses me hard. "I want you," he says.

"I want you, too."

"Oh, my God, I can't believe you said yes." He's talking fast now. "You said yes, oh, my God. I was so afraid you wouldn't. Couldn't. Oh, God, we've got to hurry."

"Okay," I say. I'm not sure what I feel. Sad, angry, excited, *thrilled*! Everything is colliding too fast. "What do we do?"

"We're leaving tonight."

"Okay," I say.

"Meet us back here. It's going to take us a while to pack. Say, midnight? Start of a new day. Start of a new life."

"I'll be here."

"You should probably let them know. Your family. Talk to them, write a note, something. Make sure they know you're all right. That it's what you want. So no one has to come looking."

"I can handle that part."

"Jade, I love you. I've got to go." He kisses me again. "Bye. God, you said yes!"

"Yes," I say.

This is what I do. This is what someone who is going to run away does, if you can call a legal adult a runaway. She walks to Dairy Queen. She steps into the coolness, where everything is red and white and there are big plastic pictures of mountainous glops of ice cream covered in various mildly gruesome-looking sauces. Where there are two boys working behind the counter, wearing paper triangle hats and flinging rubber bands at each other to get her attention. She sits at a table across from a mother with a baby in a high chair, the baby with a chocolate-covered chin, and another child, sex indeterminate, holding a wobbling, heartbreak cone. It's going over, and when it does, the kid's gonna scream. Above all, she wonders if we feel more regret for the things we do or for the things we don't do.

I sit in that Dairy Queen for over two hours. I count how many people have Chocolate Fudge Supremes, how many have dipped cones (chocolate and butterscotch), how many have banana splits (fewer than you'd think), how many have Brownie Delights (a lot). I could tell you the figures if I hadn't thrown away the napkin with the pen slashes on it (pen borrowed from boy number one. Pen snitched from Horizon Home Mortgage by someone) on my way out the door.

I walk back to the bus stop, several miles. I count sidewalk tiles. Then lampposts. I count off the words one mother had said to her kid in Dairy Queen (One Blizzard, one Peanut Buster Parfait, neither on my survey). *Justin, you are going to be the death of me,* I count, starting on my thumb until I end on my pinkie. I sit in the back of the bus, like the troublemakers do. I stretch my legs out on the seat. *People pleaser?* I say to Abe in my head. *Ha!*

It's just after eleven when I get home. Oliver is asleep, Mom is in her room with the light off, and Milo is curled up on the couch where he isn't supposed to be. The only one awake is Dad, as I can tell from the the line of yellow light under the basement door.

I step carefully to my room. I avoid every creak in the floor, and I know where they all are. I knock on my doorframe three times, oh, so softly. My mother has put my backpack on my bed and I empty it. I stuff it full of clothes, summer things, which don't take much space, and a sweatshirt, which does, so I decide to wear it. Same with jeans. I think about taking a patron saint candle, realize it's stupid. I remove my wad of money from my underwear drawer, zip it into my pencil pouch. Address book.

Small photo album. Picture taped on my computer of Hansa and Chai and Damian. Really, it's all I need. I sling my backpack over my shoulder. Creep back into the hall. But the light is on now in the bathroom. The door is open. There is the sound of peeing. Floodgates.

Oliver appears, with his aboveground-mole eyes. He squinches at me.

"Flush, Oliver."

"I forgot. I'm asleep."

"You need to go before bed," I say.

"I did!"

"It sounded like Niagra Falls."

"I'm thinking I just have a too-happy bladder," he says.

I want to laugh; instead, a loss so great overtakes me, I almost cry. He shuffles down the hall. His hair sticks up badly in the back. His pajamas have baseballs on them.

His back disappears into his room. The darkness swallows him up. And that's when I know I'm not going anywhere.

Part Four:

Toward a Lava-Lamp Sky

Chapter Eighteen

There comes a time when an elephant clan must split up. Sometimes this comes after the death of a matriarch, when bonds weaken with the new leader. More often, it is a simple necessity during a drought or the feeding season, when the group is too large to successfully find nourishment, when it is better for their survival to break apart than to stay together. Sometimes the reasons are social—positive experiences in another clan may result in an individual's decision to "leave home," to establish themselves and become members in a new herd . . .

—Dr. Jerome R. Clade, *The Fundamentals of Animal Behavior*

"You know, even if you go to him sometime, there's the chance you won't stay together. Maybe a good chance. This is your first important relationship. The beginning of the story, not the final answer. If you went sometime, there'd be that possibility—that you don't know the end result, but that that's okay anyway," Abe says.

"What do you mean, 'if'?" I say. "It seems . . . out of the question."

"If," Abe says. "It's a beautiful word. *If* is a key to any locked door."

I graduate with my class, wear the cap and gown, shake with one hand, take the diploma with the other, smile for the photo. I make a late-night confession to Jenna and Michael about my relationship with Sebastian, keeping my boundaries drawn about some parts, as Abe suggested. I cry, and Jenna hugs me, but it all seems to suggest a conclusion I don't feel. I basically live at the elephant house after graduation—between trips to the airport, that is. Good-bye to Jenna, heading to Colorado Christian University; good-bye to Akello, heading home to Uganda; good-bye to Michael, off to Johns Hopkins. I'm hollowed out, the one left behind. I realize that there is a stretch of freeway, a few miles between the airport and town, that is so laden with sadness and bittersweet joy, hundreds and thousands of comings and goings and the loss of change and moving on, so much emotion seeped into the pavement and the surrounding earth on those trips of dropping off departing loved ones, that it should be called the Zone of Heartbreak.

I started classes at the University of Washington in the fall. The large campus lined with cherry trees and brick pathways and ornate buildings studded with grimacing and grinning gargoyles was overwhelming at first. I read my map and handled it, except for one near attack when I walked into a class of three hundred students, stood at the top of the aisle, and felt like I might fall. Fall? Fail? I slept until eight, arrived late sometimes because I could, imagined I was one mere Copper River salmon in a sea of them, spawning and swimming upstream. I was happy to be indistinguishable. Happy to move because others were moving, following their direction. That way, I didn't have to think. I wouldn't have to think about Sebastian at that house on the lake, about Tess making pancakes on Sunday morning, about waking up to the smell of bacon and how much Bo was growing in my absence. I could concentrate on the professor's voice booming from the microphone, *If we take Williams literally, we may think he means that life itself is a process for discovering meaning* . . . I could focus on the words in thick textbooks and on formulas and diagrams instead of playing over and over again the sound of Sebastian's voice on the phone when he called me from Goat Haunt Lake, the crackling faraway sound of it, the *What? I can barely hear yous*. The *I miss yous*. If the person in front of me at the campus café reached for a dish of Jell-O, so would I. If I had allowed my mind to open to my own wants and desires, my insides would remember to keen over each of his sentences spoken over distance. The pain of being without him—butterflies crashing against rocks. I would then remember that other phone call, those words: *I can't come, Sebastian*. His own: *I know. I understand*.

My mother's single action on the phone that day was apparently enough to soothe her conscience. She didn't pursue it further, which meant she would be no match for Tess. My mother and

I made necessary peace. We didn't speak about it. We just let time do its little thawings. I didn't have enough energy to be angry, and she seemed sad, herself. I had thought it was because of our wobbly relationship, her loss of purpose after my graduation, leaving only Oliver for her to shadow. But then my father finished his train set.

"Come and see," he said. We all tromped down the stairs, Milo racing to get in front and making our passage down perilous. We stood in front of his miniature world, now completed. The tiny people in the tiny town, the cars, the shops, that stretch of road going out, out into the forest, to a house by a river. It was beautiful. Mom started to cry. The next day, he told us he would be moving out for a while. It would be a trial separation. They needed time to think. He had already found a house to rent. On the shores of the Snoqualmie River, on the east side, out by North Bend, where there was no big city and restaurants in every cuisine, where his commute would be over an hour each way, but where the trees got thick and the river tumbled wild and cold. He could fish there. He'd forgotten that when he was a kid, he'd liked to do that. He would teach us, too. Fishing, the expectation of good things.

"Are they getting a divorce, Jade?" Oliver asked.

Desert, cactus, lands from the beginning of time. Ancestors who survived, who were hardy and strong during every moment in the history of the earth.

"I don't know," I said.

"They can't get divorced. They have us."

"Oliver, there's something you need to know—are you listening? You know how to handle this. You can handle anything that comes your way and be okay. No matter what."

"Flask of Healing."

I tapped his chest. "Here."

Delores took to baking. She'd bring in cookies and brownies and oat bars. Muffins and breads and cinnamon rolls.

"You're too thin," she'd say. And she'd leave a second plate on Damian's desk, sticky, gooey, enticing nourishment, sometimes still warm, covered in steamed-up Saran Wrap. She was taking care of the fatally ill again, the heartbroken. Jum had pulled through her last scare, but Damian had gotten word she wasn't eating again. Our elephants were flourishing, though. Onyx was as bonded to Delores as Flora to her tire. Hansa was growing large and strong, and Tombi and Bamboo had tossed a new tree trunk into the electrical fence in spirited enthusiasm.

One day not long after my father had packed a few Hefty bags of belongings into his BMW and showed us his place for the first time (*You have no furniture*, Oliver had said. *It's like camping*, he had answered. *In a house.*), Damian calls me into his office.

"Jade. I just want to tell you that, first, I have really enjoyed coming to know you."

"No," I say. I know what he is telling me. But he can't. I refuse to hear it.

"But, Jade, I must."

"No. No, you can't."

"I have to."

"Everyone is leaving." I start to cry. I can't help it. Not Damian, too.

"Oh, little one," he says. He comes around from his desk, puts his arm around me. He is strong, from all those years of working with elephants, training them, caring for them, loving them.

"You can't go." I sob.

"I must go back to Jum. When you raise an animal, you love it like your own child. I know her thoughts, her needs. She wonders where I am, and I can't bear it."

"We need you too. Damian, *we* need you." My heart hurts. I don't know how much more hurt it can take.

"You know that elephants have your pain, my pain. They're not separate from us. Their bonds last a lifetime. I must go to her."

"No . . ."

"You, you see?" He takes my hands, grasps them firmly. "You are not vulnerable anymore like you were when you first came. You are living up to your name."

I am quiet. I don't know what he means.

"Jade," he says. "You don't know this? Jade, the substance—its nature. One of the strongest materials. Stronger than steel."

"I don't feel strong," I say. He *can't* leave. He can't. It's too much.

"Ah, but you are. You needed your herd as a vulnerable calf, but now you are so much stronger. Like Hansa!" He laughs, but I don't feel like laughing with him.

"You don't need your herd to protect you," he says. "But Jum, her herd is too small. Only my brother and his wife. I have money to buy her from Bhim and bring her home."

"I will miss you. You have given me so much." I am crying hard.

"And you, too, have given me. I am so proud. Now, you are a real mahout."

In the spring, the cherry blossoms rain down on the University of Washington campus like snow. They lie on the brick paths in drifts, as the gargoyles grin in nice-weather mischief. The air is sweet with the perfume of a girl in a summer dress, the water of the lake sparkly like it's keeping a nice secret. The elephants are happy too. Rick Lindstrom, who looked funny at first behind Damian's desk, put all the things he'd learned in grad school to use. He added auditory stimulation (classical music, cowbells, chimes—Onyx vocalized like crazy at Mozart; Delores preferred Vivaldi), built an enrichment garden full of treats, had us all hang ice blocks with bits of frozen vegetables inside (heavy!). He brought in a backhoe to dig a mud wallow (a big ditch filled with water—Tombi liked the hose, too), and had Elaine and me drape one of the pine trees with bits of fruit, like it was Christmas. Pictures accumulated on the walls of the elephant house. First, the photos of Damian with all of us around his "Best Wishes" good-bye cake, and then photos sent from faraway, with exotic stamps on the envelopes. Damian, wearing a turban now, smiling broadly. Jum, with her trunk around his waist; Jum, grabbing the hem of Damian's wife, Devi's, skirt. A new stone house. Damian with his brother. Jum in the river with Damian hugging her neck, his pant legs rolled up to his knobby knees.

I would drive Oliver out to visit Dad. We'd wind through the trees and bump down his gravel road. The river that his tiny house was on roared and churned, and you could hear the rocks under the water tumbling against each other. We would walk down the riverbank with him. Sometimes we would just walk, not talk. Other times, we would ask him questions, and he would tell us things we didn't know. How as a child he wanted to be an astronaut; that at age eight he had fallen in love with his third-grade teacher, Mrs. Edwards; that he had taken art classes in college. He bought a bed. Then a couch, and a table and chairs. Self-help books, which I gave him a bunch of shit about, were stacked up, travel guides, too. He wasn't black-and-white to me anymore, nor was he hazy shades of gray. Instead, it was more like he was beginning to have bits of color; jigsaw pieces with fragments of pictures I hoped would one day make a whole. Stereotypes are fast and easy, but they are lies, and the truth takes its time.

We'd drive home and Oliver and I would be both sad and quiet, until one day I'd had enough of the funeral and told Oliver we needed a french fry taste test. We stopped at a bunch of fast-food joints on the way home (five was all we could handle), ordered a large, and compared and contrasted. McDonald's—hot and soft and salty; Burger King—bumpier, crunchy; Wendy's—wide, thick; and so on. The winner: this little place called Hal's, where your face broke out from the grease just driving up to it. Every ride home from then on, we'd stop. Funerals are happier with fries.

My mom cried a lot and spent too much time closed up in her room. But right around the time the cherry blossoms started to fall, she came out. Spring, renewal, new life, second chances, air so delicious you wish you could drink it. She started seeing a counselor, got a job as a library assistant at Oliver's school. She made a friend there, Nita, and they went to a concert together—Mom voted with Onyx and liked Mozart.

One day I come home from the elephants and no one is around. The doors and windows are open, Venetian blinds clack serenely against the sills.

"Mom!" I call. "Oliver!"

"Out here!" she yells.

"Sis! Come on! Come out! Hurry!"

I would have been alarmed, but his voice is excited. The kind of voice you get when the UPS man drops off something large and unexpected on your doorstep.

They are in our tiny backyard. Mom has Mozart playing softly through a speaker, which is pointing out our kitchen window.

"My God, you guys. What are you doing?"

"Having a ritual," my mom says. "My counselor says rituals are good. They help us move from one place to another, marking change in an important way. This is an Oliver ritual."

Here's what I see: our old rickety ladder, the one that Dad used to hang Christmas lights (with someone holding on to the legs), sitting on the small piece of back lawn. My mother and brother, beaming and grinning, my mother's forehead shiny with sweat. Milo with his tongue lolling out, panting as he lies on the grass in a bit of shade. And our fir tree. The previously ignored fir tree, save for the times it was cursed at for dropping needles on the roof, looking somehow majestic. Sporting gear hangs from its branches, same as the pine tree in the elephant enclosure with its frozen treats. All kinds of sporting gear. Football helmets and kneepads, shin guards and soccer shorts. A basketball jersey, warm-up pants, shoulder guards. A hockey stick is falling through several limbs. Balls of every variety sit under the tree like presents. Even a jock strap dangles from the tip of one branch.

"Wow," I say.

"Look at the top!" Oliver is almost shouting.

"Well, not quite the top. As high as I could reach. Our upper-most point," Mom says.

A plastic protective sports cup, turned upside down. It has a pinecone on top, for extra decoration, I guess.

"The pinecone was my idea," Oliver says.

"We're celebrating the fact that Oliver need not do any more sports, if he doesn't choose to," Mom says.

"I wanted to burn it all, but Mom said no," Oliver says.

"We thought about burying it, but it seemed too morbid," Mom says.

I look at the tree. Take inventory. "Wait," I say. "What about karate?"

"I like karate," Oliver says.

Not long after, during finals week, I get another call from Sebastian.

"Forgotten about me yet?" His voice crackles and snaps.

"Never," I say.

"We're moving again," he says.

I lean against the warm stone of the library in the university's Red Square. My face has been tipped to the sun, soaking it in as I soak in his voice, but now I snap my chin down. Some guys in shorts and no shirts are running through the fountain, throwing soaked foam balls at each other.

"Tiffany?" I say.

"No. Mom says she's been quiet for a while. It's actually just so remote out here that Tess and I are at each other's throats. There's no FFECR, or any other meeting for her to attend, and no work for me. People have gun racks. Mattie's renter in Santa Fe got transferred. The only thing is, it's got a pool, which means we won't be able to let Bo out of our sight for two seconds. But anyway . . . Tess is nuts about the idea, because it's got a big arts community. Theater. I know I can't run forever. Sometime I'll have to go back. But for now . . . For now, this is where we'll be."

"Santa Fe," I say. The desert. An acceptance letter, sitting in an envelope tucked in my underwear drawer. It is a coincidence. A big coincidence. Maybe big enough that you could call it a sign.

We hang up, and that night at dinner, I tell Mom. And Abe, well, he was right. She *could* surprise me.

"Jade, you need to go," she says.

Chapter Nineteen

And then, after the elephants separate for the good of the herd and each other, they will sometimes later reunite. There is no doubt they recognize each other, even after long periods apart. Mothers and daughters and sisters. New sons. They raise their trunks in salute, bump and dance in greeting, entwine their trunks in warm embrace. They bellow and trumpet sounds of joy and triumph . . .

—Dr. Jerome R. Clade, *The Fundamentals of Animal Behavior*

I travel through the Zone of Heartbreak, and decide I should rename it—the Zone of Bittersweet. I am both happy and sad, and the feelings go together like a pair of hands clasped. Mom drives, Oliver and Milo ride in back. I'd said good-bye already to Delores and Hansa and all of the elephants. I rubbed their trunks and gave them apples from my pockets. My heart broke to see their saggy behinds as I looked over my shoulder before leaving the elephant house. Abe had hugged me, gave me Dr. Kaninski's golf mug—"Golfers Do It With Balls"—with a slip of paper inside, a referral to his friend and former college roommate in Sante Fe, Max Nelson, *who plays kick-ass rugby and has anxiety himself*, the note said. I gave a last wave to Titus at Total Vid. I visited Dad before I left. *I am proud of you*, he'd said, his eyes filling, something I'd never seen before. And then I watched the elephants on my computer screen one last time, their swaying, prehistorically huge forms. I touched my fingers to the screen. We are all tied together, even if we don't want to be. Animals and people. People and people. The trick is to face our necessary connections and disconnections. Humans, we need to go away from each other too, sometimes, same as they did. Sometimes, humans need to go away to study elephants. In my bag was a textbook, *The Fundamentals of Animal Behavior*, for the class I was most excited about being enrolled in at NMU.

The night before I leave, I can barely sleep. I am so heavy with the ache of good-bye. That morning, I am full of hugs and good wishes and have a stomach that feels like it could explode with nerves. My heart, too, is newly filled and nearly breaking. Tears are there, just waiting. This is what sets them off: Oliver's hands in his lap, Milo's collar askew. Mom's profile. The speed-limit sign. I remember Saint Raphael in my bag, my one chosen traveling companion, patron saint of travelers and happy meetings. Patron saint of joy. *Raphael merciful—le pido un viaje seguro y una vuelta feliz.* Merciful Raphael—I ask you for a safe trip and a happy return.

I kiss Milo good-bye. I hug his beloved, furry self. He waits patiently in the car as Oliver and Mom walk me in to the airport. We all do mostly okay, until I have to leave them.

"Sis," Oliver cries.

"My girl," Mom says. Tears roll off her nose. "This. This is the hardest thing I've ever had to do, letting you go. Oh, God—I almost forgot." She reaches into her purse. Hands me a small bag. "I was thinking about what you told me . . . What Damian had said about your name." I reach my fingers through the tissue paper, pull out a necklace from which dangles a small jade elephant.

I don't hold back my tears, and I don't give a shit who's watching. Nature is never static, I understand. Change is ever-constant, clouds zipping across a sky. It is dynamic, complicated, tangled, mostly beautiful. A moving forward, something newly gained, means that something is lost, too. Left behind. It is something Mom knows, Dad knows, Tess knows, Damian Rama knows.

But I, like nature itself, am strong and resilient. Over the eons, pieces of me had been brave, and I can be brave too.

I put the necklace on, and we hug good-bye again. And when it is time to walk down that narrow airplane aisle, I breathe, in and out, slowing the heavy hand on my chest. I breathe and picture the desert. I picture deserts and savannahs, elephants and humans; change, taking place over thousands of years. My heart is breaking; my heart is rising. I picture the landing of that plane, firm and safe, the doors opening onto ground I would walk forward on, toward the backdrop of a new, wide, lava-lamp sky. I buckle my seat belt, read the plastic safety card, am comforted to see the old lady across the aisle, reading her Bible, a crocheted bookmark on her knees. We lift off, and I grip my armrests. I close my eyes and remember that we can hold too tight, we can fail to let go, we can let go too easily. I peer out the window, which feels cool to the touch. Below, my past life looks like Dad's train set. Tiny houses, small winding roads, water you could fit into a cup and drink.

We soar higher, climb. The miniature town below disappears as we lift above the clouds. Life and our love for others is a balancing act, I understand then; a dance between our instinct to be safe and hold fast, and our drive to flee, to run—from danger, toward new places to feed ourselves.

Jordan's life is pretty typical . . . until it isn't. Her new boyfriend is turning out to be a major jerk, and her father is seeing a married woman. Both relationships will implode, but only one will go down in a shower of violence.

Ruby's always been The Quiet Girl. Dating gorgeous, rich, thrill-seeking Travis Becker changes all of that. But Ruby is in over her head, and will become a stranger to everyone . . . including herself.

When a stranger leaves Indigo a 2.5-million-dollar tip, her life as she knew it is transformed. Indigo's sure the money won't change her . . . until the day she looks around and realizes everything that matters—including her boyfriend—is slipping away, and no amount of money can buy it all back.

As if it's not bad enough that Quinn is surrounded by women who have had their hearts broken, she's just been dumped. Tired of being taken for granted, Quinn joins forces with her sisters and sets out to get revenge on the worst heartbreaker of all.

Scarlet spends most of her time worrying about other people. So when her older sister comes home unexpectedly married and pregnant, Scarlet has a new person to worry about. But all of her good intentions are shattered when the unthinkable happens: She falls for her sister's husband.

Clara's relationship with Christian is intense from the start, and like nothing she's ever experienced before. But what starts as devotion quickly becomes obsession, and it's almost too late before Clara realizes how far gone Christian is—and what he's willing to do to make her stay.

Cricket hates change. But now that she and her boyfriend aren't speaking and high school's almost over, she has some tough choices to make. It's time to face her fears and decide once and for all what she wants, and how she's going to get it.